THE
SUDDEN
WEIGHT
of
SNOW

THE
SUDDEN
WEIGHT
o f
SNOW

LAISHA ROSNAU

M&S

National Library of Canada Cataloguing in Publication Data

Rosnau, Laisha, 1972-
The sudden weight of snow

ISBN 0-7710-7580-4

I. Title.

PS8585.O8338S83 2002   C813'.6   C2001-903831-3
PR9199.4.R686S83 2002

We acknowledge the financial support of the Government of Canada
through the Book Publishing Industry Development Program for our
publishing activities. We further acknowledge the support of the
Canada Council for the Arts and the Ontario Arts Council for our
publishing program.

Typeset in Janson by M&S, Toronto
Printed and bound in Canada

McClelland & Stewart Ltd.
The Canadian Publishers
481 University Avenue
Toronto, Ontario
M5G 2E9
www.mcclelland.com

1 2 3 4 5   06 05 04 03 02

For Nelli Proch and Mathilda Rosnau

$\mathcal{T}$he story goes something like this: girl meets boy. Something sears inside her. Something empties. The ground freezes. A building catches fire. Things come tumbling down. This story begins before you arrive, and it will end after you are gone. Perhaps it begins even before I start to tell it, when we leave my father – a move that can only be followed by more leave-taking, more absence. Things fall away, leave. I try to use words to bring them back.

❧

I am seventeen, and until this year I have lived in the centre of a triangle formed by the almighty church, my mother's regret, and the vague idea of what my father may have been like. There she is, my mother, always in the middle of things. She constantly interrupts this story, imposes her own. There are no fathers in this story, although I will write them in. I may try to fill my own father's absence with other men as I have been assured I will always be compelled to do.

I still catch myself praying, although I try not to. This is what I once prayed for: a way out, hips, breasts, hair so short I could feel air moving on my scalp, love, sex that would split me open gently and then let me go, a large hand cupping the back of my head. I got almost all of those things.

My name is Sylvia Harper Kostak. I prefer to go by Harper. That was my father's last name, probably still is. Once I was Sylvia Rose Harper. Then we left and my mother took back her name, clipped it to the end of mine. Something had to go and both of us agreed it should be the Rose. I have never liked the name Sylvia either – no one should have a name with two letters so close to the end of the alphabet in it like that. So, I go by Harper.

⁓

What else do you need to know? I am probably an unreliable witness. This all starts shortly before the first snowfall.

$\mathcal{I}$ marked my own leave-taking with footsteps, counted them from locker to door. Thirty-six. If anyone wanted to stop me, they could call, "Sylvia Kostak, where do you think you're going? Aren't you supposed to be in class?" But they never did, not at Sawmill Creek Secondary School.

Sawmill Creek is a small town in British Columbia in the foothills of the Rocky Mountains, a clearing where several small valleys meet. It is five elementary schools, one high school, one mall, a 7-Eleven, a mill that goes through cycles of lay-offs like seasons and is always threatening closure, and too many churches. A place that hollowed out the pit of my stomach like hunger. People in Sawmill, as we called our town, had distinct values, a moral code that informed the whole community. Some of the things that people objected to were child abuse, homosexuality, vandalism, laziness, single moms, welfare moms, public nudity, lying, cheating, stealing, the decline of family values, zealous feminists, and most prominently, anyone who protested a man's God-given right to make a living and

3

support his family. The last mentioned were mainly the environmentalists from the city who knew nothing about the land or how to live off it honestly.

Even in a community as strong as Sawmill Creek, not everyone followed the code. There were old draft dodgers living in the hills with ham radios and Marxist manifestos, though the war they were running from had ended thirteen years before. There were those who stitched marijuana crops into the fabric of the forest and clerks at the health food store who claimed we could cure every ailment with the right herbs and tinctures. Somehow, we even had teachers infiltrate our secondary school who taught us about passive aggression, relaxation techniques, and conservationist forestry practices. These teachers were from other, bigger places – Vancouver, Calgary – and came to Sawmill Creek as student teachers, were lured to stay by the fruit-filled valley, the ski hill half an hour from town. We knew better than to tell our parents about what they taught us. We hung on to these glimpses of a larger world. Dreamed of ways to get there. People told us we'd want to return – *This is such a good place to raise a family* – but we'd been raised here and knew it wasn't true.

I was not beautiful, not yet. My hair, dark and long, was not the blue-black of Archie's Veronica but the dull brown of dug earth. Hazel eyes and olive skin, I liked to believe, were the dark Ukrainian in me. Physical reminders of the part of my mother's family that had travelled across the Black Sea from Persia to Ukraine in boats carved out of single cedar trees, large enough to accommodate entire families. This imagined history was as exotic as I could pretend to be.

From the fifth grade until this story begins, I was a toothpick, a tomboy. Not everyone knows this, but when they first begin to rise up, breasts surface beneath the nipples, as hard as rocks trapped under that darker skin. Painful, too. One usually appears first. Just when you have reached the cusp of your fear, another appears. Before I understood what the "life skills" component of phys. ed. was in the fifth grade, I was seeing the uterus lit up on a chart. An upside-down pear, two dangling gloves. The elements the teacher told us about were eggs popping from sacs and travelling tubes, cells sloughing, blood flowing. Cramps. The important thing she didn't tell us was that the firm bulbs of emergent breasts can easily be mistaken for cancer by the untrained eye and hand, under bedclothes in the dark, confused. My mother, Vera, to her credit, didn't flinch or laugh when I told her about the cancer. She simply explained to me what was happening, then bought me a training bra as though to test the very name of the thing – a bra to train and coax the breasts along. Mine never did make it to the finish line.

My hips were two bones pushing against skin and my best friend, Krista, believed I could poke an eye out with them. I didn't think that narrow space between bones could take sex into it. Sex was something thick and unknown, like beauty. My body wasn't ready for either. Sometimes, I thought I could feel the promise of something – a pain, wound like a spring in my limbs, throbbing in my legs at night – and I would wake and pound my fists into my calves and thighs, trying to knock the ache out.

Thirty-six steps down the hall to a door leading out of the school and I was free, a clap of cold hitting my cheeks as I opened the door. Krista was on the other side, waiting for me. This is the moment I mark as the beginning of this story. Then, things still seemed as simple as opening a door and walking away. On that day, the cold was the worst thing we would feel. It was an afternoon in the middle of November and the air was sharp. Too cold to sit in the park by the Salmon River and watch the water pass through town, catching on trees that swept the surface and eddying, then moving on. We walked the twelve blocks down the hill to the centre of town, small and nearly deserted as it was, to the drug store.

Krista and I had a running joke that we could pull a truck up to the doors of Community Drugs and News, walk in, unload the contents of the shelves into a truck, and drive away. The clerk would look up long enough to blink before folding herself back into a tabloid paper. There were three clerks – all women, all interchangeable – who had a distinctly middle-aged air of contempt and resignation, and they were all, it seemed, nearly blind.

In the parking lot Krista stopped walking, straddled a concrete divider, and drew the smoke from the cigarette she was smoking through her nose. I jumped on and off the concrete slabs to keep myself warm and she cocked her chin to say *watch this*. I looked as two cirrus lines of smoke snaked between her parted lips and her nostrils. Around her, a grey cloud. "Hey?" she said, eyebrow raised. She was practising French inhaling.

"Pretty good, Kris, but not quite."

"Yeah, thanks, slut."

"No problem, skank."

"Whew, you smell something?"

Krista flicked the butt and we watched its trail like a comet before we walked across the parking lot. Small bells hit the door and we started talking as soon as we entered the store. We had a routine – talk loudly enough to distract the clerks, fabricate tales that might be more interesting than the tabloids. Keep moving.

"Did you hear about Rick and Tammy?" (*lipstick slipped into a sleeve*). "You mean, after Tammy slept with Rick's dad?" (*eyeshadow tucked into a sock*). "Yeah, old news. Well, you know how Tammy's hamsters went missing?" (*facial astringent dropped into a pocket*). "Oh no, Rick didn't kill them, did he?" (*stomach sucked in, magazine tucked into waistband*). "No, worse" (*at the till, cinnamon gum pulled from the rack*). "Worse? Yes, just this, thanks" (*fumbling in pockets for change, careful not to let anything fall out*). "Worse. One word: felching, if you know what I mean." (*I did, of course – we consulted the dictionary for the words guys whispered to us in the hall.*) "Thank you. Good afternoon!" (*back out into the parking lot, laughing*).

Krista and I went from the drugstore to the public library downtown, where we emptied out our loot. We traced eyeshadow along lashes and in the crease of lids, flicked on mascara. Krista applied lipstick, her mouth gaping. "So many women miss the corners," she told me, stretching her lips tight against her teeth. "I hate it when you see the line where lipstick ends." This was a serious endeavour. "Come with me to the mall. My mom'll give you a ride home." Getting from library to mall was a challenge. There were public buses in Sawmill, but they only appeared once an hour, if that. Everything was, in theory, walkable, but the mall was on the other side of town. We lurked in the library parking lot, following people to their cars until we found someone going in that direction.

Krista's mother managed a record store in the mall and her father worked shifts at the mill. The mall on a weekday afternoon in Sawmill Creek was a quiet, dark place. It wasn't like malls in the city – ceilings vaulted and full of glass, palms looming in atriums, chrome gleaming and the sticky odour of perfume wafting out of department stores. Creekside Mall was an L with a Super Valu on one end and a Kmart on the other. The corridors were paved chocolate brown and dark orange and there was a row of benches down the middle, covered in a fabric that appeared to be burlap. The stores included JR's, which sold dark hard denim and large belt buckles, Sparklers, which sold lottery tickets, key chains and hollow jewellery, Rim Rock Records, and three women's clothing stores that all started with S and sold the same thin cotton clothing.

"Well, aren't you two looking like a couple of tramps," Krista's mother said when we walked into the store.

"Oh stop, Mom, you're flattering us."

"Harper, hon, your mom will have a fit if she sees you with all that makeup on."

"I know."

"She knows, Mom. She'll wash it off. And I believe the proper term is 'your mother will have a cow'."

"Smartass." Mrs. Delaney emerged from behind the counter. "Come here, do the till. I'm going for a smoke." She was wearing tight, high-waisted jeans with tiny, useless pockets and a white belt that was obviously not there to hold them up. The belt matched her white boots, calf-high and tasselled. When she and Krista changed places, Mrs. Delaney leaned over the counter and began teasing her daughter's hair with her fingers.

"Mother!" Krista swatted her away.

"I'm sorry, but it's flat, honey."

Mrs. Delaney and my own mother didn't know what to make of each other. Their main interaction was dropping us off and picking us up at each other's houses, and they liked it that way.

Later, my face clean from scrubbing in the mall bathroom, Mrs. Delaney drove me home, she and Krista in the front seat banging Bon Jovi onto the dashboard together. When I got out, Krista opened her door a crack, yelled, "Don't forget to pick me up for church Sunday, hey?" We never forgot to pick her up. Krista had yelled that for her mother's sake.

We arrived in Sawmill Creek when I was six and my brother, Nick, was four. We came with our mother, Vera, and the family van. Our father, Jim Harper, had given up the vehicle without a fight. We had left Alberta, where Vera and Jim had been together before and after we came along. Away from cold winters and the memory of screaming matches packed tight into the house. We were moving, our mother assured us, right into paradise. South, over the Rockies and into British Columbia. Off the flat land, out of the ragged mountains, and into smooth, rolling hills coated with green. Warm valleys, deep lakes, orchards in bloom. Fruit falling ripe from trees.

We arrived in June, the valley already holding the promise of heat for us like a gift, and we stayed at Ed's Motor Inn on Lakeshore Avenue for the first month. There was no lake at that end of the avenue but we didn't mind. Nick and I lived in flip-flops and sticky bathing suits that stank of chlorine from the motel pool. Vera wore loose sundresses and sandals with leather straps that criss-crossed up her leg. She would sit on the motel bed, her feet still strung into the sandals, wipe the heat from her forehead, and sigh. This is the only time in my life that I remember being allowed to sit in the blue glow of a TV for hours, jump on beds, and eat food that came directly out of boxes. Vera didn't know what she was doing with us yet. She was on her own with two young kids and memories of a man who told her she should allow us to do anything, let us explore our world.

We were given Tahiti Treat and Mountain Dew to drink through straws in the car, windows open and heads hanging out in the heat, while Vera went in and out of grocery stores, banks, and houses with For Sale signs posted on lawns outside them. This was a time when you could still leave children alone in cars. You could ply them with candy and leave them on benches in malls, saying *Stay right here*. Especially in paradise. Nick and I were fairly accommodating.

We all chose the house. "A farmhouse," Vera crooned over and over. There were two rooms tucked into the slope of ceiling on either side of the staircase. Nick and I liked these tiny rooms. They were like forts, and our mother's room was far away, down an entire flight of stairs. The house was on the edge of town and our yard skirted a cul-de-sac in a new subdivision. On the other side, the lawn fell into a ravine before it rose to a tiny, manicured golf course. A small abandoned field behind us ended blunt where the hill began, suddenly thick with forest. We heard Vera on the phone, telling people that she, a Prairie girl, had never lived so close to an honest-to-God forest. Nick and I didn't discriminate yet between forest and parking lot, ravine and road, back of van and bedroom. We didn't yet know the difference between moving and staying still.

Vera got a job as a secretary in Dr. Holland's office. She assured us it was temporary. She had worked as a librarian in Edmonton and she wanted to do that again. There was one small library in Sawmill Creek and apparently a lot of women who wanted to work there. I'm not sure why. By the time I was seventeen, Vera was still at Dr. Holland's office. She hadn't mentioned it being temporary for years. When I overheard her talk about it, she would say, "It's comfortable," or, "We have a good relationship. It's been so long we're almost like family."

Vera, I realized as I got older, liked to think of other people as family. It seemed easier for her to think of them as closely related to her, rather than accepting them simply as friends, acquaintances, or colleagues. I remember Dr. and Mrs. Holland being invited to dinner, Nick and I fidgeting at the table in our church clothes while the forced geniality of the adults' conversation lurched on. My mother and Dr. Holland were definitely not like family. By the time I was in high school, I only saw him when I stopped by the office, or the odd time when I was walking along the road and he drove by on his way to the golf

course. He would honk his horn and acknowledge me with a
quick, assured chop to the air, looking away before I could
wave back.

When we first lived in Sawmill Creek, Nick and I both
became aligned with a band of children that radiated from the
cul-de-sac out, into the field behind our house and then into
the bush behind the field. They came to us, and they were all
boys. With these boys, we threw robins' eggs from nests just to
collect the shards of blue, which when ground and spread on
the skin were a sure source of incredible strength and courage,
or so we believed. We collected windfalls from the abandoned
apple trees, twisted and dwarfed with lack of care, and launched
apple wars across the field. The windfalls were in various stages
of rotting and usually didn't hurt when they hit, but they made
a satisfying snap of apple skin breaking open and releasing juice
as they did. With these boys, we crawled tunnels into the brush
at the edge of the field, prodded at piles of rocks with sticks to
taunt garter snakes, caught grasshoppers in our hands and
stuffed them down each other's shirts. There is no way to
describe the feeling of a panicked insect's fine, sharp legs
against your skin, looking for a way out.

Dungeons and Dragons marked my exodus from the
group. It was played with dice and glossy manuals, warlocks
and dungeon masters dictating an entire afternoon's activities.
Play had moved inside, into the houses that circled the cul-de-
sac and lined the neighbouring streets. It was in houses that my
girlness became apparent. There were mothers who said, "Oh,
look, you've brought your sister," to Nick as though I was a
novelty or a baby-sitter. And there were other sisters. Sisters

were summoned from within the house, even from neighbouring houses. Sisters my age, or younger, or older, driving
Barbie's Star Trailer toward me or waving a life-sized bodiless
plastic head with long blond hair. "Look, we can do her hair!"
they would say, smiling in an calm and oddly convincing way.
Boys had basements where they could play D & D or manoeu-
vre joysticks and buttons through games on Atari. Girls had
bedrooms where we could pull clothes on and off dolls, seduce
Ken with Skipper, and slam their hard plastic bodies together
until Barbie raised her bent arm and slapped Ken, then
changed into a new outfit.

The cul-de-sac is where we went between school and home.
When we walked across the field to go home for dinner, we
both knew not to tell Vera all the details of our day. Once, Vera,
Nick, and I seemed to exist as a single entity. We had always
been with Vera, sharing the front seat of the van while she
drove, sharing a grocery cart while she shopped, or Nick
propped on her hip, my hand in hers as she walked. She must've
been happy to find a small house and a large yard. Somewhere
she could put us down and let us run. I don't know when it happened but by the time I was walking home with Nick across the
back field, we had become three separate people.

The following Sunday began as Sundays usually did, with
Nick's voice calling, "Harper, Harper," as he tugged at my arm.

"Go. Away." Sunday was not my favourite day. Once, it
may have been. I tried to remember a time before the valley,

before the Friends of Christ Free Church, when my parents
were still together. I couldn't remember what we did on
Sundays then but I was sure it involved getting into the van and
driving. There was no seat-belt law then and my father, Jim,
didn't want us to feel confined. The back of the van was my ter-
ritory. There was a bed back there, the floor carpeted, strewn
with stuffed animals, plastic toys, and my parents' clothes –
Vera's soft cotton skirts and blouses thin as webs, Jim's shirts,
flannel and thick. Nick would sit on Vera's lap and sometimes
she would strap him in the seat belt with her, despite Jim's dis-
approval. My father would blow smoke rings over the seat to
the back calling them fairy rings. I would catch them, then
watch as they disappeared in my hands. There was always
music playing on the tape deck. Crosby, Stills and Nash. Neil
Young. Vera and Jim agreed that they liked them separate,
Young on his own, warbling in that awful voice of his. I would
sit on the floor, back against the bed frame, and focus on the
ceiling or lie on the foam mattress and stare out the window.
Most of my daydreams had the same theme. When I grew up,
I would live in a van forever. I could go anywhere. Everywhere.
Just like my father told me, I would never strap myself in.

"Har-per!" Nick pulled at me in bed again, his braced teeth
clenched in a warning: *Get out of bed now.* The ritual of him
waking me had begun after Vera had tried to pull me out of bed
one Sunday. I had heard her voice as though from behind an
escarpment of sleep and then felt her hand tight around my
arm, towing me out. *Get. Out. Of. Bed. You lazy little bitch.* It had
been that last word, the shock of it, that had propelled me out
of the sheets and made me console my mother.

She was on the floor leaning against my bed and crying, mumbling, "I'm sorry, I'm so sorry. I'm just so exhausted." Parents are a reminder that nothing is as it seems. My mother was the kind of woman who made jam from scratch, who smiled as she handed it out to even the slightest acquaintance Mason jars with decorative fabric tied over the lids. She seemed harmless but she could wield the word *bitch* in a way that frightened me and had me comforting her at once. We said nothing that morning, the three of us, through breakfast and all the way to church. After that, it was Nick who was sent to wake me up on Sunday mornings.

～

My mother grew up in a farming community in northern Alberta where everyone was Ukrainian first, Catholic second. In the summer, I see fields waving with yellow wheat. In the winter, I see snow, flat under the force of wind. The priest in the village doesn't know a word of English. I don't know a word of Ukrainian. In that community, the Old Country is either a memory or a retold story, depending which side of the Atlantic you were born on.

Vera's parents are both from the Old Country but they meet in Canada. Vera's mom, my *baba*, travels alone by boat when she is seventeen, apples from her orchard back home folded between the clothes in her trunk. When she arrives in Edmonton by train, she is taken to the farm of friends of her family who had immigrated from her own village in Ukraine. On her first Sunday in the Ukrainian Catholic Church, Baba gives out the apples she brought from home, a rare treat in Northern Alberta then. She gives one to the priest, one to the father of each family, and two to the young man who smiled at her when she walked down the aisle to her seat. Baba is scolded later for being so brazen and uncouth. The next spring she marries this same young man and he becomes Vera's father.

What happened between Vera's mother's generation and mine was hundreds of years of difference compressed into a few decades.

Vera's parents are able to buy a small piece of land, but with no money left over, they have to clear it themselves, by saw, pickaxe, shovel, hand. They build a shack with a thatched roof and floorboards a couple of feet off the ground. A bigger house is eventually built with two bedrooms but no running water or electricity. I stared at my mother in disbelief the first time she told me. "Oh, by the time I left home, we had electricity, a telephone, even a TV," Vera assured me. A generation gap in her own generation. The television is used almost exclusively to watch *Hockey Night in Canada*, Vera's older sisters coming home from Edmonton where they are working just to watch it with the whole family on Saturday nights.

I have heard a story, passed from grandmother through aunts and mother to me, of how back in the part of Ukraine where our blood was first mixed, they believe that children aren't really ours until they make it past their first birthday. Before that they can simply be claimed. When they are taken in death, they may reappear somewhere else later – as a wolf pup, a soaring bird. If they're lucky, they'll be taken straight to Heaven and become angels.

Heaven keeps reversing its decisions, taking Kostak boys back before they can truly inhabit the farm in northern Alberta. This is a time when babies are both mistakes and blessings at once. Vera's mother loses three sons, somehow, in between the successful births of four girls. The third boy in the Kostak family to die in infancy was born two years before Vera. He lived until he was almost a year old – old enough to be admired for how well he was developing, how robust his constitution. And then he too died for no reason that Vera can ever remember hearing. Her parents, in spirit, lived between Canada and the Old Country. The part of them that still lived in Ukraine didn't question the wisdom that children can simply be reclaimed for better purposes.

And so, Vera becomes the youngest daughter in a farming family without boys. The older daughters become sons, clearing trees, manning ploughs dragged by horses. The eldest helps her father choose the first motorized tractor, drives it home, the gears rough on the road pitted with dried mud. I see her teaching him to shift on back roads, the grind and pull of gears. That daughter is still called Al – Alexandria abbreviated to the simplest form, easily yelled over fields. The next two, twins, Olga and Olesa, are identical in their enthusiasm for skinning animals, separating meat from bone. Sheep and rabbits slicked clean of fur, the twins chase each other out of their tiny, customized slaughterhouse with a heart or liver, their clothes spotted with blood. All three older sisters are good shots. In the fall, ducks and geese are strung by their necks and hang in slouching lines on the outside of sheds.

My mother, Vera, as the youngest, has to remain a daughter. She carries the eggs from the coop, ties the goats tight to a post, their necks strained and constricted, so that she can milk them. She churns butter, bakes bread every day, runs a rake through the garden to catch weeds and uproot them. When she has free time, Vera walks the fields and collects wildflowers, later flattening them in books. I can see her there, closing petals between pages. I want to warn her that she risks being trapped on that farm forever, a vestal virgin with broken English. But that's not what happens.

Life isn't easy farming in northern Alberta, but, as in the Old Country, people are true to their family, their faith. Eventually, Vera's first mistake would be, according to her family, to marry a Protestant. Her second, according to herself, was to renounce even this slice of faith for the false sense of freedom that she sought in leaving everything behind. Her third, according to me, was to return to a religious community, hoping to fetter herself to something.

In the car on the way to service, I watched my mother's hands clench and release the steering wheel. "Sylvia, I want you to try to sing today," she said, eyes straight ahead, so intent on the road you would've thought animals leapt in front of cars from ditches at regular intervals.

I said nothing.

"Just try, not for me, not for Pastor John, but for God. Try not to let Krista pressure you not to. You used to have such a beautiful voice in church, both of you." Pause while I remained silent. "Honey?"

I still didn't answer.

"God won't know what to make of your silences."

God won't know what to make of your church, I thought. If you believed Pastor John, the whole damn world would cease to be if the sixty members of the Friends of Christ Free Church in Sawmill Creek, British Columbia, stopped singing the Lord's praises, talking in tongues, and having babies.

The Free Church was different when we first arrived in Sawmill Creek. At first, there were very few of us and we met in each other's houses, or on warm days in the park by the Salmon River. We sat in a circle and talked or rose to sway and sing. I don't remember the first Sunday we joined in at the park, but I can imagine it. My mother with long braids on either side of her clean, broad face, Nick and I barefoot. We all liked to sing then and had sung throughout the entire trip from Alberta to B.C. We must have fit right in.

As more people banded together with us, we moved into an abandoned hall north of town and put up a sign. Some of the men who worked at the mill had made a cross out of hemlock, large and unadorned. It remained unvarnished, and if you ran your hand down its grain you chanced a sliver. I remember children standing on chairs, toddlers crawling up the aisle, young braided women bobbing babies at their breasts, men stroking their beards. There were few sermons then. Pastor John, who at the time was called Brother John just as my mother was called Sister Vera, would say, "Let's lift our eyes and hands and hearts up to Jesus! Make a joyful noise unto the Lord!" And we would.

Eventually, Brother John became Pastor, and with this change there seemed to come more and more sermons. We still sang and some raised their arms and shook in the aisles or spoke in tongues. It seemed to me like gradually it had been decided that some things were wrong – or perhaps they had been wrong all along and no one had bothered to tell me – things like birth control, cigarettes, divorce, sex, television.

Before the service that Sunday, the Friends were welcoming each other back after a week in the world, hugging each other and handing babies from arm to arm. The refrain *God bless* was given out like a handshake. Pastor John's wife, Trudy, came at Krista and me, her face awash with good will. "So good to see you girls," she told us through her teeth held in a smile, shaking her head from side to side as if in mild amazement. It was no surprise to us that we were there – we were every Sunday – but to the congregation of the Free Church, every teenager attending service was an act of God. We smiled back at Trudy, all that was really expected, and retreated, casting our eyes sidelong before slipping down the stairs to the basement.

We shared a cigarette in the basement, a ritual that had begun when Krista stole a pack of clove cigarettes from her mother after Mrs. Delaney had returned from a buying trip in Vancouver. The smell of cloves, some kind of strange, strong spice, hid the smell of smoke, or so we believed. In front of the mirror we practised French inhaling, pulling the smoke from mouths to nostrils in smooth clean lines. We were both getting better. When we were done, we sprayed the room with air freshener and braided each other's hair, tight and smooth, creating a spine down our scalps to the nape of our necks.

"Okay," Krista turned from the mirror in the bathroom, tucking her travel toothbrush into her pocket. "Can you smell any?" She exhaled.

"No. Me?" I breathed on her.

"Nope, you're good. Let's go sing the praises."

We slipped into the back row of chairs. The congregation had already begun singing the first song. *Spring up oh well – gush, gush, gush, gush – within my so-oul. Spring up oh well – gush gush gush gush – and make me whole-oh-ole. Spring up oh well – gush gush gush gush – and give to me your love, eter-nit-y.* While we sang, some Friends made a motion, hands splayed out from their chests as though the spirit of God was gushing forth from them. I didn't know why Krista kept coming with me. I suspected it upset her parents as much that she went to church as it would have upset Vera if I refused to go. I didn't know why I still went, either, except that I hated to think of what would happen if I didn't allow myself to be dragged from bed.

I watched Vera from where we stood. She was across the aisle and up a few rows. She didn't flail her arms but kept them at her sides, her fingers lightly tapping out a rhythm above her knee, the fabric of her skirt moving as though caught by a slight draft of air. Sometimes she would stop singing for a verse and simply smile slightly, as though remembering something small, lovely. What, I couldn't imagine. The sense of peace that seemed to overcome Vera at church made me uncomfortable, as though it threw into jeopardy my own relationship with her as my mother, all the tension and strife that relationship was supposed to bring.

Vera turned her head and looked at me in the back row. She lifted her songbook slightly and gestured to it, meaning *sing, sing*. I looked straight back at her and, without lowering my eyes to the page, began to move my lips, expressionless.

In that sermon, we were told once again that God must have lived in our valley. It was small and perfect. The seasons passed as seasons should. Winter, cold and sharp and covered in snow. Spring, wet and green, the sound of ponds thick with frogs. Summer drying everything out, releasing the scent of sap splitting the sunburned bark of ponderosa pines, fruit pulling branches to the ground. In the autumn, coyotes gathered on the hill at the end of the field behind our house and howled at the moon. No shit. God must have lived in our valley. It was narrow and closed. The musty smell of churches permeated the air. Helicopters sliced the sky, looking for pot crops, growers to bust. The valley was run on mill money and people thanked God that there were trees to cut down, that there would always be trees to cut down. The Friends of Christ Free Church was right there in the middle of the valley, holding it all in place.

GABE

Your first six years, before you moved to Arcana, California, were spent on what could loosely be called a commune in the foothills of the Rocky Mountains in Canada. Everyone has memories of childhood as a forest of legs, the faces of adults hovering somewhere far above. We have all clutched the wrong leg, thinking it our mother's, only to discover that what descends is the face of a stranger, large as a moon. In your forest, the canopy was full of smoke, the faces bearded, and the legs of potential mothers were covered in fine hair.

When your memories begin, you live between two vans. One is where your parents, Peter and Susan, sleep. The other is both where your bed is and part of the kitchen. The rest of the kitchen is between the vans, under a tarp. This tarp is enormous, stretched taut, and shelters a makeshift living room, complete with a carpet and a couch that are often slightly damp. Peter is building an A-frame cabin to Susan's specifications and there are already some other buildings on the property – a barn, sheds, sagging outhouses. Peter and the other dads are constructing a large building for all of you to gather in, and something called a sauna.

There are lots of children there. You are a barefoot, snot-nosed gang who are encouraged to speak your budding genius minds and finger paint on every available surface. Peter takes you and the other boys into the fields on Clydesdale-pulled ploughs and explains the finer points of horse farming, although it won't become clear to you until several years later that he probably doesn't know what he is talking about.

You live on what used to be a farm, and that's what your parents still call it, although it isn't like any of the farms in the books that you look at. Those farms have animals and, perhaps more importantly, farmers on them. Your farm has Clydesdale horses that the men fight about, a few scrappy chickens that continually die and are replaced, and a goat that rears its stunted horns and terrifies you. Your mother gardens in her bare feet and your father does something in the fields but there is no rooster and things aren't as shiny and red as they are on the farms in your books. There is no tractor.

The first winter in your memory, you move out of the vans and into a shack. Peter hasn't finished the A-frame. You know it's a shack because your mother calls it that. Peter does things to the tiny building – nails cedar shakes to the roof, hauls in a wood stove and cuts a hole in the ceiling for the stack. He attaches pink insulation to the inside and covers it with prefabricated walls that come straight from the store. Your mother cries a lot, and smokes. You like the smell of her hair when you crawl onto her lap. It reminds you of fires, warmth. When it gets too cold and snow falls through the cracks around the chimney, you and Susan move into someone else's finished cabin and Peter stays in the shack. The someone else is a friend of both of your parents, a man. Sometimes, all of you have dinner together and the adults stay up late, smoking and drinking, their teeth pink with wine by the time they kiss you goodnight. You keep yourself awake in the other man's loft until you hear your father leave and your mother and the friend laughing. When it warms up, you and Susan move back into the shack with Peter. By the summer, you are living between two vans again.

In the second fall of your memory, Peter still hasn't completed the A-frame. The big building is finished and is called the cookshack, though you know it isn't a shack like the one your mother complained about. Other fathers have finished building cabins and kids are showing off the places where they sleep. No one has an actual bedroom. There are lofts with ladders to them, beds built into the wall, hammocks in the corners of living rooms. Their beds are like forts, but you still have the best one – a whole van to yourself. You tell the other kids that you could drive away if you wanted to.

And one day you do, only Peter is driving. You know it was something about the unfinished A-frame. You know your mother was upset; she was smoking and crying a lot before you left, like she did the winter before. Susan must be too upset to take care of you so you go away with Peter in one of the vans, the one that was your bedroom. Now it is just you two guys, Peter tells you, free and on the road. You miss your mom.

Since then, the smell of sawdust has always reminded you of that place. There was a lot of wood there, on the farm and in the town. You took trips to town with Peter and the other men to pick up wood at a place where lumber was stacked as high as the walls of a battle fort. There was wood piled everywhere at the farm, shavings all over the ground – soggy in the spring and fall, concealed under mountains of snow in the winter, so hot in the summer that if you sank your arm into a pile of it you could burn your hand. Peter tells you that you are both going home, to the States. That where you are going there are even bigger trees. When you get there, though, you miss the wood stacked up everywhere around you. The sawdust doesn't smell the same.

$\mathcal{E}$very year when the snow melted, I heard the clatter of trucks driven up the switchbacks behind our house and the sounds of teenagers – car radios pumped out of open doors, the clink of beer bottles – in the place where coyotes sometimes yelled at the moon. Waking to the coyotes had always scared me. At first, their wails were like children laughing, rising to hysteria. Then what I heard shifted, so it sounded like children shrieking in pain, and I would have to reassure myself that it was only the sounds of animals. Except when it wasn't. To a child's ears, teenagers on a hill could sound uncannily similar to coyotes, and that was equally disturbing.

As I got older, parties became my own lifeblood. They came in two basic varieties – house and bush. House parties spilled out onto lawns and driveways, and streamed through neighbourhoods, but there was always a house to return to, a toilet to bend over, a guest bed to pass out on. Parties outside were in a field, a clearing in the forest, or a wide spot on a dirt road that led up to the hills – all collectively know as *the bush*. In the summer, the bush was a clearing near the lake where there was no sand and no gradual slope into the water, but instead the danger of falling into a mess of weeds and sinking mud. There were no bathrooms in the bush, just places to squat and pee. I have scars on my legs from making my way through thick brambles in a miniskirt. Yes, we wore those even in the bush.

The notion of celebration was irrevocably linked to the forest in Sawmill Creek. We were taught early that the forest was something to extol, something that sustained us all in different ways. Every summer during Sawmill Days men raced up trees, a blur of spiked boots and leather straps slapping against trunks propelling them at dizzying speeds. They rolled logs along the river, the cords of muscles in their legs holding a fine balance of wet bark and moving water, until all fell in but one man, triumphant. There were contests in which chainsaws were twirled and pieces of wood were thrashed into sawdust in record time. Other men rendered wood into art, grizzlies on their hind legs and broad-shouldered lumberjacks hulking above them when they were done. During Sawmill Days, the word *lumberjack* was still used and the images of fairy-tale woodcutters and the beer-bellied, chainsaw-wielding mill boys were somehow wed.

On Friday afternoon, Krista told me about a house party on the hill the following Saturday night. We were in biology class, splitting hydras into multiheaded creatures in Petri dishes. "We *have* to go. The only thing is," she said, "we can't go back to my place. My mother has declared it a No Kid Zone for the weekend. I think she's also declared it a No Husband Zone, but that's not my problem."

"What's she going to do?" I placed a drip of water on a glass disc and set my eye to the microscope. Tunnel vision.

"Fuck if I know."

I looked down the tube to where everything loomed large, bigger than I thought things could be, yet thinner, closer to disappearing. "Well, it doesn't matter, anyways. You can come to my place. The party won't start till late. We'll leave after ten. You know my mother. She'd sleep through a train wreck. Hey, you get anything?"

"Absolutely, darling," Krista said, winking. This meant that she had pilfered a two-sixer of Absolut vodka from one of the neighbours she baby-sat for, neighbours who bought liquor in cases, stored it in a stocked cellar. She had begun stealing alcohol a year before. I was fine with that. It was going to a good cause – our liberation.

"Rob and Mike'll probably be there," Krista whispered out of the corner of her mouth, her eye now on the microscope.

"So?" Rob and Mike. Interchangeable with any Matt, Jeff, or Jason at Sawmill Creek Secondary. Baseball-cap-wearing, chewing-tobacco-spitting, sport-bike-riding sons of mill executives. And that is exactly what Krista wanted. She wanted to ride hard and fast on the back of one of those sport bikes, wanted to feel her red hair tear away from her face, her screams trailing behind her. That's what I imagined. Krista was fair to my dark, at least in appearance. She had red hair, skin so pale and thin you could make out the faint lines of blood, blue beneath it. She had breasts, the promise of fleshy, milk-white breasts under all of her shirts. That holy land tempted even me.

"Oh, right. So sorry. I forgot you were above all that," she said. The bell rang. "I'll be at your place tomorrow night at eight," Krista tossed over her shoulder as she left class.

                                          —

The next night Krista and I sang along to the radio, yelping as we tried to dance in the small space, knocking hipbones and shins into pieces of furniture. Krista had brought along a backpack full of possible outfits and started to pull on a pair of tight jeans. She jumped around the room, red-faced with the exertion of trying to pull the zipper up, until I said, "Lie on the bed, I'll zip you up." I could hear water in the pipes which meant Vera was getting ready for bed. Soon we'd be able to go out. "Okay, hold," I instructed Krista. She inhaled and held the air in her throat while I zipped. "Ah shit, you aren't going to be able to move in those, Kris. What's the use?"

"What's the use? What's the *use*? Granted, walking is a little difficult but they'll stretch. Besides, look at this ass!" Krista got up and pointed to herself in the mirror. "There's nothing better than a heart-shaped ass, isn't that what Mickey Rourke says in that movie? Nothing better than a heart-shaped ass." That movie was *9½ Weeks*. Mrs. Delaney had a copy. We watched it at Krista's after school one afternoon just as we had read bits of *Fear of Flying* and *Kama Sutra* to each other, doubling over in laughter when we tried to imagine Mr. and Mrs. Delaney churning curds, as one of the positions was called. "I have a feeling my mom's churning curds with someone else," Krista had said. Unlike Vera, she was at least churning curds with *someone*.

I wore my jeans looser, which wasn't difficult with my figure, or lack thereof. The waistband of my jeans hung on the bone handles of my hips. My sweater was cropped and whenever I moved there was only skin in the place where a belt might have been between shirt and jeans. Nothing holding my jeans up or holding me in.

We worked meticulously on our faces, Krista convincing me they needed a lot of help. A light shadow beneath the brow, darker shade in the crease, liner as a frame for the eye. Mascara on the top lashes only, on the bottom lashes it was prone to smudging and would look cheap. Cheeks hollowed out with blush. The amount of effort put into covering our lips baffled me but I followed Krista's lead. Lips lined first, then filled in with lipstick, blotted, smeared, blotted again, glossed iridescent. Lips of many layers. If you bit into those lips, you would leave marks. The mark of ridges in layers of colour and gloss, a pink stain on teeth. We refined our faces until I was sure my mother had fallen asleep.

My mother slept as though night descended for her own personal benefit, designed to plunge only her into darkness, a place where all her senses were wiped black and nothing could reach her. When we were children, this frightened Nick and me. We would come to her in the night or early morning, and if Vera was asleep, she was gone from us – unwakable even when we bounced together at the foot of her bed, using her legs as a hurdle. It wasn't until exactly seven and a half hours

had passed that she would sit up in bed, suddenly and irrevocably awake. By the time I was seventeen, Vera's deep sleep was a
boon. Her sleep was my freedom and I was sure that I could
feel it when it settled on the house. The feeling of old wood
contracting, of ground shifting. Once it fell, we could walk
right out of the house, no need for cunning.

The air hit us as soon as we stepped out the door, a slow,
cold bank. It was always thick in November, before it snowed,
and hung in the fields like sheer fabric. The mill made the air
like that. The smoke was laced with a smell I identified as wood
processing and the lingering scent of trees divided and stripped
to the grain. The mill yard was always lit and, although it was
out on the highway, its light seeped into the air and everything
glowed pink. It could've been beautiful, if you didn't know
what it was from. The valley did things to the air as well. In the
summer it would hold heat, which would push the clouds out,
keep the valley arid and light. In the winter, cold would settle
on the valley floor and the air would clot up until there were
banks of it, surface upon surface of drafts, woodsmoke.

"Fuck, it's cold," Krista said, digging her hands into the
pockets of her jacket, tossing her hair around her face like a
scarf as we started down the driveway toward the road.

"Yeah, and those jeans are going to cut off the blood flow
to that heart-shaped ass."

"Uh, thanks, Mom."

"Like your mom would say that. She'd say, 'Can't you get
'em any tighter, honey?'"

"Granted."

The road was wet, no ice yet but dense, wet cold. I didn't

want to walk to the party. It was across town, up on the hill where the people with money lived. "Hey," I called to Krista, who was already walking, or mincing, her steps short and quick in the jeans. "Let's take the bikes."

"The bikes? Why would we do that?"

"Because it's so cold. We'll get there faster on bikes – and we'll be warm by the time we do." I turned back to the shed at the end of the driveway, my mind made up.

Krista yelled at me in a whisper clenched between teeth. "Harper, are you crazy? We can't ride bikes to a party. Numero uno, my jeans will split. Numero twono, hello? We will look so cool arriving on bicycles. I can hardly wait for *that*."

"We'll bike into town, park them, and walk to 7-E to find a ride," I said with finality. "We bike into town or I'm not going."

We were used to riding bikes at night. In the summer, we rode to the subdivisions on the hill, where the houses were separated by narrow corridors of lawn. Backyards full of pools. Motion-sensor lights hadn't gained popularity yet and these were people whose pets were clean and quiet, kept inside at night. The pools lay ready to be entered, fences and plastic covers the only things keeping us out. We had learned trees and fences already, ways to climb seemingly flat surfaces, ways to land with the minimum sting to the soles of feet. Pool covers were easily folded back or rolled up. It was the undressing that was the hardest part. Even though we wore only shorts over our bathing suits to straddle fences, and sandals for grip, taking those off was a final statement: we're going in; if we get caught, we'll be close to naked. We both prided ourselves on our stealth and ability to slip into water without a sound. The feeling of pool water then, in those moments of heightened awareness of slight movement and the possibility of lights, was like nothing else. The water, a smooth secret on every inch of skin.

That night, we got on the bikes – one mine, one Nick's – and pedalled to the top of a hill, bracing ourselves against the cold. The road led away from my house like a ribbon unrolling in either direction. One direction led to town. The other eventually met the highway and led out. My hair whipped back from my face and I could feel the ends meeting violently behind me, forming knots. The air was as sharp as pins on my cheeks and uncovered hands.

The 7-Eleven was new in Sawmill Creek. It had arrived on my fifteenth birthday, erected on the strip of town closest to the highway. Across the street there was a Husky gas station and diner. I had memories of Husky diners and they all involved Jim Harper. On our road trips, Vera liked to prepare food in the van to save money. She had some kind of kitchen rigged up – a cooler, milk crates full of plastic plates and cutlery, blue jugs of water, orange plastic sinks. Jim had even built a storage space into the van that held all these things together and a makeshift counter. It was Vera who did the grocery shopping, Nick in the safety seat of the cart, me in the back. She placed the food around my limbs. The last thing in was always ice for the cooler. Vera preferred a block; it didn't melt as fast. To me, grocery stores are still this: the feeling of the metal mesh of the grocery cart beneath my backside, holding ice between my legs.

Jim, on the other hand, was a great crusader for the

integrity of roadside diners. Ma-and-Pa diners were the best – the backbone of the road, and thus the spine of the North American landscape – however, Husky's presence right across the continent impressed him. He felt a kinship with truck drivers through their shared appreciation for the lure of the road. Even as a kid, I could tell that the truckers felt uncomfortable when Jim waxed poetic about this. I was most often too happy with the grilled-cheese sandwich and fries that my father always let me order to be concerned for long though. Collecting paper Husky placemats on each of our trips, I traced our routes along the map of Canada, hearts on the places where my parents got along, Xs on the places where they fought.

Sawmill Creek did not register on the Husky-placemat map of Canada. It was on the way to and from places that made it onto the map and towns that didn't, but were quainter and had more endearing names – Cherryville, Summerland, Peachland. The name Sawmill Creek had its own charm. We did have a huge carving of a lumberjack wielding a chainsaw to welcome people to town, but when the tourists found out that there was nothing there but dead boring main street and a dark mall, they moved on. On their way to bigger lakes, vineyards, and golf courses, they were able to pull off the highway, fill up with gas and eat without ever having to see the town that extended past the strip. They could get back into their cars and never get caught in the back roads that tattooed the landscape in grids, mapping out fields and orchards in never-ending squares.

The 7-Eleven in Sawmill was a meeting place for those without cars and those looking for passengers. A terminal where everyone's destination was a party. When there were no parties to be found, the 7-E become a destination in itself. Cars were parked and kids stood around in packs, blocking the No Loitering sign. Girls fidgeted and fixed their hair, glancing over their shoulders as though any minute a stranger from out of town would appear on the edge of the parking lot to whisk them away. Guys shuffled their feet, arranged their chests and called out to each other in false baritones. In the summer, the clerks would come out, walk around the side of the building for the hose, and spray us full force with water until we got back into our cars and drove away. Even 7-Eleven clerks wouldn't do that to us in the winter. We couldn't stand around outside for long in November, regardless.

Krista and I parked the bikes between a fence and hedge at a house around the corner from the 7-E. Krista looked like she was on fire, red curls tangled in a spray around her face, her cheeks and forehead a bright, glazed pink. "Fuck, these jeans are frozen to me," she said, walking toward the 7-Eleven, legs stiff and nearly straight. I opened my jacket and tried to warm myself, wrapping my arms around my waist to cover the space between sweater and low-slung jeans. Air had shot up under the hem of my jacket, a band of cold on the exposed skin as though painted with a brush dipped in water. The two of us walked in silence till we hit the parking lot. Then we had to start looking casual.

"Whose party did you say it was?"

"Jeff's. His parents are in Van. Don't turn around now, I think that's Rob's car."

"You know the sound of his car?" The car cut in front of us

to pull into a space. Rob, Matt, and Mike got out, spitting tobacco and smirking.

"You ladies ride your horses over?"

"Ha. Funny. Look, I'm laughing," Krista replied and walked past them into the store. I followed. We bought coffee to warm our hands, a carton of orange juice for mix, then loitered near the magazine rack. Two of the guys came up behind us and literally breathed down our necks. I turned around abruptly and glared. Krista turned around slowly, smiling, her expression belying her words. "And what the hell do you think you're doing?" she purred.

"Oohhh," one of the guys raised his eyebrow. "Language, ladies. That's not what they teach you in church, is it?" I didn't know how to deal with banter, the hollow, slightly malicious tone of it. Nothing was neutral to me, nothing simple or kind. A kind of battlefield, the area in front of that magazine rack, those smirking faces and bodies of boys surrounding us.

"You guys are going to Jeff's, right?" I asked, pulling their eyes off Krista as they adjusted the shoulders of sweatshirts, tugged at the brims of caps.

"Yeah."

"Okay. Give us a ride. Let's get out of here."

Krista looked at me like I had broken some kind of rule. She was crude and straightforward when she thought it would be shocking, coy and evasive otherwise. I didn't know the nuances of that language.

We started drinking in the back seat, perched on laps, too many hands everywhere. The guys had guy drinks – cans of O'Keefe Extra Old Stock, rye. We had a carton of orange juice, a two-sixer of vodka and large Styrofoam cups, recently emptied of coffee. Half-and-half, straight down. We plugged our noses and closed our eyes against the burn of alcohol, knew when it went down because of the burn down our throats, the warmth expanding in our stomachs. The party was twenty minutes away in Jeff's parents' large, pastel-stuccoed house on the hill. By the time we got there, Krista and I were laughing fire out of our noses. I clutched the door handle as I lifted myself from the car, the air welcoming me, light and electric and suddenly warm. The house twinkled with lights and sound. A wall of noise hit us when we opened the door.

We left our shoes in a pile near the door and held our coats in front of us as we pushed into the house. The guys kept their shoes on and left us as soon as they got in the door. We watched their shoulders part the crowd, their chins raised and jutted in a greeting to other guys. Then the house swallowed them, other faces and bodies turning toward and away from Krista and me in their wake. All familiar faces, no one I wanted to talk to.

Krista and I threw our coats on a bed in a spare room and made our way into the kitchen hugging juice and vodka to our chests. We opened cupboards, looking for glasses, and finally pulled two out of the dishwasher that was partially open, a ball cap perched on one of the racks. The kitchen was already smelling old with smoke. Two guys stood over the stove, one holding knives against the burner and then heating a ball of hash with them, the other holding a two-litre pop bottle with the bottom cut off, ready to take in the fumes. Girls lined the countertops, bare legs dangling out from tight denim skirts, hands on their drinks or in their hair, touching each other's shoulders and knees quickly, teasing. The stench of hash was thick in the air, the laughter of girls high and shrill.

"Let's get out of here," I said, leaning into Krista. She nodded back. We each had two huge glasses of vodka and orange. We'd be fine. We left the empty bottle and carton in the sink with beer cans, ashes, and waterlogged bits of food. We circled the house, gulping down our drinks, steadying ourselves against walls and pieces of furniture. Everything in the house was cream- and peach-coloured, gleaming with glass and brass fixtures. I suspected that before it had filled up with smoking, sweating high school students the house had smelled strongly of vanilla.

I had already lost track of time when I started to feel sick, having finished my drink so long before that I didn't know where I had left the glass. In the dining room, I found myself gripping the back of a chair. Krista was gone. One of the guys – a Rob or a Mike or a Matt – came up behind me, snaked his thick arm around my waist and gripped the chair to me, flexed some muscles.

"You dizzy?" he slurred. I could smell his breath, sour behind me.

"You better let go. I feel like I'm going to hurl."

"Oh, not such a good girl now, are you?" I tried to pull away but his heavy arm held me firm between the chair and his body. I concentrated on some distant point in the air. Through

the arch separating dining and living room, I could see a surge
of people twisting around themselves, shrieking. Soon, people
pushed their way into the dining room and the arm was gone
from my waist. I could hear yelling and the sound of two or
three loud voices shouting commands, then something being
released like a crack of thunder. There was a girl leaning up
against me, laughing so hard she couldn't stand straight, face
shining with tears. She grasped my arm.

"The couch is on fire!" she roared, spit spraying on my
face.

"What?"

The girl hiccuped. "Yeah, the fucking couch is on fire! Jeff
and Matt are using the fish tank to put it out." I pushed my way
around her and into the living room, my socks soaking up
water from the carpet. The couch was smouldering and bright
green plastic plants clung limp to the furniture. No fish in sight
but I imagined fins and tails pulsing against the upholstery.

I turned back into the dining room, pressed my palms
together and held my arms straight out, pointed them toward
the sliding glass door on the other side of the room. Putting
my head down, I pushed through the crowd with my arms in
front of me until I felt the glass of the sliding door meet my
fingertips. It slid open to dry, cold air and perma-turf sodden
with beer. Two headbangers leaned over the railing of the
deck, tapping the head of a glowing joint onto the lawn.
Hoping that the sweet, sticky smell of marijuana would fill the
place where nausea had been, I gripped the railing, leaned into
the smoke and followed my hands along the banister until I
reached the bangers.

"He-ee-ey," one of them turned to me and said this word as though it had three syllables.

"Hey," I responded, curt and cool.

They dragged on the joint and passed it between them. There were shrieks coming from the lawn, the sound of drunken people walking into objects in the dark, laughing at things that weren't funny. I wondered when they would offer me some smoke. I was sure that if I could take it into me, fill my lungs with warmth and air, the dizzy weight in my stomach would disappear. I was just going to have to ask. "Hey, can I have a drag?"

They stopped fidgeting and looked at me. "Yeah, of course, yeah, sure," one of them responded.

"We, uh, didn't think you'd want any," the other said.

I took the joint, closed my eyes when I inhaled and tasted smoke along my teeth and gums. I inhaled through my nostrils, slowly and surely. I didn't cough. I let out a long, smooth sigh and opened my eyes. The guys tried not to look impressed. I handed the joint back to one of them and watched his fingers, thick and blunt, how they could hold the tip of the joint so delicately, how they fell against his jeaned thigh when he handed it on. I wondered how that hand would feel tracing a line down the back of my neck.

Suddenly Krista was there, swaying a bit. She held on to the shoulder of one of the guys to balance herself, laughed, and then announced, "Shit," as though it was some sort of commentary.

"Hey, Kris, what's up?" I asked.

"Uh, Harp, is it okay if we go now?"

"Yeah, sure." The house throbbed with noise behind us and I couldn't imagine going back in. "How are we going to get home?" Home suddenly seemed very far away, like days would pass before we got there.

Krista turned me from the railing and gave me a nudge back into the house. She followed me through the crowd, speaking over my shoulder, her words hot in my ear. "Listen, Rob can drop us off at 7-E. Mike wants to meet me later. We can get the bikes and bike over to Harstad. Mike wants me to meet him there, will you come?"

I tried to twist around to face Krista. "Why doesn't Rob just give us all a ride to Harstad, or to my place. You guys can fool around in my living room for all I care."

"I don't know – we have to get the bikes anyway – and they're about to leave. I need to tell him. Please?"

Getting us all back into the car was a challenge. Once again, Krista and I were on laps, necks kinked to accommodate the car ceiling. As promised, we were driven to the 7-Eleven. Before getting there, I said, "It wouldn't hurt you to give us a ride all the way to wherever, like my place, would it?"

To which one of the guys answered, "You never know, it might." I didn't know how to respond, and so didn't.

⌒

The guys dropped us off at 7-Eleven, inscribing a smooth arc with tires into the frost on the parking lot. We rounded the building, cut through a yard, and groped briefly between bush and fence before finding our bikes. As we dragged them out, small, cold branches snapped from the leafless bush, a cracking sound around us.

Harstad was an elementary school in the opposite direction of my house from the 7-Eleven. We started pedalling. We weren't cold, not at first. Alcohol ran like coffee in our veins, made us hot and fast, full of energy. We pedalled until our legs tightened and our calves burned, jeans chafing against cold skin. By then, we were there. Krista and I leaned the bikes against the side of the school. Everything around us was wet and cold – the brick school, the concrete yard, each metal railing and banister. Tether-ball chains clanged against poles, the balls taken down for the weekend.

"I'm supposed to meet him over by the goal posts," Krista said.

"Oh, that's fitting."

"What?"

"Nothing – go, the sooner the better. I'll wait here. Try not to be too long, hey?"

"Fuck, I don't know many people who would do this," Krista lunged in a hug at me. "You sure?"

"Yes. Go!" I watched Krista walk into the field, air like steam around her. Then she was gone, the lights around the school only reaching so far. I sat down on the steps and realized why I was there, at an elementary school at two in the morning, waiting. What Krista wanted so badly that she would bike for twenty minutes in the cold to lie down on a wet field, I couldn't say no to because I wasn't brave enough to go after it myself. It was more than the feeling of wanting that headbanger's hand along the back of my neck. I'd been able to let go of that easily enough. I wasn't yet willing to find out what would happen if I gave myself over to someone else so completely that I didn't care, in that moment, about the consequences. And so, I tried to allow Krista that. I sat until the cold concrete sent shoots of pain into my backside, my spine. Then I got up and jumped the steps. Drunk and numb, I should have fallen, ground my face against concrete, but I didn't. The challenge of remaining in control of my own movement kept me focused, warm for a while. Then the wind picked up.

When the frigid air had made its way through every stitch of my clothing, into each pore, I walked out into the field toward the goal posts. I walked until I couldn't exactly see Krista and Mike, but a different kind of darkness, lumped on the field, then stopped and called, "Krista! Let's go. I'm freezing! We have to go." When I heard something, movement, a muffled giggle, I yelled again. "Krista, we *have* to go. I'm leaving." I followed my own wet prints back to the cement yard and waited under a light. I couldn't see more than two feet in front of me, the effect of the illumination meeting the dark, nothing in between.

Krista's voice came out of shadow, a low giggle. "I'm so sorry, Harp. You're right, it is fucking cold. I think it's going to snow soon, don't you?" I just looked at her.

Mike appeared. "Uh," he said to me. "You want a smoke?"

"Are you kidding?" I turned toward the bikes and heard Krista whisper as she said something to Mike, then let out a laugh like a cough.

The cold on the way to my house was enough to make me want to cry. We didn't speak, just rode. When we got home,

Krista followed me, wordless, to the bathroom. We stripped to shirts and underwear and sat on the edge of the tub, feet frigid, watched the colour spread from toes to ankles, Krista's feet burning magenta, mine a muddied red. Yelled into each other's shoulders when the feeling came back into them, our feet gripped with cramps. We slept in thick socks and long underwear, Krista curled into my back, and we each rubbed our feet together until we fell asleep.

I woke, heavy and hot, my body twisted in fabric – the sheets, long johns, a useless bra chafing my shoulder blades – and couldn't pull the layers off for the sweat. I struggled with the sheets until I woke Krista up.

She was moaning and cursing. "I feel like crap. There is no way I'm getting up for church."

"Bullshit, Kris. If I can bike to Harstad with you at two in the morning, you can haul your ass out of bed and come with me to church. It's communion Sunday. You know I have to go."

I held the wall as I walked across the room. "Sylvie!" Vera called from the kitchen as soon as I opened the door. "You two better have breakfast soon or we'll be late." When I didn't answer, she continued, "Nick and I will go on without you and you'll have to take the bikes." The bikes. There was no way I would take the bikes. I winced my way down the stairs and into the bathroom, held the counter and faced my bloodshot eyes in the mirror, splashed cold water on my face. I couldn't find a glass so I emptied a Mason jar of flowers out the window, rinsed it and filled it with water. I took it with a bottle of aspirin back upstairs.

"Okay, we're going to have to pull ourselves together or my mom, the bag, is going to make us bike to church," I told Krista, who was groaning and had her knees up to her chest, arms wrapped around them.

"I can't believe you let me do that last night," she said as I straightened one of her arms, opened her hand and spilled four aspirin into her palm. I held the Mason jar out to her. "What's this?"

"Water."

"God, why does it smell like compost?"

"Just drink it. Let you do what?"

"Go with Mike! Shit, he'll probably never speak to me at school again."

"He hardly spoke to you before."

"I know, but you just watch, by the time he tells the rest of them what a slut I am, no one will be speaking to me and then – this tastes like shit, I'll have you know – I guess that's just the way it goes."

"Yeah, I guess so, Kris."

As soon as we got to church, Krista and I went to the small bathroom in the basement. She leaned over the toilet gagging and spitting clear liquid into the bowl. I slapped my cheeks and opened my eyes wide in the mirror. Despite four aspirin, my head hung on to the ache. I began strapping my hair into a braid as Krista vomited, finally bringing something up, apparently from the night before as we hadn't eaten breakfast. I finished my braid, then went into the stall, pulled Krista's hair from her face and rubbed her forehead. She started to cry.

"I'm so stupid, Harper." I rubbed her back as she leaned over and vomited again. I had to close my eyes and concentrate on not getting sick myself. I would not leave Krista alone in the stall. She was the one strong enough to meet boys in fields and vomit up the evidence in a church basement the next day. Next to her, I was an observer, sitting on concrete steps in the cold. Krista coughed up again, then closed the lid of the toilet and rested her forehead against it. I braided her hair and hummed under my breath. When I finished, Krista got up, rinsed her mouth in the sink, and we both splashed our faces with cold water. Slapped our cheeks until they shone like ripe apples.

As Pastor John began his sermon that Sunday, I wrapped my arms around my stomach and gripped my waist with my hands to try to keep my head upright on my shoulders. Part way through the sermon, Amens and Hallelujahs rose up to a pitch around us. Vera had her head down, eyes toward the Bible open on her lap. I thought that she had been watching me and, as if sensing my thought, she looked up and in that moment her expression seemed to me distant, regretful.

I steadied myself, my spinning head and lurching stomach, until we rose for communion. We went to the front of the church and lined up. There were three men up there – a councillor who put wafers on our outstretched tongues, Pastor John who held out the communal cup for us to drink from, and another councillor who stood ready to refill it, a white cloth wrapped around the bottle soaking up spilled wine. The wine was cheap and smelled like composting grapes and vinegar. I knew it was bad even before I'd had a drop of anything better. Twelve of us lined up at a time and Pastor John said, "And he took bread, and gave thanks, and brake it, and gave unto them." The councillor placed fine wafers on our tongues. "This is my body which is given for you: Do this in remembrance of me." I saw Krista's body, spread out on the field, her hair bright red against the ground, stars reflected in her pale skin. I pushed the wafer against the roof of my mouth until it dissolved. I could smell the wine coming closer. A shadow came over Krista, wiped out the stars. "This cup is the new testament in my blood, which is shed for the remission of your sins." The cup was at my lips, the bitter taste of metal. I let the wine touch my mouth then backed away. "Drink of me and you shall have everlasting life." I held the wine in my mouth and felt my throat constrict. Krista was on the ground, blood bright and rising between her legs. I struggled to swallow.

"Sylvia?" I could hear Vera's voice from somewhere. I turned with the wine still held in my mouth, looking for Krista. If I could just see her, everything would be all right. I swallowed the wine, imagining the Lord travelling down my throat in wine and wafers. I felt the dark cold of the schoolyard close around me and the floor rise, hit me in the back of my legs.

GABE

On the way to a place your father keeps calling home, you stop outside Jackson Hole, Wyoming, to visit your grandparents. Your grandfather can spit, a watery shot, out of the corner of his mouth and calls your dad not Peter but the Ungrateful Little Asshole. "Well, if the Ungrateful Little Asshole isn't back again," he says with a mock punch at Peter's arm that has him wincing even though it can't have hurt. Your grandfather seems rough but he isn't cruel, kinder than your grandmother who stares at you and tugs at your clothing. She spits as well, onto her own sleeve and then grinds the wet fabric into your face. She tells you that you are too skinny, you don't drink enough milk. She tells you that your mother, Whatshername, was an ungrateful selfish little girl, who did she think she was, and where was she, anyway? Both of your parents are little and ungrateful, for what, you don't know. Later, when you remember all this, your grandparents seem implausible, as though they couldn't possibly have been that unkind. You can't tell, though, because you have no other memories of them to compare these with.

These people are not like the adults you left behind on the communal farm in Canada. Despite their age, they move a lot

49

faster, all jerking movements like they are constantly flinching from flies. They seem to have a lot of things to do. Your grandmother slams things into the kitchen counter. Your grandfather is outside, throwing open the shed doors.

"Get that boy out here!" he yells through the kitchen window. You don't know *that boy* means you. You think it might mean Peter. After all, your grandfather seems to think he is still a boy.

"Go," your grandmother jerks her chin toward the back door, frowning. As you leave the room, you hear her say, "Just like his father, slower than molasses on a frozen lake."

What your grandfather wants to show you is a gun. You have seen guns before, toys, but never handled with pride. Plastic guns could be found everywhere – in the bush around the farm left by some long-gone kid, on the edges of parking lots when you went to town. At the beach in the summer they sold water guns, hung behind the counter in a plastic rainbow of colour. You and the other boys at the farm could spot them like some people have an eye for four-leaf clovers or wild asparagus growing in a ditch. Whenever you brought them back to the farm, though, a fight would rise between someone and someone else. *We shouldn't let them believe weapons are toys.*

Play is a healthy way for them to express a natural instinct towards aggression.

They're pretending to kill each other. How can that be healthy?

If we forbid gun play, that will only make guns more fascinating. You learned what opinions were at the farm. You soon learn that your grandfather has a different opinion about guns than your father does.

Your grandfather names all the parts to the pistol and makes you repeat them. He is about to let you hold it in your own hand, on its side against your palm, to feel the weight of it, the power. He tells you it is so heavy it will pull your arm toward the floor. Your stomach is tickling with excitement. And that place below your stomach. That's when Peter comes into the shed, yells at your grandfather, and pushes you out. You stand between shed and house, waiting for someone to call for you. A dog from the other side of the fence barks and throws its presumably tiny body against the fence again and again. You don't know what you are supposed to do, where you are supposed to go. You hear your grandfather. "You're still a goddamn sissy."

Then your father. "You have learned nothing from that war, our country's failure, nothing. Don't you know what we were trying to tell you when we left, when we refused to take part in such a –"

"Refused to defend your country, to defend our way of life – a decent, civilized way of life – against those goddamn Commie bastards."

"Listen to you, Dad. Just listen to yourself –"

"No, you listen to me. You left, deserted, tail between your legs, and now you've come waltzing back in, with a ponytail and a little boy that I have no idea how you'll raise. What the hell happened to Susie? She finally had enough?"

By this time, your grandmother has come to the back door and reaches her arm right out to the middle of the yard, it seems, to pull you back into the kitchen, push you into a chair and slam a glass down in front of you. She fills it, not with milk but with lemonade, and for a moment, you think you could love her.

"Always been like that, Peter and Wilf." Wilf, you guess, is your grandfather. Sounds like Peter and the Wolf. She shakes her head, then gets up and snaps on the radio. The news comes through the kitchen in static. You want to say something then. Maybe tell her about the drive down, about all the fun you are having, just you two guys. You are going to tell her your mother is fine but Peter comes into the kitchen then, red-faced, and looks at you in a way that makes you stand up.

"Well, he's done it again," he says. "We're leaving now, Mom." It is the first time you hear Peter say this. When you came in, he called her "your grandmother." This is your father's mom.

"I know," your father's mom says back, moving toward the table in the middle of the room. When she meets it, she grips, ungrips the edge. "I know," she repeats. That was the last time you saw those two people. You don't know how much of any of that you made up.

You leave your grandparents and keep driving. When the van stops in Arcana, California, you and Peter have decided that you might stay a while. He has included you in this choice with statements like questions – "What do you think, huh?" and "We'll like it here, hey?" – to which you nod. Peter makes friends with other adults in a loud, joking way that you later realize makes people like him at first, avoid him later. You hear him tell people, "Don't have a lot of material wealth but I'm good with my hands, can do just about anything." This is how you and Peter find places to stay. He helps people with things –

greenhouses, staircases, stone fireplaces – and you both stay in their houses while he does. You eat cereal with whichever kids live at the house you're at, liking the places where they serve what Susan called *sugar bombs*, loathing the places where they feed you granola stirred into bitter yogurt. You and your instant friends – whichever children are there – read comics, build forts, and are sent outside where you run from object to object, climb things, and yell for very little reason.

You know, although Peter has never told you, not to mention the unfinished A-frame in Canada. Later, you will also know that it was more than an unfinished A-frame that came between your parents, but as a child you will attribute everything to this – Susan's crying, Peter's indifference, how you left, quickly and with so few words.

$\mathcal{F}$riends could heal with well-chosen verses, circles of prayer. Could wipe sin clean away within the length of a song. Pastor John came over the evening after I had fainted at church.

"Come in, Pastor John, God bless!" Vera chimed like a bell when she opened the door. I was in the living room waiting and could only hear them.

"God bless, Vera," he said, his tone sounding more serious. They spoke more quietly and I couldn't make out what they were saying until they were standing outside the living-room door. Then, I heard Pastor John saying, "It must be hard for you on your own, Vera. You know, I do believe that God meant for children to be raised by both a man and a woman, but we can't always know his plans for us, can we?"

They were coming into the room. "Oh, no. No we can't," my mother laughed nervously and stopped in the doorway, her hand reflexively to the nape of her neck, pulling at the fine hairs there. "Well, it is difficult sometimes, as you know, but we do try."

I thought their voices skated on the surface, thin and sharp and insincere. I greeted them with a forced smile. Vera stood in the door for a moment until Pastor John asked her to give us some time alone.

I had never seen Pastor John uncomfortable and he wasn't then. He pulled at the legs of his pants as all tall men do, making room for his knees, and set a Bible in front of him on the coffee table. "Have you been praying, Sylvia?"

"Yes." Not exactly a lie. I didn't so much pray as ask for signs.

"You will be easily deceived, Sylvia – you are young and impressionable – we understand this. I understand this, your Friends in Christ understand this, and we are here for you. But it takes more than you, it takes more than our entire congregation. No one knows you – your temptations, your weakness – better than your personal saviour, Jesus Christ." I nodded, kept a straight face. Pastor John had his hands on his knees, his eyes at some place above my head. "And no one but our true Friend, Jesus Christ, can guide you on the right path. If you ask for forgiveness with a clean heart, He *will* guide you. You must be ready, though. He'll know if you're not. Will you read Proverbs 20:1 with me, Sylvia?"

We said together, "Wine is a mocker, strong drink is raging; and whosoever is deceived thereby is not wise." The last part referred to me, I knew, the one who was deceived. There was a cure, however. I read Ephesians 5 out loud at Pastor John's prompting. "And be not drunk with wine, wherein is excess; but be filled with the Spirit; Speaking to yourselves in Psalms and hymns and spiritual songs, singing and making melody in your heart to the Lord." The Friends of Christ were doing the right thing, singing down the chosen path. A path that ended, "Submitting yourselves one to another in the fear of God."

Pastor John had me stop reading there, though the rest of the chapter was already committed to memory. Pastor John quoted it again and again to explain the hierarchy of the Free Church. Wives submitting themselves to the will of their husbands, husbands loving their wives like their own bodies, like temples. All of us flesh, bones, and blood of a greater body, submitting ourselves to Christ.

Sometimes I felt estranged from my own body, as though it were a symbol of something else. Once, it was something I didn't think of often. Something to get me up trees and onto every potentially dangerous thing at the playground, teetering on metal, standing on slides. Something that got restless in vans and cars or itchy after being in bays coated with duck crap like the ones at Sunny Bay Bible Camp. The Friends of Christ Free Church had no summer camp of our own so we were sent to camp with the lesser of evil denominations, the Baptists. We met a bus in the mall parking lot, clutched duffle bags, sleeping rolls, and pillows in quiet horror as the bus opened up, took our belongings into the bottom of it, while we climbed aboard, sandwiched into seats between strangers.

Sunny Bay was indeed in a sunny bay, one lined with cabins, summer homes, docks. The sand was fine and could burn the bottoms of our feet. Ponderosa pines released their smell everywhere. If you pull a pine needle, sticky with new sap, from the tree and place it on water, the pitch will release, propel the needle across the surface like a tiny motor boat. The camp was across the road from the lake and the counsellors wore reflective vests, walked right out into summer traffic, stop signs in front of them like shields. We would then stream across the road, flip-flops snapping against our feet, line up on the dock in life jackets and bathing suits worn thin on our backsides, later tip each other over in canoes. One afternoon, the canoe I was in was ambushed and I came up under it again and again, my body unable to conceive of any other way out of the water. I knocked my head against the over-turned canoe until I stopped, rested in the bubble of air between boat and water, alone, wet and dark. When the counsellors righted the boat, they wondered why I had stayed there, clinging to the beam of an over-turned seat. It was the first time that I knew my body was something that could also betray me. A moth and the dark underbelly of the canoe, a light.

There were strange names for things at camp: mess hall, canteen, chapel. Chapel was church and we had to go every day, after dinner. Chapel looked like a chapel should, small and white and pointed, complete with a steeple. It was like a church made from the folded hands of children – *Here's the church, here's the steeple, open the doors, and see all the people.* All God's children, with seersucker sundresses, shorts and skin that smelled of lake and dirt, lined up in pews in the heat-trapped

chapel until we stuck to each other. The pastor from the
Baptist church told us that our bodies were not our own, they
were temples of Christ. Our bodies vessels for God's will.
Shipping vessels, I thought, like pieces of the Battleship game.
I was a boat on my way to battle, God's will filling the holes so
I couldn't be hit. *A-3, miss. F-9, miss. D-4, miss.* Later, my counsellor would tell us that girls were more like vases – delicate and
fragile, God's will the water that would allow us to hold things
as beautiful as flowers. I didn't like this analogy. Flowers died
after a few days. The water left in the bottom of vases was thick
and green and it stank.

Our bodies were also temples. Each evening, after taking
horseback riding lessons or making useless crafts out of burlap,
seeds, and glue, we met before dinner for cabin talk. All it took
was one girl, a memory of her grade three teacher, his hands in
her panties behind the desk while he explained subtraction.
Four other girls choked out what was locked behind the temple
doors: a grandpa who liked a bare bum on his lap; a cousin who
played doctor until he was too old, too rough; a father who
tickled the wrong places and groaned; the feeling of back-seat
vinyl under the weight of an old family friend. Five out of the
ten of us. I tried to find myself in the numbers, hoped something would come to me that would have me choking up tears.

One summer, Krista had agreed to come with me to camp.
Each night, we sang and swayed with the rest of the kids at the
evening service. During one of these services, a camp counsellor was murmuring into a microphone about coming up to the
front. We didn't need to say anything, she assured us, we could
just rise and accept the Holy Spirit into our very own hearts.

Another counsellor was playing "Will the Circle Be Unbroken" again and again on an aged electronic keyboard. One by one, kids were going to the front, some with hands raised and peaceful smiles, some racked with sobs and being comforted by a row of counsellors, a clean-scrubbed support team nodding empathetically. Even I had felt something as I crooned and swayed. Later, I would explain to myself that I had been afflicted with religious fervour. At the time, I felt God. God had felt like air in my limbs, an expanding chasm of peace replacing whatever had been there before. I would know later that God felt a little like getting high. Whatever it was, Krista felt it too. She didn't look peaceful but her mouth was set and her eyes were focused so intently in front of her that I was sure she could rearrange air with them. She wanted something. Krista pushed past me and went up to the front, the sign that she had accepted Jesus into her heart, and stood there rigid, not sobbing or swaying like the other kids. She just stood there until the keyboard music stopped and the counsellors led us, blurry-eyed with Christ, back to our cabins.

The evening after Pastor John's visit, some young women from the church came over to talk about peer pressure and pure living. They were in their twenties and had solemn, presumably faithful husbands and an assortment of babies and toddlers. Pastor John's wife, Trudy, ushered them into the living room like a herd. Trudy was my mother's age but she continued to give birth every few years which seemed to keep her in a state of perpetual youth. We all knew Timothy 2:15: Eve's original transgression had stained women. Childbirth could save us, bleach us clean with pain. The words were given to us right in the Bible, codes to our salvation.

These were women with names like Wendy, Dawn, and Becky who shook their bangs out of their eyes, cocked their heads slightly, and nodded at the slightest provocation. Their bodies were soft-looking and smelled faintly of baby vomit and Avon creams and perfumes and they spoke in singsong, alternating between baby talk, Bible verses, and giggling. "We know how hard it can be. We were teenagers once too although, look at us now!" They beamed lovingly at each other's babies. "We're here for you, whenever you need a friend in Christ, or whatever." They each nodded toward me, feigning understanding. "Your peers will try to deceive you but His Word will keep you strong, you know?"

At the end of the evening, Vera joined us in the living room and we prayed together, a ring of faith, palms sweating between our joined hands. Then, the women formed a healing circle around me, their babies strapped in Snuglis to their chests or, if old enough, placed between their crossed legs. I lay in the middle of their joined hands, my back on the floor of our living room, limbs splayed. Each woman prayed to Jesus in a high, soft pitch for my forgiveness – "We just ask you, Lord Jesus, to let Sylvia know that we are here for her. To guide her, allow her to release her own sins, and fill her with your own spirit" – I stifled laughter after that last sentiment while the women started to sing. A couple of them began murmuring in tongues, babies gurgling their own cries and demands. I was to lie still, eyes closed. To be healed by the buoyancy of prayer and song.

Being healed felt like holding my breath. I tried to keep myself down there, on the ground, limbs spread. Tried to convince myself I was light, floating, full of the Spirit. My unspent laughter blocked my throat and I struggled to pull in air. I shot up from the floor. "Will you stop! Please, just stop." I left the room to shocked silence, babies still babbling, mothers still mumbling prayers.

I was uncomfortable in groups of girls and women. By the time we left Edmonton, I had been surrounded by family, aunts and uncles, male and female cousins, and had gone to daycare which I didn't remember as being segregated. When we moved to Sawmill Creek, both elementary school and church seemed to conspire to keep me in the Holly Hobby–themed bedrooms of classmates after school or in the middle of women's circles whenever they felt I needed support or healing.

Sometime in the sixth grade I started to develop breasts, and I felt that this would only seal my fate, take me farther away from reaching the tops of trees, balancing on the thin edges of fences. I had Vera take both Nick and me to the hairdresser in the mall. I waited until Nick got his standard cut, then took his place in the chair, and asked for the same one. The hairdresser was willing to cut my hair short but wanted to give me style, the option to curl, feather, and spray. No, I had insisted, I wanted the same cut, a boy's cut, no curls, no cute flips. I wore my hair like that, dressed in baggy jeans and T-shirts and made one last attempt to join the boys. When that didn't work, I still couldn't feign interest in Barbie's dramas. I spent a lot of time alone, sitting on the floor in various parts of the house, sketching floor plans, windows, pieces of furniture, following lines with my eyes and then improving on the design once it was on the page.

Sometimes, mothers pick up on these things, and Vera did. She started taking me along to garage sales where she would ask me what I thought of a desk, an end table, a chair. With chipped paint and mouse turd in the drawers, I didn't see much but Vera told me, "It's surprising how much you can do with a good sander and some varnish." She wasn't wrong, but after a couple of afternoons with her and a piece of furniture set on old newspapers in the basement, I grew bored of the number of times we would have to sand the paint away to bring out the grain. I flinched at the pressure of her hand on mine, showing me how. The projects we could have completed together started cluttering the basement, banks of half-finished furniture blocking our passage to the cold room. I lost interest in refinishing furniture, grew my hair out. I only had it trimmed a couple times a year after that initial cut, grew it till it reached the strap of the bra that I eventually wore, then beyond.

⚮

I was grounded for two weeks and decided not to push it. By the end of the second week, I could smell the snow that was about to fall. A hollow, metallic tang, the sharp edges of things. Each blade of grass was a small green knife. The scent of the mill was intoxicating when it was warm, sawdust and stripped wood hinting at the smell of entire forests – not only wood but dirt, composting leaves, bark. When it was cold, the mill gave off a smell like fermenting apples. It was the whiff of metal and rotting apples that brought with it the awareness it would snow.

Vera couldn't seem to meet my eyes and constantly lowered her own in both anger and a denial that she was angry. I had learned in Psych 11 that this behaviour was called passive-aggressive. Psychology was new to Sawmill Creek Secondary School. The introduction to the curriculum as an elective caused concern in a town that thought psychology was for shrinks and shrinks were for softies from the city. The class had been in some sort of assessment stage for a couple of years and would likely be until people forgot about it and found some-thing else to oppose.

On one of the afternoons of my term at home, Vera asked me to help her bring up preserves from the cold room. We filled our arms with jars of pears, peaches, jams, pickles; we bal-anced up the stairs to the kitchen and lined the bottles up in the pantry. Each summer and fall, Vera would devote days to pre-serving, finishing one batch just as the next fruit was bursting into season. Water in huge stainless steel pots would boil over on the stove, the jars inside knocking a rhythm in their sub-mersion. The thick liquid, a combination of water and seeping juices, pooled on the linoleum and coated the floor with a glue-like membrane. This mimicked the feeling of my own skin in the summer, sticky with a combination of sweat and sugar from Popsicles or Kool-Aid.

On the way up the stairs, I said, "I don't know why you bother. You can just go to the store and buy these things, you know."

Vera turned to me once she had placed an armload of jars on the shelf. "And I don't know why you would complain, Sylvia. Someday, you're going to be buying preserves like this at some over-priced market and wondering why you never appreciated them now."

"Harper."

"Yes. Harper. You just let me know when you want to start buying the groceries. Maybe you can call up your father and see if he can chip in for some of 'these things,' Harper."

"Oh, is someone touchy?" I asked

"Does someone not think before she talks?" she responded and turned back into the pantry.

My father had made several attempts to get Vera to come back to Alberta in the first couple of years after we moved to Sawmill Creek. Sometimes, I would answer the phone and Jim would start talking before Vera knew who was speaking to me. There must have been something about the way I spoke into the phone, or my expression, because Vera could tell almost immediately who it was. She would take the phone from me and I would hear her say, "Jim, no. No," apparently giving the same answer to several different questions. Eventually, it seemed to me, my father just gave up. As if to resign himself completely to the fact that we weren't moving back, he himself moved to the other end of the country, to a village in Newfoundland called Heart's Desire. "Well, I certainly hope he finds it there," Vera had said. I knew that the child-support cheques came sporadically once he was in the Maritimes. Eventually, the phone calls eased off. I hadn't seen him in years.

Vera brought a jar of peaches to the table, breaking the seal with a large spoon, and we handed it back and forth, eating straight from the jar.

"How'd you guys meet anyways?" I asked.

"Us who guys?"

"Mom, you know. You and Jim."

She looked at me for a minute, swallowed her fruit, and answered, "In a bar," and slid the fruit over to me. I fished for one of the peaches with my spoon. I had always imagined Vera barefoot and full-skirted, picking flowers in a field along the road. Jim Harper would have roared by on his motorbike, carved a sharp U-turn into the gravel road when he saw her, and turned around. He would've stopped his bike along the field and lit a cigarette by striking a match on his boot. I could see it all. It was hot when they met there, on the side of the road, a ditch between them. Prairie hot – flat and unrelenting. A buzz of insects in the ditch, whir of grasshoppers clinging to the underside of wheat, the dust pitched up by Jim Harper's turn settling on skin already covered with sweat.

I struggled to balance the piece of fruit as I brought it up out of the jar but it slipped off as I tried to jimmy the spoon through the mouth. "Damn," I said, then, "Sorry," before asking, "Really? What kind of bar?"

"Just a bar in Fly Hills. There isn't much to describe really. It was the Legion – a low-ceilinged room in the basement of a hall, tables lined up down the centre, nothing but one commemorative tray of the Queen's coronation on the walls. They didn't even play music in the bars back then. For that, you had to go to a house party."

"But, how could you fall in love in a place like that?" I asked around the slice of peach that I had finally got into my mouth.

Vera looked at me, then said, "Sweetie, I didn't say we fell in love there, I said that's where we met." She paused. "Your father was wearing a navy blue turtleneck. I thought he looked dashing. That's it. We didn't fall in love." That was all she said, all I asked.

～

I know even less of Jim Harper's past than I do of Vera's. He was the youngest son of the mayor in Fly Hills, Alberta, the closest town to the farm where Vera grew up. He went to a private academy in Edmonton, one that crawled with ivy and served tea to children, and returned home on weekends to the Harpers' brick house, the yard trimmed with roses. Not wild roses, Alberta's provincial flower, but cultured roses. I imagine Jim rebelling against refinement, cutting roses from the bushes with a pen knife, dragging the thorn along the white, fine skin of the underside of his arm, blood appearing like tiny berries. I believed that I used to run my small fingers against the white ridges on his arm. When I told Vera this, years later, she laughed, said my father had no scars.

Sometimes, I picture Jim Harper chain-smoking behind the brick private school. I see him sneaking out at night with other boys, drowning cats in the Saskatchewan River just because they can. I watch Jim Harper masturbating over creased movie pin-up centrefolds, hidden when he's done in no cleverer place than under his mattress. I hear the *swishswish, swishswish,* of a hundred private school boys' hands rubbing between sheet and skin at night, all hearing the sounds of each other, feeling too good to care. These boys are different from the ones we have now. These are boys with perpetually rolled-up jeans, hightop sneakers, freckles. Norman Rockwell replicas with longings that smell like soap, snapdragons, the pages of magazines. These boys fish in swimming holes and build tree houses and when they finally do have sex for the first time, it will be brief and intense and consensual. Granted, they will think less of the girl, but will remember the white cotton of her panties for years as the last good, innocent thing.

The first day I didn't have to return home immediately after school I felt exhilarated. Not knowing what else to do with this sense of freedom, I skipped my final class and spent it in the girls' bathroom. I stood on the toilet and smoked, exhaling out of a high window, then read magazines. I kohled my eyes until I didn't recognize them, combed my long hair until static electricity shot sparks off my brush. I knew I wasn't getting ready to go anywhere – there was nowhere to go. Krista would be working at her mom's store that afternoon, so I was at loose ends. I walked a long route home to prolong it. With my long hair collecting snow like a veil, my eyes blacked out, and my thin body rendered even more shapeless by layers of clothes, I imagined myself a young bride from another continent, trying to escape an arranged marriage in a cold country, a winter I didn't understand. When I eventually got tired of walking, I propped up my thumb, didn't think anyone would stop.

A brand new white pickup truck pulled over and Rob Hanshaw's face grinned from the other side of the window. I had to stretch up to a step to reach the passenger door. "Where ya heading?" he asked with a chuckle.

"Um, I live on Pottery Road, out by the golf course, do you know it?"

"Yeah. Sylvia, right? You go to SCSS? I gave you and your friend a ride to that party."

One high school in town; nowhere else I could've gone. "Uh, yeah. I go by Harper."

"What?"

"My name, I go by Harper."

"Hey, whatever cranks your frank, you know what I mean." Rob Hanshaw winked, showed me the tips of his teeth. "So you, uh, doing anything?" He asked eventually. I was thinking of how I would have to wash the black liner from around my eyes somewhere between Rob Hanshaw's truck and my house, wondering if snow would work, the imagined pain of that thought already pinching my brow. Rob elaborated. "I mean, now. You doing anything now?"

"No," I said in a tone that I hoped would convey that I didn't necessarily want to do anything. It was four-thirty, cloudy, the sky going from pink to a wash of grey that passed for twilight.

"Ever been to the lookout behind the course?" Rob asked.

He was talking about a bald spot at the turn of a switchback where a small fire had burned the trees to the ground, left an unbroken view of the golf course, the Salmon River rendered flat and motionless, the locked grid of town. "Yeah." It was the site of several bush parties, always broken up early because the car lights were visible from town.

"You wanna go now?"

I hoped for a shared joint, rolled thick and sweet, thought we might listen to the radio, maybe kiss a little, so I answered, "Yeah, sure." I watched the field behind my house bump by as the truck attacked potholes on the dirt road that led up to the lookout. Watched my hands fold and unfold in my lap, then stopped when I realized what I was doing.

Rob Hanshaw had brown hair, brown eyes, and brown freckles. He was one year out of high school, worked at the mill, and was the object of several crushes. He was handsome in a dull, small-town way. Cheeks perpetually flushed and a bit of dirt under his fingernails. A baseball cap and a pair of Levi's. Once the truck was parked, he said few words, his face getting closer as he mumbled something. It took me a while to identify the smell coming with him – Hungry Herbie's home-cut french fries. I identified it right before he dug his tongue into my mouth.

I pressed myself up against the passenger side and expressed no desire, hoping this would be enough. Rob Hanshaw backed away and stared at me for a moment, then came back in, one arm a vice around my waist, the other hand taking my own and pressing it against the stiff crotch of his jeans. He continued to jab his tongue around in my mouth while I tried to disassociate

from my body, but my mind remained pinned between Rob
Hanshaw and the truck door. I rubbed at his jeaned crotch to
distract him. As he moaned, I twisted my arm, which was
pinned behind my back, and groped for the door handle. I
fought the instinct to clench my jaw as I slipped my fingers into
his button-fly and began popping it open. I had to make him
think I wanted it undone as I clawed at the handle with my other
hand. Rob Hanshaw noticed and tightened his hold, pulled me
up and away from the door in one stiff, swift motion. The force
of my grip leaving the handle was enough to jerk it open.

"Oho," Rob Hanshaw said. "You're not trying to leave, are
you? We were just starting to have a good time." He tried to
stroke my hair but cursed when he caught a shock of electricity from it. The other hand kneaded my breast in a rhythmic,
robotic motion that we girls had all gotten used to after four
years of high school. Hand on breast, hand on breast, hand on
breast – pulsing there, stuck like one of those small, ferocious
dogs that, once attached by the teeth to a limb, will not let go.
Hand on breast, hand on breast, hand on breast, while Rob
Hanshaw struggled to pry open his unbuttoned fly. I started to
move back, an instinct toward fresh air, but soon he had not
only his jeans but also his briefs open and was pushing me
down there.

Cold metal buttons. Hard denim. Smooth, hot skin. Pieces
of my own hair twisted in my mouth. Fingers like a clamp on
the back of my neck. A buoyant voice on the radio announced
atrocities big and small. Sweat, pubic hair like a Brillo pad, and
the rising taste of salt.

I gagged, then struggled to breathe, hit my head on the

steering wheel. Rob Hanshaw swore and released his hand from the back of my neck only to push his whole arm between the wheel and my head, wrap his arm around my neck, a lock. My entire body bucked and roared under Rob Hanshaw's arm. My thrashing legs aimed for the door. I felt a boot hit it, the rush of cold air, the knowledge of space outside the truck. I twisted my body and bit the soft underside of his arm. When he yelped, I was able to pull myself out of the truck, dashboard and seats an apparatus to launch me out. It was completely dark by then, and when I gained balance, I stood staring back into the lit cavity of the truck. *Run*, I told myself, but I didn't. Just stood there, my breath heaving, and looked back into the truck.

I saw something pass over Rob Hanshaw's face – annoyance or embarrassment, I wasn't sure which – then watched as he gathered that up and wiped his face blank. "Ah, come on," he said. "Get back into the truck. I'll give you a ride home." His tone was like that of a tired parent coaxing a child who had just had a tantrum. I stood there, mesmerized by the wash of yellow light from the cab. Rob Hanshaw sat waiting, staring out the windshield, his arm across the back of the seat. After a moment, he turned to me. "Come on. What are you going to do? Walk? You can't walk from here, it's too far."

I turned and started walking. Behind me, the truck door closed lightly – he would've had to lean across the seat to shut it – and the engine started. I heard a low groan in the axle when the wheel was turned too sharply. Then, the truck was in motion beside me, the window being rolled down.

"Come on, I'll give you a ride home," Rob Hanshaw repeated, his arm draped out the window, hand adjusting the side mirror. He inched the truck at the speed of my stride. "Come on, no nonsense this time." I turned to him and he winked. "I promise."

It was his gall made me get back into the truck, the offer of a ride home enough of a truce. Later, when I thought about that afternoon, I tried to look for clues to my own lack of anger or indignation. My compliance seemed like something simple. I was hungry for dinner. He was offering me the fastest way home. I felt like larger things were holding me down.

The sky was glowing with impending snow when Rob Hanshaw dropped me off. Right before the first snowfall, the whole valley glows a washed-out, smoky red. I had noticed this every year since we arrived but had never bothered to ask anyone why this was or if they had noticed. I had read that in the Antarctic the sky flashes bright green the moment before the last slice of sun retreats into the horizon. That in Southeast Asia it rains at the same time every year. Even better, in a part of Mexico it rains at exactly the same time each day for exactly forty-seven minutes. I considered the red sky before snow in Sawmill our own climatic sign, something that linked us with the rest of the world, rain falling like clockwork, skies flashing and glowing in preparation for something else – a sunset, snow.

GABE

Peter insists it's different in Arcana. You hear him say, "This is where it's really happening," and of the people you left behind, your mother, Susan, included, "They're in denial up there. Think they've escaped but what they don't know is you have to come back, we have to come back and resist from within now." Of course you don't remember these exact words but ones like them. You've pieced together your father's tenets by what he's said to others.

Peter gets a job building sets for a local theatre company. You and he sleep in the van behind the theatre, shower in a stall off the dressing room, eat in a place called the green room, which is, in fact, green, the shade of cut grass. The theatre supplies endless adventures. You crawl through the spaces under the seats as though burrowing a tunnel underground and discover that parts of the stage open up, an entire dusty mystery existing under there. You have a small red padded suitcase of Hot Wheels, each car with its own slot. You send the tiny cars down the slope from the back of the theatre to the front toward jumps made out the oddly shaped pieces of wood that Peter has given you. They rarely make the hurdles but you try again and again. You do what you have always done – keep yourself occupied, keep out of trouble. You hear other people say to Peter, "Well, he's the opposite of a handful, ain't he?" and "Quiet little guy, hey?"

To you the adults here seem similar to the adults at the farm, except they speak differently, louder and with more enthusiasm. The other kids, well, "Kids are kids," as you heard someone say. You don't know how it could be any different and apply this saying to everything: milk is milk, dogs are dogs. Sometimes, you repeat this over and over throughout the day, naming everything you come into contact with. It fills something in you, some kind of space in your head, which you've recently begun to think of as the inside of a bubble of Bazooka Joe. You know other people do this too when you hear a woman say, "Let's call a spade a spade."

There is even a woman at the theatre who looks like your mother, small and blonde, soft and bony at the same time, the way birds are. Her name is Anise and soon you and Peter are living with her in the basement of an òld house. The people who own the house are old and German and lure you upstairs with fat sausages and sauerkraut. The inside of their house is coated in plastic – plastic walkways down each hall, plastic on the couches, over each lamp, plastic hugging the top of the table. It smells sour and smoky, and even though you don't like the odour you keep going back, because Mrs. Goebel has an endless supply of candy in a hallway cupboard. You sit and watch TV with her in the afternoon, curtains closed so slats of sunlight slice into the room like knives and seem equally dangerous. Fill your mouth with candy until your cheeks inside are as furry as small, unsuspecting animals.

Soon, it seems, Anise has a baby and you move out of the basement. You start going to school – a couple years too late, you find out from your second grade teacher – and this seems to bring on more babies. With each grade, Anise has another baby until you are in the fourth grade and have three sisters. You know how each of these sisters is born. Anise and Peter explain their births to you in graphic detail. You know there is blood and something that looks like snot, something else that isn't pain but, as Anise puts it, "a very very intense feeling" that makes her scream every time. They both want you to be in the room when Anise gives birth, but you refuse. Anise's body scares you, the way it expands and shrinks, expands and shrinks. The bodies of the baby girls are no less frightening – crying, pooping and burping as they do, contorting themselves into red, wrinkled creatures. It hasn't been just you guys in a long time, but by the time you're old enough to figure out how much has changed, it's too late.

As with Susan, Peter didn't have time to build Anise a house. The first baby came too suddenly, followed in quick succession by two more. Instead, you all move out of the Goebels' basement and into a split-level on a cul-de-sac. You come to understand that this is not the house that Peter and Anise wanted to move into. Whenever they tell other adults about the house, they add, "Not quite our style but it does have cedar panelling and the cul-de-sac is out on the east side of town, backs right on to forest. We'll make it our own, won't we, hon?"

Other adults are oddly sympathetic, adding their own understanding nods and words of encouragement. "Yup, yup, I hear ya. We'd all like to get a bit farther out, I suppose, but, hey, good solid build, lots of room. There's so much you can do with the place. And the forest being so close, big yard. Anise can plant a garden. You really are lucky." You have no idea why all these people are playing along, acting as though consolation is necessary. You think of the places you lived in Canada – the vans, the shack – it was your mother who complained about these places, your father who reassured her. You remember Peter speaking with pride about living so close, literally, to the land. He tutored you on the benefits of an uncluttered life on the drive south. "The less stuff you have the better, you know what I mean? The less to tie you down, keep you thinking you always need more. Look at how we're living, hey? Like kings! We have everything we need and we can explore this whole continent if we want. Kings, that's what we are, hey, us two guys?" Peter's eyes would then slowly pan the landscape through the windshield. When he looked back at you, it was with an expression of curiosity, mild delight – as though he had just discovered something unexpected and beautiful in the passenger seat.

It's been four years since you were on the road but Peter manages to bring it up every time you go out with him. You do things like pick up wood, nails, and files at the hardware store, drop things off – you're never sure what exactly – at other people's houses, go to McDonald's to eat food that you know Anise would disapprove of. Peter jokes and says, "Here we are, us two guys on the road again," even though you are just driving around town.

When your youngest half-sister is one and you are eleven, Peter and Anise get married in the back yard. Anise is barefoot and wearing a large hat. Peter is wearing sandals and jeans with an untucked white shirt that reminds you of a pyjama top. The little angels are all in tiny flowing replicas of Anise's dress. You are allowed to choose your own clothes for the day. Anise tells you, "This is a very, very special day for your father and me and I know it's a special day for you too. I'm going to let you decide what to wear. I trust that you'll know what's right." For the special day, you choose your favourite clothes – your old, comfy cords and your cowboy shirt, the one with silver snaps instead of buttons. You are allowed to wear the shirt but Peter sends you back to your room after Anise whispers something in his ear. "Perhaps you'd like to choose a newer pair of pants?" he cues you.

Later, when you look at the photographs of that day, you like the effect. Peter, Anise, and the girls do, in fact, look angelic. All that flowing white fabric, daisies stuck into hair and button holes. You, in plaid and brand new dark denim, eyes squinting against the sun and the camera, look like you have been superimposed from another place – a rougher, dustier place than that back lawn on that day.

$\mathcal{T}$he next morning, the snow had stopped falling and by the afternoon all that was left was a skiff marked with footprints, tire tracks, and reemerging vegetation in the places where the earth was inexplicably warm. I went over to Krista's for dinner, craving the kind of food I couldn't get at home. The Delaneys lived in a house that appeared to be built from a kit on a street lined with identical split-levels. Carports, swing sets, TV rooms, wall-to-wall carpeting. The kind of place where you could pretend you were average. Dinner was a fend-for-yourself affair. The freezer was stocked with TV dinners for Mr. Delaney who supplemented these with meat that he barbecued on a grill set immediately outside the patio door until it was much too cold for him to do so. We were in the season when he was still persisting, the barbecue on one side of the open sliding glass door, Mr. Delaney standing on the other in sweatpants, slippers, a jacket, and a hunting cap. There was a deep freeze downstairs with the limbs of several animals cross-hatched inside. Leg of deer, rack of sheep, salvaged part of moose found on side of road. Mrs. Delaney ate saltines, Caesar salad from a bag with a packet of dressing, yogurt, veggies and dip, Ultra Slim-Fast, and strawberry ice cream. Not a lot and never two of these things at the same time. Krista ate what she could find – boiled hot dogs stuffed into starch white buns, ketchup and mustard congealed into a brown mass, microwaved pizza, boxes of frozen burritos warmed up one by one.

Mrs. Delaney came into the kitchen in tasselled boots, black jeans, and a black sweater with a large cat appliquéd on the front in metallic brass and silver stripes. She looked around her as though she was confused, then her eyes lit up when they landed on me. "Harper, heard you've been let out of house arrest. What was it you did?"

"I told you, Mom, she passed out in church."

Mrs. Delaney snorted out a laugh, dabbed at false tears. "Oh yeah. Atta girl, Harper. Don't they love that kind of stuff? Aren't you supposed to roll down the aisles there? You weren't hungover, were ya? You, my dear, are supposed to be a good influence on my daughter. Lord, I mean, sorry, *goodness* knows I'm not going to be that influence, eh, Krista?"

"Mom, shut up, will you?"

"Do you even know what respect is, Krista?"

"Song by Aretha Franklin."

"Christ," Mrs. Delaney declared, then, "Ah shit, sorry, Harper, hon," as she left the kitchen.

Krista and I made Kraft Dinner, substituting extra butter and two spoonfuls of Coffeemate for milk, and stirred in sliced dill pickles and ketchup. We snapped open Diet Cokes and ate in front of the TV in the room three steps down from the kitchen. When we had licked the dishes clean of ketchup and cheese product and rubbed water over the bowls with our fingers, we filled them back up with ice cream. I meant to tell Krista about what happened with Rob Hanshaw, but somehow I couldn't find the right words. Instead I kept my eyes fixed on *Jeopardy*, tried to answer every question. "Where is Iceland," I asked, *Jeopardy*-style, without inflection, then, "Who is Amelia Earhart."

"Shut up, professor," Krista said, flicked upwards till she reached *MuchMusic*, all sound and bytes of gyrating hip, guitar-flexed muscle. "Okay, Harp, you know what we need? We need a change of pace."

"So, change the channel."

"Not that kind of change of pace, smartass. A real change. You know what we're going to do? We are going to go the Pilgrims Art Farm Solstice Fair."

"You might be going, sister, but no Friend of Christ is going to let me go to anything with the word *solstice* in it."

"Why not?"

"Do you know what the winter solstice is?"

"Darkest day of the year – don't ask me why, *Jeopardy* girl, something to do with the sun and the earth's rotation. If you get me a basketball, a ping-pong ball and a flashlight, I might be able to figure it out."

"I'll tell you. Jeopardy answer: solstice. Pastor John's question: What is an excuse for an ancient pagan ritual performed by pre-Christian heathens locked in darkness without the guidance of Christ's light."

"Okay, so, we'll say we're going somewhere else."

Mr. Delaney came in the door from the carport then, took one look at us and said, simply, "Trouble," shaking his head in mock seriousness as he walked by. His role as a father had been to teach Krista how to tie a fly, hit a fastball, and play poker. He had given her a couple of spankings with the belt when she was a little girl, taught her to drive when she was sixteen, and now it seemed as though he thought his job had basically been completed. Mr. Delaney was like an amiable boarder in Krista and her mother's house.

In the summer, he and other boys from the mill organized a series of backyard barbecues. It didn't matter how old they were, if they worked at the mill, they were always *the boys*. The one thing Mr. Delaney insisted on was that Krista and her mother attend these barbecues. So, it seemed, did the other old boys: they brought wives and children ranging from toddlers to teenagers. These families were statements. Look how good we're doing. We have good, solid work, families, barbecues in the backyard of what, everyone assured themselves after a couple of beers, could only be called paradise. God's backyard, really. I came along as Krista's moral support. The boys from the mill, true to their moniker, had not grown up. They slapped the backsides of their wives, the backs of their children's heads – "Hey, I thought I told you to put that down. Didn't I tell you to put that down? You better learn to listen, you understand?" – and leered at Krista and me while pulling in beer bellies, trying to convert them into abs, by then a distant memory. These men were who we would try to avoid, in no uncertain terms, until we left Sawmill Creek. When we did leave, we would simply forget them, remembering nothing but the taste of tough, barbecued meat in our mouths from those evenings. Nothing else.

I'd heard of Pilgrims Art Farm, we all had. It was fifteen kilometres from Sawmill Creek in one of the valleys that pooled between small peaks. Pilgrims Art Farm was in one of the narrow valleys that radiated out from Sawmill Creek, the mountains rising more sharply from the valley floor there. The farm informed our own perception of Sawmill Creek but most people tried not to acknowledge it. People from other places seemed more interested in what was going on out there than we did. People from the city, crews from small TV stations, artists who appeared in town with dark-rimmed glasses and black clothing, all of them looking around like they were on the set of a small town, like it couldn't possibly be real. At the time, when I thought of Pilgrims Art Farm, I thought of women with hair knotted into crowns, the smell of blood and dirt, thin listless men with erections, children like feral wolves, dried herbs, thick dark oil.

~

We had convinced ourselves that everything would change after the night of the solstice – there would be a fraction more sunlight each day until June, the Sawmill Creek Loggers would win more hockey games, and we would go to Pilgrims Art Farm, discover something there, we were sure.

On that night, Krista and I had to work the Junior B hockey game at the arena. We had managed to get jobs there for the busy season leading up to Christmas. Sometimes we were there for the games, sometimes just for public skate times. That a hockey game corresponded with the Solstice Fair worked out perfectly. We wouldn't have to invent an alibi. There were two concessions inside the arena – one large counter from which you could buy hot things – dogs spun sweating in a case, burgers, nachos hidden under bright, glue-like sauce – and one small booth on the other side of the arena where you could buy pop, chips, candy. That was our domain. Krista and I were situated in a triangular booth that was propped in an upper corner of the arena, with a window looking out on to the rink, separated by Plexiglas. We doled out strips of licorice, face-pulling sour candies, and watered-down Orange Crush with equal indifference and then went back to sitting on the counter by the window, the game a backdrop for whatever personal dramas we wished we had. We were metres away from the similarly enclosed glass box that housed the arena organist, a young Pentecostal guy who drove in from Yankee Flats. He had confessed his love for me in a lengthy letter months before but never spoke to me at the arena. I might have thought the letter was a prank but he had included a tape of himself playing his favourite organ songs and I didn't think just anyone could pull that off. He was acne-ridden and awkward and Krista and I mocked him in a way that would make me feel sad whenever I thought about him.

On that night, we were unable to sit still. We fidgeted with the radio dial, trying to find a frequency without static. The only station that came through in the arena was playing a com-mentary of the game, and we didn't want to listen to that.

When people came by, we took their money quickly, shook the coins until they slid across each other on our palms, and repeatedly seemed to miscount change. The sports writer for the local paper, an attractive middle-aged man who was known to be a harmless pervert, came by and watched us bounce around behind the counter. "God, I wish women my age had your kind of energy," he commented, one eyebrow raised, both eyes on Krista's breasts. "It's intoxicating, you know that, eh, girls?"

Krista stopped bouncing and looked at him. "Don't you have a game to cover?"

"I like a little spunk," the sports writer muttered, then smirked. "I definitely do like a little spunk," he said again as he walked off.

We pulled down the metal door that closed the concession counter before the end of the third period and left early. No one was interested in sugar at the end of games, they were already thinking of beer and salty things to increase their thirst for more beer. Krista had her dad's truck for the night. We wiped the snow off the hood and windshield with our jacketed arms and sat in the parking lot with the truck running, waiting for the engine to warm and heat the air coming from the vents. Krista leaned across me and opened the glove compartment, took out a pouch of Drum tobacco. "Where'd you get that?" I asked, sitting on my hands to warm them. She just winked and started to roll. I ripped tiny rectangles out of an empty pack of Mr. Delaney's smokes and handed them to Krista for filters. Not a bad roll job, bulbous in places, baggy in others, but not bad. The cherry cracked against the paper and we licked our lips for the sweet taste of fresh tobacco.

When we had finished the smoke, Krista told me. "I added a bit of weed to those."

"What?"

"Not much, just enough to loosen us up a bit."

"Uh, yeah, okay. Thanks for telling me."

"Relax, Harp, obviously it didn't work."

The railway tracks flanked the arena. If we drove around the building and up a block, we could come back down a street that met the tracks then dropped off immediately. A relatively small hill but one that could launch a vehicle, for a brief exhilarating moment, into the air. We circled the block and Krista accelerated despite the slip of snow beneath the tires, one last pump on the gas as we hit the tracks. The tires struck the line and then, nothing. Nothing but air under the truck; nothing under us as we left our seat for a brief moment. All in slow motion, *Dukes of Hazzard* style. Landing, the bench seat sprang up under us and, buoyant with excitement, Krista rounded the corner, fishtailing, and did the whole thing again – acceleration, jagged track, air, the spring of seats – faster. We did this three times, the third gaining so much momentum that we each hit our heads on the ceiling. The truck threatened to spin out completely when Krista lost the wheel but she somehow regained control as I doubled over with laughter. From somewhere, we heard sirens. They sounded like they were approaching so we left quickly and drove out to Pilgrims Art Farm, the feeling of air still underneath us.

Roads cut through fields around Sawmill Creek like a child's drawing of a staircase, right angle after right angle. They would straighten out in narrow valleys or come up

against hills and switch back until they met logging roads and
ascended into the forest. The volume of back roads spider-
webbing the valleys astounded me. They seemed to have little
purpose beyond meeting with other back roads. Roads as
fences, locking our small towns into valleys. The highway
passing us by.

Krista and I came down from the air we had caught over
the tracks and everything seemed weighted and quiet with the
recent snowfall. Cows plodded single file through fields, smoke
rose in straight, lazy lines from chimneys then settled around
houses and joined the smog from the mill. Fences were piled
with snow in columns on each post. "God, this place is tragic,"
Krista lamented. "Try to roll us some more smokes."

In the valley around town, the land was barely flat and wide
enough to graze animals. Farms were small and were called
hobbies. People grew and raised odd things in the valley –
ostriches and llamas, edible flowers, ginseng under taut black
tarps that collected heat by summer and were taken down in
winter leaving fields as canvases for snow. A hybrid of cows and
buffalo called beefalo grazed at a farm, their free-range,
steroid-free lifestyle attested to by large signs at the side of the
road – *We are free range and drug free!* – as though they were the
poster herd of bovines. The mill was the only thing that made
money around Sawmill Creek and that just barely. As though
resigned to this, people grew things out of curiosity, yet always
with the hope of hitting a jackpot fuelled by the quirky desires
of other people, far away. These people were rumoured to have
insatiable appetites for large delicate fungi, healing herbs, the
most organically derived meat. We'd all heard the stories of

people going into the bush around Sawmill, living in camps and spreading out into slash-burned areas to collect mushrooms. Mushrooms that were sent to Vancouver, later even Japan, and returned as gold.

No one had ever met anyone to whom this had happened but we believed the stories; they made our valley seem exotic. We wouldn't have been able to tell a mushroom picker from the pickers who arrived each summer to pluck fruit from vines and branches, or the tree planters who arrived each spring looking as soft and grey as the last year's windfalls. During the summer, the planters came in from the bush every ten days or so, dreadlocked and mac-jacketed, smelling of dirt, pine, and garlic, and went to the same bars the guys from the mill went to. We knew from the stories that sometimes the planters and the mill workers got along, found camaraderie in the commonality of livelihoods based on forms of tree and wood. Other times they didn't, knocked blood out of each other in the parking lot until the cops broke them up. By the end of the summer, the planters would be tanned and muscular, lingering longer in town, trying to get away with more at the end of the season. Most of the girls in Sawmill would admit to a love of these late summer planters, all muscle and dirt. Admit to wanting to leave with them at the end of the season, climb in the back of four-by-fours with shovels and dogs and go wherever they went back to. But unlike the planters, who returned with the next season, we wouldn't want to come back.

Pilgrims was sandwiched between hobby farms and a forest of trees perpetually ready to be cut down and planted up again, like thick gnarled lawns to logging companies. It started to snow again. "Keep your eyes out for the sign, okay?" Krista said, leaning into the steering wheel, eyes on the windshield like it was going to reveal some kind of message. The wipers cleared the glass, the snow stuck to it again. There was no wind and even the sounds coming through the radio were slow, melancholic folk songs. "Do you feel like we're time-warping, right now?" Krista asked.

"Yeah, that's exactly how I feel. If I could save time in a freakin' bottle you know the first thing I'd like to do? – break the thing open. Maybe we should just turn around and forget it."

"Nah. What use would that be?"

I paused, tried to think of a use. Like we could distill our actions into something utilitarian, something we could hold, the grip of a shovel. "Yeah, okay. So, have you ever heard of anyone ever going to one of these? I mean, who goes to these things, anyways?"

"What do I look like, a Farmer's Almanac? No one we know, but then, no one we know goes anywhere besides hockey games and lame parties. I don't know – growers, people who hang out at the health food store. I think people from Kelowna and shit. Maybe even Vancouver. They're into this kind of artsy stuff down there."

Led by a sign to the Pilgrims Art Farm Solstice Fair, we turned off a back road onto two dirt depressions made by tires. They led into the bush, then opened to a field covered in tire tracks, where cars and trucks sat, parked like resting animals. When we got out of the truck, the field clicked and dripped with the sound of recently warm vehicles shedding snow.

We had no idea what we would find at the farm, but once

we walked through the gates and closer to some buildings, we could see small wooden signs nailed to things – trees, fences, posts that appeared to be erected for the sole purpose of displaying small wooden signs – as though put there just for people like us. We peered at them, hoping they would be some kind of directions – and some of them seemed to be. A couple of signs said Outhouse and Cookshack and pointed, seemingly randomly, into a cluster of buildings, a glow coming from the other side of them. Others were more cryptic and announced, we discovered with lighters held up, *Carpe diem* and *I will go to the bank by the wood and become undisguised and naked*. "Ah, shit," Krista started. "Who wants to go to the bank naked?"

"Hi, uh, I'd like to withdraw a couple bucks. Need to get me some of them there clothes you all got on."

We walked around a building, hoping we wouldn't be late for whatever event was happening. We ended up in what appeared to be the centre of the farmyard where there was a large bonfire surrounded by bales of hay. Some people sat on these, others had gathered on the porch of one of the buildings. We looked at each other, took a deep breath, and walked past this group and into the building, looking at our feet until we got inside. It was clear that whatever craft fair had taken place earlier was over now. Long tables, like the ones in the basement of our church, were pushed up against the walls. At church, once a potluck was over, women would wash all the Corning and Tupperware before we could come down from all the Kool-Aid we had drunk. We'd go to the bathroom, almost expecting to pee lime green or cherry red, and would return to find the tables pushed aside, all the bowls and casserole dishes displayed across the taut plastic tablecloths, ready to be picked up and taken home by whoever had filled them with potato and jellied salads. God helps those who help themselves, cleanliness a virtue, idle hands and something about the devil. At Pilgrims, food still clung to dishes and platters, crumbs and whole morsels all over the table, and there were things like candlesticks, small painted boxes, coarsely woven bags amongst the food, obviously left over from the craft fair.

Like anthropologists, we examined the items on the tables, looking first, then picking through the remains as though hoping to discover something. We dipped the crumbs of chips into the remnants of different sauces – red, yellow, green dips, all with a brownish hue – turning to each other for assessment.

"What do you think that was?"

We were interrupted by a balding man with a grey ponytail and beads around his neck. "Hey, you two been on the sleigh ride yet?" he asked. Despite his appearance, or possibly because of it, we knew he was one of the worst kind: the hippie version of the sportswriter at the arena.

We looked back at him as though we couldn't have been more bored. "No, we haven't."

"Oh, you have to go on a ride. They're just about to take another one out. The moon is almost full, it's solstice, the air is clear. Oh man, I'm telling you, it's the most beautiful thing." He said all this in a slow, drawn-out way, like pulling gum out of his mouth, seeing how far it would stretch.

"Are you sure it's the *most* beautiful thing?" Krista asked, narrowing her eyes and looking pointedly at him. I suppressed a laugh. For one moment, he looked as though someone had

given his ponytail a quick jerk, then he was back to a slow blinking, rhythmic nod.

"Well, if it's the most beautiful thing, we'd better go then."
I pulled Krista past the man and we made a path to the door
through a gauntlet of large sweaters, musky smells, hair. On
the porch, people talked and smoked with the urgency that
cold brought, hauled on joints then funnelled laughter out of
their throats in tight bursts. We smoked anything anyone
passed to us, bare hands stinging when we took off one glove to
accommodate the tiny ends of joints. By the time the sleigh
pulled up to the porch, the huge horses snorting out steam
clouds of warm air and jingling with bells, I felt delighted with
the entire evening. I even started thinking in clichés about
being my mother's daughter. Vera must have stood bundled on
porches waiting for horse-drawn sleighs to pull her through
fields of snow. She may have even sneaked a drag off someone's
cigarette, imagined the flame would warm her, unsubstantiated
beliefs like that existing as they did back then.

The "sleigh" was a flatbed covered with hay, no ornately
curved sides, no furs, no burly men with bodies like bears,
teasing pipes to light and then dim with their lips. The group
of us on the porch piled on, jousted our limbs against one
another until we could find some place to sit still without being
cramped. My foot met with an ankle and someone cried out.
The man up front, reins in hand, turned and directed us to all
sit with our backs toward the middle, feet drawn in so they
wouldn't catch when we went through gates. Told us to hold on,
the ride would be bumpy. Nothing to hold on to but each other.
Nothing keeping us on but our mass, our bodies a cohesive unit.

We were pulled along snowy, moon-lit fields as we sang Christmas carols and drank hot, spiced alcohol from the wine skins that were being passed around. I was high on both alcohol and marijuana by the end of the ride, cheeks flushed with fresh air. Happier in that moment than I was sure I'd ever been in my entire life.

We got off the sleigh much as we had got on, not as individual bodies but as some multilimbed and awkward thing, tripping over itself. I found myself on my ass in the snow, laughing. "Oh, Lord," Krista announced. "You're loaded." I just laughed and fell back, started flailing my arms and legs into a snow angel. We were back in front of the building and I was lying on a skiff of snow on a gravel lot, my snow angel grinding pebbles into my back. Nick and I used to dare each other to fall into a snow angel without bending a limb, an experiment that had knocked the wind out of us both more than once. Krista tried to pull me up but I couldn't stop laughing or get any control over my limbs, which felt heavy and fluid, and soon we were both on the ground in a heap. "Help, I've fallen and I can't get up," we chorused.

That's how I met him. He and an older man came down from the porch and pulled Krista and me off the ground as though we truly needed help. The older man was behind me, his arms hooked under my armpits pulling me to my feet. When I was upright, he held me there for a moment, waiting, I presumed, until I gained balance. "What's so funny, girls?" the older man asked from behind me. When he said that, I started again, laughing so hard I would've fallen if I wasn't being held up.

"She's just fucked up," Krista explained, grinning. I saw the younger man behind her. As I tried to catch my breath I focused on his face. In that moment, that small window of rest in my laughter, his expression seemed to convey several things at once. I saw in his face amusement, sadness, and recognition, as though he was trying to place me, or wanted to say something but didn't know how.

Krista and I struggled to gain some composure but, as soon as we saw our own expressions reflected in each other's face, we spat out laughter again. It turned into steam around us. The older one let go of his hold on me and shifted so he could look at both of us. "Whew, I'd like to have a bit of whatever you two had," he said.

"You probably can," said Krista. "Whatever we had, we got it here."

He held out his hand to one of us, then the other, to shake. "Thomas." More of a statement than an introduction.

The younger one simply stared. I thought there might be something wrong with him. I cracked a grin and he beamed back. His eyes were huge. Even the crinkling of a smile didn't diminish them. Dark hair fell in thick curls over his forehead. His body was lost under layers of clothes. "I'm Gabe," he finally said but didn't hold out his hand for us to shake. He was too close to our age to do that.

"There's hot chocolate in the cookshack. You two want some?" Thomas asked.

"Oh, my God!" Krista exclaimed.

Thomas took a step back, laughing. "Whoa, Nellie. What?"

"Don't mind her," I said. "We would just *really* love some hot chocolate right now." People who are used to smoking pot forget about how extreme it can be at first, how good the thought of chocolate can taste.

"Oh my God!" Krista repeated. "Why didn't anyone tell us there was hot chocolate?"

It wasn't like I read it would be. I didn't feel Gabe's presence like heat; I didn't feel like I'd always known him. My legs did turn to water, but only because of the intoxicants. Nothing fluttering and small lodged in my chest. When I met him, what I did feel was my tongue, like a stone under a river current, rubbed smooth.

GABE

Peter and Anise have decided you should be home-schooled. They believe that the stratified, hierarchical socialization of children into one generic mass, distinguishable only by grades that reflect a limited range of abilities, can't be healthy. You are disappointed even though they tell you again and again that you don't want to be part of that kind of system. You've actually enjoyed school so far. Entering late in the second grade has been some kind of strange blessing, a buffer. Teachers make note of it and don't expect as much, so when you do well – catch on to long division quickly, excel at spelling tests – they are pleased. You have become a testament to how well the system can work. You've adapted well and fit in, you know this from the comments on your report cards.

And you do fit in. You are in the sixth grade and have made it this far without getting the tar beaten out of you. You don't consider yourself popular, or even well-liked, but you are tolerated in a kind and gentle way by both the girls and the boys. It isn't like this for everyone. There are kids who are teased and bullied ceaselessly, and sometimes brutally. Marty Cruickshank has been kicked so many times since the first grade by boys and girls alike that he has dents in his shin bones. The sad thing is that it is Marty, himself, who points this out, invites kids to run their hands down his almost hairless legs, feel the ridges. He has had his arms twisted around the tether ball pole, hands in the grip of two boys while others line up to slam his head into the pole with the ball, the chain catching in his hair. He has been teased with such fervour during a class presentation that, before the teacher could stop the taunting, Marty wet himself, a dark stain growing on his tan-coloured dress pants. Barbara Sanducci has been called Brabra since she developed at a startling rate in the fourth grade and it was revealed that she received bras in her stocking at Christmas. She has been stripped of those bras, forcibly, in the boys' change room, and once gagged with one, hands tied behind her back with her own shirt. The janitor found her there and, they say, she wasn't even crying. It is the girls who do things like this to her, call her Brabra. The boys take the "duc" in her last name and call her "the Douche."

You are not one of these kids, and while you feel sorry for them, your own feeling of relief overrides this. You don't do anything terrible to the Martys and the Douches – no one would expect you to – but you are vigilant in ignoring them. Clearly, there is something wrong with kids like that and you don't want anything to rub off on you. The other kids treat you well. You were given the nickname "Mouse" shortly after you arrived for, of course, being as quiet as one. Like other small cute things, you have become a kind of mascot for the kids in your grade. The boys pick you for teams in gym class. Not first or second, but often the third or fourth call someone will say, "We'll take the Mouse-Man" and it's not because you are remarkably good at any sports, although you have passable skills in most of them. Girls have always tried to help you with your schoolwork even though you haven't needed assistance since the first couple months of the second grade. They hover over your desk, smelling like root beer, bubble gum, dirt, until the teacher tells them to sit down. Recently, they've even approached you in the halls. They say, "Hi-i, Mou-ouse," dragging out the monosyllables, twisting pieces of their hair, giggling. They'll do this one after another sometimes, in quick succession, and then all gather at the end of the hall and giggle together, looking over their shoulders at you. Some of these girls are "going around" with boys in the seventh grade but those boys don't mind. In fact, now even they acknowledge you. "Hey, Mouse-Man," they'll nod as if to concede some strange kinship developed through the sixth grade girls giggling at you.

All this has come to an end, though. You, apparently, do not want to be in such an unhealthy, unnatural environment. You are going to learn at home, at your own pace. Because you won't have twenty-seven other kids to compete against, you will learn faster, retain more. In fact, Anise assures you that you will learn so quickly that you will only have to "do school" for half the day, the rest, you will be allowed to roam free. "Roam free!" Peter says. "Just like you did back at the farm, hey? You can explore the forest, do some fishing, help your old man in the shop." Peter and Anise have invented some kind of 1950s American boyhood for you to enjoy. They have missed an important element though. Other kids. There are more and more kids being home-schooled, they tell you, "We'll hook up with them, you'll meet some other home-schoolers soon."

One day, you go with Anise to Berkeley to buy your first home-schooling books. The girls, as they've come to be called, as though they are one blond unit, stay in Arcana with a friend of Anise's. Peter is running late on a contract so he can't come. This is the first time that you can remember being alone with Anise. This is the first time that you realize that, although she looks like her, Anise is not like your mother, Susan. She sings, slides tapes in the cassette player, then out after a couple of songs. She talks a lot. Doesn't ask you questions but talks on and on, interrupting herself with some lines from a song, then continuing. You nod. You realize that, although you used to ask Peter about Susan often – why she was so sad, when you would see her again – that you have forgotten to ask lately. You do the math. You haven't seen your mother in more than four years. Suddenly you feel as though you should be home-schooled, as though you should be punished. Something has made you forget Susan, and you don't know what. You watch as the redwood forest suddenly ends and you are driving through rolling farmland. You wonder how things can change so quickly like that, if it's always been that way.

*A*fter we regained our balance and our bearings, brushing the snow from our clothing, Krista and I went with Gabe and Thomas back into the building they called the cookshack. It was a large wood structure with a porch wrapping around two sides of it. When we went inside, it reminded me of a small community hall, two doors on either side of the wood stove in the back providing a glimpse of the kitchen. We were met with the smells of woodsmoke, of things spicy and sweet. Men and women alike wore layers of body-obscuring clothing and hugged each other more often than I was used to. People smiled at Krista and me as if they were oddly charmed to see us.

Thomas led us to a place where we could sit down, like we were elderly, or drunk, although, granted, we were the latter. He and Gabe navigated through the crowd, appeared again palming hot mugs. Thomas was handsome in a way that I thought would remind older women of being young. A way that would remind most women of horseback riding, wind-swept days by the seaside. He looked as if he had spent his childhood on a farm, his young adulthood in earnest protest against social injustice, and his current middle age in a state of simple, healthy enjoyment of life. He looked as if he could be any age between thirty-five and fifty-five. Gabe couldn't have been more than a couple years older than us. He was handsome in a strange, quiet way. I could still see the little boy in him, huge eyes blinking from behind strands of dark hair. He wasn't boyish, though. When he looked at me, it was as though there were two expressions at odds with each other. His eyes seemed to be struggling to recognize me or to convey something important, while his mouth steeled him against words. It was a look that I would get used to.

It was nearly eleven-thirty and the cookshack appeared to be in a state of transition. People who had probably just come out for the craft fair and the potluck were beginning to leave, babies on hips, toddlers hanging on pant legs bemoaning their fate – stuck at an adult party too late, believing with surprising conviction that they were not tired. Other people were coming in – people with guitars and bongo drums, one with a stand-up bass. People with bottles of wine, cases of beer, and pouches of tobacco were looking around expectantly, wondering if they had missed anything yet. And dogs everywhere, lolling near the wood stove, sucking up bits of food from under the tables, burying their snouts in people's crotches, or simply finding someone, looking up at them expectantly, tail in a slow, hopeful wag. Everything seemed slightly hazy and slow-moving, as though the smoke in the room were water. I narrowed my gaze and saw Gabe's hand around his cup, his leg against mine, the wooden bench on which we were sitting. The floor beneath us was rough-hewn. That was what I said to myself, *rough-hewn*, liking the sound of it.

Krista and I were beginning to come down, rooted to the bench by a sense of awe, relief, disbelief.

"So," Gabe started, then paused for what seemed like a moment too long. Long enough for me to notice his eyelashes, how they cast filaments of shadow on his cheek. "You from here?"

"Sawmill? Yeah." I was most definitely from here. At one time, I tried to convince myself that, because I hadn't moved to the town until I was six, I was from somewhere else. I had eventually resigned myself to being from here, the creek running in my veins, thick as the clogged water that flowed out of the booming ground at the far end of the lake.

"How do you like it? Living here, I mean," Gabe asked, looking somehow too earnest.

"Here? I don't know. I mean, I can't say I love it."

Krista leaned over from the other side of me, face red from the rising heat created by the wood stove, by more bodies crowding into the space. "Oh, come on! Are you asking how we like it here? We hate it. We fucking hate it here. How 'bout you?"

"Well." Gabe's word was cautious, a foot out onto a frozen lake, the weight shifted onto it slowly. "Well, I just got back. I don't know yet. I don't think I hate it here, though. It seems quite, um, beautiful actually."

"Yeah, fucking paradise. Wait till you stay for a while – did you say 'got back'? Are you from –" Krista's attention was diverted, which was not difficult. "Hey, what's that Thomas guy doing?"

Thomas was standing near the back of the hall, passing a cigarette around with other men with instruments. A saxophone hung, loosely and gracefully I thought, around one of his shoulders. "He's getting ready to play the sax, I guess," answered Gabe, looking slightly perplexed.

"No kidding," said Krista, incredulous.

"Uh, yeah. I'm pretty sure." Gabe suddenly grinned at me, a private joke, it seemed, that I was supposed to get.

"Hey, is he your dad?"

He laughed. "Thomas, no. Thomas isn't my dad, although I did know him when I was a kid. My dad's in California."

"Oh yeah? Cool," Krista remarked, attention then pulled in another direction again.

I had only the rudimentary threads of Gabe's story. He had been here before. His father was in California. He had come to Sawmill from somewhere else. I started in. "So, you, uh, said you were here before. Did you use to live here?"

"Yeah, at Pilgrims, when I was a kid. I mean, a little kid. I haven't lived here for, uh, twelve years? Thirteen? So, I thought it was time to move back."

Move back. Move back. He was living here, in Sawmill. My stomach engaged in the proverbial somersault. "Oh, why?"

"I don't know. My mom's here. I remember it being, well, beautiful. I don't know, I still think it is, beautiful." He paused before saying that – beautiful – even though he had said it three times already. I was keeping count.

Here is Gabe from that night: his hands, surprisingly large and strong looking for what appeared to be a slight frame, passing his emptying cup of hot chocolate back and forth, left hand, then right, his eyes down, watching his boots scuff against the floor, his thigh against my leg, the play of fabric between. There is everything else: music erupting, retreating and weaving into itself until it becomes something animate in the room, a woman swirling in the middle of the dance floor, barefoot despite the constant drafts, a large man who hugs people off the ground, two pre-teens pilfering cigarettes out of coats that have been piled on tables, and the dogs retreating to the edges of the room, feigning boredom, waiting for the signs of people who are going out. When someone does, the dogs perk up and trot out alongside them.

That was all that happened. We sat against a wall and watched people playing instruments, other people dancing. We attempted conversation. Gabe was quiet, Krista couldn't stay focused on any one thing long enough to talk. I felt as though words were difficult things, things that could become twisted and rearranged in my mouth, come out at odd angles and surprise people, so I was quiet as well. At one point, Gabe reached over and touched my hair, took a lock between finger and thumb as if testing it for something, then let it drop, grinned at me. Heat shot up that piece of hair, entered me at my scalp and travelled down my spine. We left when Krista thought she was sober enough to drive and I felt tired enough to fall asleep there on the bench, my head on Gabe's shoulder. We left in a shuffle of coat-gathering and goodbyes. Thomas

waved and winked from across the room. Gabe walked us to
the door and watched us leave.

⁓

When Vera was seventeen, her father was crushed under a
tractor while helping with the harvest at a neighbouring farm.
Too few years between horse-drawn ploughs and engines, they
say. No one is clear about how it happened, least of all the man
who was driving the tractor. The community is too small and
too free from any significant feuds to place blame. The priest
is summoned from Fly Hills and Vera's father is buried at dusk,
no one assuming that the surviving men will stop the harvesting for the day. Vera's father wouldn't have wanted that.

Vera is the only one left at home with her mother. It is clear
that, even with some help, these two women, one young and
one in mourning, will not be able to run a farm. Vera's sisters
have all married and moved to Edmonton. They each offer to
take Mother in, assure Vera that she will be off to technical
school or community college soon enough, but Vera's mother
doesn't want to move to the city. Instead, Vera and her mother
move into an apartment that the landlady calls an "efficiency,"
above a grocery story in Fly Hills.

They have left all the furniture in the farmhouse. Vera's
sisters will go back with trucks and collect some of it, sell some
of it, and leave some of it. The eldest daughter's husband will
rent the farm and the land. Vera isn't sure why they just don't put
it on the market. That's it, she thinks. That's all. Nothing else
can happen on that farm, nothing else will, at least not for them.

The efficiency apartment is furnished. "Everything is very clean and modern," the landlady tells them. And she is telling the truth. There are matching avocado-coloured appliances in the kitchen, a shower stall in the bathroom – the first Vera has seen without a bathtub – and a TV in the living room. There is one bedroom with a queen-sized bed, a bedspread blooming with large flowers, and a long, dark bureau. Neither Vera nor her mother has ever slept on a queen-sized bed and now they will be sharing one.

Afternoons, when she returns from school, her mother has baked bread, made perogies and cabbage rolls as though there is an entire family to feed. Each day, the kitchen is full of steam and the smell of rising dough, onions, and garlic. She and her mother can't possibly consume as much food as has been made but Vera doesn't ask where the rest of it goes. Each night, they eat at the kitchen table and then go into the living room and watch the television. They watch young women writhe and scream and pull out their hair for love on the *Ed Sullivan Show*. They watch hockey games. They watch newscasts that tell them that America has gone to war for freedom. Vera senses something else going on under the surface of the *Ed Sullivan Show* and the newscasts, something that connects both of those programs but is unlike either. One night, she sees a beautiful man on the screen. A man with long hair and tight jeans who is holding a flower. Other young people run behind him, police form human walls in front of the cameras and soon he is gone.

Vera and her mother both watch the TV for hours, until they fall asleep and the whine when the station goes off air wakes them up.

⌐

The next day, we found out that a puck flew over the Plexiglas in the closing minutes of the third period and struck a boy named Billy dead. A puck to the head. Billy was from Manitoba, visiting his grandparents for Christmas. Krista and I felt the sadness and guilty excitement you feel when you slow to watch a roadside accident, or when you hear hollering and what could be furniture being thrown while walking by a house and wonder if you should call the RCMP. Wonder if what you hear is something you'll learn the graphic consequences of later, on the radio while driving to church. The sense of being part of something larger than oneself. Not something larger and good, like a team or a church or even Pilgrims Art Farm, but something larger and not so much bad as unpredictable. Like the weather. We had been there moments before it happened, before death pinned a bull's-eye on Billy and sent a hockey puck there to meet it.

It might have been when we took on air over the tracks that the puck hit his head, his soul lifting at the moment we were lifted off our seats. I decided it was a portent. I looked back to the previous night, looked for other signs. All I could think of was something about going to the bank naked.

I had been near death before, skimmed the edges of it because of a late-night trip to Dr. Holland's office. In school then, I could still hand in almost all of my assignments in any class handwritten. My grade ten English teacher, Ms. Helanious, was straight out of university, however, and told us that we would be typing all our assignments soon enough and that we should get ahead of the game and become proficient at it. We had no computer at home and the typewriter in the basement had seized up since the last time anyone had used it, the keys locking in place once they were depressed.

I went to Dr. Holland's office to use the electric typewriter that Vera used. Vera drove me there after dinner, told me she'd be back in a couple hours to pick me up. What she didn't tell me was that the janitor would let himself in, that we would both shriek when confronted with each other in an office that we assumed we had all to ourselves. After we both explained our presence to calm the other, the janitor seemed kind and thoughtful. He told me he wouldn't vacuum in the waiting room while I was there so as not to disturb my writing. He did, however, wash the windows and dust every surface in the small room, talking the entire time he worked.

"So, you doing some homework? They got you typing homework these days, eh? A good skill, I guess your mother's told you that. A good skill." I didn't say anything, just looked up and nodded, but he continued. "Wish I could help my girls with their homework. They're approaching your age – how old are you? Older, I suppose – the oldest of mine is nearly thirteen, nearly, well, a teenager. Yes, I guess she is a teenager. They're growing up without me now."

I knew with a pause like that, he wanted me to say something. I consented and asked, "Why's that?"

"Oh, you know, me and their mother, we're separated now, like everyone else, it seems. She's got custody. I'm living in a basement suite. It's not like I don't see them, the girls. I do. Every weekend I take them out to lunch, you know, or to a movie. But, it's not like seeing them day to day. It's not like seeing them laugh milk out their noses or fight for the bathroom. I don't know. You'll never know the things you're going to miss once you don't have them any more." He went into the other rooms – Dr. Holland's office and the examination room – and cleaned there. I was soothed by continuous, repetitive sounds. My fingers typing out a rhythm, his vacuuming a whirl and hum in the background.

I would later find out that the janitor, whose name I can't remember, didn't go back to his basement suite that night. He went to his former house, the place where his wife and two daughters slept. He shot his wife and her new boyfriend dead in the bed, then, as they say, turned the gun on himself. How can I describe what I felt when I found out? Sadness, yes, even horror. And something else, that same kind of culpable thrill. I may have been the last person to talk to that janitor before he became known not as a janitor but as a double-murder-suicide and this notion brought with it a sense of distorted privilege.

Oddly enough, I didn't feel as though I could have done anything differently. As though if I had said more than what I did – "Oh, you scared me," "Why's that?" and "Thanks, good night" – I could've altered his course. I felt sorry for his death more than his wife's, more than her lover's. I felt a kinship with his two daughters that was probably unwarranted. I imagined them sleeping in the same bed with long white nightgowns, long hair brushed out of braids – as though they were Laura and Mary Ingalls, or two of the *Little Women*. I imagined them clinging to each other when they heard the shots, wetting each other's hair with tears. I imagined going to them some day, several years into the future, to tell them their father had loved them very much.

The town was left reeling by the events. If we didn't know how to feel, the *Sawmill Creek Chronicle* told us. We were told that we were, in turn and in rotation: "left reeling," "in shock," "mourning," and "calling for answers." Vera read the paper again and again, as though to justify her own feelings of grief, shaking her head slowly, sniffling. Dr. Holland gave her a day off work. I came home after school that day and saw my mother in the back field as I leaned over the sink, gulping down milk from the carton. I wiped my mouth and stood on my toes, bent toward the window. Vera was standing in the middle of the field, still, looking towards the mountains, not the house. It was the only time I remembered seeing her there, like that.

The afternoon I found out about the boy's death, Vera was at the kitchen table, reading the paper when I came in the back door. She looked up and sighed, before saying, "A shame, hey, what happened to that boy at the game."

"Yeah, everyone's talking about it at school," I said, hanging my jacket on the back of the door.

"You didn't tell me that happened. You were working at the game last night, weren't you?"

"We were, but," I pulled out a chair and sat across from her, folding one leg under me so the other leg swung off the floor, "Krista and I left early. There weren't a lot of people coming by." My cold skin was beginning to burn from the warmth in the kitchen.

"Oh. I didn't hear you come in. It must've been late." Vera reached out and touched the back of her hand to my hot cheek. "Are you feeling all right?"

"Yeah. I was out walking."

She looked like she wanted to ask me something else, but she got up and started to make dinner. I sat at the table and watched Vera. She was making something simple, a casserole, and she let me just sit and watch.

That night as I fell asleep, I thought about Gabe's unusual expression, how he seemed so expectant and so reserved at the same time. I wanted to find out what was behind it. I felt unsettled, so I tried to recreate small things, those which can be easily forgotten after one meeting. I thought of the shape of his hands around a cup, his long, straight fingers, flat nail beds. Gabe's lips above the rim as he took a drink. I tried to remember his smell but my mind was pulled back to his hands, the heat that had passed between his fingers and my body when he had touched my hair, the strands a conduit. I thought about my own hands as they traced bone and muscle under my sheets. They were becoming more adept at understanding the lines of my own body than they had been even a couple of years ago, though barely. There were still things that surprised me: a previously undiscovered mole, the occasional knot of something hard and sore beneath my skin, the hot slick of blood when I put my hands between my legs before knowing that time of the month had arrived, again.

Sometimes, just before falling asleep, I would feel a rocking motion, as though my body was remembering lying in the back of a moving vehicle. At one time, we had driven to Edmonton every year for Christmas. Vera would carry us out to the car in our pyjamas before we had a chance to wake up. By the time we did, we would be hours away from Sawmill Creek. When I woke, I would keep my eyes closed at first to feel the motion of the car in every part of me, my body moving with it. I thought it was the ultimate contradiction – moving yet staying still. Asleep yet on my way somewhere. If we drove straight through, Vera would be angry and close to tears by the time we arrived and would sleep through most of the next day. If we stopped on the way, it would be at an old high school friend of hers in Valemount where we would lie in sleeping bags on the floor, listening to the slow moan of snow as it slid off the roof, the muffled thud as it hit the ground.

That friend's husband once told Nick and me about how their cat had gone missing the winter before. "Sure enough, found her under the eaves, next spring when the snow thawed. Flat as a pancake. Ha! Only good cat is a flat cat I keep telling her," he motioned to Vera's high school friend. "Ha!" The husband looked confused when Nick and I didn't respond with laughter, shot us an expression that said something about *kids these days*, then cleared his throat, slurped his coffee and leaned back in his chair saying, "Hyup, yup, yup," under his breath.

Winter in Edmonton was a different kind of season than what we had become used to. Sawmill Creek's winter was a brief fairy tale of a season. The snow fell and kept falling until it peaked the mountains and smoothed out the valleys. It got cold enough to keep the snow on the ground but not enough to cause skin to tighten and burn when exposed to air. In Edmonton, the cold was so dry that the mucus froze in nostrils with each inhalation and air found drops of moisture on eyelashes and stuck them together. The snow was hard and planed by the wind. People navigated the shortest routes between car and house. They said, "Cold enough for ya?" and, "Here, this'll warm clean through," offering drinks, hot or alcoholic, as soon as guests walked in the door.

We used to spend Christmas in one of my aunts' bungalows. These houses were almost interchangeable, with all the rooms on one floor, something called an in-law suite in the basement in which in-laws rarely lived. Olga and Olesa, Vera's twin sisters, lived across the street from each other, their houses mirrors of each other. Everyone talked about how ideal this was, how convenient and delightful. Auntie Al lived a drive away and Baba was in the basement suite, insisting on having her own space down there, no matter how much more difficult the stairs became with each passing year.

Always, the guest room was transformed into the hushed centre of the Christmas celebration. No one actually spent a lot of time in that room but this is where all the coats were piled and, more important, where the dresser was transformed into a bar, complete with Christmas-themed swizzle sticks and a bucket of melting ice. A *sideboard* it might have been called by people with larger houses and more specific furniture. In any of the houses, it would be difficult for the kitchen and dining room to accommodate the forty relatives gathered and so people brought card tables and tablecloths, and lined them in a row in the centre of the living room. Every room became a dining room and people dodged legs, canes, fold-up chairs that would spring closed at the wrong time as they made their way into that guest room again and again. By the end of the night, I would have been grabbed by great-aunts who smelled of lilac powder and something like sour cabbage, great-uncles who would grind their whiskers into my cheek, and teenage cousins who wanted to tickle me to see if I'd pee like I had every other year from too much excitement, drinking too much pop and punch. Sometimes, the room that Nick and I were sleeping in was the same one that the bar was set up in and I'd push the coats aside, fall asleep under one of them, the sound of feet along the carpet, dropping ice, and splashing liquid the most peaceful I could imagine.

And then we stopped going back. Vera complained of the drive. Family members offered to pitch in for plane tickets for the three of us but Vera refused and her sisters called her proud, foolish. "They don't understand, your aunts, they don't understand that my life is here now." I didn't ask her to clarify. "And if I have to hear one more theory from them as to why my marriage didn't work . . ." she added, trailing off.

After that, I talked to my grandmother, Baba, on the phone each Christmas Eve. I felt as though she had become a grandmother to someone else, a girl who saw her more often and could understand what she was saying. I knew from those awkward phone conversations that almost all of the little English she had once known was gone and I didn't know any Ukrainian. Regardless, she spoke to me in her language. I knew that if I had been in the same room with her, I could've smiled and nodded, pointed and mimed, and at least something would have been conveyed.

In Sawmill Creek, the Free Church Christmas services were simple, pared down to the usual singing and witnessing the work of God in our own lives. Children came to the front and told the congregation about how Jesus had filled their lives that year, how grateful they were that He was given to us, born so He could die for our sins while the rest of the congregation would hum and sway, a kind of living soundtrack for their testimonies. After the service, Vera, Nick, and I would usually go to a Friend's place for dinner but no one ever ate so much they felt ill, no one ever drank. No one got red in the face and sang Christmas carols too loud, out of key, or off beat. We always left before midnight and returned to our own house, quiet and cold, the small tree blinking meekly in the living room, where Vera would say, "Merry Christmas, kids, and God bless." When the three of us went to bed, there wasn't a sound left to lull me to sleep.

Two days before Christmas, Vera came in the back door, cheeks flushed and stomping snow off her boots, and told Nick and me that we were going to get a Christmas tree. She had waited too long to buy one and so we were all heading into the bush to cut one down, haul it home, sap still dripping. She had borrowed a chainsaw from a neighbour.

"You can't be serious," I said, but Vera gave me a look that said she was nothing if not that. It was easy to forget that she was once a farm girl, from a line of farm women that only ended with her own generation when she and her sisters married men who weren't farmers.

We took the same road that Rob Hanshaw had driven into the bush, our sedan not as equipped for it. Despite the chains, when we hit potholes the car lurched to the side, jarred us against arm rests, seat belts jerking us back. The chains pulled us up to the first switchback where Vera stopped square in the middle of the road so we wouldn't have to dig ourselves out. We got out of the car and Vera took a deep breath, looked around her. "Well, won't this be good? Cutting down our own tree?"

"Somehow I doubt it," I answered.

She didn't respond to me, just made a straight line for the bush, arms swinging briskly. I realized that, farm girl or not, Vera hadn't cut a tree down in at least twenty years. Nick shrugged and walked toward the forest.

I stood by the car for a moment, then walked to the edge of the clearing and fought my way through the brush and undergrowth. Fresh snow hid stones and roots and I swore under my breath as I tripped and steadied myself. When I heard Nick calling that he had found a tree, I returned to the clearing, brushing snow off myself. Vera started to lift the chainsaw out of the trunk, then winced and held the small of her back. She attributed her lower back pain to the years she had spent sitting behind the receptionist's desk in Dr. Holland's office. She turned to me and said, "Can you help me lift this out, please?"

"This was your brilliant idea," I said. Vera just looked at me, still leaning into the trunk, one arm on her back, the other on the car. Nick bounced beside us, rangy and twitching with cold and anticipation.

Vera straightened up and said, "Aren't you in a great mood today."

"Yeah well, are we allowed to come up here and just chop trees down, anyways? I mean, aren't there some kind of regulations against that?" I asked.

Vera dropped her head and sighed, then looked up at me with an expression of forced calm. "Sylvia, sometimes a forest is just a forest, a Christmas tree a Christmas tree. We aren't taking more than we need. Now will you please help me with this."

"Come on!" said Nick, then, "Can't I do it?"

We turned and glared at him. "No," both Vera and I answered at once, then looked at each other. I lifted the saw out, then held it against my thigh. I certainly didn't know how to operate a chainsaw.

Vera took it from me and walked toward the tree. She pulled on the cord three times before it caught, the last time looking away, jaw tight, then back at the saw, fixing it with her stare. When it started, she squatted and spread her feet apart and aimed the blade at the bottom of the trunk. I stared. It was the closest I'd seen my mother to a compromising position, although what was compromised, I wasn't sure. The chainsaw whirred, the tree fell in the right direction, toward the clearing, and we hauled it back to the car. The most difficult task was securing the tree to the top. Pushing and pulling, we got it on the roof and tied it there in a way in which we had to leave each of the windows open a crack to accommodate the rope that secured it. There was also yellow line stretched out in front of the windshield, tied to the front bumper, the same in the back.

We drove back into the valley with the tree like roadkill strapped to the roof of the car. On the way, Vera told us that she had thrown the tree stand out the year before, because it had nearly fallen apart bearing the light weight of the spindly tree we had then. This being Christmas Eve in Sawmill Creek, the hardware store was closed. We stopped at 7-Eleven, hoping, and I got out to ask.

"I wouldn't think so, but do you have Christmas tree stands here?" I asked the clerk.

"What?"

"Christmas tree stands, you know, those things that keep a tree standing?"

And then there was a voice coming over my shoulder, a single word, "Hey." Gabe was standing behind me in line, his arms cradling a carton each of milk, orange juice, eggnog. "Hey, if they don't have any, I think we probably have an extra stand out at the farm," he said.

"Miss, was there something you wanted to buy?" the clerk demanded.

"Um, I guess you don't have Christmas tree stands?"

"No, we don't." The clerk looked over me to Gabe. "Sir?"

"Here, just let me get these and then you can come back to the farm and I'll find you a stand. I can give you a ride back."

"Um, okay, just a sec."

The lack of a stand had become an issue. While I was in the store, Vera and Nick were in the car trying to figure out how we would rig the tree up in the living room. When I poked my head in the car window, Nick was explaining how he was convinced that we could suspend it from the ceiling with dental floss – he had read about how strong floss was if braided – and this worked in my favour. Vera let me go with Gabe, looking straight at me with an expression that said, "I know exactly what you're up to," even if I myself didn't fully understand. It wasn't that unusual for Vera to surprise me with the things she would allow me to do, as though she were sending me out into the world partially expecting me to be shocked by what I found. To finally understand why she held herself so close.

The snow was falling when Gabe and I started driving out of town, small flakes at first then fattening to the size of coins. The flakes were black in the fallout from lights, white against trees, everything smattered with them. Snow can accumulate in valleys without wind almost instantly and it was piling up that night. When we rounded a corner for the last and longest hill on the way to Pilgrims, Gabe accelerated to make it up, a skiff of snow on the frozen road making it slick and awkward. The truck fishtailed then jerked back and started to climb before the road slipped out from beneath the tires. Gabe tried to move it forward but instead the truck shot across to the other side and into a bank of snow.

"Shit," Gabe said, looked over at me and shrugged. "I'm a California boy. You don't know anything about getting trucks out of ditches, do you?"

"Sure," I said. "What we need is a bit momentum and something for the tires to catch on." We took the mats from under our feet, then I slid over to the driver's side while Gabe got out and placed them behind the tires, then fought his way through the snowbank to the front of the truck. He pushed and I shifted the truck into reverse. We remained like this for a few moments, me with my feet holding the tension between clutch and pedal, the vehicle unmoving, Gabe in front of the truck, pushing. A miscalculation by either of us – not enough balance, not enough force – and the truck would lurch forward, bury Gabe in snow. When nothing happened, I rolled down the window and called to him, "Try jumping on the bumper."

"What?"

"The bumper. Jump. That might give us more momentum." He jumped and I played the pedals until the truck lurched and I felt the crunch of mats under tire.

Gabe hopped off and paused to see if it would slip back before he struggled out of the snow. Everything in me tensed – hands, feet, wrists, ankles – as I held it all in balance. I tried to slowly pull the truck back onto the road but even with the mats it lost traction, slumped back into the bank.

"Do you have chains?" I called out to Gabe. "We need more traction, maybe we can put the chains behind the tires."

He came over to the cab, said, "Chains, hey?" cocked his eyebrow, then, "I think there're some in here. Lean forward." I doubled at the waist and rested on the steering wheel while Gabe opened the driver's-side door and looked behind the seat. He found the chains and pulled them out. He stood outside the door with them in his hands and looked at me. I didn't want to break his gaze by saying anything or moving. Suddenly, a bright light reflected off the rear-view mirror and headlights filled the cab.

A door slammed and a man appeared beside the truck. "You need some help?"

"Yeah, thanks, man." The men dug themselves between vehicle and snowbank and began to rock the truck. This time, when the tires caught the chains, I knew not to let go. I accelerated and shot back onto the road. The guys placed chains on the road ahead of the front tires and I drove onto them, waited until they attached them.

Gabe waved to the man, then held my leg to heave himself into the truck. I tensed my quads and felt him use my muscles as a grip. I threw one leg over the gear shift and began to slide over to the other side. Gabe stopped me there with one of my legs on either side of the shift, his hand on my thigh, his body moving into the cab, filling the driver's side. When his face was close to mine and I thought he was going to kiss me, he said, "You might as well drive, you're doing a great job," and got out of the truck, then back in on the other side. He closed the door. I shifted into first and we started to climb.

GABE

You know you will never bring anyone home with you. You're never sure what you'll find when you get there. Peter and Anise have become suppliers of quality handmade toddler paraphernalia. Most days, they take their coffees out to the deck and share a thin, smooth joint; then Peter descends to workshop in the basement and Anise goes to work in the rec room, which has been transformed into a sewing and crafts centre. Peter builds cribs, high chairs, playpens, bunk beds. Anise sews blankets, diapers, corduroy overalls. Their productivity may be either helped or hampered by the marijuana they smoke, you're not sure. The house is full of sticky smoke and cloying wafts of incense. There is sawdust trailing up and down the stairs. In the kitchen, there is a sink full of bottles, glasses, and dirty dishes and a counter covered in jars breeding sprouts, bowls of fermenting soy, and the drippings surrounding a yogurt maker. NPR is playing somewhere and one of the girls is always crying. The place is a mess, even you realize this. You pick your way to your room, put in the earplugs that you took from Peter's workshop, and read Louis L'Amour and Terry Pratchett novels.

When you first move in, Peter and Anise are so concerned about the suburbanness of the split-level that they cover every wall with decorative hangings. Overlapping in each room are knobby scraps of macramé hanging from pieces of driftwood or fabric patterned with concentric circles of bright, dancing figures, assorted gods. The floors, though they are already covered in wall-to-wall beige carpeting, are laid with handwoven rugs from Amish villages in Washington State. Mexican blankets are draped over chairs and couches. Anise would like to display pottery everywhere as well, but there are three children under the age of five in the house, so that would present a problem. Over all the layers of international folk art are more layers of baby blankets and diapers.

When Anise goes through a kick that she calls Early American Folk, she has a garage sale. You are forced to work, apathetic and scowling behind the table. She sells all the wall hangings, rugs, incense-burners, and wind chimes. After this she hangs patchwork quilts on the walls and there are carved wooden Holsteins and flowers everywhere. The girls all wear floral-print dresses, no socks, no shoes. Anise isn't so concerned with what you wear. You hear her and Peter fighting at night. Your family has no money, certainly not enough money to go redecorating the place, you hear through the walls. You also hear that Peter better go and get a real job and Anise is doing work enough for three people taking care of all these kids.

Peter does get a real job, at the hardware store where he already spends so much time. He takes you there to meet his supervisor, Dave, "a great guy, a truly great guy," he tells you.

"Dave here is even willing to let me put up a little ad here and there for handyman work. I've been teaching Gabe here a bit about carpentry, myself," he tells Dave. Peter has never taught you a thing about carpentry, although a couple times, when you know he has smoked up because of the way he smells, he has called you into the shop and had you run your palms against the grains of wood, how smooth they can be, how strong.

The rec room is cleared out and transformed into a classroom. You remain at the desk in what was once the dining room and hear chaos reign below, Anise trying not to yell. By the early afternoons, you are able to finish your preplanned daily curriculum. You ask Anise if you can go out when she is in the middle of supervising body painting and colour recognition with the three girls. She always says yes.

Peter loses his job at the hardware store. You can't trust the establishment, he tells you, even if it is only a lousy hardware chain. That Dave asshole, you'd think he would understand a couple late starts, especially after all the business Peter has brought into the store, you'd think he'd have a little sympathy for a family man, the jerk. Anise cries for two days, then goes to a women's retreat, leaves you and Peter with the girls. Peter thinks you might all drive up to Wyoming, visit the old grandparents, but when you remind him that the youngest still needs diapers at night and the oldest gets violently carsick, he changes his mind. Instead, the five of you spend three days eating fast food, going to the mall, the minigolf course, and the waterslide. The smallest girls are too young for the minigolf and the waterslide so Peter leaves the two of them in your charge and takes the oldest. "Don't worry – girls can't resist a guy with kids," he tells you, winks. No girls approach you as your sisters cry and whine despite the colouring books, stuffed animals, and candy that you are equipped with.

Each day ends with all three sisters wailing at the top of their lungs until they exhaust themselves and fall asleep. When this happens, Peter invites you onto the deck and you have your first full beer, your first drag of marijuana. "I'm glad about the way things have worked out, Gabe," he says one night, referring to what, you don't know. Peter pauses, looks out to the trees leading out from the yard, continues, "I love all of you guys – Anise, the girls – think we have a good thing going here. But I'm glad you've been with me from the start, Gabe, I really am."

You have no idea how to reply to that, so you don't. Peter, you sense, is making a touching statement of some kind, but you are tempted to ask, "The start of what?" Your father has obviously been with you since the start of your own life but he didn't start when you arrived. You have no idea of his own beginnings, though his parents in Jackson Hole give you some inkling. You think about your sisters. They are contradictions to you – both part of your family and part of an entirely different family at once. Peter is the only link between the two, and he seems like a weak one at that. Your feelings for them are equally contradictory. Sometimes you feel as though you would do anything to protect them. Other times, you want to throw them, one by one, in front of traffic. And Anise. Anise is your father's wife. With not a speck of blood between you, you sometimes feel as though there is no connection there, only a shared housing situation.

When Anise returns, the girls surround her, competing to tell her what fun they've had with Daddy and Gabe. "And then, and then, and then," they each begin, sucking in breaths so quickly you wonder if they will hyperventilate. That night, you hear a headboard banging and Anise sounding like she's going into labour yet again. Although it has always disgusted you to hear them doing that, Peter gave you a tiny, little joint that night, a "pinner" he called it, to enjoy on your own as a treat for getting through the three days. You smoked it by yourself out the window of your bedroom and now when you hear them and know what they are doing, you are filled with sticky, sweet heat. You jack off to the rhythm of their bed. When they are finished and the house goes silent, you do it again, rougher this time, hoping, for reasons you can't quite comprehend, that you will hurt yourself.

Anise suggests gently, and with your consent, of course, that you move your study out of the dining room. Since you rarely do anything in your own room any more except masturbate and sleep, and this takes up little space, you move your desk and shelves in there. The dining room is emptied out and Anise arranges large cushions around the perimeter. She suggests the whole family meditate together and you and Peter agree this is a good idea. You never do and soon the girls have spilled juice, crumbs, and paints in the meditation space and things get stacked there, shoes, toys, Anise's books. Peter is exploring a new business venture and is rarely around. One afternoon when you come home, Anise is setting up a brand new TV in the corner of the living room. She tells Peter it is for educational programming. That night, they fight about money and you stay awake, hoping they will make up and the bed will begin banging again.

$\mathcal{I}$ arrived home half an hour before the service began, Gabe in tow. He insisted on walking me to the door; it was Christmas Eve, and he must have assumed that, if I had a family that was going to church, I had a family that expected boys to walk girls to doors.

I stepped into the front hall as my mother went into the bathroom, a flurry of beige nylons and slip. Gabe followed me in. I looked into the living room, where a Christmas album by Ian and Sylvia Tyson played on our ancient turntable. The tree was propped up between the end of the couch and the wall, a mess of needles dusting everything. There were boxes of ornaments piled on the floor and someone had plugged the tree lights in, left them draped across the couch.

Gabe stood beside me in the hall, each of us holding a different-sized tree stand, neither of us sure what to do next. I called to Vera in the bathroom. When the door started to open, I quickly said, "Uh, Mom, I have a friend here."

The bathroom door closed again. Vera cleared her throat and asked, "Can you get my dress off the bed, honey?" in a controlled voice that was clear, if not loud.

I handed a tree stand to Gabe and went into my mother's room. The dress was laid neatly over the bedspread, which was smoothed just as immaculately over the bed. It was a red-and-white bedspread, quilted in the pattern of a large six-pointed star. Cresting the top and meeting the headrest was a row of decorative pillows covered in Victorian lace. The bed had been in the same place in the room since we had moved in, the pillows set there just so, every morning. Returning with the dress, I knocked on the bathroom door and handed it to my mother. My arm was barely withdrawn before the door closed again. Vera was dressed and out of the bathroom within a minute, smoothing her hair and smiling toward Gabe, her grin tight, as though she already knew everything she needed to about him.

After I introduced them, Vera glanced at me, her gaze swift and sharp, then asked, in a tone of forced politeness, if Gabe wanted to go to the service with us. Before I could say anything, he accepted, as though he had been asked to come along to the fair, or a ball game, or something equally festive and wholesome.

The record ended. Vera asked, "Why aren't you dressed yet?" then said, "Never mind," and turned to the table by the door. She picked up her camera and turned it over in her hands. "I guess you have a ride. Nick and I will meet you there – Nick!" she called before she looked at Gabe and smiled quickly, asking, "You'll get her there on time?"

I heard Gabe assuring Vera that he would as I collided with

Nick on my way up the stairs. I got dressed, hands shaking and heart beating so fast I could feel it filling my chest and throat, while Gabe waited downstairs alone. In the last moment before leaving my house, Gabe said, "The lights."

"What?"

"The tree lights. Shouldn't we unplug those?"

"Oh, yeah." I went into the living room and got down on my hands and knees and crawled behind the couch, struggled for the outlet. When I backed out and stood up, he was beside me, the dim glow reflected off the snow outside the only illumination in the room. Gabe's skin looked fine and thin in the blue light. We stood like that, breathing close to each other's faces, until I said, "We should go now." We walked out to the truck. I gave Gabe directions and put my hands under my thighs, crossing my fingers, as if holding my nervousness and excitement there, tight and small.

When we filed into the church, Friends greeted each other saying, "Christ has come!" as though the birth had just taken place, the hay in the manger still stained with the afterbirth. To which others replied, "He has come to deliver you and me!" I grinned and bore it all, teeth clenched, Gabe beside me. Some Friends held their hands out to him saying, "Welcome, welcome in the name of Jesus," and pumped vigorously. The rest of the congregation tried not to stare at us – or, rather, at Gabe – but they did, out of the sides of hugs, between bending to unlayer children from coats and scarves and standing again. Gabe stood out not only because he was a stranger but because he was wearing jeans, boots, and large wool sweater while the rest of us were decked out in finery.

Gabe and I sat at the back of the church, behind and across the aisle from my family. During the service, I watched my mother take deep breaths when she prepared to sing, her back expanding beneath her dress with each inhalation. I watched Nick lean over and drum his fingers on the back of the chair in front of him until Vera swatted his hands away, gave him a look. I felt Gabe's body beside me, wondered why he gave off so much heat, if I did the same. We sat and rose, rose and sat, and I sang along to every song, although not loudly, clasped my hands together for every prayer. I focused on the flicker of candles against the banners that hung alongside the looming cross until the colours bled together. I tried not to listen to Gabe breathe but counted each of my own exhalations like a rosary.

At the end of that afternoon at the church, Gabe invited me to the farm for New Year's Eve.

Anticipation infused my thoughts, turned them into something physical, an internal upheaval whenever I thought about when I would next see him. Before that could happen, I knew I had to get through the Week of the Word. For five long days the men from the congregation met to discuss doctrine, politics, and the finances of the Free Church, the women gathered together in prayer groups and healing circles to pray the cysts, lumps, and viruses out of each other, and the children went to Bible school. Then there was us, the teens who fell into a category of our own.

Krista, Nick, and I, two boys named Danny and Scott, and

Pastor John's son, Matthew, sat every day on fold-out chairs in the foyer. Matthew was home from Bible college on the coast, wearing thick-soled black shoes and baggy jeans, walking in a way that could only be called strutting. It was Matthew who had gotten Krista and me drunk for the first time on communion wine stolen from the church basement. He had led us with the bottles into one of the fields around the church and by the time Krista and I were drunk, wondering how we would get home and what we would do once we got there, Matthew had disappeared.

"What are you doing here?" I asked him on our first afternoon.

"Don't you remember me, Sylvia? I'm the eldest son of our spiritual leader."

"Yes, and as such, shouldn't you be with the other men discussing sacred policy?"

"Don't you wish. Instead, I have been assigned the illustrious task by my father, your pastor, to lead us all in prayer and a close study of the scriptures."

"Oh, we're blessed, I'm sure," said Krista.

I bit my nails down to the skin and said, "All right, Pastor Matthew, lead away."

The week dragged on and on. The room was cold, the stacking chairs were thin and narrow, and my back and legs would inevitably ache with immobility, boredom. Though Matthew had done nothing to earn it, Nick seemed struck by awe for him. I guessed that he was looking for a big-brother figure. It didn't take a psychologist to figure that out. Vera had signed Nick up with Big Brothers when he started elementary school, but despite their rigorous screening process, it was a disappointment of colossal proportions. The first Big Brother got his girlfriend pregnant and skipped town. The girlfriend then visited us for months, Vera pouring her tea and encouraging her to find strength as she bloated larger and larger. The second, Ray, was older and had a distinct air of loneliness about him, something picked up easily by kids and, I'd suspect, dogs. He owned a sporting goods store in Sawmill and he was a clean, solid guy. Ray once made the mistake of coming by with the stain of beer on his breath. A couple of slurred sentences to Vera at the front door and Nick never saw him again. The last was the golden boy of the Pentecostal Church. He was the closest Nick would get to a good Christian example. Lean and blond, he was the closest I, at fourteen, had been to someone whose beauty looked like it could have radiated from a movie screen. On the first of July, he miscalculated the depth of water and jumped off a cliff into the lake, never came back up.

I imagined that Nick was, in a way, trying to replace a string of disappointing male role models with Matthew. I didn't guess what else he was to my little brother.

On those nights after the endless days spent at the church, I couldn't fall asleep easily. I listened to the central heating creak and sputter, the hum of the fridge, and trucks downshifting, their engine brakes making a long, sour sound out on the highway. On the fourth night, the smell of marijuana slipped through my window. I got up, went downstairs, and pulled my boots on, put a coat over my pyjamas, and was led by the smell. After that, it was simply a matter of following Nick's footsteps in the snow until I found him.

Nick, who had been gazing at the trees that separated our

yard from the ravine, letting smoke seep slowly from his mouth, gasped when he saw me and tried to pull the smoke back in, dropping his arm and twisting it behind him. He started to cough. "Ssshhh," I warned, pointing to the house. Nick nodded back, eyes panicked, and coughed with his arm over his mouth, shaking but making little sound. When he stopped, he looked at me in a way I could only describe as pleading. "You little shit," I said, without smiling, and enjoyed watching him try to figure out what to say. "Okay, well, the least you can do is give me a drag."

The joint was out. Nick fumbled in his jacket for matches, his cold hands shaking, fingers gripping the tiny end. When it was lit, he handed it to me and I inhaled deeply, easily, wanting him to know that he wasn't doing anything I hadn't done before – and had done better. I handed it back. "This stuff is shake. Where'd you get it?" When I asked, I knew that Nick was more frightened of answering than of being caught with the drug in the first place. He could have shrugged his shoulders and told me it was from some headbanger at school. But he didn't. Nick's eyes literally darted from side to side.

"Uh, I can't really say."

"Okay, fine." I left it like that and simply enjoyed a moment with my brother, thought about how lovely it all was – the smell of spruce and pine, the dark circle of dirt visible in the tree wells, sharing a joint with my baby brother for the first time. Then it came to me.

"You got that smoke from Matthew, didn't you?"

Nick shot up from the wall, stood post-straight, didn't answer.

"Didn't you, you little shit?" I said without malice. This was going to be fun. "I can't believe he brought you such crappy shake from the coast. They're supposed to have amazing weed out there. I guess not at Bible college, though, huh?"

Throughout the next afternoon, I stared at Matthew in a way I hoped conveyed I knew something. I smirked. I saw Nick squirm uncomfortably in his chair. Finally, Matthew looked straight at me, asked, "Would you like to lead us in prayer, Sylvia?"

"Of course I would. Thanks, Matthew." I folded my hands together and kept my eyes on him. "Our Blessed Heavenly Saviour, we thank you for guiding us through this week, for keeping our hearts and our minds clear in Christ. We just ask that you help us to keep our minds unclouded in the coming weeks and months, that you help us to see through the smoke-screens of our daily lives. We ask that you help us to resist the temptation to distract ourselves from a clean and clear way of living. In Jesus' name, Amen."

When I was finished, Nick kept his head down, I kept my eyes on Matthew. When he raised his head, his expression was full of something that looked like hatred.

He had a suggestion. "Okay, I think we should pair up and discuss outreach and witnessing, how we can bring our love of Christ to other teens in our community," Matthew said. "Let's mix things up a bit. Danny, you go with Nick. Scott with Krista. Sylvia, shall we partner up?" I smiled. I didn't like the candied authority in his voice. He led me into the sanctuary where the men were sitting on fold-out chairs in a circle near the front. They turned around when we came in, then away when Matthew raised his hand and nodded. We pulled two chairs into a corner.

"You enjoying our week, Sylvia?"

"Sure. What do you want to talk to me about, Matthew?"

"I don't know what you mean. We're brainstorming, remember? Coming up with ways to reach out to other teens."

"Oh, yeah. Okay, I've got a good one. Why don't we give bad shake to thirteen-year-olds and hope they see God?"

He looked back at me, his eyes level. "Yes, why don't we, Sylvia." He paused, then said. "I heard that you went to some kind of solstice ritual at that Pilgrims 'Art' Farm. I am shocked that your mother would let you go – I mean, we're all aware that she's a little misguided herself, being divorced and on her own and all. I've also heard that your mother wants to run for council. I don't know how well she'll do at advising congregates if this is the kind of thing she thinks is all right for her own daughter."

I stared at Matthew for a moment, confused, robbed of response. "What are you, the moral majority all of a sudden? Who are you to talk anyway? Giving my younger brother pot and then lecturing me. And, who's this *we* anyway? You have no idea. You are so wrong about my mother."

Matthew didn't answer. "What do those hippies tell you? Do they tell that there is no God, only your almighty self? Do they tell you that we're all one, that we should worship each other like gods? How do you worship with them, Sylvia? Do you worship with your bodies?"

"Stop it," I said through clenched teeth, glancing over at the men.

"Hard to face the truth sometimes, isn't it?"

"Shut up, Matthew."

"Nice, Sylvia. That all you have to say?"

"What is there to say? You seem to have everything already figured out yourself." I got up, knocking the chair back as I did, walked past Matthew, through the foyer, and out of the church. I made my way home, thinking not about Matthew but about Vera. When I did, I felt sadness and anger at once. I realized that Vera was being betrayed on some level by the very people that she so desperately wanted to think of as family.

⌐

Vera's desires aren't complicated. In Northern Alberta, people her age are moving off farms and into the city. They want TVs, hi-fi stereos, rumpus rooms. Vera wants something else – like-minded people, community, a simple life. She wants to meet people who understand you can live without running water or electricity, that you can live this way with community support and cooperation. She has told her sisters about her ideas, imploring them to remember a time when all of them lived like she imagines they can again. Her sisters just laugh and tell Vera she isn't old enough to remember how hard it was. She is the baby of the family and has always been spoiled.

Jim Harper is the first person Vera meets who understands what she is talking about. He tells her there are places where people haven't forgotten – where a whole new movement of young people like themselves have remembered how good it is to live simply. To live on love, community, shared experience.

At first, she is worried that he is a dreamer. Her sister, Al, has told her that men like him can't be trusted and will amount to nothing. They start to sour when the silver spoon in their mouth is no longer full of sugar.

The Harpers, of course, have high hopes for Jim, their oldest. Mr. Harper had been a lawyer in Edmonton before deciding to run an entire town, and would be a lawyer again, once he was voted out of office. The Harpers wanted to move to a small town to raise their children, to give them some sort of an idyllic, Canadian childhood – not too much of one though, hence the private school in Edmonton – in a time when everyone else was trying to move to the city. They would be cultured, yet down-to-earth children, appreciative of literature and astronomy as well as hard work and honest small-town living.

Since he can't get into McGill, the Harpers send Jim to the University of Alberta, which, they convince themselves, is a perfectly respectable institution. They rent him an apartment of his own in Edmonton because he has had to endure so many years of sharing a dorm room at the academy. Jim switches from sciences to the humanities without telling his parents. He is thinking about studying philosophy. His grades aren't the best, granted, but they represent only a small fraction of knowledge – that which can be measured quantitatively, doled out in classrooms and lecture halls. Jim returns to Fly Hills most weekends and goes to the bar in the basement to shoot pool or slide rocks up and down a shuffleboard, his slim hip cocked just so.

After their first few dates, Jim takes Vera on rides in his convertible, a high-school graduation gift, to Alberta Beach or the city. On one of these dates, he starts driving west, towards the Rockies, where he wants to spend the night under the stars, huddled together for warmth, but Vera insists that she has to be home for her mother, alone in the efficiency apartment. She is the vestal daughter, he is the prodigal son, and both families oppose their relationship – he is not Catholic, she is not middle class. Two months later, Jim Harper sells his convertible, buys a brand new 1969 Ford truck with a camper, and quits university.

Vera has the presence of mind to call her sisters – all three of them – to tell them that she is leaving and they had better figure out what to do with Mother. Before they go, Vera goes to the church each day, although never into the confessional, and stays awake all night counting out her rosary. Because she doesn't know how she will possibly explain herself, Vera writes her mother a long letter in Ukrainian even though she knows her mother has never learned to read. Her mother will wake up in the apartment alone one morning and stare at the pages for a long time. Then she will go downstairs to the store to ask if someone can help her use the phone.

For a few weeks, they live in the camper in the back yard of a friend of Jim's in Edmonton. On the day before they leave, while Jim and his friends struggle to get the heavy, wooden camper onto the back of the truck, their girlfriends take Vera out and convince her to get her hair cut. They all have pixie cuts and cropped pants, cat's-eye glasses. Vera feels like the farm girl she is with them and consents. When they return, the guys are toasting the camper with cheap wine. Neighbourhood kids have gathered around. Everyone has seen campers before on postcards and in photographs from California, but few in

Alberta have seen a real one, mounted and ready to go. Even though he doesn't say anything, Vera can tell that Jim doesn't like her new haircut. He tells her next day that she's different from those girls, that he doesn't want her to feel like she needs to conform ever again.

On their first night together they camp near the Badlands. In the early evening, they walk through the hoodoos, the setting sun rendering everything orange. Vera finds what appears to be a femur. They have been told they will find dinosaur bones here and to leave them where they are. Neither of them imagined they'd find something so large. It is half the size of Vera herself. She runs her hands along the bone, which is jutting out of a crevice. Vera is a virgin and will be until they get married. She cries at not being able to be more free, thinks she must be disappointing Jim but he soothes her in the camper at night, tells her it's okay. He assures Vera that they will be free together, that he will wait for her to unfurl, then he will be the one to keep her open, keep her face pointed at the sun.

They drive through Montana, the truck climbing and sputtering up mountain passes; stop at Yellowstone and watch, with a ridge of other people, the canyon turn bright ochre with a band of sun. The truck doesn't make the gutted road to see Old Faithful but other people tell them it wasn't much, a column of steam. They are looking increasingly dishevelled, and Jim is sworn and spat at when they stop for milk in a town in Wyoming that boasts the world's largest antler arch. In Idaho they watch potatoes the size of baby's heads cascade out of chutes into large trucks. By Arizona, Vera's resolve is wearing thin. She thinks of her will being ground into fine, fine sand every night when they stop and sleep side by side. And each night, Jim Harper comforts her, holds her close, and tells her there's no hurry, his breath ragged, the lower half of his body tight and hard. There is no hurry – they are almost in Las Vegas and soon they will be married.

GABE

Peter and Anise don't seem to notice you much. The girls are a handful, but you can take care of yourself – and you do. You realize that by cultivating this self-sufficiency, you don't call too much attention to what you are doing or when you are coming and going. You realize that you can live on the edge of your family, just as you exist on the periphery of the world of the junior high and the kids there, not truly part of either sphere. Sometimes this makes you feel free and undomesticated, other times just lonely. It's as though you could slip off either edge, fall into that chasm between family and school, and it would take a while for anyone from either camp to notice.

One afternoon you ask Peter for Susan's phone number and he doesn't get it to you for several days – whether he simply keeps forgetting or he has to locate the number, you don't know. He doesn't ask you why you want to talk to her, but you guess it requires no explanation. She is your mother, after all. Nonetheless, you wait until Anise isn't home to call. Somehow you think it might offend Anise, make her feel lacking, even though she doesn't seem to try very hard to be a mother to you. It takes a couple of calls before you are able to connect with Susan. When you do, she seems genuinely pleased to hear from you, though a bit surprised, as though you are an old friend who has just thought to call. She asks you all the right questions – how living in California is, how your schoolwork is going, if you have friends – but you don't have the right answers. You don't have the words to tell her that nothing seems as it should be, though you don't know yourself what that would be.

Perhaps this is because you are at the age when, you've been told, new and powerful hormones are being secreted throughout your body. Although you have not been to public school in two years, Anise and Peter decide you should attend the sex ed. classes at a local junior high. This seems not only unnecessary but slightly absurd. Peter hasn't told you much, but Anise has gone on and on as she does about most things. When you are finished breakfast and about to start your work, she calls out to you from the kitchen. The youngest girl is almost three, but Anise still has her sitting in a high chair. Another is colouring at the table. The oldest is running laps around the kitchen, living room, and dining room, the last of which has been converted back into your study.

Anise calls over her shoulder as she does the dishes by hand. There's a dishwasher, but it's never been used while you've lived there as anything other than storage. "You know, you'll be getting feelings that may seem strange to you, they may not, I don't remember them feeling particularly strange – good yes, strange no –" You were going to try to continue your work while she chattered, but realize she is about to start a roll. "But then, I'm not a boy, am I? Although I think a lot of the so-called gender differences between the sexes are socialized, another

reason, by the way, that you're not in school, nothing but rein-
forcement of socialized norms and stereotypes, anyway, you'll
get these feelings, I'm sure you know the ones, know what I'm
getting at." You stare at her back, her shoulders moving as she
moves dishes from sink to rack, continues talking, and you
think, *stop stop stop*. "I'm not trying to be coy but how does one
describe *those feelings*? I guess, well, okay, let's be honest here,
although I know that you know what I'm talking about – *sexual*
feelings, feelings that make you want to, well, okay, maybe we
don't need to get that honest, huh?" Anise turns and winks here,
and you look down at your textbook. "And I think, I know Peter
thinks too, that you shouldn't deny those feelings, you shouldn't
repress them or pretend they're not there, of course they're
there and they're great! The thing is, you should know how to
deal with them in, you know, an open and honest way, you
should know how to respect your body and other people's bodies
because the universe gave us these great, juicy, meaty, sexy
bodies for a reason, you know?" She shakes her hands into the
sink and turns around. "How do you feel about this? Am I over-
whelming you, I didn't mean to overwhelm you, I mean, I just
want us to be able to talk about this – all of this – openly, honestly, as a family. I know you've been talking to Peter about this,
have you been talking to Peter about this?"

At this point, you say, "Sorta," still looking at the page of
your book, equations arranging and rearranging themselves
under your gaze. Anise is crossing the kitchen, and just as you
are hoping that she won't sit down across from you in the
dining room, the girl at the table jumps down to join her sister
running laps. Unfortunately, they are running in opposite

directions and collide as they each round a blind corner. Anise
is deflected and guides your two sisters to the bathroom where
she will apply herbal salves while you look after the youngest.
You lift her out of the high chair and she toddles from the
kitchen and climbs up into your lap. You hold her around her
waist with one arm, while your other hand is pencilling equations. She is not usually a calm child, but this morning she sits
on your knee in seemingly perfect contentment while her
sisters wail down the hall in the bathroom. She even breathes a
small sigh and leans against your bony chest, her head a globe
of warmth.

You have had a few days like this, Anise telling you about
the feelings you will be having. She seems to forget who she's
talking to or that she's talking to anyone at all and sometimes
she tells you things followed by "Oops, guess you didn't need
to know that much about your old step-ma, huh?" It seems
unnecessary after all this to go to a sex ed. class at the junior
high but both Peter and Anise insist. "We know a lot about sex,
we do, I'm not saying we don't, hey, Peter? But we must be
missing something, I mean, about sexual development – who
knows what new information they have about hormones and all
that these days – not that you should take what they say as some
kind of guiding truth, Lord no, the opposite, believe half of
what you see and none of what you hear, but you want to get as
much information as you can so you can make up your own
mind. We believe you are old enough, mature enough, really,
to make up your own mind, to make choices, respectful choices,
don't we, Peter?"

Five elementary schools are funnelled into the junior high,

including the one you left in the sixth grade. All the kids from one grade go to sex ed. together in the auditorium. Most of the sexual educating is done by pointing projectors at a screen. Two gym teachers, a man and a woman, stop the films every once in a while to see if students have questions. They also read the anonymous comments from slips of paper, questions that everyone laughs at, like "Do Smurfs have sex and, if so, isn't Lady Smurf sore?" and "How do you dislodge an Oscar Meyer from an orifice?"

This is a big mistake, you know this is a mistake. You enter the auditorium shortly before the lights are dimmed but with enough time for kids to see you, for you to see other kids. You see kids lean into each other and whisper. You recognize quite a few of them from your old elementary school and you think they must recognize you too – it's only been two years and it's not like you left the country – but no one greets you like they did back then. No one calls "Hey, Mouse-Man!" or giggles "Hi-i, Mou-ouse." As you walk by, peering into the crowd for a lone seat, a couple of the girls smile at you. They do so with slightly pleading, apologetic smiles. You understand. You have become worse than the Marty Cruickshanks and the Brabra Sanduccis. At least they served some role within the group. You have become something else, someone on the outside. The screen fills with the image of a baby being pushed out of a woman, bloody and covered in pus. The woman on the screen roars with pain and then laughs hysterically. You don't think you will ever be let back in.

The last day of the year seemed like a time to look for signs – where we had come from, where we were going – or, at least, that was the popular rhetoric. I, for one, was too exhausted from steeling myself against the Week of the Word to think of much more than setting myself free and celebrating. The sky was murky that morning, clouds lying low on the fields. When I woke, I fought through the last remnants of sleep, then went downstairs to where Vera was leaning over a crossword puzzle, a coffee beside her. I asked if I could go to Krista's for the day, then to a party that night.

"Whose party?" Vera didn't look up as she asked, tracing the crossword clue with her pencil.

"You remember Gabe? Well, kind of like his family's, the people he lives with, party."

She pencilled letters into squares before she looked up at me, then took a drink of her coffee. Finally, she said, "I presume you mean the Pilgrims Art Farm?" Before I could answer she continued, "Well, I guess if it's not that party, it'll be another one. I suppose you can go. Just be careful."

When I got to Krista's, she warned me that we had to walk lightly, her father was asleep in the basement.

"What's going on?" I asked.

"Don't ask me. Mom's going by 'Therese' now and Dad's basically been hanging out in the basement since Boxing Day."

We were in the kitchen for a couple of minutes before Krista's mother came in wearing a hot pink night shirt that said Wash Me Please, I'm Dirty and what appeared to be plush bunnies on her feet. She already smelled of perfume but she wore no makeup and her permed hair was matted to her head. The baseboard heaters were pumping out air in waves, the house so hot it was nauseating. "You two want me to mix you up a glass of Slim-Fast?" she asked, smiling.

"Yeah, Mom, like we want a glass of Slim-Fast. Thanks, anyway."

"Don't knock it," Therese said, mixing powder into a pint-sized glass until it frothed pale pink. "These things are shock-full of nutrients."

"That's chock-full."

"Yes, exactly. Your loss. Or not – you two aren't going to lose any weight eating the crap you do."

"Did it ever occur to you that we don't want to lose weight, Mom?"

"That's *Therese*, honey – did she tell you, Harper? I am no longer answering to 'Mom' like some kind of robotic maid. I am now Therese – and a woman can always stand to lose a few.

You don't see those pounds now, girls, but I'm telling you, they're there, laying in wait. When you're twenty-one, twenty-two, those pounds are going to come creeping out and you'll have no idea where from. 'I used to be so blippin' skinny,' you'll say. Well, don't say I didn't warn you." With this, Therese took a long drink from the foamy cocktail and smiled at us, teeth gleaming from beneath a pink moustache. She then glanced around the kitchen as though she had just noticed where she was. "Harley's been up here. He's such a goddamn slob," she said and slammed back the rest of the Slim-Fast, turning to place her glass, unwashed, in the sink.

"Can't you at least call him Dad?" Krista asked.

"You call him Dad, for all I care. He's not my father. Try to clean up a bit in here, okay? You too, Harper." With that, Therese winked at us both and left the room.

We spent the afternoon in sweats watching videos and eating popcorn sprinkled with ranch dressing powder. Upstairs, we could hear Therese rotating Bon Jovi, Def Leppard, and Loverboy albums as she conducted her own spa treatment. Every once in a while, she would descend, toes splayed with cotton balls, polish hardening, or hair smeared in an odd-coloured treatment and covered with a plastic bag. She would perch on a chair to watch the TV, look at us with disdain and then return upstairs.

Following a series of yelps, Therese came downstairs in a T-shirt and panties. Her legs were red and raw-looking from ankle to knee where she had just waxed. From knee to crotch she was pasted in cream bleach, rank with the smell of chlorine and ammonia. She couldn't sit down like that so she stood and stared at Krista and me while we attempted to ignore her. We had moved on to eating marshmallows, expanded and browned in the microwave.

"You girls really are disgusting. Not only is that fattening, it's zit-producing. And sweatpants? No woman should ever wear sweatpants. Even at the gym, there are far more flattering things to wear."

"Yeah, like spandex, eh, Mom?" Krista took a marshmallow, placed the whole thing in her mouth, then displayed it for her mother. Therese looked genuinely saddened and left the room, stiff-legged.

"Where are your parents going tonight?" I asked.

"Oh, I don't think Harley's going anywhere. Who knows where she's going. It's so embarrassing. Just be thankful your mother isn't so embarrassing."

As far as we knew, Mr. Delaney hadn't come up from the basement the entire afternoon. We could hear the TV down there emitting cheers – there were only two channels in the basement, but each of them had been broadcasting playoffs of some sort all day.

Therese finally emerged, free of treatments and bleaches, reeking of imitation designer perfume. Her hair was sprayed into a wall that rose from her forehead and her eyes were lined cobalt blue to match the metallic blouse that hung low and clung to her propped-up, unnaturally tanned breasts. She wore a tight black skirt and high heels. She paused at the top of the stairs to the TV room and frowned toward the kitchen. "Eating again?" she asked. "You two had better clean that up before you go out." She then swept down the three steps into the TV room and leaned over gingerly to place her cheek first on Krista's, then on mine, kissing the air around us like she was suddenly European. Straightening up, she adjusted her breasts, then smiled at us with her head cocked, as though we had endeared ourselves to her over the course of our afternoon on the couch.

Krista had told me some of the things that she knew about her mother's past. Tammy, as she was once known, had grown up in the Fraser Valley on a dairy farm where Krista's grandparents still lived. She had left the valley with a leather jacket and a duffle bag full of hip-huggers and halter-tops, and she had straddled the backs of motorcycles that took her south, then east, as far away from B.C. as she could get – we had imagined her chasing heady, drug-charmed nights, desert stars on acid. We couldn't figure out what had made her return. But she did, and shortly thereafter married Krista's dad, Harley Delaney, who we knew from the photographs of him, with side-burns and tight faded jeans, must have been a catch then, though this thought repulsed us.

The newly married Delaneys moved to Sawmill Creek for the reason most people had at one point or another – Harley had gotten work at the mill. They lived at first in the trailer park that is still across the highway from the plant. Harley likes to remind Krista and her mom how much money he once made – how much everyone in forestry was making – in their first few years here. Mrs. Delaney told us about her days before Krista was born, when Harley assured her that she didn't have to work, the long summer evenings spent on makeshift patios with the girls, passing around magazines, cigarettes, and beer. We knew from the old photo albums that in the summer they hitched a small motorboat to the back of the truck and went fishing. In the winter, they snowmobiled up into the mountains, across frozen lakes to cabins. We imagined that they both loved to be outside, going fast. That they enjoyed beer around a campfire or Scotch by a wood stove. This, Mrs. Delaney had made clear, is where Krista slipped in, somewhere between a forgotten birth control pill and a couple of drinks.

The forestry market never did quite pick up, and the day she dropped Krista off at kindergarten, Mrs. Delaney enrolled in a small business program at the community college satellite campus. By the time Krista was in grade two, she was spending her afternoons in the back of Rim Rock Records, colouring books and crayons fanned around her. This is a point of pride for Mrs. Delaney and I have heard her remind Krista on several occasions that it's because she had the balls to start her own business that they live in this house and that Krista and I are allowed the luxury of watching TV all day, brushing food off our laps and onto the carpet in their rec room.

Later that evening, while Therese was getting ready, we suspected Harley was drunk in front of the TV in the basement. We imagined that the sound of her clicking heels coming though the ceiling above him would let him know when Therese was about to leave. When she was finally ready, she yelled, loud enough for him to hear, we thought, "Bye-bye, girls. Have a great night. Don't do anything I would do!"

We called out our goodbyes to her, then Krista and I tried to figure out how we'd get to the farm.

"Didn't you make arrangements with Gabe?" Krista asked.

"Um, no, not really. I just said we'd come. Can't we take the truck?"

"I don't want to take the truck. I can't drive the truck and drink – it's New Year's for crying out loud, there'll be road-blocks. Call him."

I had to call back a few times to get someone coherent on the phone. The first person who answered yelled, "Whah?" repeatedly, even when I was not saying anything, then hung up. The second prattled an incoherent joke, half in and half out of the receiver. I wasn't sure if it was directed at me or at someone on the other end of the line. Finally, the third person was able to understand me. "Just a minute, I'll find him," she said in a way that restored my faith in the ability of human beings to communicate over small distances.

"Yeah?" Gabe answered and I got caught on my own words, then was able to ask if he could come pick us up. "Um," he hesitated, "Sure, yeah, of course. I'll be there in a bit."

⌒

Pilgrims Art Farm on New Year's Eve was everything the Free Church hadn't been all week – hot, loud, crowded. The crush of bodies when we entered the cookshack made me feel strangely secure. I was anonymous there as I couldn't be any-where in Sawmill Creek. We pushed ourselves through banks of revellers. The smell was unfamiliar. Smoke, definitely, but other smells – something spicy, something that smelled like the dark, moist dirt washed off potatoes, something that might have been sweat but was sweeter.

"Come with me." Gabe leaned into my neck, his breath hot on my ear. I turned and raised an eyebrow at Krista, a motion to follow. He led us through the crowd and pulled back a curtain to a side room that appeared to be a pantry. "You can leave your coats here." He motioned to the deep freeze. Krista and I took ours off, spread them over the bluff of coats already there. When I turned, Gabe caught me between his body and the freezer, pressed the fabric on my shirt to my arms as his hands travelled from my shoulders to my hands. When he met my palms, he joined his thumb and forefinger around my wrists.

Krista laughed, said, "Okay, then," and turned to leave the pantry. When she did, Gabe took my hand, and we followed her out.

"I want you to meet my mother," he said.

"Sure," I said, feeling my hand in his. His skin. Near the wood stove people played fiddle, banjo, and guitar while others clapped and spun around. Children wove in and out of legs, stopped to regain their balance or to hiccup. I lost sight of Krista, then recognized the other man I had met the first night, Thomas, sitting across the room on a bench, a woman perched on his knee.

Gabe and walked toward them. "Susan, this is Harper," he said to the woman when we were in front of them. His hand loosened and I let mine drop from his hold.

"Oh, hello – she's beautiful, isn't she, in a slightly unusual way." Gabe's mother said, speaking in third person but directing the words straight at me. Then, "Hi, Harper, welcome to the farm." She didn't smile, didn't lift her hand to shake mine, just stared. Susan was very thin, her cheek bones cutting sharp angles into her face, giving it the appearance of an inverted triangle. Her eyes were large, like Gabe's, and webbed with fine lines.

"Harper, this is Susan," Gabe said and I held out my hand automatically, smiled. Susan looked down at it for a moment, then took it in her own, something that wasn't quite a smile on her face.

"Good to see you back, Harper," Thomas said and moved out from under Susan, his hands on her hips, shifting her weight. "Sounds like they need some help up there," he directed his chin toward the musicians. "Enough of this bluegrass, eh? Methinks we need some jazz." And he left.

"So, Harper – that's a great name – you from Sawmill?" Susan asked. She didn't look at me but felt around in her pockets. When she found a smoke she looked up, blankly, hands on her knees, as though she had forgotten who she was talking to.

"Here." Gabe reached out his lighter.

"Uh, yeah, basically," I answered, embarrassed at my lack of eloquent speech.

"Hmm," Susan said in response, no indication of whether she was thinking about my answer or about something else completely.

"Don't ask her if she likes it," Gabe said.

Susan let out one chuckle, then said, "All right, I see you two have already been through this." She paused to take a drag of her cigarette. "Well, I hope you have a good time tonight,

Harper. I'd better go . . ." Her voice trailed off, eyes already somewhere else in the room. She got up and walked off.

"Sorry," Gabe said.

"No, no. For what?"

"I don't know. Susan's not really used to having me around yet. She – I don't know."

"Nothing to be sorry about. If there's one thing I know, it's that you can never apologize for your own mother." I looked around, not knowing that I was looking for Krista until I spotted her. Across the room, I saw the pale curve between her jaw and shoulder blade when she threw her neck back, laughing. People walked in front of me and I lost sight of Krista. Then I saw her again, hand over mouth, chin lowered, her shoulders bobbing. I stared at her until she looked up and waved. I felt like I knew who I was while in a group of people if I could use Krista as a reference point.

"Do you want to sit down?" Gabe asked.

"Depends where," I answered.

He led me back into the pantry, spread out the jackets on the deep freeze and then lifted me up onto them. The curtain was pulled back, open to the rest of the room. I turned my head and watched the musicians. Thomas was up, his cheeks expanding as he blew into the sax. The banjo had been replaced by a stand-up bass. And, true to Thomas's word, the music was sounding more like jazz. Gabe stood, facing me, his hands on my thighs. I could feel him watching my face. I tried to swing my legs in time to the music but the rhythm lurched. I kept trying. The feeling of my clothing rubbing against Gabe left a small, tight feeling in my stomach. My throat expanded.

"You cold?" Gabe asked. I shrugged. He reached behind me and pulled a coat over my shoulders. As he did, I parted my legs and he slid between them until his pelvis hit the deep freeze. When he pulled the coat around me, I leaned into him. He lightly tugged on my hair, then drew me toward him with it. The way we kissed then was urgent, awkward. I could feel the edge of the deep freeze on the back of my thighs, his tongue smooth in my mouth. My desire slid down between us, jumping then retreating like the jagged music from the next room. I leaned back from Gabe for air, dizzy and giggling. I felt delirious. When I turned my head to take a breath, I caught Thomas's eyes on me from over the sax, his flared nostrils. Or at least thought I did. I thought about what he must have seen. The urgency and delirium, the laughter, and I knew I must have looked beautiful then.

We moved back into the main hall. The room was hot and humid, thick with bodies. I was wearing long johns under my jeans and felt warm, heavy, content. Gabe moved around me – a hand playing with the fabric against my thigh or the hair behind my ear, then he was gone, somewhere in the room, then back again. People played music for hours – switching off when they got thirsty, tired, or wanted a smoke. I had a glass in my hand that was refilled throughout the night. Cigarettes and joints were passed from mouth to hand to mouth. At times, I was unable to determine whether what I was saying was coherent. Other times, I could ease into the feeling, lean back and experience the solidity of the wall and the certainty of the words. I was leaning, shoulder to beam, watching people dance, when Gabe came up to me, holding my coat in front of him. "Want to go outside, get some air?" he asked.

"Sure, why not," I answered. "I'll have to get a hat and scarf, though – as much as you alone should warm me up." I smiled as I turned to the pantry.

As soon as we got outside, Gabe offered, "Smoke?" Even though I'd already taken in a few drinks and tokes, the reality of sitting outside with Gabe made me nervous and this sobered me up. I took the cigarette hoping for a buzz. Snow was falling but it wasn't skin-numbing cold. We sat on the back steps of the building, inhaling deeply, both watching the snow fall like it could tell us something.

"Hey, I probably need to go home soon – do you know what time it is? I should find Krista." I said all this quickly, remained immobile on the steps. Gabe turned and grinned at me but didn't answer. When I had sucked everything I could out of it, I ground the cigarette into a large can filled with sand. "I can't go home smelling like smoke. Do you have any gum?"

"Fresh air."

"What?"

"Fresh air will get rid of the smell."

"Yeah, but that takes time and as much as I'd love to, we can't sit out here for hours getting fresh. I really need to go soon."

"We can run through it, get the full effects more quickly. I'll start the truck, you get ready."

"Ready for what?"

"To run. I'll help you find Krista later." He paused. "Soon."

While Gabe started the truck and warmed it up, I did jumping jacks in the beams of the headlights. He flashed them and the shadow of my limbs strobing against the snow struck me as very funny. His foot was on and off the gas pedal until the engine caught and was running on its own. He then blew the horn and I yelped. "You ready?" he called as he slammed the door of the truck.

"Yes!" I yelled back.

"Then go!"

I ran past Gabe toward the field. I heard him running behind me and felt a dull knife of something like fear and excitement between my ribs, prodding my stomach. When I got to the fence, I didn't know where the gate was. Gabe was right behind me, his breath creating fog in the cold air.

"Jump over it," he said.

The fence was barbed wire. I watched while Gabe quickly found the right place to put his hands so that the wire was taut and still for a moment while he launched himself over it like a gymnast. I knew, even though the packed snow lessened the height of the fence, I wouldn't be able to do the same thing. My arms weren't strong enough, the wire would buckle and bring me down on its points. Gabe was already running straight into the field. I found a place where the ground dipped. I dropped and rolled once, quickly, feeling my coat catch on the wire and release, then I was up and after Gabe, who was almost out of sight, his figure against the snow being swallowed by the dark. I wouldn't call out; I would depend on my legs to take me to him.

I was wearing jeans, long johns, two pairs of socks, a pair of boots, the laces cinched tight. A sweater, coat, scarf and hat were all hindrances as I ran. I couldn't hear Gabe's steps, only my own breath. As I ran deeper into the field, I sank into the snow to my calf, felt the weight of it when I lifted my heel for the next step. Momentum loosened the snow and to keep myself going I imagined pushing through strata of clouds. The breath I expelled became moisture, coated my skin along with the snow that melted on contact and the mucus that ran from my nose. I tried to wipe at my face as I ran, never able to dry it.

When I saw the bank, I could think of nothing else but sliding down. At the bottom, I stopped, couldn't hear anything above the rasp of my breath. I watched it explode into steam then fall back against my face until I felt the moisture form crystals on my lashes, around my nostrils. As I sat still, the snow stuck to my lashes. There was no wind, nothing but the barely discernible hum of falling flakes and a sound that might have been water running under ice, somewhere, not near. No sound of Gabe's boots in the snow, no sound of Gabe. I looked back up the bank to where I could see the glow from the farm. I told myself that I had nothing to be afraid of, then yelled, "Gabe!"

Nothing.

"Gaa-aabe!" The thought of walking – essentially crawling – back up the hill exhausted me. "Gabriel! You asshole! Come find me and carry me back!" I heard a laugh, somewhere near me. I turned and tried to orient myself. "Gabe, I heard you!"

To the right, there was a grove of trees like a shadow. I could make out the twisted lines of the first trunks against the snow but branches, needles, and trees eventually deepened into grey, then black.

From somewhere in there came Gabe's voice. "Aha, you think you're a princess, do ya?" I tried to follow his voice with my eyes. "Think I'll carry you? Then you have to come find me, princess." The voice shifted but there was no other noise or movement. It was cold enough that the snow that fell stayed dry and light but not cold enough that it squeaked underfoot. This was the all-encompassing snow of folk tales, of losing all bearings – it covered tracks, obliterated sound.

"Gabe!" I yelled again, not knowing what else to say. When he didn't answer, I chose forest over bank. When I entered, I thought I heard something and stopped. Nothing but my own breath, boughs creaking under the weight of snow. And then something – a sound that could have been anything but I decided it was him. I stopped in my tracks, feet in the depression my boots had made in the snow, and understood the exact meaning of that phrase. Another sound, this time like rough fabric against wood, but I couldn't tell from which direction or how far away. I began moving again, keeping my breath small, my steps light. I could see the glow of the field behind me, felt reassured by the presence of light. I took one step forward, two steps to the side through the trees, not wanting to stray far from the field. Gabe said, "Pssst," from deeper in the trees. I knew he was leading me in. I didn't call out again, didn't want to miss the next clue. I took a couple of steps farther into the forest then began to walk with the field still in sight on one side of me. I needed to know where open space was.

Movement, sound, and sensation began to blur. I thought I heard something, thought I saw something. Thought I felt the presence of someone else nearby, of eyes on me, but when

I stopped there was nothing but the aural memory of my own footsteps in the forest. I stood unmoving, barely breathing, waiting for the next hint until I surprised myself by becoming scared in earnest. Rather than call out, I started to make my way back toward the field until I heard him again. "Prinnn-cesss." This time, the word was whispered from close by and when I spun around I could see Gabe running away from me. I let out a call like a laugh and a gulp at once and ran to follow. He darted around trees and cut a crooked, narrow trail in front of me. I was close. Branches were still springing back from his passage and I had to keep my arms up to shield my face.

Avoiding a large branch, I ducked, swerved, and slipped. When I struggled up out of the snow, he was gone. I laughed, then stopped, listened and again there was nothing. I looked around. Nothing but the cross-stitching of dense young trees. I could no longer see the field. We were deep enough into the forest that the trees were creating their own warmth. I could hear melting snow drip from needles, chunks of it slide from trees, the shifting of branches. I wondered what time it was, where Gabe had gone to, and which direction I could take to the road. I reasoned with myself that the farm was small – in any direction I would meet with either field or road. Then I felt something approaching fear.

"Gabe, you asshole!" I yelled. "I'm not your princess and I am definitely not having fun any more." The words didn't seem to be carried far before they were absorbed. "Aaahhh!" I shouted, stopped, stomped my feet in the snow, my body getting cold, rigid with fright and anger. I wouldn't cry. I closed my eyes and turned around then I stopped and walked in whichever direction I was facing. Field or road, field or road, field or road. I no longer listened for sounds or searched for clues.

He was behind me before I heard him. He circled my waist and turned me around. I was about to yell into his face but he clamped one gloved hand over my mouth. His other arm roped around me, pushing me back into a tree. He held me like that for a moment, looked into my eyes without speaking, his own irises black in the lack of light. I held myself stiff but didn't struggle. He loosened the arm around my waist, drew it out from behind me slowly, his hand moving along my side, my neck, the scarf now hanging loose, my jaw. When his hand reached my cheek, Gabe slid his other hand off my mouth equally slowly until both were holding my face and I was looking at him. We stood like that, me trying to glower at Gabe, Gabe staring at me.

"So, you're not my princess, hmm?"

"No, I'm not – but you still have to get me back before midnight."

Gabe moved his hands with the same slow precision, off my cheeks, along jaw, neck, shoulders, down each arm until he reached my wrists and pulled them back, around the tree, pressing his chest and thighs against me as he did. I could hear my heart in my ears. I moved up toward Gabe's mouth, up out of the confined space between chest and trunk, toward air. I found his face, his lips moving back to my ear and biting me lightly. Gabe continued to hold my arms tight against the tree. I struggled then found his mouth, met him there. Heat and moisture and teeth against teeth. I waited until everything loosened – his hands around my wrists, his thighs against mine – until everything, our two bodies, the tree, the ground became liquid then I took his bottom lip in my own and sucked until Gabe let out a small sound from his throat. Then, I bit down into his lips and I tasted salt.

I slipped out from between Gabe and the tree, moved away from him as he came toward me. I felt no anger but the remnants of fear, and this mixed with a prickly heat between my legs, my chest and throat throbbing, the feeling of pins and needles along my neck. Gabe wiped his mouth and laughed, took my hand.

GABE

Sometime along the way, you manage to make friends again. When you were first at home, Anise tried to hook you up with other kids being home-schooled, but they turned out to be either kids whose Christian fundamentalist parents didn't want them coming to your house or kids who had "behavioural problems" and who you didn't necessarily want coming anywhere near you. You have been wandering the streets of Arcana looking for something to do. Some of the junior high boys remember you and others have heard of you, know that you don't go to school and think you're cool because of this. They ask you what you do all day, if you can hook them up with weed and girlie mags. The assumption is, since you don't go to school, you have access to things other kids don't, and to your initial surprise you discover that this is true. Anise and Peter's supplies of weed are fairly easy to find and there's enough, in enough different places, that they don't notice when some goes missing. And the girlie mags. By a stroke of instinct, you ask one of Peter's buddies – a younger guy who is involved somehow in the conservatory – if he can, um, if he can, uh, okay, get you some, um, magazines? You turn red and falter and he laughs and slaps your back and tells you, "No problem." He brings a couple of magazines every time he visits your house, slips them to you when Anise and Peter aren't looking with a wink and a click-click from the side of his mouth.

You wish you had a normal family, two parents who worked, sisters who went to school. Anise has started AMAHALI – Aware Mothers At Home And Loving It. So far, there are four other mothers in the group and they rotate houses on weekday afternoons. So far, the mothers have sat in the living room or on the deck and drunk tea or coffee while the kids have either run around the yard or watched videos that could loosely be called educational.

You loathe the days when they descend on your house. Someone always gets hurt, someone always cries. The mothers attempt to laugh it off and tell each other the kids are learning social skills. For all of their awareness, the mothers don't appear to be loving it. They roll their eyes, coax kids out of the living room and talk about things – childbirth, menstruation, tantric sex – that you can't help but overhear and this embarrasses you. When they are there you try to leave, smiling and asking Anise if you can pick anything up for her at the store. You hear her telling the other mothers what a help you've been, how like your father you are.

Your sisters have developed, to your surprise you'll admit, distinct personalities. The oldest is wilful, stubborn, and sneaky. The middle one is wistful, dreamy, and a whiner. The youngest, your favourite, is a charmer, a ham. She sings and dances and puts on one-girl shows for anyone who will watch. They are six, seven, and eight – ages that you can remember being – and this makes them seem more like little humans to you, and, in turn, you feel more protective of them. One of the mothers makes a joke about the kids being "feral" – about how free they are, how untamed. You want to tell your dad, Peter, something, warn him, of what you're not sure. That Anise rarely helps you with your home-schooling and probably won't help the girls much either. That they should have more super-vision than the loud, laughing group of hippie moms that watch the brood now. But, you remind yourself that you are not quite a part of this, that you have a lot of freedom where you are. Freedom you're not sure you want to give up.

Peter isn't home a lot. He did start that new business venture, after all, although you have little idea what it is. Anise tells the mothers that Peter has gone into the holistic growth of organic herbs and medicinals. This is news to you. Peter refers to where he goes a couple times a week as "the conser-vatory." He loves to use the word, as though what he is doing is so grand, so lovely that it should be set to music. When he is home, Peter is in the shop.

You gain a reputation from the guys as someone who is always able to come through for them. The weed, the maga-zines, and other things – your house to hang out in on the rare afternoon when Peter, Anise, and your sisters are all out. You have even let them start up Peter's power tools and point them at each other.

The guys tell you what has happened to girls since you've been out of public school. Sure, there were a few years when they all seemed to walk into things – desks, chairs, doors, any-thing really – when a couple of girls were spotted with bur-gundy stains on the seats of their pants and some of them cried for no reason in phys ed. Most of them, though, are through that now and the guys let you know that you should be thankful that you weren't around for those years. Now the girls have asses instead of butts, tits under thin T-shirts. Almost all of them wear bras, the guys tell you, but there are always a few who think they don't have to, think they're too flat-chested. This is good too. If you are ever near one of them when it's cold, they swear, you will be able to see the ridges of their nipples clean through their shirts.

These same boys are fighting substantial battles with acne. Oil seems to noticeably creep down their roots and along each hair even in the few hours that you spend with them after they're out of school. By the time you part, a couple of the guys look completely water-logged, skin and hair gleaming. It seems unfair to you that it is these same boys that are able to share classes with the girls they tell you about. They are able to look at them from behind locker doors. To sit behind them in algebra and smell their hair that always has the essence of something sweet, fruity – green apples, peaches. These boys are able to ask if they can borrow a pencil and watch while the girls' rose-tipped fingers sift through pencil cases, imagining all the while what those same fingers would do to their bodies.

It doesn't take you long to figure out a couple of things. One, since Peter and Anise trust you and you have had a certain amount of "freedom" for a couple of years now, there is no stopping you hanging around the high school when classes get out, meeting your buddies, running your eyes up and down those girls. Two, that when you do show up at the high school, the girls are as fascinated with you as you are with them. You are a legend now.

It is Saffron Fraser who lets you in on this. You are waiting for the guys, a few minutes before the final bell, when she appears from around the side of the school. "You waiting for your loser friends?" she asks. You answer that yes, you guess you are. "Don't then. Come with me, walk me home." You walk her across the field and down a road that will eventually lead you to her place. "You remember me?" she asks. You do. She was in your elementary school, always in another class, called Saffie then. That's about all you can recall.

"Yeah, sure."

"Yeah, well, I remember you too, Mouse. A lot of us do, you know." You didn't know, stay quiet, afraid to blow whatever is going on. "You're so lucky that you don't have to go to school." You start to explain that you still have to do schoolwork, that instead of being in class you are in a house with three younger sisters, but then stop. "We're not –" she continues, then pauses. "We aren't so lucky that you're not at school, though. The boys there are, well, never mind, they are your friends, unfortunately. Hey, you should come to one of the dances. You know, the lame ass school dances, I don't know if you'd want to but –"

You are in front of her house by then and this is when you turn to face her, instead of walking side by side. "Yeah?" you say. "Sure. Just let one of the guys know when." While you are looking at Saffie, who you're sure you once chased screaming around the schoolyard of your elementary school, her neck turns pink.

"Yeah?" she says, as a question.

"Yeah," you say, as an answer. When you do, she takes your hand and pulls you into her carport. There, she kisses you on the lips – your first real kiss – it is fast and wet and your top lip bangs against your teeth. She bursts out laughing afterward.

"Oh, my God," she says. "No one is going to believe this." You don't ask her why not.

This first kiss, that rising pink on her neck, knowing that you can make her laugh for no reason at all, is intoxicating but it doesn't make you confident, it makes you awkward. Anise notices. She has started directing what she says to Peter instead of you. "Peter," she yells to him in the next room, right in front of you, "You know, I thought Gabe already went through puberty but there seems to be something else going on now, doesn't there?" This last question she points at you with her eyes, laughing at the corners. You don't know how to answer, leave the room. Anise has never been more annoying.

She thinks you're having sex. This becomes clear after a few of these cross-house announcements to Peter. "I think your son – *our* son – is becoming, well, a man, so to speak. Huh, Gabe?"

"Shut up, Anise," you tell her one day. It is the first time you have ever said this to her. It is the first time you have seen her look genuinely surprised at anything you've done.

You are not having sex but you think about it constantly and Anise seems to pick up on this, which drives you nuts. You discover, however, it isn't only her. The other women in her mother's group pick up on it too, although they don't yell things across your house, thank God. Instead, they poke their heads into your room on their way back from the bathroom down the hall, ask you how your work is going, and move into the room further. You have twice had mothers sitting on your bed asking you about basic laws of physics, watching your lips move while you explain. One of them tells you that you have lovely eyelashes. Eyelashes? No one will ever believe this. Not even you believe it completely. You don't know how adults get anything done. Your days are saturated in sexual suggestion and you haven't done more than kiss Saffie in a carport and wipe the saliva off your mouth when she wasn't looking.

When Gabe and I got back to the cookshack, it was one in the morning and the truck that we had left running had stalled. We had missed the countdown. Krista was dancing, stripped to long johns and a shirt like most of the other people in the room. I didn't want to stop her.

"You can spend the night here, you know," Gabe offered. And we did, Krista and I both sharing Gabe's double bed with him in a converted shed. I slept in the middle. Gabe and I kissed until Krista kicked me, saying, "Would you two cut it out." We stopped, and Gabe fell asleep first, as Krista and I whispered to each other about what fates awaited us for not returning home. When I finally did fall asleep, I was too happy to care.

The next day, after dropping Krista off first, Gabe took me home. I went into the kitchen and poured myself some cereal, listening to the Cheerios hit the bowl as I tried not to think of what was coming next. No new snow had fallen. The ground shone, sun off a tight skin, and I didn't close the blinds, squinted into the glare.

They arrived home with a cough, a splatter of keys, boots dropping. Nick pounded up the stairs and Vera came into the kitchen, reached for the coffee maker, registered the sight of me sitting at the table, then walked back out. When she came in again, she did nothing but stare, tight-lipped. I looked back at her; she was only a silhouette while my eyes adjusted from the light out the window. When she finally spoke, what she said was this: "Well." She said this quietly, straight at me.

"Hi," I said.

"Well, yes, hi," she responded, poured herself a cup of coffee and slammed it into the microwave. "You were with him last night, weren't you?"

"You already know I was at Pilgrims last night and yes, I was with Gabe. It's not what you think, though."

"Sylvia, I trusted you to spend the evening there, not the night, and I'm trusting you now to tell me the truth."

"I wasn't doing anything."

"Well, you certainly must have been doing something. I just hope you know what that was, or what you think you're looking for."

"Looking for? Is that what this is about? And what did you think you were 'looking for' when you moved us here and joined the Free Church? Tell me that."

Vera stared at me without saying anything, then sighed. "Speaking of which, I met with Pastor John yesterday. Matthew was there. I went to talk about the possibility of being on the council, and instead we ended up talking about you. They're concerned that with me being responsible for you and Nick on my own, I won't have enough time to focus properly on the church, and I can't say you're helping matters any."

"Why are you telling me this?"

"You know it's hard for me, Sylvie. I can't keep track of your every move. Do me a favour and don't play innocent with me now."

"I'm not playing at anything. Did you ever consider that? What are you trying to say?"

"I'm talking about that farm, the drugs, the New Age nonsense that they're feeding you."

"New Age nonsense! Yeah, they're brainwashing me, Mom, stripping me naked and painting me with menstrual blood. What did Matthew tell you, anyway? What do you think is going on?"

"I don't know, Sylvia, but I don't think you do either. Why don't you try to explain to me what *you* think is going on."

"Well, for one thing, Matthew is lying to you."

"I understand, you confided in him, but let's not talk about Matthew, let's talk about you."

"What about me? It was New Year's Eve. I got tired. I didn't want to face coming home and going to church *again*. We went to church all last week. I didn't want to face you and your accusations, all the Friends' fake smiles, the self-righteousness. I can't believe that you would take Matthew's word over mine. I'm not even going to repeat some of the things he said to me."

I refused to let my emotions misfire and make me cry. I realized that Matthew, hypocrite that he was, had been counting on me not saying anything that would implicate my brother. Without even being there, he had me pinned. Anything I said now would come off as an attempt to protect myself. I wanted to tell Vera that the pastor's successor was dealing dope to her son. Instead, I blew. "You are so self-righteous. Why don't you ask some of your so-called friends exactly what they think of you and then see if you still want to take all this out on me. Mom, open your eyes."

I saw something register in Vera's face. She blinked quickly, like coming up out of water. "This is not going to help, attacking me, turning everything around." Vera sat without moving, her lips pursed, before continuing. "I don't know what's happened to you, Sylvia, but I don't like it."

"Maybe you'd better ask yourself what's happened to you. Your life is nothing but that church and they don't even think you're fit to sit on council. I suppose you think that's my fault. Nick and I are going to leave eventually and then what will you have? No kids around, shitty job, no husband and no hope of one, and a church full of hypocrites. Oh yeah, and poor. That sounds great. That sounds like exactly what I'd like to aspire to." I told myself that I didn't mean to make Vera cry. No one likes to see her mother cry – mothers are supposed to be resilient, immune to anything as weak as tears. I simply wanted to expose things, bring them to the surface. For years, this had meant happening upon words and situations that could disarm her. Once I did, though, I couldn't take what was bared, so I sought easy exits.

I got up from the table and walked toward the door, pulled my jacket off the hook. Vera was behind me and as I reached for the door her arm shot around, pulled the handle closed. Her other hand dug into my arm and turned me around. "Sylvia," she said, speaking through her teeth, eyes wet.

"Let me go." I twisted my arm out of Vera's grip and my shoulder slammed back against the door. "We obviously can't talk about this, so let me go."

"We *are* going to try talk about this." She now had me by both arms against the door, her spit a spray on my face. I struggled out of her hold but she turned and blocked me. As I tried to open the door, she grabbed my coat and I instinctively thrust my forearm toward her. Vera shoved it away, then we each got a hold of the other's clothes and fought with little more than fabric, our meek blows blunted by uncertainty. At some point, she faltered and I ducked, pulled at the door, and ran into a slap of cold air. I slipped as I rounded the path around the house. Tears gathered in the back of my mouth. I swallowed, turned, and kept running.

I fell two more times on the hard-packed road before I got to the corner store and called Gabe. When he picked me up, I shivered while he drove wordlessly, pulled me over to him on the bench seat and rubbed my thigh with his one free hand. I glanced up repeatedly at the rear-view mirror, not knowing why I expected to see Vera's car appear there. "I don't want you to have to keep doing this," I said. "Coming to get me. I don't want you to feel like you have to bail me out." Gabe kept rubbing my thigh, his eyes on the road. When I started to cry, he pulled my head down onto his shoulder. As he drove, I could feel his muscles shifting, and, in me, something altering, steeling me against tears.

I didn't ask Gabe to take me to the farm. He didn't ask if I wanted to go. He simply drove there, brought me into the converted shed and then said, "You can stay here as long as you need to." He ran his hand through his dark hair, twisted it into accidental curls and watched me like he had no idea of what to do with me, or what I might do.

The next day, we returned when Vera was at work and Gabe waited for me in the truck. It didn't take me long to pack. When I had, I left the way I had come in, locking the door behind me.

My arrival at Pilgrims was virtually unnoticed by most of the people there. I figured the people who lived at the farm expected mutable family situations, transitory living conditions, people moving in together within a month of meeting.

As the son of one of the first families on the farm, Gabe had been given, though not a cabin, a relatively good shed to live in. It was close enough to the outhouses that it was convenient, far enough away that the smell didn't reach him. It had electricity wired to it from the cookshack, a narrow wood stove, good for heat and boiling water, and a space heater. There were no storm windows, but it was relatively airtight, which was more than could be said about some of the sheds on the property. It was split down the middle, vertically. One half was a narrow, insulated room – a makeshift home – the other was a essentially a workshop with a concrete floor, tools, implements.

He told me that around the farm, there were various living

accommodations, some more lacking than others. As I would soon find out, the old Pilgrims establishment lived in charming log cabins with lofts and wood stoves and window panes in formations – Stars of David, pyramids. There was a tree house that rotated tenants. The hayloft in the big barn had been converted into an apartment and that was where Thomas lived. The rest, Gabe explained – the grown-up children, the hangers-on, the volunteers who appeared in the summer to receive a back-to-the-land experience like a benediction – lived where they could. In tents and vans during the summer. In sheds and outbuildings the rest of the year.

For the first two days, I did little more than sit on the bed, look at the walls, and nap often. I was exhilarated by thoughts of a new kind of freedom, but I felt stripped of both energy and emotion. I couldn't comprehend what I had done in any way that made sense. I had called home and left a message with Nick to tell Vera that I was fine but I wouldn't be coming home soon. That I was now at the farm, eating and sleeping there as though this were normal seemed both inevitable and at odds with everything that had come before. Gabe brought me food, the remnants of dishes other people had made, mostly vegetarian and stinking of garlic, hot with ginger. I didn't eat a lot of this, preferred the bread and peanut butter in the mini-fridge, soups I could add water to and heat up in the microwave. At night, Gabe and I pressed up against each other. I kept on a T-shirt and long johns, moved away from him when I got too hot.

On the third day, as if to rouse me from my lethargy, Gabe said, "I need you to help me with something."

"What kind of something?" I looked up from the bed.

"We'll be outside."

"Oh, I get it, it's a mystery," I said as I started to get my coat, my sign that I was willing to go along.

Gabe wanted to keep what we were doing a surprise so I followed instructions. He gathered an armload of old hockey sticks from the back of the truck. "I just picked these up yesterday. This guy at the arena's been collecting them for me."

Old hockey sticks did not excite me. "I know, we're starting a league – the hippies against the religious freaks." He just looked at me and rolled his eyes.

In the shed, we made holes into the blades of the sticks, Gabe holding the shafts against the workbench, me drilling. It was the first time I had ever used a drill. I loved the way the point entered the wood, how it could render something that had once been solid into shavings. When we had eight drilled, Gabe said, "Okay, I think that should do it," and weighed large hammers against his palms contemplatively, put a bag of large nails in his pocket. He found a place on the porch of the cookshack where a plastic-coated wire emerged out of a small hole. Gabe nailed one of the hockey sticks to a post on the porch, blade up and turned out, slid the wire through the hole. "We're going to string this wire back to the shed. You good at climbing trees?"

"Show me what to climb and I'll climb it."

"No, actually, you stay on the ground, I'll climb. You can hand me the sticks. I'll have to nail them to the trees so it could be hard."

"Whatever you say."

It took longer than I expected, Gabe finding foot- and

handholds that would lead him up trees, me handing hockey sticks to him from the ground. "We have to get this high enough so that it won't be in the way." I looped the wire through the drilled holes first, then handed Gabe the sticks. He reached as high as he could, nailed the shafts to trees. The last stick was nailed to the shed. "Okay, we just have to bring it in now," Gabe said. We went back inside and Gabe knocked on walls, stood back and peered, knocked again. Eventually, he drilled a hole in the frame of one of the windows in the workshop and pulled the wire through. "Ta da!" he said when he was finished, his cheeks bright with cold and exertion and what I could only describe as glee.

"Ta da!" I repeated. "What is it?"

"A phone line! It's been ready to go for a few years now but no one's ever bothered to wire it over. Now you can talk from here, you won't have to go to the cookshack to call Krista, or whoever. I mean, it's not quite ready – we'll have to get a guy to come out and put a jack in – but almost!"

Gabe seemed oddly excited about the prospect of having a phone in the shed, and so happy then. Perhaps it was his way of welcoming me. His gesture meant something else. He expected me to stay long enough to use it.

⌁

Susan thought so as well. She came into the shed on the fourth morning without knocking and sat down on the edge of the bed. Gabe wasn't around.

"So, you planning to stay for a while?" she asked.

"Um, I'm not sure, things aren't great for me at home and –"

She cut me off. "Yeah, well, they never are, are they?" When I didn't answer, Susan continued. "We don't expect much here at the farm. Everyone does what they can – that's about all you can expect from anyone, really – and Gabe has a bit of money, as I'm sure you know. Just pitch in where you can." I nodded, not quite following along. How I was to pitch in was unclear, as was the part about Gabe having some money.

Susan continued, "Okay, well." Paused. "Gabe tells us that you go to that church out on Pleasant Valley Road." I nodded. "Now, I don't know much about your church but I know they have some pretty strong beliefs and we don't want anyone butting in here, Harper. We don't want this to become an issue."

"Oh, no, I, you don't –" I started, but Susan cut me off.

"It's okay. I'm sure everything will be fine, I just wanted to make that clear. I'm sure everything will be fine. Just let us know if you need anything." With that, Susan got up, left the shed.

When I couldn't sleep that night, I got dressed, went to the cookshack and used the phone. I called home twice before Nick answered. When he did, I asked him to wake Vera.

"Come on, Harp. You know how hard that is."

"I know, but you can do it. You *have* to do it. For me."

A few minutes later, Vera was on the phone, her voice coming through a haze of sleep. "Sylvia?"

"It's me, Mom. I just wanted to call – I wanted to let you know I'm at the farm. Pilgrims Art Farm."

"I know. Your brother told me." She sounded more awake now but her voice was still quiet. "What is it, Sylvia? What is it you think you're doing?"

"I'm going to stay here for a while." I stopped before continuing, "I need you to understand that this is what I have to do right now. I just wanted to let you know." I could hear her breathing on the other end of the line. "Mom?"

"Yes. I heard you. In case you wondered, the school called to ask me why you haven't been going to classes. How do you think I felt when I couldn't give them am answer?"

"I'm going back to school. I'm going back. Don't worry."

"Sylvia, listen to me, I am going to worry," she said. "You can't just leave the way you did, not come home, and expect me to be fine with it."

"I was suffocating. Look, I love you but I don't want to live in a house where all that seems to matter are the mistakes you made in the past and how the church can absolve all of us from them. The church isn't going to do that, Mom. They're still blaming you for those mistakes."

Vera was silent for a moment before she said, "I'm sorry that you feel that way."

"I'm sorry, too. But you can't go on trying to protect me from making my own mistakes. I really need some time to sort some things out on my own, without you or anyone from the church."

I began to feel dizzy with exhaustion, my mouth dry, an ache stretched taut across my forehead. We were not going to reach a resolution. I wasn't going home, and while Vera wasn't giving me her blessing, she wasn't insisting I return either. I have wondered many times since, what that must have cost her.

After we said goodbye, I sat at a table in the main hall of the cookshack in the fallout from the kitchen light. When I went back to the shed, I didn't wake Gabe as I slipped into bed. As I fell asleep, I thought about rites of passage, about baptism. In the Free Church, we were baptized more than once. The first time as babies or – in the case of Nick and me or other kids who hadn't been part of the church as infants – as young children. A liquid brand to remind our parents that we were marked as one of His. The second time was when we could accept Christ into our hearts on our own and be conscious of Him entering our bodies. For this, I was baptized in the Salmon River. Even though the Friends of Christ had no problem with bathing suits, to be baptized everyone wore clothing head to toe, then pulled on a long white smock like an enormous Victorian nightgown. I stood in the river with Pastor John, my hands on my heart and my back to him while Vera smiled so hard it brought tears to her eyes and other women thanked the Lord.

It was the middle of the summer and the river looked swollen and unmoving but the volume of water hid a tricky current on the riverbed. After Pastor John said his part and I fell back as planned, expecting his palms to cup my head and keep my eyes tipped to the sky, I simply floated downstream. Pastor John had lost his footing and gone under. I paddled back to the shore and struggled through river weeds, weighed down and waterlogged. I made my way back to the congregation upstream, relieved to see that Pastor John looked jovial in his wet robes. "God works in mysterious ways," he chuckled. Other people laughed but Vera didn't. She looked at me as though what happened had been my own fault. After I was dipped again, we ate hot dogs and drank warm Pop Shoppe soda through straws. Vera had forgotten to bring me a change of clothes, so I spent the afternoon drying, river scum trapped in my underwear. I never forgot the look Vera gave me that day.

The next morning I woke sweating, the sheets soaked. When I pulled off my clothes, the feeling of the blankets against me was a dull ache, the air that slipped through pricked my skin. I moaned and when I did, my teeth began to knock against each other, seemingly of their own will. Everything ached – even my hair hurt, felt like it was forcing out from my scalp, breaking the skin. Gabe woke up and began to ask me questions. Each of my responses was a moan. I struggled against the blankets and he pushed me back under them, then got up and added new wood to the stove, blew until fire cracked, then he left the room. He returned with aspirin and water and told me he'd boil up some tea. I fell asleep to the sound of liquid rolling, the wood snapping and hissing.

I woke with my hair wrapped around my neck, in my mouth, or stuck to my face. I woke again and again, fighting it off. It held me there, roped me to the bed. By the second night, everything seemed to smell of it – the pillow slips, the sheets, the blankets. Even Gabe smelled like it.

I sat up in bed and announced, "I need to wash my hair right now or I'm going to go crazy."

Gabe came in from the workshop. "Wash your hair? Okay. You want me to bring a basin in here or you want to go to the bathhouse?" The bathhouse was between the cookshack and the kitchen garden and adjacent to the sauna. It had been built with the sauna in mind – a place to wash off impurities steamed from pores, not a place to bathe daily. As such, it was a fair-weather structure, not at all airtight.

I craved hot water, wanted to scald the last of the fever out of me, to force each pore open and drain myself. I couldn't get water that hot with a sponge bath. "I'll go to the bathhouse," I told Gabe.

January and February were the coldest months in the valley. I put on layers of long johns and sweats. I wore boots, mitts, and a hat, and wrapped a wool blanket around myself. The path from shed to sauna was slick with hard snow and ice. Because both hands held the blanket I couldn't balance myself. Gabe steadied me down the path. He started the shower and steam was created instantly by the contrast in temperatures. I got undressed under the blanket that he held around me. I no longer felt sick but the steaming air was a sharp pain all over my body. I yelled, laughing and crying at once. Gabe held me, then gently pushed me into the shower where I continued to shriek, this time because of the heat. I shook with laughter, sobbing, as extreme cold and heat ripped across my skin, but after I was under the water for a minute, I felt my body release. I stood in the pounding stream for a long time then reached for the soap and tried to wash myself but even holding the bar made my muscles contract. Gabe was waiting on the bench beside the shower with his jacket, hat and boots still on. I called to him. "Gabe? Will you wash me?"

He opened the shower curtain, "What?"

"Will you wash me? Please?" I repeated, my head directly in the water, not opening my eyes to look at him. A shiver rode my skin. I felt the shower curtain close and heard rustling, movement. When it was pulled back again, I opened my eyes. Gabe was there, shirtless, reaching for the soap. He still had on his boots and jeans, hair sticking out of his hat. He grinned.

"All right, hold out your body parts." This was the first time Gabe had seen me completely naked, but I was too sick to care. It was as though the ache washed away any self-consciousness. I held out a foot first, steadying myself by bracing the walls. Then I extended a leg. The other foot, leg. Hands, arms. I leaned forward and he washed my breasts. I turned around and he washed my back. While I was turned, he slipped a hand around my waist, then between my legs and up, washed me there. He washed me there for a long time, until my hands against the shower walls felt as though they would push it out, until the hot water was not only all over my skin but pouring inside of me as well. He was just hands. Nothing else, the rest of his body held away from me, out of the water. He was just hands and when I shook and my own hands slipped from their hold on the walls, he held me up, held my hips like smooth handles.

When I got out of the shower, Gabe was fully dressed again, his hair curling around the lip of his toque. He was ready, holding towels out. He rubbed me so vigorously, I was unable to sense the cold. In my state, I thought I could feel the dead skin balling up and ripping off. I felt the sharp points of hair that seemed like they were freezing on contact with the air, then Gabe had me lean my head over so he could wrap my hair in a towel. The moisture on my face was thick, at some consistency between liquid and ice. I started to shake and Gabe wrapped me in the blanket, forced socks and boots on my feet, and brought me back into the cookshack. The fire was lit and I stood by it shivering, the wool blanket rough against my skin, the water seeping out of my hair and soaking the towel. I wanted it gone, the hair, the mess of water it released.

I tossed my hair out of the towel, said, "Gabe, cut it, will you?"

"What?"

"My hair. I want it off."

"I don't know how to cut hair. I'd be scared to."

"There's nothing to be scared of. I just want you to cut it all off. I don't want any style to it." My hair hung wet and cold, drops of water on the floor around me. If it was gone, I would be clean and dry.

"What am I going to cut it with?"

"There've got to be scissors in here somewhere."

Gabe went into the kitchen and I leaned toward the stove and shook my hair, listened to the water sizzle on hot surfaces. When he returned, Gabe opened and closed the scissors behind me, a swish of blade against blade, and I turned around.

"Okay, where do you want to do it?"

"Right here, right by the fire."

Gabe pulled a chair over beside the stove and I sat down,

let the blanket fall off my shoulders and bunch around my waist. He collected my hair in his hands, held it there as if weighing it.

"You're sure? I'll do it if you want me to but I don't want you to be angry with me if it doesn't work out."

"Just do it." I felt a slight pull on my hair, then the scissors entered it. It was not one smooth motion of blade. My hair was thick, wet and tangled. I could feel the scissors struggle against it, then the change in pressure, the tug against my roots release when the scissors made it through some of the hair. The weight of it changed as Gabe made his way around me. He worked silently and I felt hair dropping. It fell in clumps, strands, and knots, got caught on my shoulders, breasts, stomach, back, collected on my lap.

When he stopped to brush the hair off my body, I felt as though there was more air than had ever made it to my skin before, as though my senses were clearer, the awareness of my surroundings more acute. Then the scissors began to move again, more easily and quickly. Soon, there were no more long wet strands falling, just short pieces of hair. These were even itchier. Gabe brushed me off and continued cutting. Brushed and cut, brushed and cut.

He kept going, and as the scissors got closer to my head, he began cutting more slowly, the cool pressure of the blades against my scalp. Gabe hummed. My eyes had been closed the whole time. The stove cracked and sizzled behind me. My skin was hot and clean. The sound of the scissors and Gabe's humming became a strange lullaby. He tilted my head in every way, held my ears lightly, bending them away from the blades.

When he put down the scissors, he began to brush all the stray hair off my scalp, shoulders, face. He blew on me then got the fan used for fuelling the fire and sprayed me with air. My scalp felt electric, like it was going to split open and release something. I raised my eyes and the cookshack slowly came into focus around me. There was dark hair everywhere, fanned around us. Gabe was watching me, scissors in hand. I could smell the stink of hair that had landed on the stove and begun to burn.

GABE

Despite your initial success with high school girls, it takes you longer to actually *do it* than it does most of your friends. Surprising, as these friends are the losers Saffie was referring to, their acne dried into patches with medication just in time for them to get laid. They use their classes in common with the girls to their advantage, ask them over to study, then get them in the mood with wine, Beat poetry, old Doors albums. They begin to refer to the girls they've slept with as the girls they've made. They tell you that girls love an underdog, especially the ones who recite poetry, even though they themselves know it's a bit of a hoax. You believe them too, although you wish you could convince yourself they were lying, that you are not close to becoming the last virgin in your group of friends.

You can't invite any girls home with Anise and your sisters always there so you go to the school dances and the parties. You do the things you think you are supposed to – lead girls under bleachers or onto guestroom beds. It is relatively easy to get them to come with you, but since you have become a legend, you can't use any kind of underdog status to your advantage, no matter how nervous you feel. The girls are most often already drunk, slightly sloppy. You want to be able to experience the awkward moments of slowly gaining their trust, but instead they lie like dead weight, giggle and slur, "Oh, come on, you can take me, Mouse, take me!" but something always happens. They start to laugh or cry or, worse yet, they don't move at all. There you are, kissing and sucking and kneading, and they are almost immobile, nearly silent and, while you struggle with your fly, everything seems so overt and so pointless at once that you can feel yourself deflate. This is not what is supposed to happen. Your desire should be insatiable. You know this from everything you've ever read or heard.

You like the magazines better. You and a joint and a centrefold. It's not the centrefold, herself, though she is alluring, but everything she represents. She represents those same high school girls under the bleachers with you, their small breasts and narrow hips, but instead of blubbering or uncertain, they are sober and confident, with an uncanny knowledge of exactly what to do with their hands and their mouths.

The young guy that Peter works with at "the conservatory" – you've found out his name is Gord – has been keeping you supplied with magazines for more than a year now. It is Gord who brings it all together, gives you that one invaluable tip. He knows you love both girls and pot, so one evening when Peter and Anise are having a barbecue, your sisters running screaming around the lawn and the adults closing their eyes and bobbing their heads to music, Gord joins you on the deck, props his feet up on the railing and gives you the clue. "You been sharing that weed you skim off the old man?" When he asks you this, you must respond with a look of pie-eyed terror because he reassures you. "Relax. I'm just wondering if you're sharing it with any of the young ladies. I'll tell you this, if I tell you anything, nothing gets the young ladies hotter than a little toke. Used to think alcohol was the thing but that just makes them silly. It's the ganj that gets them horny. Give it a try."

You don't know what possessed Gord to prop his feet up and tell you that but you soon find out that you have no way of thanking him enough. The next time you lead a girl into a guest room, you share a joint – rolled with a bit of tobacco like you've heard they like it. You play with her hair and trace a path around her lips slowly, barely touching, and soon enough she has thrown a leg astride yours so she can straddle you. Soon enough she is popping open your jeans, each button releasing like a sigh. If the other guys, the ones your age, have taught you anything, it's to think of the table of elements or the Dewey decimal system while you're doing it. You make it all the way to Mercury and explode.

By September of the year that you would've been a senior, you have already acquired all that the school board authorities expect you to have learned in high school and you have nine months to study for the state exams on your own. You know you will do well. You have been a success in this experiment. Anise didn't have quite the same results with the girls, although she did her best – Peter assures her of this on a daily basis. With the oldest girl it's a power struggle. The middle girl is always daydreaming and can't focus. The youngest, still your favourite, continually calls attention to herself. When she isn't singing and dancing, she is running away, setting things on fire in the yard, balancing on wobbling banisters and breaking small bones in her body – clavicle, wrist. Anise reads books on the psychology of first, second, and third children. She reads books on home-schooling the wilful child, the artistic child, the performative child. She reads books on holistic parenting, on parenting with love, on adaptive parenting. Eventually, she and Peter decide it will be best for all of you to send the girls to school for a year or so. It will be something new, a growing experience for everyone.

For the first two months that the girls are in school, Anise sleeps through most of the day, reads self-help books, and eats in bed. When she stops making any meals, you pack the girls lunches and Peter makes rudimentary dinners, suggests counselling. Anise looks for a job instead. She goes back to the small theatre company where you and Peter met her years before and gets a part-time job at the box office. When she isn't working she volunteers at the theatre, designing sets like she used to. You hear her saying on the phone, "It was my one true love – getting lost in those worlds I could create with paint and wood. Once I always had that and now, well, now I guess I have five true loves and no way of getting lost anywhere, no matter how hard I try."

Your family – you have come to know these people as that – seems all right for a while, you might even say stable. Peter has work at another hardware store, one that truly values him. Anise throws dinner parties for "theatre people." The girls bring reports home that say they are adjusting well. Then Peter's grow operation is busted. You must have known all along that "the conservatory" was a marijuana crop. You've taught yourself Economics 11, calculated your family's net yearly income, their expenses and taxes, and have always ended up with the wrong numbers. Thankfully, the conservatory was cultivated in a basement, behind false walls, in someone else's house. It is Gord that is busted with the intent to traffic, but they know there is more than one person involved. They are questioning him and you hear Peter tell Anise again and again, "I just hope the kid doesn't crack."

*M*aybe Vera was right, I didn't know what I was looking for, but there was one thing that I was certain about: the farm would be different than the place I was coming from. I wasn't seeking a place I could belong. If anything, I was seeking a place where I could feel comfortable not belonging. A place where I could take a couple of steps back, and rest there.

I couldn't figure out exactly how many people lived on the farm during the winter. There was Gabe's mother, Susan, who spun wool on a wheel to make sweaters. She also hooked rugs, the kind you would imagine you'd see in farmhouses, oval, made of concentric loops of an unknown and sturdy fabric. Another woman, Brenda, was a potter. What she liked to make were oddly shaped vases – vessels, she called them – and teacups shaped like squat, full-breasted women. What made money, however, were uniformly shaped soup bowls, cups, and saucers, all with the same pattern and glaze – a blooming dogwood twig, the trim a wave of green and blue. These sold in several gift shops between Sawmill Creek and the coast.

Thomas was a musician, his loft full of instruments – the sax in a stand, an old piano, several guitars in various states of repair leaning against walls. They were artists, but made money other ways. Brenda left early each morning to work at an answering service in Vernon. Susan worked in the fall and spring at a tree nursery, pulling uniform bundles of tree roots from rows in the ground, later sorting them off a conveyer belt, each pile of tiny trees representing a bigger paycheque. These same bundles were collected in boxes by Thomas in the late spring. A tree-planting foreman for five months of the year, he would tell his crew where to plant them, how deep and how quick.

There were children on the farm, their lineage all uncertain to me. Children lived with two parents, or one parent, or a parent and a friend, or the person who was the most like a parent to them. There were children who came to the farm only on weekends or holidays. Gabe told me that there were more children like him, who had one parent or two return to the States after the Vietnam War, for whom Pilgrims Art Farm was a strange memory, quaint and Canadian.

Before moving there that winter, Gabe had visited Pilgrims only during the summer. Summer on the farm, he told me, was four months of people speaking about sucking the marrow out of life, of seizing the day, living for the moment. Young men and women would arrive in small packs of volunteers to learn to garden organically, companion-plant, and farm with horses. They spread themselves around the property in vans and tents, under tarps. Young artists arrived individually to apprentice with Pilgrims residents – a woodworker, a potter, a playwright, several musicians – and they were the ones who most often ended up staying for more than one season. The farm was transformed into a kind of adult summer camp. Those young women we saw in town in the summer, bells on their ankles, thin cotton revealing the shadows of legs thin as twigs, those men with dirt under their nails and hair gnarled into dreadlocks, they were the transient members of the farm. They came in vans or station wagons stickered with slogans, wanting to get out of cities or take a break from cross-continent road trips. Young and vibrant, they would stay for a month or two, seeking unconventional romance and clean air, collecting welfare cheques so they could pursue these through volunteer work and shared meals. They would leave, Gabe told me, after they found someone else sneaking into their lover's tent, or got drunk around the firepit and threatened to kick the shit out of someone, or when they simply grew bored with the feeling of moist clay spun between hands, loamy soil.

When I asked Gabe what they expected, he said, "I don't know. Everything to be sweetness and light, something like that." What did they get? "Same shit as everywhere else, different pile, I guess."

Gabe told me that in the summer when the volunteers came, there were regular meals in the cookshack, food in exchange for labour. In the down times, like it was in the winter when we were there, it became the place where people without adequate kitchens came to cook. Gabe and I were two of those people. I wasn't entirely clear on how the division of food worked. Farm food was marked with a *P* for Pilgrims. Common food was marked with a *C*. There was food belonging to individuals marked with initials, and then there was unmarked food. There was no food marked with Gabe's initials or, for that matter, my own. Gabe told me to help myself to anything unmarked or marked Common. I couldn't get over the feeling that I was stealing.

Sunday was the first day I was feeling reasonably well. Mid-morning, and the kitchen was empty. I found a loaf of bread with a C on the bag, a jar of unmarked peanut butter and set to work. It would be my first solid food in three days. While I was forcing the thick peanut butter across unbuttered bread, Thomas came in without me hearing him. When he cleared his throat, I jumped and sent the knife across the counter.

Thomas laughed. "I'm sorry. Didn't mean to startle you."

"It's okay."

"So, you're staying at the farm."

"Yes, I guess I am." I battled with the bread as it caught on the dry peanut butter, rolling away from the crust.

"Great, great." Thomas broke his gaze and began moving around me in the kitchen. He plugged in a kettle, pulled a paper bag out of the freezer, spilled coffee beans into a grinder. When the whirring sound started, I left the kitchen, bread in hand. During the day, the cookshack was a different place than at night, bleaker. The sun came in the front windows in patches of dust motes. Things seemed dirty – the kindling, paper, and ashes around the wood stove, the dried herbs hanging from the ceiling, the old couches slouched against the wall. I ate the bread and felt small in the room.

The grinding, whirring, and hissing ceased in the kitchen. Thomas came out and put a mug of coffee in front of me and one across the table, then he poked at the fire. He threw on two more logs and blew. I had finished the toast and was staring at the mug.

"That's for you," Thomas said when he sat down. "Cream and brown sugar."

"What makes you think I want that?"

"Young women. They – you – usually like cream and sugar." He paused. "Uh, we have a lot of young women through here, volunteering. A lot of kids out of high school or college who want to dig around in the dirt, or drive nails into outbuildings, you know?"

I hadn't touched the coffee yet. "Actually," I stated, "I take mine black." I had just made that decision.

"Well, then," Thomas said and, smiling, exchanged my cup for his. "I like your haircut."

I instinctively reached my hand to my scalp and tried not to smile. I took the coffee into my mouth and willed my face blank as it scalded my tongue and seemed to coat the inside of my mouth with a bitter film.

"So, where've you come to us from?" He asked.

"Just my mom's place in Sawmill."

Thomas took a sip of his coffee and shook his head. "Whoa, that's some sweet brew. Okay, so, you've left your mom's place. You going to stay here then?"

"I can't say I know. I mean not for good, but maybe for a while."

"No, no one really stays here for good."

"Don't you?"

"Me? Yeah, well, it must look that way, but no. I've been back and forth for the last – man, what is it – twenty years? But I don't stay. Got a few other places I go to. A person couldn't always stay here, it'd drive you mad."

"Why's that? Seems pretty relaxed here to me."

"Oh yeah, it is for the most part, but, you know, every group has its own politics. You'll probably see that eventually." I was beginning to enjoy the taste of the coffee. It made me feel sharp, bold. Before I could think of anything else to say, Thomas continued, "It's just close quarters for a lot of people. A lot of decidedly eccentric people. I don't mean to scare you or anything. It's not that. The farm's a great place. The people here, great. It's just well, yeah, close quarters."

After not going to classes the entire first week after the holidays, I decided to return. I called and woke Krista up that morning to make sure she would meet me in front of the school. I had left home, missed a week of school, lost a head of hair. I felt that I needed to know she would be there. Gabe drove me to SCSS. I had rarely been dropped off at school before. It was something that rich girls had done for them, or girls with tight jeans, too much makeup, and older boyfriends in Camaros and Firebirds. I had always noticed those girls, the ones who were dropped off by men, just as I knew I would be noticed.

Krista was waiting outside the front doors, hands tucked under her armpits, blowing her breath into the air in disappearing currents of steam. She looked at my hair, smiled, shook her head and didn't comment. I smiled back and she hugged me in a kind of urgent, jerky movement, then released me and rubbed my short hair. "Shit, I've missed you."

"Yeah, me too," I said and opened the door.

"Oh, I bet. No time to even come to school any more." Krista shouldered people through the hall, giving them sharp looks when they stared at me.

"No. No, it isn't that, Kris. I was really sick last week. Still am a bit. I haven't even got my appetite back."

We were walking towards Krista's locker. "Word's got around," she said. "About you running away. Some girls are actually jealous."

"Jealous? Of what?"

Krista opened her locker and began pulling out books. "I don't know. I guess because you're not living in town."

"Yeah, I'm living out of town where there's even less to do. Speaking of which, you should come out this weekend."

The bell rang. Krista waited for it to stop, closed her locker, then said, "I don't know. There's a party Friday and then I might be doing something with Mike on Saturday."

"*Mike* Mike?" I asked. When she didn't respond, I said, "I guess he's not ignoring you then."

"No, I guess not. Listen, I've got to get to class. Talk to you later?"

In the hall, I avoided eyes and faces. In class, I wasn't called on. It was left up to me to ask each teacher individually what I had missed that week and how I could catch up. Each responded with the same lack of interest, feigned or genuine, I didn't know, as they listed chapters and assignments, rearranging pens and paper on their desks or packing their own bags to leave as they did. I nodded, wrote it all down.

Vera and Jim are married in a chapel in Las Vegas, something she will regret for years afterward. By the time they get to Vegas, Vera is hot and tired and longs for something – stability, sex, something – and she hopes marriage might be that unknown. She spends a day touring the wedding chapels in Vegas while Jim gambles – "Going to win us our honeymoon, baby," he says in a tone she knows is meant to be ironic. She is looking, Vera realizes partway through the tour, for a chapel that resembles her Ukrainian Catholic Church in Northern Alberta. She finds several small, ornate, white churches but none with the distinctive onion-shaped dome, the ornately painted ceilings. She chooses instead a chapel that looks like the kind that children draw – double doors, pointed roof, a straight, simple steeple. Jim doesn't understand why she wants to get married in a church at all. If he had his choice, he'd marry Vera either in the desert at sunrise, perhaps with a Native American shaman officiating, or in a heart-shaped hotel bed, simply for the campiness of it. He loves Vera though, and loves the Catholic, flower-picking farm girl in her, so he agrees to marry her in the Chapel of Eternal Love. He doesn't pressure her on their wedding night, their first night as man and wife. They have gone this long and he knows it won't last forever. When she cries and admits her fear, he placates her, smooths her hair to her head until she falls asleep. When she does, he slips out of the room and back down to the casino. Jim Harper hasn't won anything yet, but neither has he lost.

In San Francisco, they park the camper by Fisherman's Wharf and walk each day through North Beach to Chinatown and back, each hoping someone will stop them, invite them to the place where everything is happening, neither of them saying this to each other. On the second day, they stop at City Lights bookstore, Jim excited about touching the pages of limited editions. The clerk appreciates his enthusiasm and tells them about a poetry reading in another part of town, near the park. The evening is the culmination of everything Jim hoped to find in San Francisco. They listen to poetry in a base-ment café that offers three drink selections: coffee, whisky, red wine. Women come up to Vera and welcome her, grasp hands and gaze into her eyes. When they ask where she's from and she answers, they respond, "Canada? That's cool. So, you know, unspoiled and clean." The men talk about poetry, the Romantics, the rise of the Beats, the birth of the movement, the meaninglessness of existence. Jim is intoxicated by it all.

That night, he tells Vera again how much he loves her, how happy he is that they found each other and this whole scene, people who understand, who believe. They smoke a joint together in the camper, heads ducked as they try to sit upright on the bed. Jim has already had several joints, but it is Vera's first. He shows her how to inhale. She spits out the smoke and coughs and he tells her it's all right. Eventually, they are both laughing and soon after that, it seems, Jim is pushing himself inside her. He calls her "My sweet, sweet farm girl," and planes the hair around her face with his palms as he moves. The camper rocks with them. Vera clenches her teeth and feels waves – waves off the Pacific, the wave of motion in the van, the wave that hits her body full force. She feels a hot slice of pain, then Jim makes a noise, rolls off her. Vera fights sleep. She wants to stay awake for this first real moment of man and wife even though Jim is already snoring beside her. She prays to remain fully conscious but wakes up the next morning, her neck cramped, the light through a narrow window hot on her eyelids.

Jim Harper is well-liked, a shining star. Though he speaks softly and slowly, people gather and listen. In the course of that month in San Francisco more and more of his anecdotes have to do with Fly Hills, Alberta. He talks about the town as though it were a close-knit community, simple and uncorrupted, even though both he and Vera know they couldn't wait to get away, that they are travelling so they can find a place better than the one they left behind. Jim often uses Vera as an example. It is he who tells people how she grew up without water or electricity, he who talks about how she could homestead if she chose – she can grow a garden, milk a cow, kill a chicken, skin a pig, and preserve enough food to last a Canadian winter. He exaggerates and it embarrasses Vera, but she does feel a strange thrill when other women look at her with envy, the men with admiration, as Jim tells his stories. He throws a hand around her shoulder, looks at her with the expression that now tells her, without him saying as much, "You're different, pure. That's why I love you."

Vera does begin to feel she is different, but not in the way Jim thinks. She feels different because she doesn't understand what is so great about San Francisco. It seems to her that very little is going on. She is becoming bored with sitting on the sagging couches in so many different pads, listening to music and squinting through smoke. She is becoming bored with hearing Jim's stories again and again, even with the poetry readings and jam sessions that he assures her will make history. "We can say we were here, babe. That we saw it all begin." She is getting tired of the long-haired, glassy-eyed women who hug her, hold her hands in theirs and stare into her eyes, tell her she is beautiful. The same women stare at Jim, laugh at his stories or nod and say, "You are so right, man."

Vera starts excusing herself early. The pot makes her tired and she wants some time alone. They are constantly with groups of people and Vera starts to cherish the few moments that she is in the camper by herself. One night, when she stumbles back into the house to use the bathroom, she passes a partially open door and has to back up to make sure she is seeing right. She is. What she is seeing is Jim Harper sitting on a bed, legs apart. There are candles and incense lit and there is a woman kneeling on the floor in front of Jim, her head between his legs. Jim's eyes are closed, his hand rhythmically stroking the woman's hair. Vera continues to the bathroom, throws up in the sink, brushes her teeth with someone else's toothbrush, then feels terrible for doing so. She rinses the sink and the toothbrush with hot water for several minutes then scours the bowl with Comet and decides to take the toothbrush with her. She'll throw it out later.

When Jim comes back to the camper that night, he finds her clutching her abdomen, gasping for air between tears. She confronts him and he tells her it's different, it's not sex. He tells her that he would never want her to do that to him, that she's too good for that. Vera cries and tells Jim that they are leaving San Francisco. She has never been more certain about anything in her life. They are leaving tomorrow together or she is leaving on her own.

They travel up the coast in record time. When Vera and Jim drive through the B.C. interior on their way east and north, they both feel better. The landscape is like a tonic, an elixir. Here are the small communities, roaring rivers, rolling hills, blue lakes, and valleys of fruit that Vera had expected to find in the south. They stop at fruit stands and roadside pull-outs, sit on picnic tables, faces angled to the sun, and Jim tells Vera how much he loves her, how one day they will move to one of these valleys, a place as beautiful as she is.

~

At first I thought I would find a way of knowing Gabe. That was what was supposed to happen between two people who spent time together – a gradual stripping away of things on the surface. It had always happened with friends and I expected, though I had no personal experience on which to base this, that the same would apply to boyfriends. For a while, I tried to convince myself that we were getting to know each other on a level that I simply wasn't aware of yet. But it seemed the longer I was at the farm, the tighter Gabe held himself.

He confused me. He would tell me about his life before coming to the farm, his thoughts and memories, but it was as though he were talking about someone else. It didn't seem as if he cared how I reacted, or what I thought about anything he told me. "Men are like that," Krista told me with authority on the phone one night. I was talking to her in the cookshack, ducking my chin and the receiver into my chest and talking quietly when other people walked by. "That's what Therese says – I know, like we should be taking advice on men from my mother but – she says that they'll pursue you like you're the Holy frickin' Grail when they think you're unavailable, but once they've had a drink, well –"

"Oh, come on, your mother is offering dating advice from Arthurian times and you're passing it off as wisdom?"

"My mother does not know the word Arthurian. That was my own saying – what's that called, is that a metaphor or a simile? – thank you very much."

"Simile."

"Yeah. By the way, he called. I *am* going out with Mike on Saturday."

"Oh, now look who's talking about being unavailable."

"I know, I'm asking for it, but what can I do?" With that, Krista made the yowling sound of a cat in heat and hung up.

What flustered me most about Gabe, though, was his desire. How it flared up and became something larger than his own body, a presence in the room. He seemed to pride himself on his control over it. I would hear the intake of breath, feel the rigidity of muscle when he pulled it back in. Then, he would be closed to me. At first I felt relief. If popular wisdom was to be trusted, moving into the shed with Gabe was laying myself open. The equivalent of spreading my legs and forfeiting all personal boundaries. That didn't happen. I felt vindicated, as though I alone had known there was something good in the world, something gentle. Not everyone had ulterior motives. Then I began to worry. I wondered if it was me that made Gabe pull back, reel his desire in, just as mine was rising to the surface.

～

"So, I'll pick you up around three-thirty?" Gabe would ask every morning when he drove me to SCSS, both of us struggling through the thick haze of morning, coffee in plastic 7-Eleven cups our beacons. "Yeah, thanks," I'd answer. We each tried to pretend that his taking me to and from school wasn't a given, that we were living from day to day, making plans to meet like friends would after school. Sometimes I drove the truck there, but he always took it with him, then came back to get me.

"What're you going to do today?" I would usually ask. The answer was almost always vague. Work in the shop, draw up some diagrams, or, simply, "I don't know." His dad was a carpenter but had never taught him a thing, so Gabe was trying to learn on his own. There was a woodworker on the farm who'd offered to teach him how to make shelving, cabinets, even

chairs, but Gabe wanted to make a guitar. Even I knew that was
absurd. He had taken apart one of Thomas's old guitars and
was drafting diagrams, weighing and measuring things,
holding thin wood up to bright light. I saw the pieces scattered
across the workbench each night. Nothing seemed to change.

Sometimes I asked him questions, led him into speech.
Once: "Tell me about making a guitar. How's it going?"

He answered by telling me what it felt like to take it apart.
"I don't know how to describe it, Harp. Each piece on its own
is so perfect, you know, each curve. I know this will sound
stupid but I don't know if I want to put it back together. It's like
I can never get it as perfect as it is now, in pieces. You know?"
I nodded, not really knowing.

Another time Gabe told me about how he looked forward
to the spring, when the ground thawed and he could start
putting up fencing, like he had when he visited the farm in the
past. How he loved the feeling of hard ground breaking open,
of pounding the post in. "I like the routine of it, the certainty,
you know?" He talked about the Clydesdales. They were used
during the winter for tourists visiting the ski hill sled rides and
brought in a little bit of extra income. In the spring and fall,
Thomas and some of the other men were experimenting with
horse-logging, using the Clydes to pull trees out of the forest
one at a time. "We'll get better at it," Gabe told me, as though
he had been working with the guys. "Steve's read everything
about it and Decker, he's taken an eco-forestry course in
Oregon. One day we'll get the trees out the right way – not
have to go in and cut them where they're felled because we've
gotten them stuck." Gabe chuckled and I joined him.

Once back at the farm after school, I spent afternoons doing homework at the table in front of the window in the shed while he puttered in the workshop on the other side of the wall. Sometimes, I would do schoolwork at Thomas's loft, or I would avoid it, sit on the couch and read his magazines – *Utne Reader, The Economist* – and ask him questions about the articles. Gabe and I would piece together dinner – rice and beans, stir-fries – then smoke a joint and watch an old TV in the corner of the cookshack. The TV had to be at a certain angle to get any kind of picture, and even then lines of static would appear and pick up their high-speed descent on the screen. In the times that I wished we were talking, we were taking turns getting off the couch and slapping the side of the TV with an open palm, trying to rid it of static. Late at night, if we had struck the right balance between smoking and sobriety, the talk would come. This was when Gabe told me what he remembered about being on the farm as a kid, about growing up in California and his family there. They were other people, far away. They seemed separate from him, distanced both by geography and by the way he spoke about them. They were a series of stories he told to put himself in a context for me, other than the one I knew him in that winter at the farm.

On some nights, the cookshack filled up around the space in the corner of the main hall to which we had laid claim. Thomas and other musicians would jam or people would sit around the long table, drinking wine or impossible amounts of tea. Through their conversations, I discovered the things that were respected and revered. I learned about arts festivals up and down the coast, protests in various endangered areas, alternative theatre companies that performed in fields or on beaches, artists who lived and created in every conceivable small space – tree houses, boats, geodesic domes built into the ground. I learned that people made houses out of used tires, pop cans, and bales of hay. That there was an entire informal network across North America of people who inhabited the periphery. The things I had learned about the world so far – that church and family were the most important things, and after these a good education and a job – no longer seem to apply.

One night, a few weeks after I had arrived, Gabe left during one of these cross-table conversations and didn't come back. When people got up to leave, I stood and looked out the window toward the shed. There were no lights on there. I decided to wait in the cookshack.

Thomas stayed behind with me. He came out of the kitchen, two mugs in hand. I knew his ploy already. "Black, right?" he asked, handing me one. I nodded. Even the small lies stick with you. I took the mug and watched his hands. I had a new fascination with the wrists of men and boys. How fine or coarse the hairs could be there. How, sometimes, I could see the shift of small muscle around bone.

"Do you know where Gabe went?" I asked.

"Back to the shed, I'd guess."

"I don't think so," I said, motioning with my chin toward a window from which the shed was visible. "No lights on." I went to the stove and started poking at the wood, adding a couple more pieces. I was practising my fire-building skills. As I blew and nudged the wood, I could imagine Thomas's eyes on the curve of my spine, my waist, my butt where it met my heels as I crouched.

"Have you talked to your mother recently?" he asked.

I turned, remained on my knees. "Yes. Well, kind of. I told her I didn't want to come back, that I needed to stay away for a while, but I don't know . . . I said some things to her that I probably shouldn't have and I don't know how I can talk around that." I stood up.

"Have you tried talking through it?"

"Yes, a little." I shifted in front of the fire. "We tried." I held my palms open behind me to collect warmth.

"What are you going to do here, Harper?"

"What do you mean, what am I going to do here? What everyone else does, live. I'll help out, too. I just don't know how yet. I'll garden in the summer, I don't know, maybe help Gabe fence. Maybe Susan can get me work at the nursery. There's got to be something I'm good at."

"That's not what I meant. You're welcome here, Harper. You don't have to do anything until you're ready. I just don't know if this is the right place for you."

"Really? What do you think would be the right place for me then?"

"It's just not the right place for everyone, that's all. To be honest, not much happens here. We play music, people do their own thing, every once in a while we put on a play or a craft fair. Not much. There are so many other things you could do. I don't mind it. I like meeting the people who come and go. I like things simple – good food, good music, good people."

"I like things simple too," I said, heard my own voice pleading.

Thomas laughed when I said this, then stopped. He put down his coffee mug and cleared his throat, but instead of saying anything, he took one step toward me. I watched as his hand reached for my jaw, felt the tips of his fingers along the outline of it, then trailing down my neck lightly. I felt something tighten. A cord between chest and neck and his fingers, a taut string. Just as quickly, his hand dropped. "You'll figure things out," Thomas said, then left the room. I heard him rinse his cup in the kitchen, his footsteps out the back door.

GABE

The kid cracked. Gord told your family that they took him into a room and interrogated him like they do people on TV. Hard-nosed, suspicious cops, one-way glass, grey light, and stifling air spotted with dust. Gord tells you he can understand why people buckle, tells you all he's so sorry. You learn first-hand that there is a wholesale war on drugs and that drugs tear families apart. Peter is taken away for questioning, then arrested. After that, everything changes.

Anise cries for weeks. Peter asks you from the other side of the glass to be strong, to be there for Anise and the girls, just like a scene from a movie. The girls experience personality reversals of the kind you thought only existed in Anise's books, the ones you flipped through when they were left open on the kitchen table. The oldest becomes kind and compassionate, wanting to devote all of her free time to nurturing her mother and sisters. The middle one snaps out of years of daydreaming and transforms into her older sister's former role, stubborn and demanding. The youngest one becomes quiet and withdrawn, and, as much as she was beginning to grate on everyone's nerves, you all miss her theatrics. You find out from another mom that the girls are being ridiculed at school, that people are calling your father a stoner and a drug lord. She tells you because you are the one who answers the door. Anise is in her room, not able to get out of bed to see anyone. Moms – older women – still like you and this woman tells you how strong you've been, asks if you need a hug. If there's anything you don't need now, it's a hug. You thank her politely and close the door behind her when she leaves.

They don't fine drug traffickers in California. It makes no sense. Drugs make money, so traffickers could just pay the fines off and go deeper underground. They send them to jail; it is a crime, after all. Your father, it is believed, is being used as an example. He has been sentenced to nine years in a state correctional facility – a phrase you have only heard on TV, read in books. He will be eligible for parole – another one of those phrases – in three years. By that time, you will almost be legally able to drink and to vote.

Peter and Anise have a lot of friends – theatre people, people for whom Peter has built things, young families, and all the decent, simple-living folk that "the conservatory" supplied. You find out that your father was a good supplier, an honest man. He charged a fair price and never sold to kids, gangs, or other dealers, just to people like himself and Anise. People who simply wanted to relax every once in a while.

Several of Anise and Peter's sundry friends drop by in the months after your father's arrest. They bring care packages for your family – Mason jars of soup, frozen vegetarian lasagnas, squash and zucchini from their gardens, loaves of bread, cookies, and homemade granola bars. Eventually, Anise is able to get out of bed for these visits. She emerges from her room looking like some kind of prophet in billowing pants and long loose tunics and tells her friends that their visits sustain her. You are the one who takes the care packages, puts the food away, makes tea and brings out cookies on plates to pass around. Anise makes a point of telling everyone how she could never make it through this without you. If the girls are home, they glare at you, whine, or launch tantrums.

All of their friends tell Anise that Peter's been done wrong and that they'll do everything in their power to get him out sooner, although none of their friends have a lot of social clout. "They should be concentrating on the real criminals, the guys dealing hard drugs. A little smoke has never hurt anyone," one of them says.

Another concurs, "It's alcohol that kills – with the drunk driving, assaults – you'd think they'd know that by now. They should be thanking Peter, not arresting him."

"It's Reagan and his almighty war on drugs, nothing but misinformation and propaganda. Another instrument of oppression by the right wing."

"Well, we know he's being used as an example. He'll be out as soon as they find another one."

Talk like this can go on for hours, Anise cross-legged on the couch, nodding and dabbing tears from her cheeks. If their friends come over after dinner, they bring bottles of wine and raise glasses to Peter over and over, reassuring themselves that that's what he would want them to do. No one, thank God, lights up. Even these friends have more tact than that.

After one of these evenings, Anise scares you in the kitchen. You have been washing the wineglasses in the dark, letting them drip-dry by the sink on a tea towel. When you turn around, she's standing there, not moving, not making a sound. She looks like an apparition with those white clothes on. You jump at the sight of her and she doesn't say anything but comes toward you and gives you a hug. Anise rarely hugs you, and when she does, it's usually when other people are around as if to show how close you all are. This time, she's hugging you in the dark, not letting go. What follows next is like a scene from another bad television special. Your life has become surreal, full of awkwardly dramatic moments. Anise sobs softly then tells you how much your support has meant to her, how proud your father would be. As she says this, she strokes your hair and not in a particularly maternal way. She leans back to give you a meaningful look and then draws you in, shifts until she meets your mouth. Anise's lips are surprisingly soft, her tongue quick. While she kisses you, you think of the magazines, bad porn movies you have watched in the basements of friends' houses, all of you jerking off together under blankets. You think of Hamlet.

When you pull away, Anise sobs on your shoulder until your shirt is soaked through. "I'll get you a drink," you finally say – this is something Peter would do at a time like this. You pull a bottle down from the cupboard above the fridge and a can of pop from under the sink and make a gin and tonic, feeling suave and adult for doing so.

"Go ahead, make yourself one too," Anise says, almost in a whisper. The two of you sit at the kitchen table in the dark, listen to the crickets in the yard and the ice in your glasses until the alcohol melts it away.

*A*fter Thomas left the cookshack, I stayed, waiting for a light to go on in the shed, telling myself I wasn't looking for it. I kept the fire going, sat with my boots off, feet balanced on an upturned log in front of the stove. I felt desire as certain and sharp as a knife then. Not necessarily for Thomas, not even necessarily for things sexual, but desire like a fine, absolute edge between something, and something else. I thought about Thomas's hand along the line of my jaw, my neck. That was mine. I knew he meant that gesture to be mine and no one else's.

Then I remembered a baby-sitter Nick and I had when I was in the second grade. Her name was Melody – not Melanie but Melody, like a song or something hummed – and I had idolized her. She had hair that was long and layered in a way that if she parted it down the middle, curled each layer into a wave and combed it from her face, it would meet in a perfect line down her scalp to the nape of her neck. This was just one sign of her perfection. Melody smelled like the colour pink – sweet and slightly spicy at once, like bubble gum and cinnamon.

I had decided that Melody, at thirteen, was the perfect woman, something that I, as a girl who aspired to be a boy, was sure I could never become. How could one aspire to be both? Melody made it easier. She would attempt to curl my lank hair, dab purple eyeshadow on my lids and pink gloss on my lips, then announce to Nick and me that we were going to war. We weren't allowed to play with toy guns so we made do with our hands, shaped them into pistols or wrapped them around air grenades, and battles would ensue that led the three of us, ducking, diving, and climbing, across every inch of the property. After this, when Nick and I required baths and scrubbing to come clean, Melody needed only her white leather purse. Out of this she would pull her fat Goody comb, sweep her hair back into place and hold it there with a deft shot of Tame hair spray from the same bag. A layer of lip gloss and she was as beautiful as she had ever been.

I discovered that lip gloss was one of the things that gave Melody her smell. Her purse was full of different kinds of gloss. She had lip gloss shaped like a crayon, one like a chocolate chip cookie that twisted in two, plastic tubes of liquid pearl that were applied with a wand. It was the gloss disguised in a pack of gum that fascinated me. One evening, instead of launching grenades from the ravine, I snuck back into the house, pulled the plastic pack of gum out of her purse and hid in the broom closet. There, I crouched and slid it open to two perfect rectangles of sweet, pink gloss. I don't know how long I was there, applying thin layers to my lips and licking them off for the taste. I believed I could taste everything to come – a teenage-hood of jeans as tight and pliant as skin, white leather purses, strawberries, and cinnamon. I slipped the gloss back into the purse and waited inside the house, saying I didn't feel well when Nick and Melody came in red-cheeked and out of breath. I felt like I had stolen something elusive and unnamed. A small part of whatever made Melody perfect. The unattainable. It filled me with the same sense of buoyant peace. A full, clean place inside me that no one else had access to.

It was nearly midnight when I returned to the shed, turned on the space heater and lit balled newsprint and twigs in the woodstove to start the fire. I got into bed to keep warm and waited. Gabe came in when I was slipping into sleep and he unplugged the heater and added wood to the stove.

"Where were you?" I mumbled, turning over.

"Thinking."

I opened my eyes, but they hadn't adjusted to the dark yet. I could hear one boot drop, then the other, the sounds of denim and buttons. "Where, though?"

"It doesn't matter. Go back to sleep." I heard him rub his hands against his skin, then inhale quickly, as though testing cold water. I had begun wearing fewer and fewer clothes to bed, piling on more blankets, collected from around the farm. By this time, I was sleeping naked.

When he got into bed, I turned to him. "Why do you want me to go back to sleep?" The whites of his eyes were four quarter moons. He was propped up on one shoulder where his skin caught what little light came in the window and shone, looked buttery and thick.

"I just didn't want to bother you," he whispered and dropped onto his back, eyes to the ceiling. He shivered once and I rolled on top of him, wanting my heat to blanket his skin. When I did, I realized Gabe still had his long johns on. I sat up and rolled them over his hips, down his legs, over ankles, then crawled back up slowly, letting my breath settle on his skin. He stared at me, pressed his hands into my hip bones. When I put my head between his chin and collar bone, I could feel something tense there. My will was strong – a drive to keep him open, to warm whatever seized up in him. I moved against Gabe, put my cheek against his, my breath on his ear, didn't say anything. I breathed lightly there, felt the alchemy of his skin and my breath become heat, and waited.

When a low sound came from Gabe's throat and he pulled me to him, I rolled away, then slid up against him, met his chest with my back, his mouth with my neck. I guided his hands to my hips, palms on the bone, fingers pressing into the dip there, moving in. I threw one foot over his ankle, hooked it around his leg, arched my back. Then we moved together, rocked until there was no difference between the rhythm of bodies and breath, no difference between his skin and mine. When he entered me it was simple, something catching, then pushing through, the tug of something held tight unravelling. Things are never as they say. I expected pain, tearing apart. Instead, I felt pain as heat, both liquid and solid at once, and tasted metal in my mouth. It was as though there was something else moving between my legs – a big fish, tail pounding. When it broke the surface, I gasped, threw my head back so it hit Gabe's collarbone. He bent his head toward me, opened his mouth and I could feel the crest of teeth against my shoulder. Then we both collapsed into the mattress. After that night, sex became a place. A place that was wide open and safe only because it was stolen, held so close.

I had became a kind of low-level celebrity at Sawmill Creek Secondary. To my admittedly limited knowledge, prior to staying at Pilgrims I had been known as two things: a religious freak and a prude. Two attributes that said *Stay far away*. Then I became a religious prude turned pagan whore and had cut my hair off to prove it. The Matts, Jasons, and Jeffs who had ignored me in the hall before leered and made low noises in their throats when I walked by. The girls cornered me in the change room to let me know they had seen Gabe in town and thought he was so cute. To ask if there were any more like him out there and if they could come party with us. These were girls who used the word *party* as a verb. They spoke to me in sugared condescension, their smiles like pats on a puppy's head.

Krista was spending more time with Mike and some days I wouldn't even see her at all between classes. On those days, I felt slightly untethered, but I couldn't describe the feeling as wholly good or bad. I thought perhaps this was simply how it felt to get older. In the past, we had spent numerous weekends watching corny romantic videos on Krista's couch, squeezing each other's arms when the young lovers on the screen finally kissed. We thought this desire, this ache we felt, would go away when we were finally with boys and men, kissed in ways we could only imagine. Perhaps, though, joining our bodies to someone else's just brought that ache closer to the surface.

I thought that if I could share with Krista the fact that I had slept with Gabe, the new loneliness I felt might be abated. I walked the halls looking for her, then staked out her locker. When she appeared, I asked her what she was doing after school.

First, Krista simply stared at me, looking almost annoyed, then she said, "I need to work at my mom's store, why?"

"I thought maybe we could do something. I could come with you to the mall and we could hang out after you're off."

She paused as though considering it before answering, "Yeah, all right."

We went to the food court before she started work and as we plucked french fries from the tray, filled our mouths with them, I told Krista about Gabe and me. While I did, she dipped her fries into the mound of ketchup, moaning and clutching the side of the table.

"Will you cut that out?" I said.

"Oh, so sorry, Your I've-been-laid-by-Gabeness. It sounds all right, though. It couldn't have been good, not at first, hey, but trust me, it'll get better." Krista was looking around the food court as though distracted, or searching for someone.

"Actually, I don't know. It wasn't bad."

"Okay, Harp, if 'you don't know' and 'it wasn't bad,' then it wasn't great. When it's great, you'll know." She shook her head slowly, still looking away, and scanned the tables.

"Well, what about your first time?"

Krista's gaze snapped back to mine. "My first time, *my* first time? Shit, you remember that prick Derek Jeffries, no pun intended, just jammed it in me before I knew what was happening – remember, grade nine?"

"Oh yeah, shit, Kris, I totally forgot."

She ground the last remaining fries into the soup of ketchup and vinegar on the tray. "Yeah, well, I wouldn't expect you to remember, it was utterly forgettable. No big deal. It got better, that's the important part." Krista looked up at me as she put the fries in her mouth.

"So, it's good with Mike?"

She nodded, chewed. "Yeah, most of the time," she said through the remnants of a mouthful, then swallowed, continued, "I mean, I can't even feel the rug burn when we're going at it on the floor, that's how good it feels."

"That's not what I meant."

She looked at me. "Oh. Well, I don't know what else to tell you. I haven't had any spiritual insights, if that's what you're after." Krista got up from the table quickly and told me to meet her at Rim Rock Records at five-thirty. She left the tray behind and I tipped it toward and away from me, watching the ketchup and vinegar slide across the plastic.

Later that afternoon, on our way to Therese's car in the parking lot, I saw them, a trail of women and children from the Free Church coming out of Kmart, a bantam parade of

noise and colour. Two young women pushed children balanced in the seats of grocery carts. One had a baby strapped
to her and kids skipped and jumped around the rattling
freight of cleaning products, large boxes of food, and plastic
bags of diapers.

"Sylvia!" Becky from the Free Church said, her baby
strapped to her facing outward, blinking and pumping its limbs
like it was emerging from her chest. The other woman, Wendy,
smiled slightly and looked over her shoulder. The four of us
stood like that, without speaking, until Becky went on, "We
sure would love to see you two back at service." Wendy nodded
in agreement.

"Uh, yeah, maybe –" I said, my voice trailing to a silent
point, thankful when one of the kids started shaking the metal
frame of a cart, causing the baby in the seat to wail. The women
tried to keep up some kind of meagre conversation but the
children tugging, crying, and vying for attention made it
impossible. Therese drove the car up beside us and honked
once, quickly. We said goodbye to the women and I felt sombre,
though I couldn't imagine why. There was no reason to be – I
had left behind the possibility of becoming one of those women,
cloaked in children and groceries, pushing loads through cold,
wet parking lots.

When we were almost back at their place, Therese started
in, "All right, Harper, you little devil," winking at me in the
rear-view mirror as if to signal she wasn't serious, though I
would've known. "Tell me. You up and ran off to a hippie
commune. Your poor mother must be shittin' bricks, pardon
moi Franchais."

"Therese, it's not a hippie commune," Krista said. "It's a – what is it, Harper?"

"An arts community."

"Well, all righty, then. Sounds like a commune to me. Bunch of long-hairs and draft dodgers, 'farming' as they call it – Harper, did I ever tell ya how close I was to going to Woodstock?" We had pulled into the carport and Therese yanked on the emergency brake.

"Only about a million times, Mom – Therese. Harper doesn't want to hear about it again." Krista got out of the car, slammed the door and went into the house.

Therese just looked after her, and continued as we both got out of the car and went in. "So, I get stuck in New York City. Heard the Stones were playing. I'd take seeing the Stones over standing around topless in a muddy field any day. Course, we never did find them. They were probably up in Woodstock, the jerks, but, oh, Mick Jagger – what I wouldn't give! Those skinny little hips – oh, can that man move."

We were in the kitchen and Krista joined us there, saying, "Uh, Therese, fascinating as this is, Harper doesn't want to hear it."

"Mouthy little wench, isn't she? Harper, pull up your jeans, let me see your legs."

"Mom, come on!" Krista said.

"Harper doesn't mind, do ya?"

"Nah, I don't mind." I lifted a leg of my jeans. I knew what Mrs. Delaney was checking for.

"Attagirl, still smooth. Don't let those hippies convince you to stop shaving your legs. I don't care what anyone else says, men do not like women with hairy legs, not even those longhairs out there. If they tell you any different – the men, I mean – they're lying."

"Therese, you are an absolute font of knowledge," Krista said to her mother.

"And you, my darling daughter, are an absolute font in the ass." I couldn't help but laugh at that. Mrs. Delaney beamed back at me.

Krista said, "Harp, I don't know if we can hang out tonight. I have an essay due for English." She turned away from me before I could say anything, and asked, "Therese, can you give her a ride home?" When she left the room, Therese looked at me and shrugged before picking up her keys again from the kitchen table.

That evening, when I returned, I joined Gabe in the workshop half of the shed. A guitar was in pieces on the drafting table and he was measuring each one, laying them on partially unrolled spools of paper.

I stood by the table, touching the edge lightly with my fingertips and shifting my weight, but he didn't say anything. Finally, I asked, "Can I help?"

Gabe looked up, blinked, and I was sure I caught the beginning of a grin. "You want to help?"

"Sure."

"Okay, well, um. You're probably good at sketching, huh?" I nodded. "Why don't you sketch a piece. It doesn't have to be perfect, but as close to what it actually looks like as possible, okay? And if you figure out the measurements, you can write them alongside, or I can tell you what they are." I nodded and picked up the face of the guitar. It was curved and wouldn't lie flat, but I placed it on a piece of paper, traced the curves, with a pencil, then followed these with a compass carefully, while I tried to remember what to do from there.

At some point I asked, "What's the story with Thomas?"

"What do you mean?"

"You know, where's he from, how'd he get here . . ."

"I don't know much. I know he moved here years ago, when my parents did. He was with someone then. I don't think it was his wife but, you know. I think she died in childbirth."

"Childbirth? I didn't think anyone died in childbirth any more."

"Yeah, well, I guess someone did. I'm not sure though, something like that. He never talks about her and I don't ask."

By the end of the evening, I had sketched the front, back, and neck of the guitar. I had given up on the equations of figures, leaving that to Gabe, and made alternative versions of each piece. The first sketch would be the bare outline, in proportion. In subsequent drawings I would elaborate, add the grains of wood, the notes that would reverberate from the strings.

~

After a couple of weeks, I suddenly felt as though I wanted to see Nick, as if to find some connection to a place I'd been before. I couldn't remember the last time I'd seen him at school. Granted, he was in grade eight, skinny, and awkward. Boys like him must have willed themselves invisible. Either that or they were still outside playing like they had in elementary school. I wouldn't have known. I preferred parking lots and streets leading away from the school to fields.

Then, I remembered. Nick was a skinny boy who smoked dope. He would probably be with the other skinny boys who smoked, outside the back door to the metal workshop, the one that opened onto a loading zone and a couple of dumpsters. I had to go into the parking lot to access the concrete and chain-link yard that smelled of sawdust, metal filings, garbage, and cigarette smoke. There he was, not with the headbangers but with a couple of lean geeks, squatting, handling dice and cards. It was still January and the temperature hovered around freezing, if we were lucky. It felt colder.

"Hey, Nick," I called out, hoping my tone conveyed a kind of casual authority. He looked at me, back to his friends and rolled his eyes, then shuffled over. We walked to the chain-link fence separating the loading zone from the field and both seized it with ungloved hands, stared outward and both leaned back, pulling the links. The fence was so cold it burned. I turned around then, bounced my back off the fence.

"How's it going?" I asked, not knowing how else to start.

"All right. Nice hair, Harp."

"Yeah, thanks. Nice life."

"You're one to talk. You still at that commune?"

"It's not a commune. It's an arts community. How are things at home? Miss me yet?" I rubbed my hands together, looked down at them.

"Yeah, right."

"How's Mom?" I rubbed my hands slowly. They felt unnaturally smooth in the cold, unreal.

Nick stared at his feet as he spoke, kicked at lumps of unrecognizable material – snow, dirt, sand, something for it all to cling on to. "She seems a little, like, sad. People have been talking about how you've been deceived, that they're brainwashing you up there, that they're a New Age cult and you've been, you know, taken by sin, that you've – what's that word? summoned? to temptation." He looked up at me quickly, then away again.

"Succumbed." I pulled one of the unrecognizable lumps toward me with the tip of my shoe, then punted it skidding across the pavement lot.

Nick watched its progress then turned to me. "So, you going to come back?"

"I don't know, Nick. Not now anyway." I bounced off the fence and stood upright, groping in jacket pockets until I found a small piece of paper. "Here's my number, though, you can call, although I don't know why you'd want to."

I already had the number written down. I was going to give it to the first friend of Nick's I saw, if I didn't find him. He took the piece of paper and stuffed it in his jacket pocket and we both stood rubbing our hands together. Nick looked over at his friends again and I knew he wanted to go. "See ya," I said, not moving.

"See ya, Harp." He twisted his mouth in a way that could have been a smile and turned to walk back to his friends. I watched him, his gait awkward and self-conscious, chin stuffed into the collar of his jacket.

I knew Nick would never call me at the farm but suddenly he was the person I loved most in the world. That must be the way it is with siblings. You might not have much in common with them. You may hardly even talk, but suddenly a love can rise up in you for them that is so strong and clear that it can make you believe all those sayings about blood and water and the way they both flow.

GABE

In a few months, the visits taper off until there are only phone calls a couple times a week, people checking in to see how everything is going. Everything is not going well but there's no way to say this. People don't want to hear it so you tell them that you're all pulling through.

You have thought about Anise's kiss, her darting tongue, since that night. She was a better kisser than any of the girls you've been with and it disgusts you that you are even able to think that. Anise is wearing fewer and fewer clothes around the house, even though it's getting colder, and sometimes she looks straight at you when she crosses and uncrosses her legs. The girls mimic their mother. The heat is cranked up so the four of them can walk around the house in T-shirts and underwear, eating and watching TV in Anise's bed together.

You were going to wait until the house sold and they found another place but you know now that you are going to have to leave soon. You have no idea what Anise is going to do and this unpredictability scares you. First, she will have to find a much cheaper place to live in with the three girls, then she will have to find full-time work. She'll visit her husband in jail and become a single mother, after eleven years. It all sounds like more than one person can take, especially if that person is Anise, and you had assumed that you would stay and help. Much as you like to believe that you raised yourself, she was always there for you, after all.

It takes you a few days to get a hold of your mother, Susan, in British Columbia. When you hear her voice over the phone line, she sounds like a stranger, which she is. You have only seen her four times since you were six. Twice you stayed for a couple of weeks. The other two times, you stayed the entire summer, learned to ride a horse, put up a fence and use a swede saw. You could probably count the times you've talked to her if you tried. Susan sounds tired and resigned when you talk to her on the phone, says, "Sure, of course, come on up. Won't be able to help you out with cash, though, but you know that."

You tell Peter before Anise. You no longer have to talk to him on the other side of glass, so you walk around the fenced yard together. When you tell him, your father stops walking, looks through the wires out into the trees and tells you he understands. When he turns back to you, there are tears in his eyes and he tries to smile. You don't think you've ever felt a true emotion before this moment. The sadness that you feel burns through every organ and cell in your body, feels like weight and heat and sharp pain at once.

A couple of weeks later when they say goodbye at the Greyhound station, the girls each give you a gift. The oldest gives you a traveller's journal, complete with a lock, and is proud of her choice. The middle girl stares at her feet and thrusts a drawing at you. It is of the three girls, Anise and Peter, all standing on the back deck, waving. You are in the picture too, the back of your head in the lower right-hand corner, your hand raised in a wave. You can tell that she had trouble drawing the hand, the paper is thin and balled there from being erased several times. The youngest gives you a shiny, purple stone. When the bus comes, you hug the girls, then Anise, who holds your face in both of her hands and shakes her head from side to side slowly.

With what little money there is, Anise bought you a ticket for the entire trip but after a night on the bus, you get off and hitchhike. As a single young man, you are picked up by a succession of freaks. No one hurts you, but one man asks politely if you'd like to blow him, then simply smiles when you refuse, slips a John Denver tape in the deck and sings along, something about filling up his senses. Another drives with one hand on the wheel, the other either reaching for a can of beer, lifting it to his lips, or throwing an empty out the window. You didn't know people like this actually existed. With each ride you feel your childhood strung out behind you, a trail of exhaust.

It all goes well until you hit Kelowna, in the interior of British Columbia. After that, no one slows down except to glare at you. Twice, men in pickups give you the finger. After spending an unprecedented six hours by the side of the road, you walk back to a minigolf course and phone Susan. "Welcome to the Bible belt, sweetie," she says. The minigolf course is open late enough that you can wait there while someone drives the hour to come get you. On the course, you try to launch a ball into a castle and hit the moat every time. Later you shoot at things in the arcade until you are confusing sound and colour and have to get some fresh air.

Thomas comes to pick you up. He may or may not be the man from your first memories, the man that you and Susan stayed with in the coldest months of the winter while Peter slept in the shack. You know he's been around the farm for years but was always working out in the bush when you came up those summers. He laughs and nods his head when he sees you. "Gabriel Miller. Gabe Miller," he says and shakes your hand.

Once you get into the truck, Thomas says to you, "That's rough about your old man." You tell him that Peter may be out soon, that he has some friends pulling strings back in the States. You don't know why you say this. It's a lie. Peter's friends have no strings but it's as though you want to impress Thomas. This is when he tells you about the money – that Peter has been sending up a bit here and there for Thomas to put aside for you. He's opened up an account in your name in Canada and, though you're by no means rich, you'll have a bit to live off for a few months.

"No offence, but why you? I mean, why not Susan, or I don't know . . . Why didn't he tell me?" you ask. Even after such a short absence, your father is seeming more and more like a stranger. Peter never disclosed what he did for a living and now you find out that he was feeding a trust fund off that money, and not telling you that either, not even during those last times you saw him. Thomas speeds up to overtake a car, then mutters about slow drivers in the passing lane. He doesn't answer your question and you don't repeat it.

You get to the farm after midnight. Susan is up, drinking coffee and smoking in the cookshack. She cracks a grin that cleaves her small, taut face when she sees you. You greet her with feigned nonchalance and, for the first time, when you hug her, you have to bend down. Susan looks older than you expected. Her hair and her skin look thin, her eyes huge, the rest of her features receding. She puts out her cigarette when you come in but lights another one soon after, coughing between the two like someone who has been smoking for years.

As you walk back to her place she tells you that she is sorry about what happened to Peter. She says his name quickly, non-committally. She lives in an A-frame cabin now. After you and Peter left, she built and wired it herself. "Well, not entirely myself. Took me three years and as many men to get this thing off the ground," she jokes. "I've set up the spare room for you, for now, but we'll get you set up in another space on the land. I'm sure you didn't come up here to live with your mother." Susan laughs lightly and you join her, wonder who she is saying this for, you or herself. It's true, you don't think you came here to live with your mother, but you may have come to escape your stepmother, the uncomfortable things growing between her and you. You've come to forget everything you've left behind.

Susan helps you carry your things into the spare room, then leaves you alone. The room has a bed, a desk piled with books, old newspapers, and shoeboxes, an open trunk full of balls of wool, and everywhere photographs of you. Some are framed, some are pinned to the wall. One of Susan holding you is blown up on thin paper and hangs above the bed. There are several of you as a baby and toddler, barefoot and in overalls, the standard uniform for children of your generation. A few look like they were taken shortly before you left, doing boyish, farmish things – sitting on the horse-drawn plough, chasing a goose, standing on top of a stump. The rest of the photos are from one of four ages – eleven, twelve, thirteen, or fourteen – the years when you visited. In each you look even more awkward and scrawny than the last. As you get older, you look away from the camera and your mouth betrays smiles pulled down in embarrassment.

You have a hard time falling asleep with images of yourself looking down on you. The boy in those photographs isn't the same one you left behind in California. None of those photographs exist in Arcana. It's as if there were two of you, who never met.

During lunch breaks, I returned to the loading zone behind the shop classes. By then, Krista usually spent the entire lunch period with Mike. Sometimes, they would ask me to come along to the food court, but after a couple of lunch hours spent deflecting the advances and snide comments of Mike's tobacco-chewing buddies while he and Krista made out, I declined. Nick was always in the smoking area, though almost never smoking. Most often, he was huddled in one of the doorways with a couple of other geeks, playing cards or hand-held video games. Once, I had been able to dissolve into the neutral, unnoticed masses in the school. I couldn't do that any more and I would have rather smoked with the freaks than be stared at as I walked the halls alone.

Very few girls hung out with the skids and nerds in the loading zone in sub-zero temperatures. The ones who did could be grouped into two broad categories: tomboys who loved wood and metal and were almost indistinguishable from the guys, and girls lacquered in heavy makeup. Those girls smoked and glared and spoke in a sparse language, never quite turning to look people in the face when they did. Nick's friends simply stared at me like any thirteen-year-olds would at a seventeen-year-old girl who had deigned to talk to them.

They all acknowledged me soon enough. The tomboys ran their eyes over my shorn hair and I registered their acceptance immediately. The tough girls shot their chins out and said, "Hey, what's your story?" When I mumbled something about leaving home and living with a guy, I knew I was in. Then I made the ultimate in offers, "Drum?" and held out a pouch. I had gotten it off someone at the farm. Drum was what most people smoked there, that or American Spirit. These were somehow acceptable forms of tobacco.

There wasn't a lot of talking in the smoking area, and at that time of year none of us spent the entire lunch hour out there. Sometimes, one of the guys would slide an electrical cord under a shop door and bring a stereo outside to play speed metal – a soundtrack for the dumpsters, the chain-link, and the white, abandoned field, for the leather jackets and heavy eyeliner. Each group would exchange a few muttered comments, smoke cigarettes while looking away from the school, shuffle their feet, and then leave after fifteen or twenty minutes, complaining of the cold. Nick and his friends huddled in a doorwell with their games until someone offered them a butt – it was always someone offering, never them asking – at which point they would nod, trying to appear indifferent, and three or four of them would share the smoke together. I had begun rolling cigarettes, thin as pencils, for Nick and his friends, throwing them to the boys like candy to kids at a parade.

At the beginning of February, Nick caught one of the cigarettes and walked up to me. "Can I talk to you, Harp?"

"Sure." We walked over to the concrete steps leading to an unused door to the gym. We sat on our hands on the top step. The cold was going to drop lower yet, I could feel the edge of it coming on. "What's up?" I asked Nick.

"I think you should call Mom."

"I know, I know. Why now, though?"

"She's just acting strange. For one thing, I think she's having trouble sleeping. You know how weird that is. I hear her walking around at night. It kind of freaks me out a bit. I think she misses you or something. Who knows why." Nick turned his head away from me and spat, as though to show he had some handle on the situation

"Nice gob, hero. Okay. I'll call Mom." I put my hands on my lap and turned them palms up. "Don't say anything to her though, okay?"

"Yeah, okay, I won't." Nick pushed himself up from the concrete step. "See you around." This time, he was up and down the stairs before I had given him an unspoken cue to leave.

⌒

I remember in surprising detail the first time that I left a place without letting anyone know where I was going. I was in the first grade. It was during the transition when we had first arrived in Sawmill and were still living at the motel. Vera wanted to make us feel like we belonged. She thought new friends could do this and so made it her mission to find some for Nick and me. Her means were simple. Any adult – the real estate agent, a cashier at the supermarket, the guy who pumped our gas – was a potential parent, their children potential friends. Nick and I were dropped off at strangers' houses, encouraged to play with kids with whom we often had no more in common than our age, and sometimes that was a stretch.

One afternoon, Vera dropped me off at a girl's house. I don't remember who she was, or ever seeing her again. We were playing in her carport, metres away from where Vera had dropped me off. We didn't interact as we roamed the carport like detectives, in silence, picking toys up and putting them down. When I picked up a glossy red plastic change purse, it was so smooth, so gleaming that I couldn't imagine not having it, holding it in my pocket, a space within a space like one of the stacked Russian dolls my baba had sent me for Christmas.

I slipped the purse into the pocket, felt a hot itch on my face and neck, then took it back out. I wanted to leave, get out of that carport with the silent girl stranger. Vera found me later, walking from the girl's house to wherever the road would take me. "Sylvie, honey, where are you going?" She bent to me, grasped my arms until they hurt, the van still running on the side of the road.

"I don't know. I wanted to go home. I didn't like it there." I was glad she had found me. I don't think I would actually have walked home if she hadn't. The memory of holding that purse in my pocket was propelling me in some other direction.

For years, Vera would tell the story of finding me walking on the side of the road. To her, it attested to my innate wilfulness, stubbornness like a steel bar in my spine. To me, it was about a fear I couldn't name. About wanting something so badly that I had to walk away from it, lose my way.

⌒

I called Vera on a Sunday evening from the cookshack. There had been a potluck and I had helped clean up afterwards. The kids had reached the point when they were beginning to stutter and become delirious, running wide wobbling circles in the middle of the room.

"Hello?" Vera answered.

I had to raise my voice to say, "Hi, Mom. It's me."

Silence on her end, then she asked, "How are you?"

"I'm okay. Listen, Mom, I don't really want to talk like this, over the phone. There are people here, you know, and –"

"I know. Maybe we could meet. Here, at home."

"At home?"

"Yes, honey, the place you used to live?" Vera said sarcastically, then shifted her tone quickly once she caught herself. "I mean, if you'd be comfortable here," she said. I could hear something thin and tight in Vera's voice, as though it were strained through a crack. I felt as though I couldn't push her any further.

⌒

I walked to Vera's after school, having agreed to meet Gabe at the café downtown in an hour. Entering through the front door seemed too formal so I went around the back. Once I got there, however, I felt presumptuous simply walking into the kitchen, so I knocked first and waited a moment before letting myself in. I almost expected Vera to be at the table waiting, but she wasn't. I started to take my coat off but decided against it. Then I heard some movement from the direction of the living room and called out.

I could hear Vera get up and walk down the hall toward the kitchen, her steps neither fast nor slow. She stopped inside the kitchen door, smiled, then took a step toward me. "Hello, Harper. It's good to –" Vera began to reach for me, then let her arm drop. "How are you doing?"

"I'm – are you sure you want me to answer that question?" I asked.

My response must have relaxed her a little. I saw the slight shadow of a smile pass over her face as she shook her head. She moved toward the table, pulled out a chair, and sat down. "Yes, unbelievably enough, I really would." She pulled an empty cup toward her, tilted it and peered in. She looked up at me and asked, "Are you going to sit?"

I considered this, took my hands out of my pockets and held the back of a chair, then pulled it out and sat down. "Okay. I'm doing well at the farm. I like it there."

"Good. That's good, really."

I looked at Vera to see if she really meant it but her expression was wiped flat. "How's Nick?" I asked.

"As far as I can tell, Nick is fine, although it can't be good for him to see his older sister walk out on her family."

Instead of addressing this, I asked, "And council? Have you decided anything about council?"

"No, I haven't." Vera looked out the window, then turned back to me and asked, "Has it ever occurred to you that I might have some kind of comprehension of what you're going through?"

"I knew it would come back to this."

"Sylvia, it isn't coming back to anything. Whether you like it or not, you are my daughter. You've been very vocal about what you think is wrong with my life. Now it's my turn to make my observations about yours. Would that be all right?"

"Sure, as long as you're really looking at me, Mom, and not at yourself."

"So, you think you have it figured out, do you? You've already made your mind up with what you think you know about me. Where does that leave us?"

"Here, I guess."

⌁

By the end of February, the valley had been socked in with clouds thick as gravy for two weeks solid. The temperatures had begun to rise under this blanket, enough that skin didn't ache when exposed to air, but the clouds shed no new snow. The dirt roads were either mud or frozen mud. The paved roads were gritty with old salt. The snow was yellow and grey and melting. In the fields, leafless plants and patches of brown broke through the snow.

I felt restless, as though only movement could shake off the dormancy of weeks of grey and brown. Having convinced myself it was a fresh start, I hadn't skipped any classes since moving to the farm. But one afternoon in February, in a windowless classroom in the belly of the school, the teacher's drone began to join with the hum of the fluorescent lights and I knew I had to get out. I knew too that I would end up at the Catholic Church downtown, oddly enough.

Before moving to the farm I had skipped class to go to the church on the corner of Pine and Twenty-seventh, Our Lady of Perpetual Help. I seemed to be perpetually in need of something and once I had thought it was help. Going through the doors meant crossing over into everything the Free Church had left behind – idolatry, blasphemy, ritual. Our Lady was the only church with unlocked doors on weekdays when I needed a place to sit alone. I went there for silence. The Virgin would welcome me, hand half-opened at her heart, a passing gesture frozen. The Mother of God didn't mean the same thing at the Free Church and she was resolutely not worshipped. The women who were named in sermons – Bathsheba, Jezebel – were the bad ones. The good ones – Esther, Ruth – were given to girls in Sunday school parables, stories as sweet and tart as powdered candy licked off lips. Esther was my favourite. She was beautiful enough to pass between worlds, smart enough to bring peace to both.

My fascination with the Catholic Church had begun one summer when we returned to Alberta after moving to Sawmill Creek. Then, Vera's family had still been able to convince her to bring us to services in the Ukrainian Catholic Church. Vera explained to Nick and me both, although it seemed to me that my little brother could barely understand English at that age, that this was our relatives' church, not our own. We didn't believe we needed special smells, and chants, and signs to talk to God. It was their church I liked, though. The priest walked down the aisle, swinging a lantern of smoke that smelled both sweet and old. The congregation all knew the same mumbled language and would kneel down and stand up in unison, chant in a low hum. The ceilings were painted with heavenly hosts and on the panels on the walls still-faced, sombre saints all held a hand open at their chest in a gesture I assumed to be a small wave, an acknowledgment.

On one of those Sundays, I had asked God for a sign. It took me most of the sermon to try to think of what I wanted a sign for, and I never did come up with anything specific. I just wanted a sign; that seemed like enough to ask. We had been told that God didn't like specifics, that He knew best. Ask and ye shall receive. So I asked and received a sudden band of sunlight, like those shafts of light that spill from clouds as though made from the stuff of angels. The band shot through a window, picked up the red from the stain on the glass, and created for a moment a wall of light that wouldn't allow me to see through it. The priest intoning in Ukrainian on the other side was invisible. That's all. Eventually, my eyes adjusted and I couldn't even see the red tint to it. The light became just something else in the air.

On that day in late February, I wanted something. Not a sign necessarily. Even a wash of light would do. But I wouldn't recognize what did come to me that afternoon.

Though I had seen a lot of Krista, we hadn't spent much time alone in the previous two months. Before last period I waited outside of her class, catching her before she went in.

"Come downtown with me," I whispered, as students crowded around us to get into the class.

Krista looked at me without saying anything, glanced into the classroom for a moment, as though considering her options, then she shrugged. I took this to mean she would come. When I smiled, she moved past me, and turned. "Meet you outside in a couple minutes," she said.

We walked downtown. When we were at the bottom of the church steps, Krista and I stopped talking and went in. She didn't ask any questions, just followed me. Not knowing what they were for, I lit some candles on one side of the altar and Krista followed my lead, lit some on the other, then we sat in empty pews across the aisle from each other. I had forgotten what it was like to chase prayers out of my mind. Sometimes when Gabe turned me over and I spread my legs and arms and gripped the sides of the mattress, everything heat and liquid, I heard myself saying, "Oh God, oh God," but I didn't really consider that praying.

Something about sitting in a pew brought the words back to me. Words that asked for things to be given, then asked for others to be taken away. Words that implored, then apologized. I wanted to wipe my mind clear of each one. I thought that the absence of thought would be better than trying to sort out what exactly it was that I wanted to believe. I tried paying attention to my breath instead as it passed through my nostrils. Tried to see clouds moving, skies about to clear, waves rolling and abating until the water was smooth as glass but the prayer started anyway. *Our Father, who art,* the Lord's Prayer started up like a recording, *in Heaven, hallowed be*, and kept breaking through, even though the Free Church had only adopted it a couple of years before, *Thy name*, when Pastor John had decided that something about the rhythm of those words would bring us closer to God, *Thy kingdom come*, come – I was still uncomfortable with that word for what happened, *Thy will be done*, that word for the liquid we both expelled as though the impact of our bodies against each other forced something out, drained us in small ways, *on earth as it is.*

I opened my eyes and looked across the aisle. Krista was shaking slightly in the pew, arms wrapped around herself. I closed my eyes, opened them and looked again to see her still shaking. Not knowing what to do, I lay down on the pew, stared at the ceiling, and waited.

When I heard Krista get up and walk down the aisle, I followed her out. I touched the arm of her coat in the foyer and we exchanged a glance – one in which I asked *Are you all right?* and she answered *Leave it.*

Back outside, we took runs at the remnants of packed snow on the sidewalks, trying to get a good slide in, in spite of how we both felt, or perhaps to cheer ourselves up. Most of it had already melted and the few patches that remained were grainy with dirt and salt, not great for gliding. Krista coasted a small way, then spun around to face me, breath flowering the air, cheeks bright. "Let's go to Community Drugs."

I could tell by the way she raised her eyebrow as she walked backwards what Krista wanted to do. "I don't know, Kris –" I started.

Krista shifted so she was walking beside me. "You don't know? I come with you to the Catholic church for no particular reason and now, you don't know?"

"I just don't feel like it today," I answered.

I stopped on the sidewalk for a moment and Krista kept walking, then said over her shoulder, "Well, I'm going. You can do whatever." She shrugged and headed in the direction of the drugstore. Something about that shrug, her turned back, made me follow.

Perhaps it was our haste or the lack of recent practice but we got caught that day, a clerk hollering at us as we tried to make it out the door and across the parking lot unnoticed. There being little else for excitement in her life, the clerk insisted on calling the police after she got us back inside and had us empty our clothes of loot.

"Cry when the cop gets here," whispered Krista.

"I don't know if I can."

"Of course you can. Whatever you do, don't act cocky."

"Huh! Look who's talking," I shot back in a whisper.

When the officer arrived, Krista cried enough for both of us. He agreed not to press charges but insisted we call our parents to pick us up. I felt my throat constrict and I squeezed out, "Um, officer, I don't live at home."

"Okay, then, your guardian," he said, without missing a beat. He must've picked up kids all the time who didn't live at home.

I tried not to expel my relief too quickly. I called the cook-shack and let the phone ring. The officer wasn't going to let us go until we both had rides. I called the farm again and again. We were trapped in the Community Drugs staff room, surrounded with positive affirmations, kitten posters, and the smell of perfume samples. When I realized that I wasn't going to get anyone in the cookshack, I asked to use a phone book and looked up Thomas's number.

"Uh, hi, Mr. Steele" – I talked quickly – "I was, uh, well I've been caught shoplifting – I'm, uh, sorry – and the officer wants you to come pick me up. I'm at Community Drugs, okay?"

Thomas showed up shortly after Krista's dad, Harley, and we all crowded into the staff room, the clerk smiling and offering them coffee like it was a social event. Both Harley and Thomas seemed to be trying to hide their amusement as the officer spoke to them about the seriousness of our crime. Harley said something about "talking this over at home" and "there will certainly be consequences," which we all knew wasn't going to happen, then they shook the officer's hand.

Harley elbowed us both as we walked into the parking lot. "Little shit-disturbers, eh?" He turned to Krista. "I guess you don't want me telling your mother about this?"

"Uh, yeah, Dad, you guessed right."

Harley didn't ask who Thomas was and why I was going with him. He must have thought he was a member of the Free Church. We got in their respective cars – Harley's truck, Thomas's old Suburban – and drove opposite ways out of the parking lot.

"Shoplifting, Harper? Really, I thought you had more class," Thomas said, no indication of whether he was trying to make a joke or not.

"Are you going to discipline me?" I didn't mask the edge of flirtation in my voice.

Thomas didn't say anything for a moment, then asked, "Has Susan talked to you yet?"

"Susan? No, about what?"

"Social Services has been by."

"What for?"

"I guess your mother – or one of your people – called them."

"They're not 'my people.' They can't do anything, though, can they? I mean Social Services can't actually tell me where I can live."

"I'm afraid they can, Harper. You are technically a minor. They can't force you to move back in with your mother, true, but, if you don't, it'll be them who'll decide where you'll live. Sorry to burst your bubble."

"Oh fuck, this can't be happening."

"Do you like it at the farm enough to make a case to stay?"

I was about to answer, "Yes, of course," but stopped. I saw several images at once: lines of static moving across the television in the cookshack, Gabe's back turned away from me in sleep, Thomas's hand on my jaw, the slope of the ceiling above my bed at home, Vera sitting at the kitchen table.

When we got back to the farm, Thomas headed for the cookshack, and I scanned the yard for Gabe's truck. It wasn't there.

"Come on, I'll make you a coffee, the way you like it," Thomas said.

I followed him in the back door, into the kitchen. "You know what, Thomas? I don't actually like my coffee black. I like it with lots of cream and sugar just like you said I would."

Thomas laughed. "Harper, you really are something else." He leaned up against the counter, looked at me and crossed his arms over his chest. I registered that flick, the quick etching of my body with his eyes.

"Yeah, a liar and a thief, who knew?" I moved toward Thomas slowly. "I'm also probably desperately looking for a father figure." I stood directly in front of him and unfolded his arms, put them at his sides. I made sure I didn't touch Thomas but stood close enough that I could feel the fabric of our clothes shift against each other when we breathed. I lifted up on my toes and turned my head so that my cheek and mouth were against his neck, not pressing but just placed there. I could feel the heat off his skin. We stood like that, unmoving.

"Harper," he finally said, his voice quiet and rough, hot on my hair. "What are you doing?"

"Nothing." I moved my face back a bit and stared at him without expression. I could see things pass across his face – desire, something that looked like pain, perhaps that was restraint. I wanted to stand there like that for a long time, watching the emotions change his features in small ways. I could do this to Gabe but that was unintentional, a side effect. I wanted to be able to will Thomas to feel things, my body a conduit. He broke the spell, his face moving towards me. He stopped when his mouth was almost on mine. I wanted to open up to it, to crawl inside. Instead, I pulled back, turned and left the kitchen. I went into the shed and waited for the sound of truck tires in the yard.

GABE

After the first week, you move out of Susan's spare room and into a shed on the farm. At first you think it might be the shack from your childhood memories but you ask Susan and she laughs, says, "Don't be ridiculous. That thing was used as kindling years ago, thank God. Not good for much else." You are relieved. That would have been too much of a mockery, returning to live in the place where your parents were last together.

The shed is livable – half of it like a bachelor pad, complete with mini-fridge and microwave, half of it a workshop. This might be even more of a mockery, Peter in prison and you basically living in a workshop. It is the first space you've ever had completely to yourself. One night, when you are listening to how quiet it is, you realize that you will probably never have to hear Peter and Anise having sex again. You will never hear that sound that comforted and disgusted you at once.

You will also never have to go through the torment of the girls' nightly antics to keep themselves out of bed. This was called "carrying on," and ranged from launching water wars in their shared bath, to running down the hall screaming, nighties trailing behind them, and falling into a laughing heap, to asking for glasses of water repeatedly. The girls' tactics variously worked and didn't work; the unpredictable results, you are convinced, providing an incentive for them to try again. There was always a chance their ploys might be successful. Sometimes they were up for hours, delirious with exhaustion, slurring their words and laughing at inappropriate moments like miniature drunk people. Sometimes Anise or Peter would set aside their belief that they should never raise their voices long enough to yell, "Not another word! Get. To. Bed! Now! I mean it!" and you would feel strangely vindicated.

You wonder if it is homesickness that you feel, but it is something more akin to relief and loss at once. You wouldn't want to go back there, though there is no "there" to go back to. Anise has sold the split-level, moved into a low-income housing co-op with the girls. There isn't even space there for you to come back and visit. The offer is extended, nonetheless.

After a couple nights of insomnia at the farm, you seek solace in the cookshack, hoping there will be other people doing the same. The farm isn't like it was those summers that you visited, though. Most of the people here are families or older, like Susan. There are no wisecracking young philosophers smoking around the long table in the cookshack. Unfortunately, there are also no young women doing yoga by the wood stove in transparent clothing. There is a television. Two channels and, thankfully, one of them gets Letterman. You watch Dave toss cards and clean his teeth, the idiot band leader stumble through words and grin maniacally, and stars teeter in tans and heels, throwing their torsos forward when they laugh, holding their tiny garments against their chests and flashing the camera thousand-watt smiles. You become foolishly and unrealistically nostalgic for the States or, as you've come to think of it, *America*.

Things pick up. In December, everyone at the farm assures themselves that it's the winter solstice, absolutely not Christmas, that they are excited about. After all, Christmas is simply the co-opting of a pagan winter celebration by the Christians. At Pilgrims, they are determined to celebrate the original holiday, as though it were more worthy, more real. The cookshack is transformed into a craft barn. For several evenings there are people baking without using refined sugar, playing music by the wood stove, and weaving baskets, mixing oils, firing pots, knitting scarves. Each activity is stretched out, strung through days and weeks with breaks for herbal tea, coffee, smokes, and banter. The women your mother's age wink at you, pinch your ass, and say, "You've grown up very nicely, there, Gabriel Miller," and you can tell they feel racy for doing so. You already know this game, and these women are the most familiar thing here, the element that makes you feel most like you're back at home.

By the time the annual Pilgrims Art Farm Solstice Fair rolls around, you are embarrassed to admit that you really are excited. You know you shouldn't be. It will start off full of women and children and deathly boring, and will end a freak show of aging hippies, like any one of Peter and Anise's gatherings. You avoid the craft fair and go to the potluck afterward, pleased that everyone else seems as eager as you to get the food out of the way and start drinking. Thomas asks you if you want to hook up the horses and help him take people out on sleigh rides. He is letting you know that he trusts you, that he thinks of you as a man able to handle large animals and small crowds of people.

You meet her after the sleigh ride. Actually, you don't notice her in the mass of people that piles onto the sleigh, although you are disappointed that your radar didn't alert you to the presence of teenage girls sooner. It is afterward, when you have already lit up a smoke on the porch that you notice them in the yard. You hear her laughter first. It comes at you almost as an assault. When you turn to the noise, you see the two of them on the ground, all hair and sweaters and thin teenage limbs. You look at Thomas and he raises his eyebrows, says, "Well, seems we have two damsels in distress. It would be wrong not to help."

When you help her friend up and hold her against your body, you think of how good it is to be close to another person, a girl, but it is the one you later find out is named Harper that you are looking at. Harper is the one laughing so hard she can hardly stand, Thomas trying to keep her upright. The way she laughs – like there is nothing as large and all-encompassing as her laughter – makes you want a piece of it. You think, if you can get close to her, her laughter will open you, empty you, and fill you back up with something light, something good. You will tell me this later.

$\mathcal{S}$omething shifted with the weather. It was the beginning of March, a time in the valley when pressure builds up – warm air moving in fronts, colliding with cold – so that banks of clouds meet and press up against each other and the sky seems as though it will split. When it did, it would be spring. But until then the TV weatherman droned on about the barometer, people got restless, and though November yielded the highest number of suicides each year, in March more people escaped from the south wing of the hospital – the psych ward – than at any other time.

The air got warmer but things seemed to be held in stasis. Tight, still. Then they tore open.

The people at Pilgrims decided to throw an event to cheer everyone up. We called the party Raise the Roof, believing we could lift the ceiling of clouds and the roof of the cookshack simply with the power of celebration. What I had never realized until then was how quickly things we feel are solid can topple, however small the push. I didn't recognize the precariousness of all that holds us.

I called Krista to invite her to come, telling her she could bring Mike if she wanted. "Are you kidding?" she answered, as if it was a ridiculous suggestion. I didn't know if she meant it for herself or for Mike.

"No, why? Did I miss something – you two are still together, aren't you?"

"Why wouldn't we be? I just don't think Pilgrims Art Farm is the right place to bring Mike. He'll probably get drunk and threaten to 'boot-fuck some fairy.' God, he is too embarrassing sometimes."

"Krista, you do realize you are going out with someone who has terms like 'boot-fuck' and 'fairy' in his vocabulary? I don't know how you can do it."

"Oh, listen to you. This is Sawmill, Harper. Not everyone can be with some sweet, sensitivo guy from California. The rest of us take what's available."

"Sorry, I didn't mean to –"

"Ah, forget it, Harp."

"You'll come, though, right? To the party?"

"Yeah, of course. Hey, can you pick me up? Therese has taken up – get this – line dancing and I know she'll take the car to the Wildhorse. She never gets picked up at home, always goes either by herself or picks up her 'friends' – those skanks that hung out behind shop – Oh, sorry! I didn't mean you."

"I know. Yeah, I'll come by with Gabe and pick you up. Eight o'clock."

⁓

The next night, I helped make posters in the cookshack. We gathered around one of the big tables and I tried to keep up conversation, laugh at the right jokes. I wasn't used to being around so many people on a regular basis. I hadn't even thought of the implications of this when I first came to the farm. Gabe and I kept to ourselves in the shed or in the one corner of the cookshack that we had taken over. I decided I would make more of an effort to feel like part of the community. It would just take some getting used to.

Poster-making was like a kids' craft class – the table spread with paper, coloured pens, things that sparkled, glue – except a few people had to smoke up first to get back to a childlike feeling, one of "expansive weightlessness," as Brenda, the potter, called it. I thought about that for a moment. I didn't recall feeling particularly expansive or weightless as a child, confined to various small spaces – car, classroom, bedroom – reluctantly led by others through grocery stores, church services, school days.

I offered to put up posters at the library and on the main street. I was armed with stickpins and a large roll of tape, left a trail of sparkles. When I had pinned a poster to the Community Announcements board outside the Super Valu, I turned and saw Pastor John striding toward the store, his legs kicking out from his knees. He was approaching the black mat that would swing the doors open. When he turned and saw me, he smoothed a smile over his face, the same kind of expression that he had in the pulpit, too uniform to convey any real emotion. He nodded and said, "Well, hello. Sylvia."

"Hi," I said, and smiled back, hugging the posters to my chest.

Pastor John had one foot on the motion sensor and the door was wide open, making lurching movements as it repeatedly attempted to close. He looked into the store, squinting as though he was trying to locate something or someone. I wondered where his family was. The last time I had seen him without the entire troop he had been in my living room. He moved away from the door and took a step toward me. My instinct was to move back but I couldn't. I was against a row of grocery carts. "Let's sit down for a moment, shall we?" Pastor John said, his voice level and light, a forced smile on his face. He looked around as if to motion to a bench, but there weren't any.

"Sure," I said, and sat down on the curb between grocery store and parking lot.

Pastor John followed my lead, bent his long legs until they brought him to the curb. He cleared his throat. "Sylvia," he started, then stopped. "Your mother, all of us, really, are trying hard to understand what you're going through. None of us want to pressure you into anything, but as a minister it sincerely saddens me when one of my congregation leaves. I feel partly responsible, especially for a young woman like yourself, and for what this is doing to your family."

"Um-hm." I nodded and pushed my foot through the slush gathered at the curb, watched it part around my boot. Pastor John had no idea what was going on with his own family and he knew even less about Vera and me. I noticed that he was wearing shoes with odd rubber sole protectors on them and wondered if the moisture had seeped over the line between protector and shoe.

"I'd like to help you, Sylvia, to talk about the decisions you've made and the choices that I think Christ wants to give you the strength to make, but I can't do that unless I believe you are in a place where you can really hear what He has to say." When I didn't say anything, he continued, "I've told your mother that she needs to get you back into her home if you're going to work this through, but she seems oddly reluctant to allow Social Services to intervene."

"Oddly reluctant?" I said. "Maybe she knows that social workers are going to be about as understanding as you've been. You don't really want to help either of us, do you? If I stay away from home, you can simply point at me and keep Vera off council." I started to get up, a bit off balance because I was still holding the posters, pins, and tape against my chest with two hands. "Thanks, but I don't think I need your kind of concern." I was standing boot-deep in slush, my feet beginning to ache from the cold.

Pastor John didn't respond, simply looked for a dry place to put his hands to hoist himself up from the curb. When he was standing, he said, "Well, I'm sorry you feel that way, Sylvia. I'll be praying for you. May you go in Christ."

"Goodbye," I said in return and turned, walked away.

Posters for Raise the Roof were put up in cafés up and down the valley – Cherryville, Salmon Arm, Kamloops, Kelowna – and people that Krista described as nutbars showed up from everywhere. Some brought instruments and formed bands on the spot with names like Nellie May's Backyard Blues Busters and the Salmon River Jug and Squirm Band. Tables were pushed back against the walls, a space by the wood stove was cleared for jamming, and kids and dogs ran an obstacle course around furniture and through legs.

In the shed, I smoked a joint with Gabe and Krista until we fell back on the bed laughing at our lack of ability to control basic motor functions or transfer simple thoughts from mind to mouth. Gabe told us that Thomas had some magic mushrooms.

"Oh, my God," Krista answered. "If I'd known there'd be shrooms, I would've brought a change of clothes. I always piss my pants when I do shrooms."

"Hey, since when have you done mushrooms?" I asked.

"Since a few weeks ago, with Mike and them."

"Why didn't you tell me?"

"I don't know. I didn't know it was such a big deal. Besides, we can do them now together." Krista seemed herself again, as though the awkwardness between us, her tears in the church, getting caught for shoplifting all had no bearing on the night ahead.

When we made our way to the cookshack, we found Thomas in the kitchen, leaning on the counter with a beer in his hand and a woman pressed against his thigh. Gabe pushed me forward, whispering in my ear, "You ask him. I'm not charming enough to get his attention now." I stood so close behind the woman that I could smell her scent – jasmine. Thomas was looking at his beer bottle while he drank from it. When the liquid slid down his throat, he raised his eyes and saw me there.

"Harper, hi," he reached around the woman. "Just a minute," he said to her as he pulled me between them, placed his arm on my shoulder and pinned me momentarily between the woman and his thigh. She moved away.

"Hey, can I talk to you?" I asked. He nodded and turned me around so he could guide me out of the kitchen, his hands on my shoulders. I saw the woman roll her eyes and shake her head. I smiled at her. We pushed through the room, winding our way through bodies, bumping up against them. I felt Thomas's chest against my back whenever we stopped. He brought me to the pantry, drew back the curtain, and we went in. This was not a neutral space. I moved out from under Thomas's hands, hoping that Gabe and Krista were close behind.

"What is it, Harper?" he asked.

"Uh, Gabe said you had some, um, mushrooms that we could do together. Gabe and Krista – have you met Krista? – and I were wondering if we could get some shrooms off you. I mean, if that's okay. Gabe said, um –"

Thomas threw back his head and laughed. "Drugs. You want drugs." His Adam's apple bobbed in his neck.

"Yeah, I mean, if that's okay." I backed up and reached for the curtain separating us from the rest of the party. When I did,

I hit the deep freeze and remembered being against it with Gabe. I felt the curtain being pulled out of my hand as it was moved aside. Krista and Gabe came into the pantry, blinking as their eyes adjusted to the lack of light.

"Oh, good," said Thomas, his voice suddenly jovial. "You must be Krista. I remember you from that first night you girls came out here." Gabe slid in to stand beside me. "So, Harper tells me you're interested in indulging," Thomas continued in a mock English accent, and paused. "Gabe, you think it's a good idea for these young ladies?"

"It's up to them, really."

"All right, then. How many grams does everyone want then? A couple grams each?"

Gabe's arm moved around my waist, drew me to him. "Maybe just one for Harp, hey, sweets?" he asked me.

"Sure. I mean, no. I'll do however many you do."

Thomas took our hands, opened our palms, and placed dried mushrooms in them.

"Just like this?" Krista asked. "I'm used to having them in chocolate."

"Well, well," said Thomas.

"We can brew them in tea," Gabe offered. "That might be better for Harper."

"No, it's okay," I insisted and lifted the dry bits to my nose. They didn't smell like much. While the other three watched, I shook them into my mouth, chewed. A mouldy, bitter taste hit the back of my throat and I gagged a little as I swallowed. Gabe and Krista laughed and gulped theirs down, then we made our way back into the room. Thomas was behind me.

He caught my hand for a moment, brushed his fingers against my palm. I drew it away slowly and followed Gabe's dark head through the crowd.

I had a bottle of beer as though it was a way to anchor myself to the room, smoked part of a joint to ease my passage into the effect of the mushrooms. I held Krista's hand, wanting her beside me when the drug hit. Gabe moved like water through the cookshack, one moment beside me, breath on my ear, hand on the small of my back, the next on the other side of the crowd or out of sight completely. Krista and I circled the room slowly, trying to find a place to sit down together. We made a nest out of jackets, coats, and scarves on top of one of the tables and sat there, waiting to get lighter.

When it happened, I felt air rise inside me like carbonation until it pricked my cheeks and filled my mouth. I held it as long I could, looking straight ahead.

"Aha!" Krista whispered. "It's hit you, hasn't it?" and began to giggle.

I avoided looking at her for as long as possible but faces and bodies began to merge, waver, and when they did I needed to look at something familiar to regain my bearings. When I turned toward Krista and saw her shining eyes and crazy hair like banners announcing her face, I burst out laughing.

"What?" Krista asked, joining me.

"Nothing! I just feel so fucking good!"

"I know! Isn't it great?!"

"Are we yelling?!"

We collapsed back on the table. Krista's head hit the window sill but this just made her laugh harder. I had my legs folded under me and I threw my head back, my spine arching like a bridge. When I tried to move, the laughter lodged me there. I imagined vocal cords straining against skin. I rolled myself over, onto Krista, so I could breathe again, then sputtered and laughed even louder. No one seemed to notice. The impromptu bands played on, people danced, children ran, babies wailed, and the sounds of the dogs that had been shooed outside came in through the open door.

The cookshack became a kaleidoscope of sound, colour, and movement. Gabe was with me, then he wasn't. Krista was beside me, or I forgot that she was at the farm at all. Every once in a while, I was caught up in the music and tried dancing but I felt self-conscious, my body foreign, unwieldy as it moved around me. I saw faces and mouths moving, and tried to listen, even feign conversation but I couldn't speak much, except to Gabe and Krista. We would gather in corners or along walls and attempt to relay conversations as we had heard them, but other people's words never formed the same thing in our mouths. This, in itself, was funny enough to have us laughing so hard we would fall to the floor, bend in on each other, get stuck in an inebriated version of Twister.

At some point, I saw the curtain door into the pantry pulled back, a corridor of people stretching beyond me. When I went toward them, I could feel cold air and searched for its source. The night was visible through the open door and I pushed my way through the pantry, gasped at air when I got outside. People were leaning up against the cookshack smoking cigarettes and joints. With the smell of cedar and the sensation of heat radiating from somewhere, I realized that someone had

started up the sauna. The sauna! I wanted to find Krista and
show her the bathhouse and sauna, show her where I showered,
practically outside, even in the dead of winter. As I moved back
toward the pantry, I heard someone yell, "Close the door, it's
freezing in here!" and watched as it slammed in front of my
face. I tried to turn the handle but it was stuck, locked from the
inside. People yelped in the bathhouse and each time the sauna
door was opened, I could hear wood cracking in the stove.

I went looking for Krista and Gabe. I wanted to see him
again, to feel his hands on me. I couldn't remember how long I
had been looking or where. I watched my feet, making sure that
I was still on the ground, but then I would walk into things and
remind myself to look up. I would never find them if I wasn't
looking up. I stopped on the porch, more than once, for a
smoke. A smoke to clear my head, bring me down, to help me
remember where to look.

I was crying when Thomas found me and brought me back
to the sauna. There were moments of blindness – the shirt
being pulled over my head, the first dark of the sauna. When
the air struck my skin, Thomas's hands tried to rub the cold
away, then led me into the heat. My mind seemed unable to
follow basic mental processes but my body took a fierce hold of
every sensation and experienced it acutely. "It's okay," I told
myself, feeling air on every part of my stripped body. "Everyone is naked in here. It's a sauna. It's okay." I sat between
Thomas's legs on the top bench, sobbing unevenly while he
rubbed my back, the skin and muscle stiffening, folding, yield-
ing. I could feel him growing hard. The stove opened and

closed to accommodate more wood; water was thrown on the rocks, creating a sputtering vapour. By the time the steam rose to the top bench, the wet heat pawed at me, the press and lick of flames. The sides of my throat seemed to be straining to meet each other, block out my breath. Muscles gripped bones and everything began to ache. I gasped and clutched at my neck, trying to find air. The heat pressed against me like walls.

Shh was the sound of Thomas's voice as he led me out of the sauna. *Shh* was the sound of the water over my head and in my ears. Who was in there with me? Later I would remember Thomas and Gabe both being there, but decided they couldn't have been. *Shh* was the sound I made when I saw Gabe's face on the other side of the steam, thought I saw him, clothed and standing outside the shower, like he had on the night he washed me and cut my hair. If he wasn't there, whose hands were washing me, who was holding me up? I heard the sounds of muffled yells, of words caught. My own throat wouldn't open. When I tried to force words up, out of it, when I tried to say something to Gabe, they lodged there. *Shh* was the only sound I heard as someone held me back, the feeling of lost words and water, skin and heat becoming one in that cramped place. *Shh* was the sound of someone dressing me, wrapping a blanket around my shoulders and holding me until the shaking stopped. It was the sound of someone rubbing my jaw to ease the clattering. *Shh*. It was Thomas's hand on my face again, the sky above us clear and pricked with stars.

I would understand, when I tried to piece together the night later, that Thomas was the person who walked me back to the shed. I thought I would be all right then. The fresh air entering my lungs reminded me of how it would feel to be sober, clean. I was sure sleep would come quickly and that when I woke everything would be back to normal but when I saw Krista's boyfriend, Mike, swaying and obviously drunk in the yard between the cookshack and shed, my mind skipped, tried to find a reference point. Behind him Rob Hanshaw bounced from leg to leg, spat into the dirt. I was confused, things colliding in my mind. Mike and Krista in the schoolyard the night after the party in November. My neck in the vice of Rob Hanshaw's arm in his truck. I pulled away from Thomas then reached back for him at once. As I did, Mike approached me, his words coming as though from different directions.

"Sylvia Harper. If it isn't sweet Sylvia Harper."

"Harper, this a friend of yours?" Thomas asked.

"Who the hell is this?" Mike said, pointing at Thomas with his chin.

Instead of answering I said, "I'll go find Krista," and moved away from all of them. "I'll go find Krista," I said again as though this was a reassurance, for myself or someone else.

"Why don't we all go try to find Krista, shall we?" Mike said. "It'll be a little game, eh, Hanshaw?" Rob Hanshaw didn't say anything, just stood behind Mike with his hands in his pockets, smirking. Thomas turned and made a motion with his head for me to follow. When we were on the front veranda, Mike got hold of my arm and snapped me back towards him.

He and Rob stood watching my reaction, laughing. Thomas had just gone in.

"Stoned, Harper?" Mike asked. He had his lighter out, flared it in front of my face. "Seeing lights?"

Then, with Mike still holding my arm, Rob Hanshaw leaned in. "Know what I'd like to do to you?" he asked. When I stared back at him, Rob continued, "I'd like to go down on you when you're on the rag, suck up all that blood, and then spit it back into your mouth."

I tried to hold my stare, to have them believe I wasn't intimidated, but Mike let go of me and I fell back. As they laughed, I stumbled up the steps to the porch and into the building. I wanted desperately to be sober again. To be safe. It would be all right, I told myself, all I had to do was find Krista. She'd know what to do. It would be all right. I pushed my way through the hall into the kitchen and found her. She was coming in the back door with Gabe, their cheeks taut, glazed with fresh air.

I looked at Gabe quickly then gripped Krista's forearm and said, "Mike's here." My hand shook as I did.

"What?" both she and Gabe said at once, then Krista continued, "Oh, God, I didn't think he would come. I bet he's drunk. Shit." I was still shaking, wanting to collapse against something or someone but Krista and Gabe were already moving out of the kitchen and back through the cookshack. When I got to the front porch, I could hear Mike before I could see anyone else.

"You slut. What did you think you were doing – you think I wouldn't figure out what you were doing?"

"No, Mike, I –"

Mike motioned toward Gabe. "And, what, everyone shares everyone out here? Bunch of fucking freaks."

I stopped in the door frame and watched the porch like a stage. Things seemed to move in slow motion. Mike's mouth gaping then clamping shut, the words coming out fast, his face twisting around them. Rob Hanshaw beside him, scowling and shifting his weight from heels to balls of feet, arms and hands twitching. Krista recoiling from Mike's words, her head turning from side to side, red curls bobbing and springing in a way that seemed almost cheerful, inappropriate. I lost focus when my eyes found Gabe. He seemed less defined, a blur of colour and shifting texture, as though I couldn't quite place him in the surroundings. I stepped out onto the porch in an attempt to get things into focus, people gathering behind me, pressing.

Mike caught one of Krista's wrists, held it stiff between them as though wielding a weapon against her. That was when things sped up. I moved quickly and somehow I got her away from Mike. Thomas came between Krista and me and the guys, telling them in a slow, controlled voice that they should leave. Mike stood, fists clenching and unclenching, releasing his breath in short, violent bursts, and stared around Thomas at Krista. "Come on, let's just move along," Thomas said again.

"Come on? Move along?" Mike said, shifting his gaze until it was directly on Thomas. "You think you've got it made out here, eh? While the rest of us are out working, busting our asses, you can just sit back, watch your weed grow, living off pogey. And now you've got these sweet teenage girls to pass around. Share and share alike, right? Can you even get it up, you old hippie? You scared we're going to take them away from you, huh?"

That's when Gabe lunged at him, knocking us aside as he did. Thomas tried unsuccessfully to hold him back. The rest of us stood as though paralyzed. In the light of the cookshack, it was Gabe's face that I watched, the set of his jaw, twist of his mouth. Somehow, those hostile expressions looked natural on Mike. Seeing them on Gabe frightened me. I closed my eyes and heard boots against wood, fists against fabric, then air expelled, guttural sounds bursting from chests, throats. When I opened my eyes, I saw blood on Gabe's face. "Stop!" I yelled, still holding Krista, who was struggling out of my grip. "Stop!"

Krista tore away from me and stood in front of Gabe and Mike, small movements betraying the conflict within her – as though she were lurching forward and holding back at once. The guys had paused and were staring each other down, transferring their weight, hands pumping fists, each waiting for the other to strike. As Gabe glared at Mike, it was as though all thought and emotion were wiped away, his expression revealing only an instinct, a need. And in this, I saw something familiar. I had seen the same thing happen to his eyes when we had sex – in that moment right before he came, an instant when his eyes were wiped of recognition, his need fierce, sharp and anonymous. Gabe struck out again, and I felt nauseated. Mike dodged him and Krista moved between the two of them, arms held out as though to protect herself, wild panic and anger across her face. She turned to Mike and yelled, "You bastard! Get out of here!"

Gabe and Mike stood mirroring each other, shaking the men off, still staring each other down. Their stances began to slacken slightly – breath slowing, shoulders and hands loosening – but they seemed intent on holding their hard gaze. It was Gabe who broke it, turning abruptly and pushing people out of the way as he went back into the building.

"Come on, Hanshaw," Mike said when he did. "Let's go. These people aren't worth our time." He stopped at the top of the steps, turned to Krista and said, "I'll leave your diaphragm at the end of my driveway. With the trash," and walked down the stairs. Rob Hanshaw cocked his head, looked at me, spat once on the porch and followed.

Krista and I were against the railing, holding each other. Ordinary things – the banister, steps – started coming into focus, blunt and heavy. My throat felt raw. I could feel Krista shaking in my hold. "Bastard!" she yelled out again. I wasn't sure if it was intended to reach Mike or if it was simply a statement.

Thomas came through the crowd, stopped and turned, said loudly to the people around us, "Would you clear out of here? Come on already." With a few more glances in our direction, everyone filed into the building or moved to the other end of the porch, lit cigarettes, tried not to look at us.

I pulled away from Krista and asked, "You okay?"

Krista nodded and swallowed. She said quietly, "I just want to go home. Can I get a ride home?"

"Of course you can," I said.

"Where's Gabe?" asked Thomas.

"He went inside," I said. "I'll go look for him." I looked at Krista, ran my hand over her hair and asked, "Will you be okay for a sec?" When she nodded, I turned back into the cook-shack. The party had begun to die down. I asked people if they had seen Gabe, but no one had. He must have gone out another door. I was drawn through the building and out the back to the edge of the field, as though it were a magnet and I was a piece of something hard, metal. I clung to stretches of wire between barbs, listened to the sound of the wind. The field stretched from white to grey to black.

The effects of the drug reared up again. I went back into the cookshack but couldn't find either Gabe or Krista. I was alone and the world was jumping, sounds and images all flowing into one stream, everything becoming a buzzing in my ears. I sat down against the wall and pulled my knees to my chest, wrapped my arms around them to stop the movement but my own shaking wouldn't cease. There is a space here in my memory, a missing piece. Someone found me there, stopped the shaking. I remember being put to bed, the blankets smoothed tight under my chin. *Shh.* That sound again. I don't know who put me there. *Shh.* The sound of sleep.

I dropped into slumber quickly and was pulled out just as abruptly by yelling, growling engines, tires in the yard, sirens coming from somewhere. I battled the blankets and reached for Gabe to ask what was happening but realized that he wasn't there. The yelling wouldn't stop. It was joined by what sounded like commands and another sound, like wind, roaring wind. I sat up against the wall, pulling the blankets around me.

"Gabe?" I called out, knowing no one would hear me. The wail of sirens was getting louder, coming closer. I reached under the blankets to feel my body, ran my hands over each limb – they felt normal, fine. I decided I was no longer stoned. Someone had dressed me in long underwear and wool socks before putting me to bed.

The sirens advanced, the shouting continued. The fact of Gabe's absence seemed more frightening than whatever was going on outside, or as if it was a cause of it. I heard a sound like the sky snapping, things cracking. I pulled myself out of bed and groped for clothes I could put on, for things I could hold in the spinning room. I pulled on jeans, sweaters, boots, and reached for my coat on a hook at the door. I held it for a moment with both hands, pressed my forehead to the wall, which was sur-prisingly hot, then moved again. I knew that I had to get out. I knew too that there was a fire and that I had been forgotten – that someone had brought me back to the shed and put me to bed and then hadn't come back for me. I opened the door and then stood against the shed as a fire truck roared into the farm-yard. Without moving, I watched firefighters run at the flames that jumped and rose around the cookshack and sauna, pulling hoses with them. I tried to lay my body flat against the wall, tried to become part of something solid and standing, and heard the roar of the heat that coated me.

As I watched, the fire seemed to be moving from the back of the building to the front. I could see through the two huge front windows that the kitchen was gone, a wall of flames. As the fire moved forward, I could see the wood stove, tables, couches. Things became black forms against shades of red.

The heat was too much and I was too close. I knew this, but felt unable to move. Firefighters were flooding the back of the building when the two front windows burst out of their frames. With the sound of shattering glass, I ducked.

It was as though the fire had taken a giant gulp of air. When I raised my head again, I couldn't see any more shapes, only flames, and I watched as one rode the wire between cookshack and shed, the wire Gabe had hooked up for the phone we never installed. The flame hit a tree between me and the building and began consuming branches. A firefighter doused the tree before the flames spread, the spray from his hose loud and violent. I remained immobilized, my body reacting to the fire and my fear with momentary paralysis. That was when the firefighter saw me. "What in God's name are you doing!" he yelled. "Get out of here – you have to go!" He pointed his finger behind me. When I turned, I could see people in the farmyard, all moving toward the field where the cars were parked. Some ran, hands over mouths. Others reminded me of people coming out of the arena after a game, as though there was no huge rush but no reason to hang around longer either.

I searched for Gabe's figure among the group, wrapped my arms around my chest and ran towards them, coughing up smoke. Susan went by at a kind of slow jog, then stopped and backed up when she saw me. "My God, Harper, you're still here? We have to go. They're clearing us out of here."

"Where's Gabe –? Have you seen Gabe?"

"Yes, he's fine. Come on, we have *got* to go."

"What about Krista, do you know about Krista?" My words raced with my mind. "Maybe we can wait for them. The fire's almost out. Look." I turned and saw the black outlines of men against the dying fire, smoke. The cookshack was nearly gone, a skeleton of what had stood there before, the remaining frame buckling with the force of water blasted at it. I couldn't understand how the place where we had gathered together a few hours before, the heart of the farm, was simply gone. The centre charred.

Susan sighed heavily, turned to walk briskly toward the field where trucks and cars had been parked. There were only few vehicles left and they sat revving engines, doors open while people yelled out. "Harper," she shouted over her shoulder. "There's no time for this now. Gabe will catch up with us. We have to go." I turned one last time to look at the fire. What remained was mostly smoke, some struggling flames being choked out. How odd, I thought, that something that had likely begun with one careless action had taken so much effort to stop.

GABE

Things keep coming back to you at the farm, as though now that you've returned to a place that's supposed to be "home," memories follow you there, lodge themselves around you like fence posts. Images are driven into your mind but you resist finding the links between them, don't want the connective tissue to form a fence around you.

You see the van leaving the land thirteen years before, dust rolling behind it, a vantage point you never would have had. You didn't know then that you should have been sad, that you were leaving your mother and everything you knew behind. It seems like years passed before you remembered to miss Susan at all. What kind of person are you, you wonder. If you don't miss your own mother you must be capable of other insensitivities. Even now, when you seek Susan out, it is for appearance's sake only. You don't enjoy spending time with her. She chain-smokes, speaks in a string of sarcastic comments, and looks at you with too much need in her eyes, though she will never admit to wanting anything from you.

You see your old house in Arcana, the yard backing onto forest, your legs kicked up on the railing around the deck. In this image, your face is missing. You see your hands instead, wrapped around a cup, the sight of steaming liquid so authentic that you can smell the coffee. You were allowed to drink it too soon, you now believe. Something was stunted in you, some ability to connect with other people. You set yourself apart from Peter, Anise, and the girls, out on that balcony, your back toward the house, eyes looking into the trees. You try to recall how free those times felt, despite the girls shrieking in the background and the voices of Peter and Anise in various states of disorganization. The rest of your life was still open then. What you thought of, those times alone on the deck, was leaving – the possibility that your life, genuine and waiting to be fulfilled, existed elsewhere, just waiting for you to step into it.

You have always imagined where you are at any given time as a point on a map. In your mind's eye, the map lies flat, north at the top, and you are simply a speck on the page. You've often wondered how other people visualize where they are – if they see it in more than two dimensions, if they can see the land rising up, rolling out around them rather than just paper. You can't imagine phone lines stretched over landscape so you draw them as straight lines on your mental map. You haven't talked, really talked, to anyone from California since you've been in Canada. Peter doesn't have long distance calling rights and neither of you is good at writing letters. As for the guys from home, there is nothing you can talk about with any of them on the phone. Yours were friendships that were dependent on place and situation, fuelled by running commentaries that required the assessment of girls, magazines, or dope to keep you going. Anise has put your sisters on the phone a couple of times but it's as though none of you know what to say to one another. The worlds that you are all now living in, you on the farm, they in the housing co-op, are different from the place you knew together. The split level on a cul-de-sac, a memory.

Images of Anise and the girls wandering the house in T-shirts and panties seep into the edges of your days. You can see the smooth limbs of your sisters twisted around each other in sleep, piled up on Anise's bed where they all slept in those weeks before you left. Any of your other thoughts can peel back to expose Anise's legs crossing and unfolding. You are ashamed to admit that you miss her more than you ever did Susan. You try to convince yourself that it's the years of her raising you, the years when she acted as your mother, that you miss, but what you remember is the smooth lick of her tongue in your mouth. Thankfully, you have read enough "Letters to Penthouse" to realize that this isn't unusual. Fantasies about sex with forbidden partners are standard issue, sexy stepmothers up there in that category. But you did more than fantasize, returned to her more than once. Your tongue looked so rough when held out to your reflection in the mirror, all bumps and crevices, but in her mouth it felt wiped flush. You returned just to feel that.

You spend a lot of time thinking about all of this. Too much time. All those images and memories continually shift around you and you are never on stable ground. You like to walk at night, the fields glowing with snow, to regain some sense of your footing. Night seems the right time to do this, everything slow and conceivable then. Days sear with too much urgency. Sometimes you try to sleep through the insistence of daylight, the sky bearing down on you, even through the curtains. Other times it is the sheer mass of clouds that keeps you horizontal. Brenda, a woman at the farm, tells you that this is natural, you are experiencing SAD, seasonal affective disorder. You have wondered more than once how people can grow up and continue to live in this valley, pushing through banks and banks of heavy grey every winter. Even the sun provokes melancholy. You know it is bound to be marred by cloud cover soon after it appears and it seems to demand something of you in the meantime.

For all the pressure that you feel, no one has actually asked anything of you. Even Harper, who lies beside you at night, asks little. She slides next to you in the bed, arches her back and moans in ways that make you wonder if you've hurt her, and turns away satiated by what little you offer. You try to tell her some of this but, because she has asked for so little, you know this would be more than she could be expected to understand.

You had always assumed that adulthood was about discernible burdens, demands. You realize now that pressure doesn't come in neat packages, distinct and identifiable, easily separated. Instead, pressure builds like a invisible layer on your skin until it forms a membrane. On the night of the fire, you try to break through it. You lash out in an attempt to lose sight, to render yourself blind to everything going on around and inside you. Without this sight, you feel free, as though there is a purity to your actions. There is nothing but your anger and his, muscles and fists tensed. Bone, teeth, skin, blood. Later, you won't be able to describe how good it feels. Better than sex because that act brings so many other things with it.

When we were evacuated from the farm, we were told to go to Motel 6, where we crowded into the lobby, tired and reeking of smoke at three in the morning. There was a fire department official at the desk with the receptionist, taking our names. "Your whole family here?" he asked Susan when it was her turn at the counter.

"No. My son, Gabriel Miller. I think he'll be back at the farm now. I don't know if he knows where to find us."

"There're still a few guys there. Fire's taken care of and it seems no one was hurt. We'll have them bring him and the others here in short order. And her?" he gestured to me.

"She's with us."

I was put in a room with Susan and Brenda. They shared a bed. Susan sat on top of the covers, completely clothed, not saying a word or glancing in my direction. I watched as she opened the drawer in the bedside table. She slid out the Gideon Bible and pulled pages from it, folded them into small origami cranes, her fingers moving quickly. I watched as she drew the crease delicately through her pinched nails. Sometimes her nails would catch the fine paper and it would rip. She would curse and toss it aside. I fell asleep watching her hands move, attempting to guess how many cranes made for each page ripped.

Gabe must have come in sometime during the night. I woke in the morning to a warm place beside me in the bed, the sound of Susan and him talking on the other side of the motel door, Susan's voice slightly raised. A pile of crumpled paper and origami cranes, tattooed with words, spilled over the bedside table and onto the floor. Gabe came into the room at the same time that Brenda emerged from the bathroom.

"Love motel bathrooms," she announced. "Little soaps, little shampoos, everything folded and white – like your life can be so compact and manageable here."

"Susan's gone to the diner for breakfast. I think they're giving it to us for free," Gabe said to Brenda while he looked at me. I looked back, saw his cracked lip, the cut above his eye.

"Little shampoos, free breakfast – what could be better, hey?" Brenda said as she left the room.

Gabe sat down on the side of the bed. I reached out to touch his face, the places where he was cut, then stopped. "May I?" Gabe just shrugged and looked away. I let my hand drop.

"They started the fire, didn't they?"

"Those two assholes? Yeah, who else would've? Jerks. Went to a party in town and bragged about it afterward, no less. Susan's pretty pissed off that they ended up at the farm."

I sat up in the bed and asked, "Where were you last night? I woke up in the shed alone."

"I was giving Krista a ride home," he answered evenly.

"Oh, my God – is she okay?"

"Krista's fine. Her boyfriend's a total psychopath but she's fine – I got her out of there before the fire even started."

I tucked the bedspread under my arms and smoothed it across my chest. "Oh, well, I'm glad you were looking out for one of us."

He paused, his eyes on me for a moment before they settled in a corner of the room. "Listen, she was really strung out. I can't be everything for you, Harper."

"I didn't know you were trying to be," I said and then realized how far I was already from my original intent. "Are you okay?" I asked.

When he shrugged and continued to look away, I asked, "What happened? What made you blow like that? I'd expect that kind of thing from Mike but –"

"What happened?" Gabe's eyes were back on mine. He shook his head and said, "Well, I guess I could ask you the same question. Last night was fucked up, right Harper? And I'm not talking about just the fight, or the fire, although those certainly both qualify."

"Oh. I get it – change of subject. What are you talking about then?"

"Harp, you can't keep falling back on this innocence thing."

"Okay, Gabe, I'll fall back on the ignorance thing. I don't know what you're talking about." He gave me his best cold stare. I mirrored it back. As I did, I could feel it slip, could feel the heat of the sauna, the smooth path made by a soaped palm on my back. I looked down at my hands, then at the pile of paper cranes.

When I didn't say anything else, Gabe said, "Yeah, right. Okay then, Harp." After a few minutes of silence, he said, "Look, do you want to go for breakfast?"

"No. I'm not hungry. I'm just tired, so tired." I slid back down to the pillow.

He turned and looked at me, and I when reached my arm towards his face, he leaned in. I touched the cut above his eye. I let my fingertips rest there, feeling the heat under his skin. Gabe watched my face, then brought his hand down slowly to my temple, pinched pieces of my hair between thumb and forefinger. Without a word, he folded back the sheets, got into the bed with me. It was what I had wanted him to do the night before. I let him wrap around my body from behind, closed my eyes and tried to create warmth, forget everything else.

Susan and Brenda returned from the diner and woke us from our brief sleep.

"Well, they've fed us, now they're giving us the boot," Susan said. "Seems they've caught the little bastards and I guess there's not much else they can do for us now."

Gabe got out of bed and dressed as though no one was there, not me or Susan or Brenda. I dragged the sheet from the bed, wrapped it around me, trailing paper cranes as I went to the bathroom. I adjusted the water so it was as hot as I could bear, then stood under the spray without washing. When I got out of the shower, the room was heavy with steam, and I could hear Susan and Gabe talking.

"She hardly even knows them for God's sake. Mike is Krista's boyfriend. Get off this already."

"All I'm saying is that not everyone belongs at the farm – I mean, not everyone chooses to live like us and we don't choose to live with just anyone."

Brenda interjected. "We just can't ever know how things will turn out. Who's to say they wouldn't have been there? Who's to say that someone else wouldn't have started the fire? Maybe it was simply supposed to go. We never know why these things happen."

I chose this moment to emerge from the bathroom and they each turned to look at me. Without saying a word, I crossed the room to the bed, picked up my clothes, dropped the towel, and got dressed.

I called Vera from the motel, knowing she would hear about the fire soon. I told her that I was fine, that I was going back to the farm and she shouldn't worry, though I knew those two things were no doubt mutually exclusive. We drove back to the Pilgrims without speaking, Gabe, Susan, myself, and Brenda, who sang along to the bits of lyrics she knew on the radio. We all listened when the news came on. ". . . While it is now safe to return to their homes, many of the residents have lost belongings in the fire. Needed are food and kitchen supplies as well as building materials. Donations can be dropped off at the Sawmill Creek Community Centre. Two local youths are being questioned in connection to the blaze."

Susan snapped the radio off, laughed once and said, "Local youths," nothing else.

I had heard expressions about ashes settling but never realized that it did, in fact, take time. When we pulled into the farmyard, the air was grey, still mottled with ash, and each step we took unsettled it. Susan asked Gabe if she could speak to him. Telling me he'd be a minute, he followed her to the A-frame. I talked with a couple of people who were milling in the yard, looking at the place where the building had been. We crossed our hands over our chests and heaved sighs. I went to the shed alone, sat on the bed, the sheets and blankets still the mess I had left them, and felt my back rise and fall against the wall as I breathed in, out.

When Gabe returned, he sat down on the bed, reached out for one of my ankles, then held it, rubbing light circles around the bone.

"She okay?" I asked.

"All right. She's just upset about the cookshack and everything." Gabe dropped his head and, keeping one hand on my ankle, he rubbed the other across his forehead, again and again.

"I know. We all are, I guess."

He stopped moving and looked at me. "Yeah, but we can't understand what it's like for them – for the people who've been here for years. I mean, my parents helped build the thing. I guess Thomas will be telling you all about how he's feeling soon enough, though."

"Is that what this is about?"

"You tell me, Harp."

"Listen, I don't know what happened between me and Thomas last night. Whatever it was, I was stoned and I can't even remember. It was the first time I did mushrooms. You can't hold that against me."

"No, not this time."

"There won't be another time." I paused to gauge his reaction, but Gabe was looking away. "I guess it would've made things a lot more comfortable for you if I'd never come, wouldn't it?"

He groaned. "Harper, give it a rest," he said and fell back against the mattress, covering his eyes with his hands. "What do you want me to say to that?"

"I don't know."

"No, it wouldn't have," he said to the ceiling.

"Look at me when you say that."

Gabe sat up, then looked at me without wavering. "No." In that moment, he seemed tired. Tired in a way that it didn't seem sleep would be able to help. I knew we were leaving things unresolved, but I didn't want to press either one of us then.

The entire cookshack had burned to the ground along with the sauna and the bathhouse. The fire made the front page of the *Sawmill Creek Chronicle*. In the photo, specks and clusters of newsprint grey conveyed a pile of ashes and charred wood. At the farm, the fire site didn't seem as simple. Parts of the cookshack were completely gone, yet some pieces of furniture seemed virtually untouched by the fire. They sat eerily, waterlogged and grey, where they had before. The deep freeze was there, streaked with black, with no pantry left standing around it.

In the article, Rob Hanshaw was named as a suspect who was being charged with arson but Mike was a young offender and couldn't be identified. I would hear the story repeated and elaborated as it moved from newspaper to second-hand accounts in the high school hallways. Most versions had Mike and Rob going to a party in town and bragging about burning the commune down, expecting, it seemed, to be commended rather than arrested.

As I walked through the halls on Monday morning, people approached me with a mixture of sympathy and excitement but it was Krista I wanted to see. I had tried to call her repeatedly the day before, each time going to Brenda's cabin instead of the cookshack as I once would've done. Each time not getting any answer.

I found her waiting at my locker. "Thank God. Where were you yesterday? I was calling all day," I said.

"I didn't feel like talking to anyone. I told Therese not to answer the phone."

I put my bag in my locker and the bell rang. We waited until the hall cleared, then I slid to the floor, back against the lockers, and Krista followed my lead. We bent our legs off the floor.

"So," I said.

"So," Krista responded.

"I just wanted to know if you were okay." I looked at the

side of her face while she stared ahead. "I mean, that was horrible what Mike did, the way he treated you and everything."

"I'm fine, Harper," she said and pulled her legs closer to her chest.

I dropped my knees and balanced a heel on the tip of the opposite shoe and transferred my weight from foot to foot. "Are you sure? I mean, it was a pretty crazy night. It's okay if –"

"I said I was fine."

"Oh," I said, stopped moving my feet. "Okay."

After we hadn't said anything for a minute, I asked, "So, have – have you talked to Mike?"

"Of course not." Krista got up from the floor quickly. "What kind of person do you think I am?"

I tried to tell her that I hadn't meant anything by it, but Krista had picked up her bag and was already walking down the hall.

The old Kostak farmhouse, the one Vera grew up in, has been rented out since her father died. When she and Jim Harper return to Alberta, it is sitting empty, a neighbouring farmer using the fields for a small fee. It is Vera who comes up with the idea. She still can't shake the feeling that the so-called *scene* in San Francisco was a sham. They had to go there and return to find out what they really want, where they belong. She wants to move back into the farmhouse, not as her old house but as her new home.

They move into the farmhouse, Vera's brother-in-law charging them less than he would someone who wasn't family. Jim Harper's father hooks him up with some work for the district. Regional Works and Maintenance it's called. Jim drives around in a truck all day, stopping every once in a while to fix things, as far as Vera can tell. She sees him off every morning, then sets to work, rids walls of yellowing wallpaper, heaves the linoleum off the floor – not easy as it is so old it has been worn right into the wood in places – sands every bit of wood down to the grain. When the entire interior of the house is stripped of what was there before, of even the lingering smell of her father's pipe tobacco, Vera feels an incredible sense of peace. She doesn't paint, paper, or furnish the house at once. She wants to remain in this space, wide-open and free, it seems, of everything that came before it, everything to come. Sometimes, when she sees Jim off to work, she stays out on the porch with a cup of tea. The fields are turning golden with the changing season, the air has an edge. Vera feels like she is a full season away from the girl that she was in this same place. The same person, but everything is different.

When she gets pregnant, her sisters assure her that she'll be sick and tired most of the time but she surprises everyone, except herself, when she isn't. She moves through the first trimester without morning sickness and in the fourth or fifth month, mania hits. Vera rolls paper onto the walls, using an intricate system of stepladders and chairs to reach every corner. She paints each frame, sill, and bit of trim with precision, after a while not even using tape to keep her edges straight. She goes to bed late, exhausted. She is relieved that Jim is usually already asleep. She hasn't wanted to have sex in weeks. There are bigger, more exciting things to think about.

By the time I am born, the farm house is a new world, brightly painted and sparkling, homemade baby preserves lined up in jars in the cellar. And then, something happens. It's as though in pushing the baby out of her, Vera has pushed out her ability to desire anything. The house is finished and furnished, Jim has work, the baby, who at one time seemed as simple as a room she was thinking of redoing, is there. And the baby is much more complicated. She is a little human and Vera isn't quite sure how she feels about her. Two years later when Nicholas is born, paint is already chipping, the walls need washing, and Vera sends Jim to the grocery store for a supply of Gerber food.

She has braced herself for another bout of post-partum depression and when it arrives Vera tries to tell Jim how she feels but he says, "It's nothing to worry about. Lots of women get it. It's natural." For Jim, if something can be described as natural, then you shouldn't try to change it. He kisses Vera on the forehead and goes back to Fly Hills in the evenings to meet the guys from work at the bar. He still stitches a fine story, attracts a following wherever he goes. Jim likes it in Fly Hills – the simple, honest work, the simple, honest friends. The farmhouse on a piece of land, a beautiful wife, two infants toddling around in various states of glee or torment. It's all so natural, so easy.

Vera has got to get out. The wide-open peaceful space in the farmhouse has filled up with laundry, dishes, and toys. Few friends come out to visit her on the farm, and she has no vehicle to get in or out of town. She spends most of her time with two people under the age of four and she is afraid that she will start to babble and wail along with them.

I don't remember much from that time, though I can piece together a few uneven memories. We go for walks down back roads, Nick's stroller rattling on the dirt or rough asphalt. Vera tells me things – the names of plants that grow in the ditch; how one day we'll move to a place where there are other kids to play with; how to tell a girl bird from a boy bird. On one of these walks, Nick starts to cry and won't stop. We walk for a while, Vera talking over his wail, then she leans down to the stroller and shakes it, saying to Nick, "What is it? What *is* it?" This scares me. They are both red faced, Nick with tears, Vera with an emotion I can't identify. Then Vera stops shaking the stroller, takes Nick's knotted face in both of her hands and her frustration dissolves. She picks him up and holds him. Nick doesn't stop crying and Vera drops to the ground on the edge of the road, breath leaving her nostrils like blows to the air, then slowing. We all sit there for a long time. Eventually Nick stops crying and Vera's breath lengthens and quietens. I stand at my mother's side and pat her shoulder like I've seen people do. After what seems like hours, a car goes by and, as if this is our signal, we get up off the side of the road, keep walking.

It was Gabe who told me what the word equinox meant. The word did not refer to pagan ritual as I had been led to believe but something that happened in the sky. Things that lined up, equi-distances, the equator. The days leading up to equinox felt like walking up the unsteady plank of a seesaw. In some ways, I must have never wanted to reach the middle, that place where things finally levelled out, only to slide down the other side. I never wanted to find out that there was no middle ground, no resting place.

In the aftermath of the fire the absence of the cookshack had become an entity itself. Something that demanded attention, like a hum or high-pitched buzz. When you looked for its source, you couldn't find it, yet it was always there. The grey hollow place where the building had once stood couldn't be overlooked and it set things off balance somehow, threw into relief what was left behind. We all tried to find our place at the farm again without the cookshack as a reference. It may have been easier for me. I had never quite found my place there.

For others, the absence of the building at the centre of the farm seemed to initially confuse them, then bring them together. I saw people in the farm yard between buildings more often, stopping when they walked by, sometimes carrying on conversations for up to half an hour while standing, shifting from foot to foot and rubbing their hands in the cold. People dropped in on others more often. Brenda even came over to the shed one night. It wasn't the best space to receive visitors, but we did our best, Brenda and I sitting on the bed, Gabe on a chair, as we talked, tried to sort out what it all meant. Thomas kept to himself and I didn't see much of him. Gabe and I went over to Susan's for meals a couple of times, but although his mother could never be accused of being blatantly rude, I didn't feel comfortable there.

As we moved toward spring, Gabe was like a silhouette of a person; a shadow against snow. He didn't talk about his memories or his ideas any more and when he talked about the other people on the farm, it was most often to drop an off-handed cynical comment – *He's been here so long, he doesn't know what's going on in the rest of the world*, or *She thinks that throwing clay can cure cancer.* I continued to go to school and he would still appear, truck idling on the edge of the parking lot, to pick me up but he would rarely disclose what he had done that day. Even when I asked, he answered with a shrug or a non sequitur. I missed even those bewildering rote explanations that he used to give me – his descriptions of taking apart the guitar; how flawless the pieces were when separated from the whole, or about of his research into forms of wood and ways to make trees fall in the forest with minimum impact.

"How's that eco-forestry thing going?" I asked one afternoon on the ride home. "You think you guys will start it this spring?"

Gabe didn't answer me at once, then said, "I don't know if it'll be that easy."

"Oh."

"Sometimes, I think we should all be able to just do things, you know. Just decide to do things and then do them. Sometimes it seems like I'll never be able to just make a simple decision and act on it in my life."

I couldn't make sense of what he was saying but I said, "I know what you mean," nonetheless.

Evenings, I bent over homework, tried to gain understanding of the two subjects that had continued to elude me since the ninth grade: algebra and French. If I could accept how numbers and symbols could be assigned values, if I could form thoughts in another language and bring them down the canal from mind to mouth, perhaps I would also have the capacity to comprehend what was eating away at Gabe. Perhaps I would be able to escape my own patterns of thought long enough to glimpse his.

Sleep came like dreams of falling, except I didn't jerk awake before landing. Later in the night I would wake, and even when I opened my eyes, the sensation of the bed tilting or swaying under me didn't stop. I would reach out for something steady to hold on to and would often find that Gabe was already gone from the bed, the blankets on his side carefully folded back. Sometimes, there was no light, no sound to indicate that he had gone or when he came back, only puddles of melted snow around his boots in the morning. Other times, light from the workshop half of the shed was a slice under the door, sounds I could barely identify strained through the wall. I imagined what they were. That is the sound of diagrams traced in pencil then torn from paper; that is the sound of thin wood snapping.

Gabe and I no longer had a kitchen. We used the microwave in the shed, Susan's kitchen when we had to. She was civil to me, never warm. A couple of weeks after the fire, she asked me over for coffee.

Susan placed a cup of mug in front of me and sat down. She had already stirred in soy milk and brown sugar. "Harper," she started. "I know you must feel – or, I don't know but Gabe's told me – that you feel as though I'm excluding you in a way."

"Well, not exactly. I just get the sense that you don't want me here. That you blame me somehow for the fire."

"I know you had nothing to do with the fire, Harper. Those two probably never would've been here if it weren't for, well – but I know you are in no way responsible." When I didn't say anything, Susan continued. "It's not the fire, it's Gabe."

"What about Gabe?"

"He just moved here. He hasn't even been able to get his bearings yet. I just don't know if this is the best time for him to be in a relationship."

"Oh." I thought for a moment, then said, "Don't you think Gabe should be the person to decide that?"

"He's so young. You're young, Harper. I just think that you and Gabe should take a step back, think about this."

Anger rose in the back of the throat, but my voice came out quiet and thin, as though strained around the sensation. "And I guess you want me to take a step back right off the farm. Well, I'll go when Gabe asks me to. Don't be too surprised if we leave together."

"Harper. It's not –" Susan reached out like she was going to touch my hand. I got up from the table and thanked her for the coffee that I hadn't taken even a sip of and walked out the door. The path to the farmyard was slick with melting snow and new mud. From the small rise on which her A-frame sat, I could see past where the cookshack had been, the fields going on until they met forest or road.

Gabe's truck was gone from the yard. I went into the shed

to check if he was there, nonetheless. When he wasn't, I left, walked the dirt driveway to the road, crossed it and jumped the fence into the neighbouring cow pasture. The cattle had etched paths across the fields and I found easier footing on them than the wet ground mounded with hummocks. I followed a cow trail that led up a hill covered in low scrub, my legs weak from a winter of relative inactivity. The cows had eaten a path up to a small outcrop of rocks at the top. I sat there and looked down, watching vehicles corner ninety-degree angles on the roads and climb, telling myself I wasn't watching for Gabe's truck. The sky was a high wash of white. Sawmill Creek was surreal under the haze of mill smoke. It began to get dark and still he hadn't returned. I made my way back to the farm.

When I entered the gates, I walked across the dirt yard past the barn where Thomas's loft was. I hadn't gone to see him since the fire and I decided to then. I knew the narrow door on the side that opened to the steps leading to the loft would be open. I didn't knock but stopped midway up the stairs, called out to him and waited until he said something. From where I stood, I could see a kettle on the stove, a lit burner.

I heard movement, papers shuffling. "Come in," Thomas said, his voice sounding flat, resigned. When I came the rest of the way up the stairs, he was sitting at the table, papers spread out around him, staring at the space at the top of the stairs where he knew I would appear. He watched me look at him and blinked back without expression.

"Are you busy, Thomas?" I asked. "Am I bothering you?"

"What is it, Harper," he said, a statement rather than a question.

Though he didn't sound very welcoming, I walked into the room and sat down across from Thomas at the table. "Um, well," I started and stopped, then started again, blurting, "I think Susan wants me to leave the farm. She doesn't think Gabe should be in a relationship now."

Thomas looked at me carefully, then got up and walked to the counter, turned around, and leaned back, crossed his arms over his chest. "And I'm taking it you don't want to leave."

"No, that's not it. I mean, no, I don't want to go but that's not the point. The point is, what does she know about Gabe and me? How can she know when he should or shouldn't be in a relationship?"

Thomas turned so that one hand was on the countertop and dropped his head slightly. He appeared to think for a moment before he said, "Harper, to be honest with you, I don't know if I'm the right person for you to talk to about this." When I didn't say anything, Thomas continued, "Look, you can choose to stay here, at the farm, you know that, but there's nothing I can do for you. You have to realize that this is probably about more than just you and Gabe. That fire has affected a lot of people. Some people have spent years making this their home and to have such an important part of it gone, just that like that, well, it causes us all to reconsider things."

"I know." I looked down at the papers spread on the table.

When I touched the edge of one with a finger, Thomas offered, "Insurance" by way of explanation.

Withdrawing my hand as though he had reprimanded me, I pushed away from the table and moved toward the stairs. At the top, I paused. "Thomas." He was turned toward the counter then, both hands flat on the surface. I took his lack of response as a sign to continue. "Did anything happen the night of the fire? I mean, anything between us that I can't remember?"

Thomas turned around. Steam rose from the kettle behind him. He looked straight into my eyes for the first time since I'd been there. "No. You were stoned. Gabe was nowhere to be found. I got you out of the cold and put you to bed."

I felt something flare up in me then – disappointment or resentment. The kettle began to wail. I didn't know if Thomas was being completely honest with me. "Too bad." I said. Thomas continue to look straight into my eyes. "I hope you're all right," I said and turned, walked down the stairs. I hadn't said what I wanted to say, but I wasn't sure I knew what that was.

GABE

Your first complete memory is this: It is fall and Peter and the other fathers on the farm have collected a spring and summer's worth of fallen trees, leaves, dead wood. Twigs and dry vines that the garden has expelled off the edges of its harvest. They are going to burn it all in a bonfire in the middle of the farmyard and sparks will scale the sky. In the late afternoon, before it is lit, you and the other kids circle the pile and mimic things that make the adults wonder whose children you are, where you have learned these roles. You are Indians pounding the earth with your feet, hands clapping open mouths to mute war cries before letting them burst out again. You are soldiers who believe that the pile holds power, that to bow down before it is to receive strength for battle. And so you do – drop to the ground and gather dirt in your fists, smear it on your faces, then argue whether it is war paint or camouflage, if it can be both.

At some point during this ritual, you realize that this has happened before. Last year, the fathers gathered the things that hadn't lived through the summer and burned it all before the first snow fell. Then, as now, you united around the unburned pile with other kids and shared a sense of reverence, excitement. You knew then that it would be gone soon, and in such a

spectacular way. Fire climbing so high it would challenge the
night, spark new stars. It all makes sense to you now. In a few
weeks, the snow will fall. After a few months, the farmyard will
turn to mud and things will smell wet and achingly green. This
will be spring. Summer will follow, when the yard turns to dust
and the sun makes you so delirious that you stumble through
the heat until your mother finds you, demands you accept shade
and water. And then, it will all happen again.

You arrive at a sudden understanding of seasons, there in
front of the scrap pile. You may have had some inkling of them
changing before, but never before this moment have you realized how certain they are, how persistent. How they will
happen every year without fail and each time one passes, you
will be older and already into the next without knowing how
you got there. You have no idea of how to explain how happy
this new knowledge makes you, how peaceful. You want to tell
someone – the other kids, Peter, Susan, anyone – but you can't
find the right words. Years later, you will tell Harper what this
meant to you. You tell her when you have returned to the farm,
the place where you began, and this early memory comes to
you, complete.

You are determined that this memory will always remain
whole. Now that you have retrieved it, you will keep it intact.
Unfortunately, other recollections have unravelled to such an
extent that you don't seem able to follow the threads of your
own thoughts, your own stories. How much have you remembered correctly? How much have you already forgotten?

You are tired of this – tired of trying to sort out where the
past ends and the present begins, which memories are accurate,

which you've embellished. You are tired of trying to figure out
what other people are thinking, what they think of you. It's
dangerous to try to imagine the coordinates of another mind,
even more so to lodge yourself in there.

*G*abe hadn't told me where he went the night I saw Thomas but that wasn't so unusual, and I'd become used to not asking. I knew the answers already – different versions of needing space, a place to think, time alone. I had convinced myself that we were each mature, independent, free. We didn't need to know where the other was at every moment.

Late that night when he returned, I simply said, "Hi," and started to get undressed for bed, as though his presence was all I needed for sleep.

"Hi," Gabe answered and did the same until we were both naked and lying in bed. We watched one another, our gaze moving from mouth to eyes and back, slowly, carefully, as though trying to discern if the other was a threat or a solace. I saw that the cut from eyelid to forehead was almost healed. It would leave a scar, a delicate white ridge to trace with a finger. I wanted to say something, to put words in the space between us, something to which we could respond or react. Because I was too tired to conceive of a way to broach the subject gradually, I said, "Your mother doesn't think you should be in a relationship."

"What?" He sat up quickly.

"I said, your mother –"

He cut me off. "I heard you the first time. How am I supposed to respond to that?"

"What do you mean, how are you supposed to respond? Try honestly. Try telling me what you think. Did you tell her that?"

Gabe didn't say anything for a moment. He stared straight ahead before turning to me. "Okay, you want honesty? No, I didn't tell her that, but I don't know if I should be in a relationship either. How's that? I don't even know if *I* want to be here let alone whether you should be here or not. I don't know where I'm supposed to be – I just feel so much pressure from all sides, and I know I shouldn't. I know I have no right to. I'm sorry, Harper – and I'm sorry about Susan. She had no business saying that to you."

"Too late." I knew what would come next, what usually came when we had exhausted our ability to use language. We stared each other down, emotions colliding until they became one thing, the desire to touch one another, or perhaps simply to touch something warm, malleable. Gabe started crawling up my body, pushing me into the mattress as he did. He balanced on his arms, kept his upper body weight raised as if challenging me to push him off or pull him down. He moved slowly, watching my face. I let him, kept every facial muscle still, held my eyes on his. It wasn't until his entire body met mine and pressed me to the bed that I tried to bring my arm up, shove him away. I wanted to think for a moment, to breathe. I moved my mouth away from his.

Gabe propped himself up and pinned my wrists to the mattress, the weight of his forearms on mine. When I tried to pull free, he held my wrists tighter. "Harper, what do you really want?" he asked. I watched his eyes for a long time, then turned my head and let my body yield under his. When I did, I concentrated on how our torsos met on the same breath, fell away. I closed my eyes and tried to forget everything else. Fingertips, hands, mouths on skin, the only ways left to communicate. This was a different language, one in which it didn't matter what was said, only how we felt and how it grew. It didn't matter if the emotion was anger, frustration, tenderness, as long as it intensified to the cusp of release. I sought that – release – the kind that words and conversation could never seem to bring to me. I opened my eyes again and kept them on Gabe as we built to that point. Kept them on him until the moment before orgasm. When I saw that he was gone from me, I closed my eyes. When I came, I tried to join him in the place I thought he had gone to.

The next morning, I felt a sense of calm so complete, it seemed to lift me off the bed. When Gabe woke, I pretended to be asleep. With my eyes closed, I held that sensation of buoyant calm in me. He dressed and left the shed, probably to go to Susan's for breakfast or to walk in the forest, plotting which trees to attempt to fall once the snow had completely melted.

The feeling of lightness, of peace, seemed to come from a sudden instinct that I had to leave. I wasn't sure for how long I

would go but I felt like I was riding a balance then and that I
needed to leave before things slipped, went bad. I knew that
despite what Gabe had said, he wouldn't ask me to leave. The
only person who could convince me to go was myself. I considered doing the rounds to say goodbye but I didn't want to have
to explain anything to anyone. I called Krista from Brenda's
place, not wanting to go to either Susan's or Thomas's. "I'm
going to spend a few days with a friend," I explained to Brenda,
although she didn't ask. "Then, I don't know. I might even go
home. I might be back." I left Krista's number with her, telling
her to give it to Gabe if he asked.

"Remember, whether you're with Gabe or not, you're
welcome here any time, love," Brenda said, then paused.
"Where is Gabe?"

I shrugged, and said, "I don't know, but I think he'll understand why I'm going. I just –" I stopped.

"Take care of yourself, Harper – and be true to your own
heart, no matter what anyone says." I hugged Brenda because
that was what she expected and told her I would, although I
hardly knew how anyone could be true to a heart, it being a
vague and inconstant thing. Something that pumped blood and
moved it around.

❧

I was standing in the farmyard when Krista and her mom
pulled up in their truck. "She wanted to come," said Krista,
jerking her head toward Therese as she jumped out of the passenger's side.

"These things have to be done quickly, honey," Therese said. "We don't want anyone changing their minds." She came toward me, then stood with her hands on her hips, surveying the site of the fire. She looked out of place with her white boots and pink ski jacket. "So, that's where you've been staying since that building burned down?" she asked, motioning to the shed, a forced but reassuringly cheerful note in her voice.

"No, that's, uh, where I stayed all along."

"Oh," she said surprised. "Oh, well, that's certainly – okay, well, I'll just wait here for you two then, eh?"

It didn't take long for Krista and me to gather my belongings. When we were finished, Krista took most of my things and left me alone in the shed. I stood in the middle of the room for a moment, unmoving, then went to the table where Gabe and I had eaten our microwaved dinners, where I had done homework. I shifted dishes and papers in order to make sure I had everything that was mine. Among the scrap paper and various diagrams was a shiny purple stone, under this a letter, still in the jagged-edged envelope, as though torn open with a crooked finger, addressed to Gabe from Anise.

I stopped and read the letter, knowing Krista and Therese were waiting for me outside, knowing I shouldn't. It began with a page and a half of description of the girls – they were adjusting relatively well, finding outlets for their emotions. The oldest could now executive a flawless back handspring, the youngest had joined a children's theatre troupe and the middle one, she would find herself soon enough. I smiled at the description of these girls, their names on the page. Aubrey, Sage, and Mia. It was as though separating myself from their half-brother made them more than simply part of his story, but more real to me, whole and alive somewhere.

My smile slipped when I came to the end of the letter, the words there. *The girls miss you, Gabe, and so do I. I don't know what I want to say. I just wish you were here with us, with me. You helped me so much in those last few months. And the way you were with me. The way you are. When we were together – some things probably shouldn't have happened but I'm not sorry they did. I guess I shouldn't tell you things like this.* I felt a knot of nausea lodge in my throat and tried to swallow it. I read the words again. *The way you were with me.* I thought of all the time I spent with Gabe. *The way you are.* The stories we told each other, how our mothers kept creeping in, stepping on our toes as we tried to leave them behind. *Some things probably shouldn't have happened.*

Gabe came into the shed then, scaring me with his, "Hey," and I jumped up from the table, guilt radiating from me. He didn't seem to notice, though, looked at me for a moment with a puzzled expression then started to take off his jacket, went into the workshop to hang it up. I scrambled to slip the letter back into envelope as he did.

Gabe came back into the room and said, "So, I saw Krista and her mom outside," and sat down on the bed, leaning back on his arms and looking up at me, squinting slightly. "You're going."

"Yeah. I guess I am," I answered, looked out the window to the tract of field, the patches of brown growing larger by the day. "I left Krista's number with Brenda. I'll be there for a few days, at least. You can call me there, you know." I got up from the table and stood in front of Gabe.

"So, you were just going to leave?"

"You know what you said the other day about wanting to make a decision and then be able to just do it? Well, this morning when I woke up, I realized I had to go. I feel like there's too much pressure on both of us here – like we're trying to be something for each other we're not. You need to be in this place now, but I think I need to not be here. I know things are complicated for you, I don't want to be in your way."

He took both of my hands in his then, and parted his knees slightly. I shifted so that my legs were against the mattress, Gabe's on either side of mine. I looked straight at him. He tried to smile. There were so many things I wanted to say – that I had read the letter; that whatever had gone on with him and Anise, it was wrong; that I didn't care. I hoped that my going would relieve some pressure on at least one of the sides.

"You've never been in my way," he said, running his hands up my arms so that I instinctively leaned towards him. I was about to put my hands on his thighs when he said, "You don't have to explain yourself. I mean, especially after what I said last night. I'm sorry, Harper. I think that I will –" He stopped and cleared his throat. "I'll probably go too once I sort some things out."

"When, where?" I felt a hit of panic then, a feeling of losing footing, handholds, and crouched down in front of Gabe, between his knees.

He turned his head to the side, that muscle in his jaw clenching like it did on men in the movies, pulsing there. "I don't know." He looked back at me, put his hands on my shoulders, then slid his palms down my arms to my wrists where his hold tightened, slackened. "I guess neither one of us really belonged here, hey?"

I was dizzy with something – longing, loss. "I should go now. Krista's waiting." I started to stand. Our faces were so close. I rested my forehead on his, raised my hand, touched his face. I wanted to kiss Gabe then, but didn't. Instead I placed a finger on his mouth and he parted his lips, sucked it into the space between his teeth and bit. I smiled, withdrew my finger and placed it on my own lips and then straightened up.

"I'm not going to say 'see you around,'" I said.

"Okay, Harper. But keep in touch, okay?"

"I will, Gabe. You too."

"I will."

On the ride back to Krista's, the sense of calm settled into numbness, then exhaustion. I fought sleep until we got there, then climbed under Krista's pink gingham bedspread and fell asleep on top of the blankets.

When I woke, I went downstairs. Krista and Therese were in the kitchen. Therese dished strawberry ice cream into a bowl, the closest I'd seen to her preparing food, and offered it to me. Krista spooned out her own and we took it upstairs and ate on her bed, the pink canopy matching the ice cream. I felt sticky and hot.

When we finished the ice cream, Krista asked, "So, what do you want to do now? I mean tonight."

"I don't know."

"Okay, then, let's get out of here. Harley's at hockey practice with the Old Timers. Therese is going out line dancing. We can't hang around this empty, boring house. It'll just make you more depressed. Let's just go." Krista dumped the contents of her backpack onto her bed and left the room with it, coming back wearing it and holding my jacket out to me. I put it on and followed her out of the house.

While we walked, Krista's backpack sloshed and clinked with the sounds of liquid and glass. We climbed out of her subdivision until the streets ended in orchards and we slipped a fence. The orchards were wet with melted snow, the trees twisted and bare. Orchardists had figured out how to both increase the yield of fruit and make picking easier by pruning small, bottom-heavy trees. It had warmed up enough that the ground released the smell of rotting windfalls from the last season. We filed our way through rows of trees to an old picker's shack on the edge of the property where the hill rose up out of the orchard and into the forest. We had been there before, although not since the previous summer. In the early fall when harvesting began and the shack was populated by pickers, we stayed away.

"Wait," Krista opened her backpack. She had an old beach towel wrapped around bottles. She spread it out for us on a makeshift porch of flats and plywood and we sat on the pattern of black palm trees against fluorescent lines of setting sky. "Here," she said and handed me a beer. "Don't drink it all at once, we need them for chasers." I looked at what Krista was pulling out of her bag: a mickey of gin, four beers.

"Krista, I can't drink gin. It's gross, I'll hurl."

"Sorry, Harp, tonight you're drinking what I say you're drinking." Krista tightened her jaw and stared straight at me, daring me to cross her, then she threw back a gulp of gin, chased it down with beer. I followed but when the alcohol hit the back of my throat, bile rose up. As I tried to wash it away, I choked on my beer, forcing it out my nostrils.

"So," I said when I had regained some composure. "What's going on?"

"You tell me," Krista answered.

"I don't know what I can tell you. Things weren't working out at the farm. Gabe doesn't seem the same, but I don't know if it's that. Maybe I'm just seeing things differently. It's not like we were fighting or anything but –"

"Men," Krista started. "They just don't know how to be in relationships – most of them are convinced that they should be living in a cabin in the woods hunting their own game or blasting around in some sports car getting a blow job but, come on, like most of them could pull off either of those things successfully."

"Yeah, but it's not just that. I don't know if I can have a normal, relaxed relationship with *anyone*. And the farm – as different as it was, it seemed like people couldn't just be honest there either, and that's exactly what I was trying to get away from. But what, do I just go home and call it a day?"

We kept going without talking, pouring drinks down our throats and controlling gag reflexes, until we were both red-faced and dizzy. It started to get dark. "Okay, your turn," I said. "What's going on? With you this time."

Krista stopped drinking, then looked straight ahead for a long time before saying, "What if I told you that I did invite Mike and Rob that night, that I invited them so I'd have someone around when you abandoned me for Gabe, or Thomas, or whoever?"

"I don't know," I said, then, "Why didn't you tell me you felt like that?"

"We didn't seem to be telling each other much of anything any more." Krista held a nearly empty bottle out in front of her and peered through it. "There's something else." She paused, then said quietly, "You know how I was crying that day in the church?"

"Yeah?" I chided myself for not asking sooner.

"Well, oh, God – well, okay, so one night about a week before the fire we do shrooms, Mike and me and Rob. We'd also had a lot to drink and, well . . . Mike and Rob disappear for a while and I'm left watching some dumb movie by myself – that one about the girl and the horse, she becomes a champion, horse dies, you know the one – in the basement. I keep drinking, 'cause you know how that makes you feel less stoned sometimes?" She stopped and took a drink, then said, "Are you sure you want to hear this?"

"Of course."

"Okay, so they come back and, before I know what's happening – I mean, seriously, I really didn't know – Mike's holding me down on the floor and Rob is on top of me." I was silent, staring straight ahead, unable to feel anything but hatred toward Mike. "At first I think it's some kind of joke and I'm like, ha ha, Mike will you get this guy off of me, but then I realize they're serious and, and Rob – well – and then Mike gets on me and – you know."

I clenched my fists to feel my nails dig into my palms. "He never should have done that to you, Krista."

"Then Mike tells me, when he's done, that he's sorry, that Rob was supposed to just get me 'ready' for him, he promised he wouldn't actually do it. He kept apologizing and apologizing and saying how drunk he was and how it wasn't supposed to happen that way and, I don't know, it's like – I don't know what it's like."

"And you stayed with him after that?"

"That's the worst thing. It's like I had to see him hurt someone else, commit arson, before I could convince myself to ditch him."

"What he did wasn't your fault, Krista."

"I know, it's just that sometimes –"

"It wasn't."

We were quiet then, passing the bottle back and forth until we had finished all the alcohol. Then, I moved toward Krista and held her while she shook. When both of us could stand, we threw the bottles from the porch into the orchard and wove our way back to Krista's, stopping to rest several times. I stayed on the back step when we got there. I wanted to find a steady place where the world would stop spinning. When it wouldn't, I went inside. The bathroom light was on at the end of the hall. Krista was sitting on the edge of the tub, head between her knees. I gripped the counter to maintain my balance. Krista lifted her head and pointed to the toilet with a wan smile. "Be my guest," she said. I puked up gin, beer, and what appeared to be strawberry ice cream while Krista crawled into the hall.

When I was finished, I tried to wipe down the bathroom, misting disinfectant and air freshener to try to get rid of the smell, then made my way into the hall and dropped to the floor beside Krista. At some point, encouraging each other, we dragged ourselves into her bed. I remember a moment of throbbing pain in my head as I laid it on the pillow, a fleeting thought that I should seek water. I couldn't move though, and as I began to fall asleep I thought of my own bed, a place where I could sleep alone, spread myself until my limbs met every edge. No fear of meeting another body in the night and not knowing in that state of sleep whether it was known to me or not.

～

The next morning, Krista and I missed the bus. We slept in until our hunger led us to the kitchen where we ate sugared cereal and drank instant coffee. I was hoping that Gabe would have called the night before, but there were no messages on the machine. When Therese discovered us, she gave us a ride to school, Krista and me pale and shaking with hangovers.

"I don't even want to know what you two were up to last night," Therese told us as she backed out of the carport, adjusting both the rear-view mirror and the sunglasses she wore for driving.

"Ditto," groaned Krista from the back seat. "We're not interested in what you did either."

Therese looked at me and said, "Harper, tell me honestly, did I give birth to this monster? I mean, where did this smart-ass come from?" She motioned with her chin toward Krista.

Krista had given up sitting straight and was trying to lie down, wrapping her arms around her stomach and moving her torso slowly towards the seat. As she did, she said, "Look in the mirror, Therese. I sprang from your very own sweet loins – and can you not take the corners so quickly? I'll puke, you know."

"Loins!" Therese laughed. "Is that what kind of language they were teaching you in that holy-rolling church – please tell me you two aren't going back there now, are you? Christ – loins, my ass." With this, Therese turned up the radio and started singing along to an ancient Tammy Wynette song, pounding the steering wheel for emphasis. I opened the window in an attempt to swallow air and release some of the noise.

"Mom!" Krista said. "Can you turn that down? You are such a bitch."

"Not my problem you two are hungover," Therese answered but she turned the volume down. "I'm sorry, Harper. I just like to take the piss out of her, sometimes. Has to learn she can't get through life so lippy, eh?"

I sleepwalked through all my classes, numb with too much sugar, not enough sleep, and something that seemed to be akin to grief, or some experience of loss. I spent the class after lunch crouched on a toilet in a stall in the girls' restroom. I had taped an Out of Order sign to the door, but it wasn't the most con-ducive space in which to formulate clear thoughts. I thought about calling Vera, if only to have her say, "It's okay, sweetie, everything will be okay," but I didn't know if she would and didn't want to find out.

~

It takes Jim a couple of weeks to tell Vera he's lost his job. He is still getting up early, taking the lunch she packs for him, but instead of going to work, he ends up going to the Legion. When she finds out, instead of yelling, she calmly tells Jim she'll leave him and take the kids if they don't get out of Fly Hills.

Jim complies and we move into a rental in Edmonton. While Jim continues to collect unemployment insurance, Vera gets part-time work at the library. I sit with other kids on a carpet and listen to my mother read, so proud that I actually live with the Story Lady, I think I'll burst. She gets more and more hours and Nick and I go to a daycare in the same building, one with primary colours everywhere and stuffed cubes for chairs. We hear the fighting at night, fragile things hitting hard surfaces and the sound of glass splintering downstairs. Nick and I share a room so I get out of my bed and comfort him, my hand touching his hot head, the hair stuck there. Furniture is put out with the trash – an end table, a coat rack, small broken pieces.

While Nick and I finger paint, stack blocks, and eat snacks at a low circular table in the daycare, Vera talks with the other librarians about how she will leave her husband – the hushed tones, the quiet of the library making everything serious and peaceful at once. And she does leave. When she decides that she's talked herself hoarse trying to be understood, that she doesn't have the energy to throw one more plate, Vera packs the van with some of our things, straps us in and drives away, talking to Nick and me the entire time about how Mommy needs some time away from Daddy, Mommy needs some time to think.

We move into Auntie Al and my uncle's house, along with their three teenage kids and my grandmother. I worship the teenagers. They seem far more savvy and smart than the adults. They have quick retorts, can disappear in an instant, and have more subtle, convincing ways of getting me to do what they want than any parent, aunt, or grandparent. The adults' world is louder, more rushed – aunt, uncle, and mother passing plates of food, car keys, coats to one another in the kitchen. Baba is a formidable woman, and even as a small child I realize that she's not the same as the rest of us. It's been explained to me a few times that she's not from here. Our grandmother comes from a place very far away called the Old Country. Sometimes she even thinks she's back there. The teenagers live in a subtle world of secrets and exhilaration, Baba in the Old World, and Nick and I aren't sure where we belong.

The Saturday afternoon that we sell most of our things in the driveway of Auntie Al's house, I feel rich and important. People keep coming and buying our belongings, giving us money. I know, because Vera has explained it to me, that this money will help us get away and start a life on our own. I say goodbye to my cousins, my idols. It will take me a few years and a few summer visits to realize that they aren't teenagers any more. They are nice enough adults but they will never be teenagers again.

We spend our last night in Edmonton at my father's small apartment. Nick and I have been staying with him every weekend and we know how to help fold out the couch. Jim snaps the sheets over us and laughs as he unfolds them and then stays to tuck us in after he's made the bed. "Last night on your old man's couch for a while, hey?" he says and reaches out to touch both of our heads, holds his hands there for a long time. We want stories, not our father's silence, so Jim stumbles through one, never telling it as well as Vera, then kisses us each on the forehead before he turns out the light. Later, I wake up and hear them. My parents are talking and laughing in the next room. That muffled sound in the dark makes me so happy that I rub my feet together under the blankets. I want to go see them in there, to lie between them and listen to them laugh. I am afraid that I will ruin it though, that if I go into the room, they will remember that they don't get along and they will stop laughing. Perhaps if they get along again, we can stay.

Nick and I wake almost on top of each other, forced into the sagging middle of the mattress by the sheer will of the fold-out couch. We are grumpy and tired and we don't know where we are going. Vera mutters about the lack of breakfast food in Jim's kitchen while he sits in the living room and tries to talk to us. He asks if we are excited, if we will miss him. We don't know what to answer so we nod and look at our feet. He tells us not to worry, and promises that we'll see each other all the time.

Vera comes into the living room with peanut butter sand-wiches already made and sealed in plastic. We'll eat them on the road, she says. We have to get going. When we have gath-ered our things and hugged him goodbye, my father freezes in the middle of the room and starts to cry. They are frightening, those huge, racking sobs. He doesn't even sit down like most people do when they are crying. My father just stands in the middle of the room, shaking, covering his eyes with his hands. It is mid-morning; I remember the light. I stand in the hall and watch him, watch how the bright light shakes with his silhouette. None of us say anything, not even Vera. She reaches out and touches his arm and Nick and I stand side by side, uncertain, then we just turn and leave, closing the door gently behind us.

☙

It had taken us three weeks to drive to paradise. We stopped often, Vera insisting that we look up and take in all the beauty around us whenever we did. Each time, I wondered, is this where we will live now; is this where we will start our new life? We kept driving. We sang and took turns telling jokes or we would make up stories together, each of us saying one sentence and then passing it on. We patched together narratives from Vera's logical sentences, my flights of imagination, and my little brother's nonsense. One night when we were falling asleep on the foam mattress in the back of the van, Nick and me on either side of her, my mother said, "We've had enough of this, haven't we?" I didn't know what to say but it didn't matter. She continued, "We've had enough moving around. Won't it be nice to stop?" I answered by shifting closer to my mother on the mattress, finding a place to rest my head against her arm, and falling asleep. When we got to Sawmill Creek, we stopped.

GABE

You believe that beauty is in the details. So you make a list of things beautiful: Peter's knuckles, tensed over wood and blade; Anise's slender fingers around the globe of a wineglass; the pale skin of Harper's scalp appearing between the slide and catch of scissors.

You make a list of beautiful things while you start the truck and warm it up. It doesn't take nearly as long for the engine to warm as it did even a month ago. New Year's Eve, how long did the truck take to stall while you and Harper ran through the snow and into the forest? That is one of those things you can't know, like a tree falling in the forest and how much noise it makes. You mark these two things down on your mental list: a truck stalling in the snow, a tree falling in the forest, the silence that follows. You decide that silence is another beautiful thing, though not a detail. Details can't be quite so all-encompassing.

Now is the time in this story when you start to go. When the engine is warm and you leave in the truck. You think briefly of notions of leave-taking and quickly surmise that things can't leave unless they have first arrived, can't wither before they have come bursting through soil like the plants on a science film you once watched on your own, a sped-up version of growth and decay. In that short reel, plants grew and bloomed, underwent the force of weather patterns, then wilted and died while a disembodied voice explained what was happening. This is how you see yourself going – like things unfurling, bursting open, and sloughing away: all as functions of the same force.

You always liked to drive. It was Anise who taught you. With Peter, tension would build with each word spoken, each instruction given, until the car was skidding sideways along back roads, your fingers going white around the bones from the force of your grip on the wheel, your feet mad with the uncertainty of gas pedal and brake. When Peter tried to give you lessons, things in the car seized up, both of you included. It was a dangerous situation for everyone, and neither of you wanted to endanger passersby. Anise employed the tactics of a true teacher. She brought along things that she knew would help, or at least hinder your propensity for speeding headlong into danger. She brought small pinches of pot as rewards for you to enjoy later, still oblivious to the fact that you skimmed off her supply all the time. She brought your sisters, lined them up in the back seat, their blond heads in the rear-view mirror the opposite of blind spots – you could always see them, reminding you to drive safely. Anise reassured you that you were doing just fine.

You had always liked to drive, liked the swift confidence in the execution of shifting the gears. There is something both calming and exhilarating about transferring smoothly from one gear to another, as though each transition lets you know that you are a master of your own fate, moving effectively on your course.

You shift into reverse, back the truck away from the shed. Shift into first, begin to move forward out of the yard. You stay in second on the road out. The thaw has begun urgently and awkwardly, as it does some years. The snow melts but frost still covers the ground at night. The sun yanks it off in the morning so the dirt roads are pocked with holes and even pavement heaves a bit, cracks. On the road, you shift into third, fourth, take on the corners like a personal challenge to your driving ability, pleased with your precision. You cross the centre line. Not because of a loss of control but because you can.

You want to climb and then come down. You are familiar with the jump in your groin that happens when you drive over a rise in the road quickly, descend just as quick. A little thrill there, like so many other shivers, shudders, and stabs of pleasure. You drive up switchbacks, wanting to take on an entire mountain. To come down from it in one extended leap of sensation. Like other things, you want the feeling to last.

You feel the back of the truck fan out behind you, the flick of a fish's tail. You use this analogy to reel it back into your line of control. Control is what you want now. Exactitude. You turn around on one of the pullouts. A crescent of gravel drops into nothing, the valley below. Your mind clears as you calculate exactly how close you can get the tires to the brink without meeting air. If there were someone in the passenger seat, she would probably be screaming by now about how near you are to the edge. Your calculated turn is swift and certain. You gear up again as you move the truck back down the mountain. Second, third, fourth, then fifth. The space between, that slice of time when feet pass each other on the upward and downward motions of clutch and gas, is expansive and crystalline, even in that briefest of moments. Or, perhaps, because the moment is so brief.

It is a rare clear day in the valley. Most days, clouds lie like soup, obliterating even the notion that sky might exist above them. On this day, though, even the people in the valley below will be able to see straight up. Will be able to glimpse the top of the mountain that you drive the truck down. The road you navigate is not quite a ribbon or a snake from below, the corners too sharp for things that smooth. It is more like a zigzag. A child's drawing of a zipper. Yet from where you are, even the sharpest corners have some degree of roundness. You trace the road with your eyes like you might the image of a woman. Your sight becomes more than one sense. Becomes something that can taste and feel things. You take in the curve of the sides, the conviction of the centre line, the solidity of asphalt.

Just when you think you can taste it, when it is about to fill your mouth and become something you can swallow, you leave the road. You leave the road, taking the truck with you. You leave the road at such a speed that you are able to experience what nothing but air under tires feels like. You are able to experience what falling feels like. Able to experience certainty so clear and absolute, it is blinding.

*T*he moment I find out, something divides in me. It's as though, in discovering that I never really knew you, I realize that I can never know myself. And so part of me splits off, becomes a stranger. With the other part I try to keep myself together, try to stitch things into place, as though I can create some kind of fabric, a context.

～

It was Thomas who told me. Near the end of French class, the school counsellor, Mr. Robinson, knocked on the door and spoke in a low voice to my teacher, then called me out. I couldn't figure out what Thomas was doing in the hall, looking from me to his fingernails, then down the row of lockers. I noticed small things then, tiny things – a rogue piece of Thomas's hair twisting up, the tip pricked with fluorescent light, Mr. Robinson's gaping pores.

"What's going on?" I asked, looking from one to the other.

Mr. Robinson drew in his breath, then said, "Mr. Steele has something to talk to you about." He exhaled, then reached out his hand as though he were going to place it on my shoulder. It seemed to come at me very slowly and I was able to see the coarse hair that pushed out of his knuckles. I looked away and winced at his touch. He let his arm drop and said, "I'll let your teachers know that you've had to leave early today."

I looked to Thomas but he only offered me a slow nod. "Thomas, what's going on? Tell me," I implored.

He looked from me to Mr. Robinson, uncertain, then said, "Harper, let's get your coat. This isn't the right place." I kept my eyes on Thomas and this time when Mr. Robinson reached out to touch me, I wasn't fast enough to move away. He squeezed my shoulder, then left Thomas and me in the hall.

As we walked to my locker, Thomas pulled at his jacket as though he were hot, or his clothes were constricting, and repeatedly cleared his throat. I looked straight ahead and said nothing. Heat rose from my chest, along my neck, to the top of my head until my scalp seemed barbed with it. I swallowed and tried to breathe deeply but my mouth could take in only short gasps. My hands shook as I dialled my lock combination and it banged against the door. While Thomas waited, I pulled out textbooks and looked at them, trying to figure out if they'd be any use. I felt as though I was about to be taken somewhere I'd never been before, and I had no idea what to bring.

As if reading my thoughts, Thomas said sharply, "You won't need those today. Just get your coat and let's go." His words were like a slap.

I fumbled with my coat then yanked it off the hook, turned to him and said, "Thomas, please, just tell me what's going on. I know it's something about Gabe. It's something about Gabe, isn't it?"

Instead of answering, Thomas took the coat out of my hands and held it out to me. I looked at him for a moment, wanting to say something, but I saw his red-rimmed eyes, the way the corner of his mouth was twitching slightly, and I took the coat from him, walked towards the door.

Thomas drove to a place where there was a small park propped up on a bank rising from the Salmon River. In the late summer, you could launch the green spiked armour of horse chestnuts from the bench there, watch them bob once on the current and go under.

We got out of the truck, walked to the edge, looked down at the river. "Harper," Thomas started, stopped, then started again. "Harper, Gabe was found . . . His truck went off the road. He went off the road on the way down from the mountain."

I stopped walking and asked, calmly, "Which road?" Then stared down at the water. Dizzy, I put one arm out to a tree, felt the bark rough under my palm. The river was completely thawed, but the snow pack hadn't melted off the mountains so the current wasn't strong yet. When Thomas didn't say anything, I said again, evenly, "Which road, Thomas?" pausing after each word, then, "Which road, damn it! Where is he, Thomas?"

"Harper, he's –" Thomas started, then turned me to face him and took my hand.

"Please don't touch me!" I shouted and wrenched my hand away, as if raising my voice could stop me from crying but the tears came anyway. "He's gone, isn't he? He's gone and this is what you've come to tell me." I started to kick at the exposed roots near the top of the cut bank.

"He went off one of the switchbacks," Thomas said. "He must've been going too fast, miscalculated the turn."

I looked up at Thomas through a blur of tears. "He was a good driver, Thomas," I choked out. "He just wasn't used to these roads."

Thomas took both of my hands in his. "I know, Harper. He was. I know."

✨

I had been at Krista's for more than a week. Her home had been a kind of neutral place, a buffer zone between the reality of the farm and the reality of home. After the news about Gabe sank in, I didn't have the energy to even consider packing the few things I had. The thought of going home exhausted me. Therese phoned my mom and told her what had happened. I stayed back from school for a week, lying either on Krista's bed or on the couch in the rec room, or wandering aimlessly around the house. When they were home, Krista and her mom did their best to cheer me up.

Susan called me at Krista's one evening. I was surprised to hear her voice but remembered that I had given the number to Brenda. I thought she would simply tell me when the funeral was going to be held but she asked if we could meet. Though I didn't feel ready to see her, I agreed.

We met later that afternoon in a café downtown. We greeted each other with small smiles stretched tight across our faces. Susan looked pale and even thinner than usual and sat looking down at her napkin, which she was twisting into a helix. We sat in silence for a moment, then I said, "I don't know what to say. I'm so sorry, Susan."

She looked up. "I am too, Harper. I am too," she said, then paused. "I know that you cared for him. I never should have said what I did to you. I had no right. We try to do the best we can to understand a person. I'm not sure I could ever read my son, but I could see you were there for him."

"I don't know if I was, Susan."

Susan looked out the window and continued as though she hadn't heard me. "I was so young when I had Gabe. *We* were so young," she started. "Peter and I thought we could solve everything, save the world, by coming here before he got drafted. But, aside from knowing that we didn't believe in war, we didn't know yet what we wanted, what we were looking for." She paused and then moved her gaze from the window to me. "Turned out we wanted different things and when the war ended, and Peter wanted to take Gabe back to the States, I thought – well, to be honest, I don't know what I thought. Maybe that simply by nature of him being my son, I would be able to see him whenever I wanted to, like it would be inevitable. But, neither Peter nor I had a lot of money, California's a long way away and, God, I hate to say it – I got used to living without him." When she looked at me then, there were tears in her eyes. "And now –"

I took her hand in mid-sentence and Susan stopped talking. She put her other hand over mine and we sat like that, looking at each other.

After a few minutes, Susan took a breath and said, "I don't know if the funeral's going to be here, Harper."

"What do you mean?"

"Peter's wife wanted me to ship, to ship the – his – body down."

"Anise?"

"Yes, Anise. She thinks that Gabe should be buried down there, in California. I'm just so tired. He's my son. I didn't want to have to fight over his body."

I suddenly hated those people, his family in California whom I had never met.

Susan looked out the window. "They say that there was no ice on the road, no packed snow. It was clear and dry. Clear and dry." She pulled more napkins from the holder and unfolded them, smoothed them flat in front of her. "No skid marks, none, but that could mean anything. I don't even know what he was doing on that road."

"He was probably just going for a drive to sort things out. He was driving too fast, that's all."

She steadied her voice, hardened it. "There are no guard-rails on that turn, you know, knocked off in some other accident, that one not fatal," her voice caught like skin on a nail. "They haven't replaced them." She started to tear the napkins into small pieces. "Thomas knows roads, he's been on every goddamn road in this province. He says it's sheer luck that this didn't happen sooner."

I had been told often enough that there were no accidents, no coincidences. At the farm, people mouthed things about the universe, karma, cause and effect. For the people at the Free Church, it was the hand of God. As a child, I thought the hand of God was just that – a giant hand descending from Heaven, moving things, picking people up, putting them down. I saw that hand on the way down from the hill, saw the thumb meet the forefinger in an O and flick Gabe's truck off the switchback.

Susan was bordering the pile of napkin bits with the sides her hands, creating edges. She looked at the pile with her head to one side, then at me. "I'm flying to California on Monday," then paused as if to gauge my reaction. I just looked back and nodded. "We agreed that the funeral would be on Tuesday. This wasn't really his home. Maybe he should go back."

⁓

When she joins the Friends of Christ Free Church, my mother doesn't know if she'll stay. She wants something for the kids, a place where they can feel as though they belong. She has taken them away from everything they have ever known – their father, their house, their family, their province. She has taken them because she had to leave and the three of them are inextricably linked, strangers in the same car of a moving train. They have only each other for now.

She passes by the park one afternoon when a group of women from the church are singing, their voices carried by the river. She is drawn to the women by their voices, and by the circle of children around them. Friends, she thinks. She has never wanted to isolate herself or her kids. When she finds out that the women are, in fact, part of a group with Friends in the name, she takes this as a sign.

After a couple of Sundays, she tells some of the women her story. They gather in a circle on the carpet in someone's living room, and listen while she tells them everything. Or, not everything, but the basics: her father's death, eloping at eighteen, the drugs and the women who filled their mouths with her new husband in San Francisco, the first child at twenty, second at twenty-two, the isolation in the farmhouse, the move to Edmonton, the fighting. By the time she has finished, the women start to tell their own stories, echo each other's words, sentiments, experiences. She cries at each retelling, then feels a release throughout her whole body, the kind that only too many tears can bring. The women have gathered around her in a circle, are telling her to lie down, let it all go, surrender to Christ. When she gets up her limbs feel heavy, yet liberated with a strange new light, and she knows that she will stay among them. She hopes her kids will thank her for it someday, for finding them all something that feels like community, but when she looks at them, she realizes she will never know what they are thinking. She watches the furrow in her son's brow when he concentrates, smells the musky sweetness of her daughter's hair when she sneaks into her room at night, and she realizes she doesn't need to know.

Several times, I woke when my mother was doing this, leaning over and smelling my hair. I always pretended I was still asleep. I knew, even then, that those moments, though they had to do with me, were only for her.

I saw Gabe's hands around the steering wheel, thought of all the times we had driven together. As I did, I could feel the slip of road under us on that night, Christmas Eve, when the truck had lost traction and slid into the bank. The wheels spinning under us, the grind of tire, road, engine.

The day after I talked to Susan, I took Krista's parents' Camaro without their knowledge or consent. Mr. Delaney was at his shift at the mill, Therese was sleeping. Krista gave me the keys. Even though the muscle car was an embarrassment to be seen in, it was true that it cornered well, shifted smoothly. The car worked with the precision of something well kept and loved. I thought of how God is in the details, how Gabe and I had differed on this. He believed that it was only beauty that one could find in the details.

When I got to the farm, I pulled into the empty spot where Gabe's truck should have been, and went into the shed. I stood looking at the bed. The sheets and blankets were a tangled mess, as though Gabe had slept with them coiled around him in ropes. There was a glass of water on the floor, half full, half empty, catching the dim light from the window. I thought of the afternoon in the Catholic Church when I was a child and had asked God for a sign, opened my eyes to a wall of red light. I felt that I had lost my ability to believe in anything I couldn't touch. I didn't want to ask for signs any more. Signs can be misinterpreted. So can memories, words, the stories we tell each other.

I started with the bed, pulled blankets and sheets off. I saw in them all the nights we had slept together, heard in them how little we had actually said, and overturned the mattress. I went to the shelves where Gabe's clothes were piled. As I yanked them off, turned things inside out, his smell seemed to fill the room. I turned toward the table and saw the letter from Anise sitting exactly where I had left it. Not wanting anyone else to find it, I picked it up and went back into the workshop. I kicked at tools on the floor, my breath heaving. I emptied screws and nails from jars and then moved to the drafting table, sweeping the wood and diagrams off it with my arm.

With the letter in my fist, I looked at the thin slices of wood that were on the floor. At one time they were supposed to represent a guitar. They never would, just as I could never put the pieces of this story back together in a way that made sense. I tore up the letter and let the scraps fall around me. It took several matches to keep the torn paper and thin wood lit on the cold, concrete floor. Once it started, I watched the fire, not knowing what I would do next, then it caught the edge of the drafting table. It crawled up one of the table legs. I held my hands above the flames, waiting for them to suck on my fingers.

The door of the shed opened. "Harper," I heard Thomas say, "I didn't know whose car was in the –" He started, then he saw the fire and pushed me aside, threw his jacket against the table leg and kicked the fire out with his boot. When he turned and looked at me, his face flushed, all I could manage was, "I don't know what happened."

"Harper –" he started, reaching for my arm. I pulled away from the possibility of his touch, wrapping my arms around myself instead. Then, though I clenched my jaw, I felt glands opening in the back of my throat, sharp pain behind my eyes.

When I realized that I was crying, I dropped to the floor, defeated.

Thomas crouched with me. When he put his hand in the middle of my back, it was as though a huge, balled fist had pounded me there and a sob tore out of me.

⌒

I drove the Camaro back to the Delaneys', and realized when I got out that the tires had tracked new dirt and sand into the carport, marking my passage. Later, neither of Krista's parents said anything, though they must have known I'd taken the car. Part of me wanted to stay in a place where it seemed nothing was demanded of me, but I knew it was time to go home. It felt at once like a relinquishing and a relief.

Krista helped me pack. When I asked if she could give me a ride home, she said that she'd had her driving privileges revoked for letting me take the car. I tried to apologize but she said, "Between us, no more apologies."

Therese drove me home. She helped me with my bags when we got there. "We can take them around back," I said. "My mom usually forgets to lock that door."

"Pretty naive, eh," Therese said, picking her way in high heels along the path to the back yard. "Either that or trusting." The last of the snow had slid off the roof and had melted on the spot, creating a small bog.

"A little bit of both," I answered.

The back door was open. We went in, set my things down by the kitchen table, then Therese stood in the doorway, an awkward smile tugging at her face. "Well, I know she'll be glad to have you back, anyway. And, after what you've been through, well . . ." Her words trailed off. She reached for my hair, stroked it, then pulled her hand back as though surprised at her own gesture. "I'm really sorry about Gabe, Harper."

"I know. Thanks for everything, Mrs. Delaney."

"That's 'Therese' to you and thanks shmanks. You're welcome at the Delaney Home for Wayward Girls any time, honey. Next time, just be prepared to pay some rent, eh?" Therese winked and wiggled her French-tipped nails at me, then went out the back door and made her way around the house. I could hear her swearing as she went, imagined her high heels sinking into the uneven, muddy ground.

The house was empty and buzzing with appliances. I looked around, everything familiar and foreign at once. The kitchen was small, orderly, gleaming. It looked like a safe and clean place, no herbs hanging from the ceiling, no footprints etched in ashes tracked from the woodstove. This was a place where one woman and a teenager ate. The fridge door layered in school notices, peanut butter and bread occupying a permanent corner of the counter. An efficient space, the clutter slight. It smelled familiar – of lemon, burnt toast, Vera's perfume. Weak sunlight strained through clouds and windows, the hum of the fridge. I quickly gulped down milk out of the carton and my head sliced with pain. I was going to leave it empty on the counter but changed my mind and threw it in the trash.

In the bathroom, I leaned over the sink to the mirror to see if I looked different, if I had changed. My hair was growing out oddly, in misshapen chunks. I stripped off my clothes and balanced on the edge of the tub, toes gripping porcelain, hands holding the shower curtain rod, to try to see my entire body. I decided that my breasts were a bit larger, though that may have been wishful thinking. It did seem as though my body had more mass, as though there was more flesh to hold me to my bones. I expected something else, to be marked somehow, the faint traces of a map or a code smudged into my skin.

I left my clothes where I'd removed them, at the side of the tub, and climbed the stairs wrapped in a towel. Photographs of Nick and me at various ages lined the wall going up the staircase, the oldest ones near the base, the most recent ones near the top. The last one is a photo of Vera and me arm in arm outside the church on Christmas Eve. Vera had asked Gabe to take it. She isn't smiling in the photograph and looks as though she is uncomfortable, wondering when he is going to snap the shot. I am grinning bravely in spite of the cold, my cheeks flushed and my eyes looking straight into the camera. It was Gabe's face I was trying to look at, not at the hand he waved as he said *Say cheese!* He was practically a stranger then, just a party and a church service between us. I wondered if, after everything, we'd ever got far beyond that.

I went into my room. The manufactured heat in the closed space felt stifling, so I opened a window wide, hoping to let in the wet scent of the field thawing, mown grass. The snow had melted off the golf course and they had begun cutting the green down. I climbed into my bed and immediately fell asleep.

When I woke, it was getting dark, my door was open and Vera was there, standing beside my bed. I shifted, holding the blankets to my chest, then said simply, "Hi."

"May I?" Vera asked, motioning to the bed.

"Sure, go ahead," I answered. She sat down and we were both silent for a moment.

"I knew you were back. I saw your bags at the door," Vera started, as though I needed an explanation. "And your clothes by the tub." I just nodded. She reached out, took my hand and held it loosely at first, turning hers around it, then gripped it so tightly it hurt.

I grimaced but didn't pull away.

"I guess I can't hold you that tight, hey?" she asked, then sighed and let go of my hand. "I don't know what I can say to you now, Harper. Are you all right?"

"Gabe's gone, Mom," I said quietly.

"I know." She paused, then said, "I can't even pretend to imagine what you must be going through." We sat on the bed in silence for several minutes, then Vera continued. "I know you've always thought that when I look at you it's myself I'm seeing at your age. Maybe I have seen you that way at times, but I've never believed that things are that simple. I've never tried to make my mistakes be your own. I just hope that you don't think that you could've done something to make things turn out differently for Gabe."

"I don't." I thought for a moment, then said, "He was never really here, you know. I think he thought he could find what he was searching for by coming here, but that didn't happen, even when I was with him. No matter where Gabe was he was probably always somewhere else."

"Your father liked to say 'Wherever you go, there you are.' Used to bother me so much, him repeating it. There was one night, though, when you were a baby and we were living in the farmhouse, when we were all lying together on a mattress on the floor and he said 'Wherever I go from now on, here we are.' He was talking about the three of us, how we'd become a unit. We never thought that would change."

"Things always do though."

"Yes, they always do."

We sat together quietly on my bed. It was completely dark by then.

⚊

When my mother told me about her childhood, there were stories of picking wildflowers, pounding dough into bread, walking through the snow to a one-room schoolhouse. A different world than my own. But there were other things she told me about. How difficult it was to grow up with parents from another continent, another culture and time. How she once found herself waking up from an unconscious state on the kitchen floor and didn't know why. And there was a male neighbour – I don't know whether he was man or boy – who gripped her wrist between his thumb and forefinger and pulled her towards him. That's as far as she ever got into that memory before her voice would trail off and she would clear her throat. She would cringe whenever Nick or I grabbed her that way, hand around wrist, and shake us off.

But that was not that event I imagined to be the defining moment of Vera Kostak's adolescence. It was this: she is at the farm, digging potatoes in the garden in gumboots and hand-me-down work jeans from one of her sisters, hair held back with a kerchief. She hears a car in the dirt yard out front. This is during the time before they have a telephone, a time when people "dropped by." She hears the voices of young men, her mother saying, "She here somewhere, I call her," in thickly accented English. Vera runs to the outhouse before anyone sees her and stays there while her mother calls, the boys wait, and eventually the car drives out of the yard, pebbles spun out by the tires. She crouches over the hole in the outhouse for a long time, long after she has heard the vehicle retreat down the dirt road, imagines a cloud of dust rising and then falling, small things flattened under tires. Vera didn't want to be seen dirt-smeared in a kerchief and gumboots, looking like both a *baba* and a farmer at once. Because of that, she has lost her chance. Those boys are gone now, gone to wherever they wanted to take her.

~

I started walking to school again, wary of taking rides with friends and strangers alike. Most days I made it through all of my classes. I took long routes home and walked until I found a kind of comfort in the cadence of my own steps. While I did, I tried to call up memories of my father but he kept turning into just a name. I tried to retrace my mother's past as a way to connect her to my own. I tried to remember your story, to frame it in a way that would bring part of you back, but it kept slipping back into me.

On one of my walks, I meet Krista at a corner downtown.

She balances on the curb like a pro, turns quick pirouettes on the edge of light traffic. We no longer walk to drugstore, library, or mall, seeking instead parks, fields, the edge of the lake. One day while we walk we remember the heat of late summer. We remember flip-flops, jean cut-offs, and bikini tops. We can feel backpacks sticking to the sweat collecting on our backs as we imagine ourselves hitchhiking out to the lake, shielding our faces from the sun. We know that by August the lake will no longer be refreshing. The top layers will be hot, pollen clinging to the surface. Below, cool silk. We will lie on the dock, the sun on every part of us. When we jump in, it will be sweet relief. I'll let myself drop, and open my eyes to the layers of green to blue, until I feel the slick pull of milfoil at my ankles. Then I'll kick back to the light, split open the surface of the lake with a gasp of air. Krista will turn over as I crawl onto the dock, the wood already hot under my wet hands. I'll lie on my back and join her in facing the sun, water evaporating on my skin, the dark pools that stain the wood lightening around me.

Needing to understand where we all started, where we came to, I try to trace a route back to a place I once thought I knew, to map my way with words. When you lose something before really knowing it, what is unrecoverable becomes the shape of longing, a story you have to tell yourself. I follow the fingers of several valleys, but all of them round in on themselves again, seeking some kind of centre, the lowest point, a place where things gather.

ACKNOWLEDGEMENTS

My sincere thanks to:

The three other Ls who complete the square – Lorne, Lorna, and Lucas – and my huge and hugely supportive extended family. Karen Wall, mentor extraordinaire. Catherine O'Connell. John Lent, without whom.

Nancy Lee, the first person to read this manuscript in its infancy and my constant companion and kind critic throughout. Charlotte Gill, Lee Henderson, and Chris Tenove, whose minds, hearts, and humour will always astound.

Jennica Harper, who so graciously lent me her name. Jason Dewinetz, for reminding me to pay attention to the details. Anastasia Hulsizer, my first American reader. Vanessa Timmer, Michelle Patterson, Khaylish Fraser and Jody Wettig, sources of support, diversion, glee. All those who lurked and laughed in the offices of *PRISM international*.

Keith Maillard, George McWhirter, and the faculty and students of the University of British Columbia's M.F.A. program. Residents and staff of Green College 1998-2000, who fed, housed, and entertained me through the first drafts. The faculty, participants, and Scotch drinkers at Banff Centre for the Arts Writing Studio 2001.

My agent and literary godmother, Anne McDermid, for falling in love at first read. And Ellen Seligman, for the insight, endurance, and humour necessary to push the book farther than I thought possible.